THE KILL GAME

Also by the Author

Broken Dolls
Presumed Guilty
Watch Me
Hush Little Baby
Prey

James Carol

THE KILLING GAME

bookouture

Published by Bookouture

An imprint of StoryFire Ltd.
23 Sussex Road, Ickenham,
UB10 8PN, United Kingdom

www.bookouture.com

ISBN: 978-1-83888-093-4
eBook ISBN: 978-1-78681-031-1

This one's for Karen,
The Killing Game!

PROLOGUE

So, how are you going to play this one?

First you switch off your cell phone, then you take a deep breath and count to ten. Knee-jerk reactions are not your style. You need time to process what you've just heard, a moment of quiet reflection before leaping into the hurricane. Once those ten seconds are up you're going to make two lists, one for the pros, one for the cons. Then you'll take everything you've learned and put it in one column or the other. Inevitably, you will end up with more cons than pros, otherwise you wouldn't have got the call.

Your clients don't live in the real world, which is just as well. That one simple fact is the reason you've got a convertible Maserati Spyder, a suite of offices up with the clouds, and a condo with views across the valley in one of LA's more exclusive zip codes. These people believe their own hype. They think they're gods, but they're not. Deep down they have the same insecurities and flaws as the rest of us, and, like the rest of us, they screw up occasionally. The big difference is that when they screw up it makes the headlines. This is where you come in. Trying to stop those headlines is an exercise in futility, but you can angle them to your advantage. And *that* is the Art of Spin.

So, what do you know?

You know this particular client isn't a regular A-lister, he's in the A+ category. There's rich, and there's Learjet rich, and this client is most definitely Learjet rich. He's got the leading man looks, the healthy, twinkling smile and a great body. He made his name playing the all-American good guy and has basically rehashed the same role in every movie he's ever made. However, so long as he keeps packing out those movie theatres, this doesn't cause the studio bosses a problem.

Mr A+'s whole reputation rests on him being seen as whiter than white. According to the media he doesn't drink, doesn't smoke, doesn't do drugs or screw around. He eats healthily, exercises regularly and does plenty for charity. He married his high school sweetheart and they have a couple of kids, a boy and a girl. You've seen the photos. How could you miss them? There's the four of them with their perfect teeth, perfect skin and perfect smiles, living their perfect life. There's even a cute little pooch at Mr A+'s feet to complete the picture. Mr A+ came from nothing and now he's sitting right up there at the top of the mountain. This is the American Dream made real.

If something looks too good to be true, it is. That's something you've seen time and again in this town. So it comes as no surprise that Mr A+ is currently languishing in a Beverley Hills police cell, nursing a hangover and wondering what the hell he's doing there. As far as he's concerned he hasn't done anything wrong. As far as the law is concerned, he has. This time the law wins big. Being caught in a sleazy motel with a dead hooker and a large bag of cocaine definitely contravenes a law or two.

And you know one more thing. Rather than phone his lawyer, Mr A+ phoned you.

Your clients fall into two broad categories. First up are the quiet ones. They know they've royally screwed up and will do anything you say to make the problem go away. Then there are the clients who roar like lions. In the end they'll do what you tell them, but it takes time and persuasion to help them see the light. Mr A+ is a lion, and then some. Before he can wind himself up into a righteous fury, you tell him to shut up and listen.

Home truth number one: things will get uglier before they get better.

Home truth number two: he'll lose contracts.

Home truth number three: for the foreseeable future his career will resemble a car wreck.

Judging by the silence on the other end of the line, you've got his attention. No mean feat when dealing with an A+. Now he's listening, you lighten your tone and tell him to hang on in there because things will get better. So long as he plays the long game and doesn't get suckered into short-term thinking, everything will work out fine. You repeat this a couple of times to make sure it sinks in.

Next, you tell him he has to follow your instructions to the letter. No ifs, no buts. You're in the driving seat now. You're calling the shots. Unless he does everything you say, he can kiss his precious career goodbye. The grunt coming from the earpiece indicates that he isn't convinced. Not a problem. What he thinks is irrelevant.

You let the silence stretch to breaking point, then tell him you want a million dollars, the whole amount up front, the money transferred to your account immediately. His first reaction is to tell you to go to hell. You keep quiet and give him all the time he needs.

'You're really that good?' he asks tentatively.

'For your sake, you better hope I am.'

By the time you hang up he's a believer.

Your first call is to the presenter of America's highest-rating daytime chat show. Not her office, the woman herself. You promise a soul-baring confessional. You promise tears. You promise great TV and a ratings bonanza. She tells you she'd be delighted to do the interview.

Your second call is to the National Enquirer. Half a million dollars secures them exclusive rights to a fuzzy video still of Mr A+ using a plastic straw to administer cocaine to the hooker in an unusual and imaginative way. For your strategy to work, Mr A+ needs to be seen to have hit rock bottom. As with all great tabloid stories, the more spectacular the fall, the better.

Your third call is to a five-star rehab clinic.

Your fourth call is to your pet pap to give him an ETA for Mr A+'s arrival at the clinic. As usual, the split on any photos sold is seventy/thirty, the percentage in your favour.

Once the important calls are out of the way, only then do you call in the lawyers.

Your name is Jody 'JJ' Johnson and this is what they pay you the big bucks for.

13:00–13:30

1

JJ dropped her car keys into Victor's waiting hand and checked the time. Four and a half minutes late was about right for this particular business lunch. Just late enough to come across as the busy professional she was, not so late as to appear rude.

Victor slid into the Maserati, started the engine, then pulled away from the kerb and reversed expertly into a nearby slot. The valet was in his late fifties, an ex-Marine cruising gracefully towards retirement. He doubled as Alfie's security guard, which basically amounted to keeping the paparazzi out. In all the years JJ had been coming here there had never been any trouble inside the restaurant.

The four feet of sidewalk that separated the road from the entrance was covered with a large plain white canopy to discourage aerial photographs. It also provided shade from the relentless onslaught of the LA sun, a definite advantage on a day like this when the temperature was pushing into the nineties. As usual, Tony Bertollini met her at the door with a kiss for each cheek.

'JJ, my darling, you look spectacular. There's something different. No, don't tell me. It's your hair, isn't it?'

Tony was larger than life in every way. He weighed in at close to three hundred pounds, but carried it like it was two hundred. He was in his late fifties, with a full head of neat white hair and permanently flushed cheeks. His blue eyes twinkled with boyish mischief. The camp, affected, high-pitched Italian accent sat just the right side of annoying.

'It *is* your hair,' Tony added. 'You've had highlights put in.'

JJ smiled and shook her head. 'Tony, my hair's the same as it was last week. And the week before that. And it's the same as it's going to be next week.'

And it was the same. Black and short and not a highlight in sight. Time was too precious to spend worrying about hair. This philosophy carried over into her wardrobe. All her suits were black and tailored to fit, and more or less identical. The uncomfortable truth was that she operated in a man's world, and she found it easier to do that in pants rather than a dress.

That said, she did own a couple of black dresses for those rare occasions when she needed one, or it worked to her advantage to wear one. Pragmatism was a theme that ran through both her wardrobe and her life. Whatever got the job done. And, anyway, she liked black. It brought out the green in her eyes.

Tony took a sharp, dramatic intake of breath and slapped a meaty hand across his mouth. 'Don't tell me you've finally come across to the Dark Side and been Botoxed, darling.'

JJ laughed. 'No, I have not been Botoxed.'

'Well, whatever it is, you look amazing.'

'Since you brought it up, you're definitely looking younger today, Tony. Anything you wish to share?'

'Only that after all these years of searching, I might finally have found the secret of eternal youth.'

'And what's his name?'

Tony answered with a smile, then took her by the elbow and led the way inside. 'Dan Stone has already arrived,' he whispered. 'He's handsome. And ten minutes early, so he must be keen. And, if the rumours are to be believed, he's hung like a donkey.'

'Behave,' JJ whispered back.

She followed him into the dining room, the parquet flooring creaking underfoot. The walls were a cool, neutral grey, the ceiling a gentle off-white. Large Pollock-inspired paintings hung around the room, dazzling white canvases streaked with bold splashes of colour. The smells drifting through from the kitchen were to die for. There were a number of reasons why Alfie's was her favourite restaurant, but right there at the top of the list was the food. Chester, the head chef, was either a miracle-worker or he'd sold his soul to the devil.

The restaurant was small and intimate. That and the fact there wasn't a single window had made it a favourite haunt of the Hollywood elite. The entertainment industry was all about being seen in the right places, and, ironically, sometimes the best way to be seen was by not being seen. From the second Tony welcomed you through the smoked-glass doors, the outside world ceased to exist. The waiting list for a lunch reservation was currently running at six months. The wait for dinner was closer to nine. People tried to queue jump, and invariably failed. Tony was immune to both bribery and flattery. The only person he bent the rules for was JJ.

A few years ago there had been an incident involving a rent boy, and she'd made it go away. She had even waived her fee, which was a first. Tony had pledged his eternal undying gratitude, and she'd told him that she was happy to help. She'd been even happier to accept his offer of a lunchtime table once a week. She had actually been angling for a table once a month.

Since then they'd become BFFs. JJ loved Tony's irreverence and the fact that he had a heart the size of the sun. She loved that he could make her laugh so hard that she worried she might actually pee herself. Tony knew plenty of her secrets, and she knew plenty of his. What's more, she knew that he would never betray her trust. It was good to have someone she could just relax and be herself with. In a place as superficial as Hollywood, a friendship like that was as rare as a unicorn that crapped diamonds.

Usually there were only five tables, three on the upper level and two on the lower, all five spaced far enough apart to allow the guests total privacy. Today there were six. As a special favour to JJ, Tony had squeezed in an extra two-seat table on the lower level. She glanced over at it as she breezed past. The couple sat there were too wrapped up in themselves to notice her. They appeared to be getting on, although it wouldn't have mattered if they hadn't been. What did matter was that anyone looking at them saw two kids who were crazy about each other. Tony led the way to her favourite table. It was tucked away in the far corner of the upper level and was perfect for surreptitiously watching the other customers.

Stone stood when he spotted her. He gave her a cold hug, his lips brushing against her cheeks, then sat back down. Everything about the agent screamed *look at me*. The expensively casual clothes, the large TAG Heuer on his wrist, the diamond pinkie ring. He was in his late forties, but surgery made him appear a decade younger. His eyes were blue, his black hair finished in a widow's peak, and his fingernails were perfectly manicured. The dimple in his chin was pure Travolta. Stone was both handsome and rich, and anywhere else in the world he would have been a prime catch. But this was LA. Standards were different here. There were plenty of men who were handsome enough to make him look plain, and plenty of those were rich enough to make him look like a pauper.

Tony pulled out a chair and JJ sat. Seconds later, Holly, the head waitress, swooped in, deposited two menus and a vodka and tonic on the table, then swooped off again. It happened so effortlessly that JJ barely noticed. It happened before she even had a chance to flash a plastic smile at Stone.

'Sorry I'm late, Dan. Traffic was a nightmare. You know how it is.'

'Tell me about it. You know, I took delivery of a new Ferrari last week. Beautiful car, but what's the point in being able to do 180 miles an hour when you can't get up to twenty?'

JJ was only half-listening. While Stone talked, she stole glances over his shoulder, checking out names and faces against the databank in her head. Sorting, categorising, collating. There were people she knew, and a few she didn't. There were people she wanted to know better and people she would prefer to avoid.

Gary Thompson was a prime example of the latter. He was one of the top people over at DreamWorks, a bully and a grade-A asshole. They'd had a run-in a few years ago and ever since she had done her best to avoid him. The movie exec was cutting into a steak at the table nearest to hers. As far as JJ was concerned, that showed what a Neanderthal he was. You have someone like Chester working miracles in the kitchen and you order a steak. It was wrong on every level.

Excluding herself and Stone, there were fifteen customers today. It was the usual lunchtime crowd of actors, directors, producers and agents. There were two pairs, a threesome and two foursomes. The split of male to female was pretty much fifty-fifty.

There was even a face from old Hollywood. Elizabeth Hayward had been a star in the fifties, an era when everything looked golden but was made from the same tin as today. Multiple facelifts had left the ageing actress with skin stretched so tight it glowed, and eyes pinned open in a look of permanent astonishment. She was part of the group of four on the lower level. There was some sort of celebration going on. A birthday party was JJ's best guess, although she doubted Hayward would be celebrating her real age.

It was sad, but JJ understood why the actress had taken such extreme measures with her appearance. Once upon a time Hayward had been one of the most beautiful women in the world. But time could be cruel, especially to Hollywood actresses. As her looks had faded, the parts had slowly dried up until nobody wanted to hire her. That was why she'd done everything in her power to halt the ageing process, getting increasingly desperate with every passing year.

The depressing reality was that JJ knew more women who'd had surgery than hadn't. A nip here, a tuck there, a little Botox. Up until now she'd resisted the temptation, but there would come a point when she'd need to get some work done. She was thirty-eight and the years were catching up. There were lines and wrinkles that hadn't been there six months ago. Lines and wrinkles that could easily be erased.

The problem with plastic surgery was that it was a slippery slope. Where did you draw the line? And it wasn't just women who succumbed to the lure of the knife. Men were not immune. Take Dan Stone, for example. And he wasn't alone there. Admittedly, it was easier for men to age in Hollywood, but more and more of them were getting surgery these days.

Ed Richards was at the next table. As well as being one of the most handsome men in the world, he was currently the most bankable star in Hollywood. His last three films alone had grossed over a billion dollars. But he was pushing fifty, and not getting any younger. Richards was adamant he hadn't had surgery. He'd told JJ this to her face, and been totally convincing. However, she had it on good authority that even he'd had work done.

And then there was Alex King. The actor was sitting at that little two-seat table on the lower level, enjoying a lunch date with Simone Kristiansen, a stunning Norwegian supermodel. King was the new kid on the block. If his career continued on its current trajectory, he'd definitely end up an A+. *Killing Time* had been the summer's surprise blockbuster. The film had launched him as the new must-have action hero.

King was the real deal, the complete package and then some. He looked great on screen, had an amazing body, and he could act. His was the sort of stellar talent that only came along once a generation. He was currently on three million a film, but that figure was rising fast. It wouldn't be long before he joined the eight-figure league. JJ glanced over again, just to make sure he was behaving himself. So far, so good. He was sitting there with a look of rapt concentration, as though his date was sharing the secrets of the universe with him. The kid could certainly act, she'd give him that much.

JJ had planned the whole thing like it was a military campaign. The paparazzi would be waiting for the couple when they left Alfie's, and by the end of the afternoon the pictures would be all over the Internet. Tomorrow night they'd get 'spotted' leaving a nightclub, which would confirm that Alfie's wasn't a one-off. An intimate snap of them making out beside a pool would prove this was the real thing.

By this time next week they would be Hollywood's next golden couple. The new Brangelina. JJ was still looking for a suitable tag. Simonex didn't work, and Alsimone sounded like something you might use to treat haemorrhoids. She would come up with something, though. It was just a matter of time. Like so much of what she did, this particular love story was very much a work in progress.

2

Alex King smiled at Simone, then glanced around the dining room, trying to take it all in. There were moments like now when he still couldn't quite believe how much his life had changed. It was insane. Totally off-the-charts crazy. A couple of years ago he would have struggled to get a busboy's job in a place like this, and now here he was eating lunch. Hell, a couple of years ago he would have struggled to pay for a meal at McDonald's.

Since *Killing Time* had gone supernova, he'd felt like he was living in two universes simultaneously. In one, he was Alex King, the action hero. In the other, he was Alex King, a trailer-trash white boy from Ohio who was never going to amount to anything. A part of him was just waiting for the dream to end. At any moment he was going to wake up and find himself back in that crappy two-bedroom apartment in downtown LA that he'd shared with Sapphire, a drag queen whose hands were too big and whose Adam's apple stuck out too much, and who'd snored so loudly he'd almost shaken the paper-thin walls down.

Simone said something, then paused. The pause went on long enough to indicate that she was expecting a contribution from him. King nodded, hoping this was the right response. And then Simone was off again, talking at a hundred miles an hour.

King tuned her out and let his gaze drift towards the upper level. He spotted JJ and his blood froze. She was at a table right at the back, talking to some dude who was trying way too hard to get noticed. What the hell was she doing here? He shrank back in his seat and prayed for the ground to swallow him up. Today was going to be hard enough without having this to deal with. How was he supposed to focus with JJ watching his every move? How was he supposed to concentrate?

He tried to shift position so JJ wouldn't see his face. Not that it would do any good. She'd already seen him and it would be crazy to pretend otherwise. She would have spotted him the second she walked into the room. He took a deep breath and tried to push JJ from his thoughts, but no matter how hard he pushed, there she was, larger than life and twice as scary.

There were thousands of restaurants in LA and she'd come to this one, on this particular day, at this particular time. Thinking it through, it made perfect sense. After all, it was JJ who'd suggested he come here, JJ who'd somehow managed to secure a last-minute reservation. She was obviously checking up to make sure he behaved.

'Everything okay, sweetie?' Simone asked.

King forced a smile. 'Yeah, everything's fine.'

Simone was peering across the table, candlelight softening the fake concern in her face. Her accent was an odd mix of Norwegian, English and Valley Girl. King reckoned she'd probably overdosed on too much US TV as a kid. Judging by the way she kept going on about those lame reality shows, she was still addicted. Reality shows aside, a love of all things TV was one of the few things they actually had in common. His childhood had been a living nightmare. TV hadn't just been a mother and a father to him, it had been his lifeline, a promise that there was a better life out there just waiting for him.

'Are you sure you're okay? You look pale.'

King forced an even bigger smile, then leant across the table and touched her hand.

'You are so beautiful. Do you know that?'

Simone smiled in a way that made it obvious that this wasn't exactly front-page news. And it wasn't. She was one of the most beautiful women in the world. All her life, people had been telling her how attractive she was.

For the thousandth time, King asked himself what he was doing. Millions of red-blooded males across the planet had wondered what it would be like to get hot and sweaty with Simone, and this afternoon he would find out. The thought was enough to make him feel physically sick. The only way to survive the next few hours was to treat it like any other acting job. Smile for the cameras, deliver the right lines at the right moment, and make sure he hit his mark.

Lights, cameras, action.

He hated JJ for putting him in this situation. Hated her crazy-assed schemes.

'Could you excuse me for a minute?' he said. 'I need to use the restroom.'

'Sure, sweetie, but don't be long.'

'I'll be back in two seconds.'

King folded his napkin and placed it on the table. Wrapping his head around the do's and don'ts of eating somewhere like this was so stressful. And dumb. You had to use the correct fork, the correct knife, drink from the right glass. It totally messed with his head. Where he grew up, napkins were made from paper, and you only ever got them on burger night.

A waitress saw him stand and moved into a position where she could steer him towards the restroom. King walked clumsily across the room, feeling like everyone was watching him, which they weren't. They were all far too involved in their own dramas. Even Simone was ignoring him. She'd slipped a compact from her Gucci bag and was busy fixing her make-up.

He hurried into the restroom and pulled the door closed behind him. It was good to have a few moments to himself. He felt safe here. There was nobody watching him. Nobody talking at him. No one making demands. The men's room was small and clean and smelled of oranges. And it wasn't anything like he'd expected. In places like this, the restrooms were usually totally over the top, but not here. The walls were plain white, the taps made from stainless steel. There was soft lighting, a shelf with some towels on, a bowl of mints, and that was about it.

King locked himself into the cubicle in the far corner and sat down on the toilet lid. He took a deep breath, told himself to get his shit together, and did his best to push back the feelings of uselessness that seemed to be constantly hovering in the background. He *could* do this. He'd been through much worse and survived. It was only a date, for Christ's sake. Okay, it was a date with one of the world's most beautiful women, but, when all was said and done, it was just a date. It wasn't like he was being asked to murder anyone.

It had been so long since his last real date he wasn't sure what to do anymore. Before *Killing Time* everything had been so much simpler. Back then, he'd been in a steady relationship. He could go see a movie, go to a bar, just hang out and have a good time, and nobody would care.

Nowadays it was so much more complicated. The people he went out with only wanted to be with him because he was Alex King the movie star. They didn't want him, they just wanted to brush up against his fame. And the few times he had been with someone who'd seemed genuine, they'd ended up playing dodge-the-paparazzi, which was a real mood-killer.

He forced in another deep breath and the world retreated to a more manageable distance. It was just a date, he told himself again.

Just a date.

3

Christ, he goes on. JJ didn't let her smile falter, not for a second. She had a strong urge to leave Stone here talking to himself, but he probably wouldn't even notice she'd gone. Right now, Dan Stone was sitting slap-bang at the centre of the universe, which was his favourite place to be. JJ remembered why she'd put this meeting off for so long. The guy was so self-obsessed he'd turned it into an artform.

Unfortunately, keeping narcissists like Dan Stone happy was a tedious but necessary part of the job. Agents like Stone were her bread and butter. They looked after the talent, the very same talent who had a knack for getting into trouble on a regular basis, the very same talent who kept repeating the mistakes of those faded stars and starlets who'd gone before them.

You'd think they'd learn, but they never did. This was something JJ thanked God for each and every day. If anyone ever came up with a cure for stupidity, she'd be out of business. This was a line she had heard a hundred times from the late, great Johnny Wiesner. Out of the few people she actually admired in this town, Wiesner topped the list every time. He'd survived more than fifty years playing the Hollywood PR game, which was no mean feat. The fact that he survived with his integrity more or less intact was nothing short of a miracle. You'd have to search hard to find someone who had a bad word to say about him.

Wiesner was already well into his seventies when he'd hired her fresh out of college. To this day she didn't know why he'd done that. There had been plenty of people out there who were better qualified, and more experienced. Clearly he'd seen something, though. He'd taken her under his wing and been both a mentor and an inspiration. It was Wiesner who'd re-branded her as JJ. 'From time to time you're going to have to break balls,' he'd told her in that gruff, warm voice that had saved and made a thousand careers. 'No one called Jody could ever break balls.'

It was Wiesner who'd persuaded her to strike out on her own. She'd visited him in the hospital after his first stroke and he'd told her to go for it. 'JJ,' he'd said, 'you're never going to be truly happy until you're the captain of the ship.' The stroke had made it difficult for him to speak but he could still sell an idea. He'd gone on to tell her that she reminded him of himself back in the day. He also told her that he'd point a couple of clients in her direction.

Six months later, Wiesner had had a second stroke and died. By then JJ had been renting a small office that was as close to the action as she could afford. Her roster of clients numbered six, all courtesy of Wiesner. Those early years had been tough but fun. The business got bigger, the client list expanded, and she moved to larger premises. Brightlight was a long way from being the largest PR firm in town, but it was one of the most respected. JJ liked to think that Wiesner would have been proud.

While Stone droned on, she sipped her vodka and tonic and watched Simone out of the corner of her eye. The model was gazing around the room like she'd died and gone to Disneyland. A flirtatious twinkle here, a flirtatious twinkle there. Simone and King really did make a great-looking couple. JJ reckoned that a three-month relationship would be about long enough.

The beautiful thing about this plan was the fact that even after they split up the headlines would still keep coming. First up, there would be the inevitable kiss and tell, where Simone would inform the world what a stud King was. Or not, as the case might be. Even a negative story wouldn't pose a problem, since King's legion of loyal female fans would assume it was sour grapes. Then there would be all the speculation as to whether or not they were going to get back together again. Spin it hard enough and they'd maintain traction for at least another six months. Wiesner would have loved it.

King was still in the rest room. Either that or he'd done a runner. JJ wouldn't have put that past him. Getting him to come here today had been like pulling teeth. She knew everything there was to know about the actor. She knew all about his trailer-park past. She knew all about the beatings and the abuse. She also knew that it didn't matter how sparkling the future was, the past always had a way of sneaking up on you when you least expected it. The past defined you, it shaped who you were. It didn't matter how good an actor you were, there was no getting away from that fact.

King's handlers were going to have to be careful. If they kept him on the right path then everyone would make a ton of money. Get it wrong and he'd end up being yet another casualty of the Hollywood machine.

'I'm going to turn Carmine into the biggest thing ever,' Stone was saying. 'We're talking bigger than Marilyn.'

Sure you are, thought JJ. This was Stone's favourite theme. Every new client was going to be the next big thing. His evangelical optimism was tiring.

'And when does shooting begin?' she asked.

'Already started. Carmine's up in Montreal as we speak. By all accounts, the dailies are incredible. I'm telling you, JJ, she was born to do this. The director loves her, the crew loves her, everyone loves her.'

JJ wondered how long that would last for. If Carmine Hart followed the usual trajectory then it would last just long enough for her to start believing her own hype and turn into a prima donna bitch from hell.

'Sounds like you've got a real diamond there, Dan. You make sure you keep hold of her.'

Stone laughed. 'The contract I got her to sign, even Houdini couldn't escape from it.'

JJ reached for her menu, which was Stone's cue to pick up his. She knew the menu by heart, but anything to shut him up, even for a minute or two.

Someone suddenly screamed and JJ's head snapped up. The scream sounded all wrong in the rarefied atmosphere of Alfie's. It was jarring and surprising, and completely out of context. Conversations stopped, cutlery rattled onto plates, the room fell silent. All eyes turned towards the woman who'd screamed. Her hands were over her mouth and she was staring wide-eyed towards the corridor that led to the kitchen.

JJ followed her gaze and saw a suicide bomber. For a second, she just stared. Three details demanded her complete attention. The black balaclava, the silenced submachine gun, and the explosive vest.

The kitchen staff were walking in front of him, hands in the air, expressions of fear and disbelief etched onto their faces. Chester was leading the way. JJ couldn't remember a time when she hadn't seen the chef smiling and laughing. He was one of the gentlest souls she'd ever met. Holly the waitress was there, too. Tears streamed down her face, and the only reason she was managing to stay on her feet was because she was being supported by one of the kitchen hands. She couldn't see Victor. Hopefully he was okay. JJ's fork clattered onto her plate, and every single muscle went taut as she braced herself for the explosion. A millisecond of intense light and searing heat, and then nothing. It would happen so quickly there wouldn't be time for pain. One second alive, the next vaporised.

An image of Tom flashed up inside her head. Despite all the therapy, despite her best attempts to lose herself in her work, the memories were always there, lurking just below the surface. For a split second all she could see was the rippling reflections of the lights on the pool, and his still body floating face-down in the water.

JJ pushed the memory away, swallowed back the guilt, and searched for a good memory. If she was going to die, then she wanted her last thought to be a good one. The memory she locked on to was one of the best. It came from a time when the dark days would have been inconceivable. Back then, there had been plenty of laughter and love, so much that JJ had thought it would last for ever.

She was sitting with Tom by the pool, hypnotised by the most glorious sunset she'd ever seen. She had turned to Tom, expecting him to be as transfixed as she was, but he wasn't watching the sun go down, he was watching her. He didn't say a word. He didn't need to because the look on his face said everything that needed to be said. JJ had never felt more loved than she had at that moment.

4

JJ wasn't sure how much time had passed. What she did know was that by some miracle she was still alive. She opened her eyes and saw the bomber push through the kitchen staff. He strode into the middle of the lower level and turned through a full 360 degrees, clocking faces, his gun tracing a lazy circle around the room.

'Okay, folks, let's get some things straight. First off, this vest is packed with enough explosives to take out this restaurant, the rest of the block, and the next block, too. I press the button and your families will be lucky to get enough pieces back to fill a matchbox. From this moment on I am God. I have the power to giveth life, and you better believe that I've got the power to take it away.'

The speech felt rehearsed, and the way it was delivered made JJ think of Samuel L. Jackson. Same delivery, same level of gravitas, and pretty much the same accent, too. The bomber spun through another 360 degrees, aiming the gun as he turned to drive home the fact that he was in charge now.

'Secondly, don't even think about playing hero. Push me hard enough and I will flick the switch. So, here's how this works. You are going to do exactly what I say, and the reason you're going to do that is because you've all got a lot more to lose than I do.'

The bomber shook off his backpack and placed it on the floor. He motioned Tony forward with a wiggle of his index finger.

'You. Come here.'

Tony walked over. There was no hesitation, no debate. He kept eye contact with the bomber the whole way, staring him down like he was a rattlesnake.

'You're the owner, right?'

'Yes, I'm the owner.'

The camp Italian accent was gone, replaced with a harsh New Jersey grate. This was disorientating, but didn't come as a complete surprise to JJ. Back when they were first getting to know each other they'd had a long evening together that had stretched through until morning. They had polished off a couple of $2,000 bottles of vintage red wine and the best part of a bottle of Courvoisier XO Imperial, and had ended up playing Truth Or Dare.

Allegedly, Tony was the son of a New Jersey factory worker, and in his younger days he'd been a boxer. Fifteen fights and fifteen wins, eleven by knock-out. The first two confessions JJ had believed, the third she wasn't sure about. Like a lot of Hollywood's wildlife, Tony existed in that grey area where fact and fiction collided.

'Put your cell phone on the table,' the bomber said.

Tony pulled out his phone and dropped it on the nearest table. It landed with a clatter and rattled to a standstill. JJ couldn't get over how loud this sounded. She figured it was all a matter of perspective. Everyone had fallen as silent as they could. There were a few stifled sobs, the occasional creaking of a chair, and that was it. The smallest of noises had taken on extra weight and significance. Her own breathing was deafening, and the gentle hum of the air-conditioning sounded like a jet engine.

'I want the grilles down and the doors locked.'

Tony didn't move. The bomber raised his gun and pushed it into the restaurant owner's chest. JJ's heart froze. What the hell was he doing? Someone points a gun at you, you do what they say. You don't argue, you don't hesitate, you just do it.

'At least let the women go.'

The bomber paused like he was giving this some serious consideration, then he flipped his gun over and rammed the butt hard into Tony's face. The flat crack of metal connecting with flesh and bone filled the room. Tony collapsed to his knees, blood gushing from his nose and staining his mouth, chin and clothes. JJ shrank back in her seat and took a sharp intake of breath. She slapped a hand over her mouth, but it was too late to stop the noise getting out. There were tears in her eyes. Tears of fear, and tears for Tony. *Please God, don't let him die.*

The bomber aimed the gun, and JJ repeated the short prayer in her head, over and over, pleading and bargaining and wishing for a miracle. *Don't let him die, don't let him die, please God don't let him die.* Just when she reached the point where she was convinced that God wasn't listening, the bomber lowered the gun. JJ let out a long breath and sagged back in her chair. That had been way too close for comfort. Tony grabbed hold of the nearest table and hauled himself up. Without another word, he turned and headed for the front door. A couple of moments later, the grilles came down with an electric rumble. The silent stillness that followed was like the end of the world.

5

Alex King inched the door open so he could hear what was going on, just enough so that he could close it quickly if he needed to. Everything had gone quiet. Too damn quiet. He shut the door, pressed his forehead against the cool wood, and tried to work out what the hell he was going to do now.

This was unreal, totally whacked out. Stuff like this happened in Syria or Afghanistan, not LA. It was like something from a movie, with one big difference. This was actually happening. Fear washed through him. He didn't want to die. It wasn't right. He was only twenty-six for Christ's sake. His whole life was supposed to be ahead of him. He had to get out of here, had to get out now. But how?

His heart was pounding like it was about to explode. Cold sweat stuck to his skin. This was so screwed up. There was a suicide bomber out there, and any second now he was going to hit the switch and that would be game over. King cracked the door open again. It was still all quiet, which somehow made everything a million times worse.

Think.

But it was impossible to think. His head was filled with white noise and every time he caught hold of half a thought he imagined the bomb going off and whatever was in his brain would disappear. The only thought he seemed able to keep hold of was the fact that he was going to die.

He shut his eyes and for a brief moment he was back in Cincinnati. He could hear his mom crying in the next room, and he could hear the sound of heavy footsteps in the narrow passageway that led to his bedroom door. His ears were still ringing with the meaty slap of flesh hitting flesh and the sound of her screams. He hated his mom, but he'd still wanted to rush in there. Partly because it was the right thing to do, but mostly because he wanted to make the noise stop. The problem was that if he had, her boyfriend would have started in on him.

King's eyes sprang open and he was back in Alfie's, a crazy guy with a bomb in the next room. He wasn't sure which was worse, being in here or being in that Cincinnati trailer park. When you got right down to it, there wasn't much difference. He'd been powerless to do anything then, and he was just as powerless now.

6

Alex King wasn't here.

The thought caught JJ off guard, sending a jolt of electricity sparking through her. She glanced around the room and saw she was right. He hadn't come back from the restroom. She wasn't sure if this was a pro or a con. If he decided to play hero then it was a serious con. Nobody had been killed so far but she didn't doubt for a second that the bomber could and would pull the trigger.

She put all thoughts of King aside and tried to get things into some sort of perspective. The problem was that this was just too big and too crazy to comprehend. Even for LA where crazy was a way of life, this was in a league of its own. In order to even begin to make sense of this situation she needed to detach herself from it. She was terrified, more scared than she'd ever been in her entire life, and it was good to recognise that fact. However, getting emotional never solved anything.

She closed her eyes, took a long, deep steadying breath, then counted to ten. The shit had well and truly hit the fan, so ten seconds wouldn't make any difference. When she opened her eyes she felt calmer. Her heart was still racing, but she could think more clearly.

So, what did she know?

Firstly, and this was important, this was no terrorist attack. If it had been, they would be dead by now. Suicide bombers didn't operate like this. They climbed quietly on board a bus or a train, sat down without making a fuss, mouthed a few prayers to whichever God they believed in, then detonated their bombs. They didn't go around waving guns and making well-rehearsed speeches.

Secondly, she could see the bomber's hands and the skin around his eyes, and it was as white as hers. Judging by the crow's feet and bags, she'd say he was at least fifty. And that was a Deep South Baptist preacher voice. Tennessee or Georgia or Louisiana. According to CNN, terrorists were either Arab or black, and none of them spoke like they'd been born a stone's throw from the Mississippi. And most were young, in their twenties or thirties. Some were even younger, just teenagers, and the reason they were so young was because younger minds were easier to brainwash. Head down to Guantanamo Bay and that was the demographic you'd find.

That said, domestic terrorism was a definite possibility. Maybe this guy was the next Timothy McVeigh, or the next Unabomber. McVeigh had killed well over a hundred people when he'd set off a bomb in Oklahoma City back in the nineties. The attack had made him infamous the world over. And that was another possibility. Maybe he was just out to get his fifteen minutes of fame. After all, almost forty years had passed since John Lennon was shot and people were still talking about Mark Chapman.

JJ had noticed something else that chilled her to the bone. The spark of obsession in the bomber's eyes was combined with an aura of complete, unquestioning self-belief. It was something she'd seen plenty of in this town. The big difference was that there usually weren't any bombs or guns in the equation.

'Everybody on your feet.' The bomber nodded to the restaurant's upper level. 'I want everyone up there now.'

JJ stood up and watched everyone from the lower level hustle up the stairs. Counting herself, there were twenty-five people in total. This broke down into sixteen customers, eight members of staff and Tony. The ratio of male to female was still more or less fifty-fifty.

'Blow out the candles, move the tables and chairs to one side, then get down on the floor.'

JJ helped Stone lift their table out of the way, while Tony dragged the chairs to one side. The restaurant owner's face was a bloody mess and he was in a lot of pain. She caught his eye and mouthed, 'You okay?' He gave a small shrug and did his best to dig up a smile. She finished moving the table and sat down with everyone else on the cold wooden floor.

'You. Come over here.'

The bomber was pointing to a middle-aged black woman who was wearing a bright orange headscarf that matched her skirt. JJ recognised her straightaway. Natasha Lovett was an Oscar-winning film director whose critically acclaimed movies dealt with the heavier social issues. They were big on art, but not particularly commercial. It was the sort of thing the Academy loved. Lovett stood up and walked over to the bomber. She was trembling from head to toe and looked absolutely terrified.

'Please don't hurt me.'

'So long as you do exactly what I tell you to do, you'll be fine. Take out your cell phone.'

'I can't. I'm sorry.'

The bomber raised his gun and pointed it at her chest. 'And that is the wrong answer.'

'No, please don't shoot.' Natasha was talking fast, her words tripping over each other. Her cheeks were wet with tears. 'I don't have my phone because it's in my bag. Back at my table.'

'Well what are you waiting for? Go get it.'

Natasha walked unsteadily down the steps to the restaurant's lower level. She was moving quickly, almost jogging. Stolen glances at the bomber, stolen glances at the gun. She reached the bottom of the steps and looked back. The bomber lifted the gun and made a show of aiming at her head. She turned away quickly and got moving again. JJ could hear her mumbling something under her breath. She caught a couple of hurried words. *Hallowed be. Kingdom Come. Power. Glory. Amen.*

The bomber still had his gun trained on her, following every move. Natasha reached the table. She lifted her bag from the back of the chair, unzipped it. The bag was the same shade of orange as her dress and headscarf.

'Stop.'

Natasha froze with her hand half-in and half-out of the canvas bag. The bomber aimed the gun and JJ felt her heart stutter. She was convinced he was going to pull the trigger. She'd never been so sure of anything in her life. Her blood was pumping and the adrenalin was making her tingle. Her senses were operating in a heightened state. Sight, smell, hearing. The smell of food still filled the room, but where it once tempted, it now made her feel sick.

'I think it's best if you bring that bag up here, don't you?' The bomber reaffirmed his grip on the gun. His eyes had narrowed to suspicious slits behind the balaclava. 'How do I know you don't have a gun in there? Now, that would be far too much like temptation, don't you think? A quick squeeze of the trigger and I'm a dead man. And you become a hero for your troubles. The mayor would probably give you a medal. Is that what you're angling for? A nice shiny medal to show how clever you are?'

'I don't have a gun.'

'Just bring me the bag.'

Natasha climbed the steps to the upper level, slowly and unsteadily, like it was a real effort to put one foot in front of the other. She held out the bag and the bomber snatched it from her. He tipped it up and her whole life clattered onto the floor. Make-up, a script, packets of tissues, all sorts of junk. The cell phone was one of the first things to fall out.

'Well, well, it looks like you were telling the truth. Wonders never cease. Maybe there are still a few honest people left in this town after all. Okay, pick up your cell.'

Natasha knelt down and picked up the phone. She was holding it between her thumb and forefinger like it was radioactive.

'Okay, here's what you're going to do. You're going to get down on the floor and point that cell phone at me. Then you're going to do a quick sweep across all these fine folk sitting nice and quiet like the good little mice they are. I reckon fifteen seconds of footage should do the trick. The thing is, it needs to look like I don't know I'm being filmed. Can you do that?'

Natasha nodded, and the bomber nodded back. Even though most of his mouth was hidden behind the balaclava, JJ saw enough to know he was grinning. The sick bastard was actually enjoying this. She could hear it in his voice.

'And make sure you get the gun and the vest in. That's important. Okay, on the floor.'

Natasha got down on her knees. Her eyes were wide with fear and she was trembling worse than ever. She pointed her cell phone at the bomber. He'd positioned himself with the gun visible and his masked face turned away from her. The explosive vest was wrapped all the way around his body, so there was no problem getting that in the shot.

The director swept the phone in a narrow arc that took in everyone huddled on the floor. Some people were looking directly at her, some were looking pointedly away. Everyone looked scared to death. Natasha finished filming and lowered the cell phone.

‘Show me,’ the bomber said.

Natasha held the cell phone up. JJ couldn’t see the screen, but she could tell from the way the bomber was nodding that he liked what he saw. Had Natasha been chosen at random? It could be a coincidence, but she wasn’t convinced. In her experience, you created your own coincidences. When it came to making films, Natasha was by far the best qualified person in the room. And earlier, the bomber had known that Tony was the owner. On that basis, he’d clearly done some sort of reconnaissance. The question was how much, and why. It was certainly something to think about.

‘You did good,’ the bomber said. ‘Go sit with the others.’

Natasha hurried over and dropped to the floor.

‘Okay, hands up who watches CNN?’

No one moved.

‘Come on people, it’s a simple enough question. Who watches CNN?’

A couple of uncertain hands went up.

‘What about Fox? Any fans of Fox News here?’

The hands quickly went down and a couple of new ones took their place.

‘Me, I prefer TRN. They might be smaller, but that means they try harder.’

The bomber took a scrap of paper from his pocket and typed something into Natasha’s cell. If JJ had to guess, she’d say that TRN was about to be given the scoop.

7

Alex King's cell phone vibrated in the pocket of his jeans and a surge of hope flooded through him. Not only did he have his cell with him, it was switched to silent, thank God. He pulled the phone from his pocket, saw his agent's name lit up on the screen, and let the call ring through to voicemail. His agent was the last person he wanted to talk to.

The fact his phone had been on silent was a lucky break, just one in a long line that had started a few years back when he'd got the audition for *Killing Time.* If he had to pinpoint a moment when things had started to turn in his favour, that was it. Since then his life had been a rollercoaster ride. There had been the occasional moment where he'd been able to catch his breath, but most of the time he'd just been holding on tight while he flew through one turn after another. And, man, it had been a blast.

It had actually reached the point where he'd started to believe that good things should happen to him, that he deserved them to happen. This was the big payoff, and, after everything he'd been through, he'd earned it. Then today had happened. In some ways this shouldn't be a surprise. This was how it worked. You thought you'd finally got everything sussed, then something like this came along to prove that life really did suck. King stopped himself there. The last thing he needed was to plunge into a downer. Yes, this situation was screwed up, but it wasn't all bad.

For a start, the guy with the bomb wasn't a suicide bomber. That much was obvious. If he had been, they'd all be dead by now. And that was a massive positive. While you were still breathing and your heart was still beating there was always hope, right? If there was one thing he'd learnt from his shitty childhood, it was that. Another positive was the fact that he had his cell with him. He punched in 911 and pressed the phone to his ear. The operator who answered was female with a nasally high-pitched East Coast whine.

'911. What's your emergency?'

'I'm in Alfie's,' King whispered. 'The restaurant. Some crazy guy has come in with a bomb. A terrorist. We need help.'

'Can you speak louder, sir?'

'No. I don't want him to hear me.'

'Are you safe?'

'I think so. I hope so.'

'Okay, stay where you are and I'll get a squad car despatched straightaway.'

'*One* squad car?' King hissed. 'Didn't you hear me? There's a terrorist with a bomb out there.'

'I know this is difficult, sir, but please try and calm down. I'm going to need some details. What's your name?'

'Alex King.'

'Like the actor.'

'I am the actor.'

A pause. 'Sir, I have to warn you that it's an offence to make hoax calls to 911.'

King sighed and shook his head. The white noise in his head was back, and it was more deafening than ever. 'Listen, ma'am, this is for real.'

Silence on the other end of the line.

'Jesus Christ, this isn't a hoax. I repeat, this is not a hoax. My name really is Alex King, and I am really in Alfie's, and there really is some lunatic out there with a bomb.'

'Okay, sir, please stay calm. Whereabouts are you in the restaurant?'

'I'm hiding out in the restroom.'

'And the rest of the hostages?'

'They're in the main part of the restaurant.'

'How many are there?'

'I don't know. Twenty. Thirty, maybe.'

'Is the bomber on his own?'

'How should I know? Weren't you listening? I'm trapped in the restroom.'

'Okay, I'd like you to stay on the line. Can you do that?'

'Yeah, I'll stay on the line.'

Something creaked on the other side of the door. It sounded like a footstep. King killed the call and stuffed the phone into his pocket. He'd seen enough hostage movies to know how this one played out. The bomber would discover him hiding here, and then he'd kill him. The hostages who stood out got into the most trouble, and being caught in a restroom making calls to 911 definitely qualified as standing out. That said, if he was going down, he was going down fighting. He was no longer that little kid from Ohio who'd curled into a ball and wished himself dead while his mom's boyfriend had beaten him. That kid got left behind the day he'd climbed on board a Greyhound in Cincinnati and got the hell out of there.

In *Killing Time*, he'd played Max Murphy, a Gulf War veteran who turned vigilante after his girlfriend was murdered. The film was a cross between *Rambo* and *Death Wish*. Max Murphy hadn't been any old grunt, he'd been the youngest ever member of Delta Force. He was an expert at hand-to-hand combat, a crack shot. Basically, he was a one-man killing machine. King had done his homework. He'd learned to shoot and he'd learned all about hand-to-hand combat, and he'd worked out every day with his personal trainer. Right now, he was in the best shape of his life.

And he had the element of surprise on his side. He pressed himself up against the wall next to the door and waited. His plan was simple. When the door opened he would hit the bomber with everything he'd got. The last thing he'd be expecting was for someone to fight back.

Long seconds passed and nothing happened. King pressed his ear against the door and listened hard. Since that first squeak he hadn't heard a thing. No more squeaks, no footsteps, no voice telling him to come out with his hands up. But that didn't mean the bomber wasn't out there right now, gun in hand, edging along the corridor.

Any second now the restroom door was going to burst open and the shooting would start. King had been shot once before. Not for real, but it was real enough. Near the end of *Killing Time* Max Murphy got winged by one of the bad guys. What King remembered most was how much it had stung when the special FX blood bag on his bicep exploded. Man, that had hurt like hell.

He pressed his ear against the door. Still all quiet. He gave it another thirty seconds, then inched the door open and peered through the crack. The corridor was empty. He shut the door and smiled to himself. So far, so good. He'd been called lucky so many times lately that he was thinking of adopting it as his middle name.

Alex 'Lucky' King.

His smile turned into a wide grin. Lucky didn't even come close to covering it. What he had went way beyond luck. He wasn't just lucky, he was the original nine-life cat.

8

The bomber held Natasha Lovett's orange canvas bag high in the air so everyone could see it.

'Okay, people, put all your valuables in here. Watches, rings, necklaces, bracelets, everything. Oh, and I want your cell phones, too. All of them. The last thing I want is for one of you fine folk to call in the cavalry. My mama always told me that the best way to deal with temptation was to keep it out of sight. What the eye don't see, the heart won't yearn for.'

He grinned another of those invisible grins then walked over to Ed Richards. JJ couldn't get over how composed the actor looked. Either he was braver than she'd given him credit for, or he was acting. A third possibility was that he'd become so detached from reality he'd lost the ability to tell the difference between fact and fantasy. Thinking about it, that last explanation seemed most likely. Richards was Hollywood royalty. These days he only had a passing acquaintance with the real world.

Richards dropped his watch, phone and wallet into the bag. He hesitated a moment, then pulled off his wedding ring and put that in as well. The next three people all had their valuables ready. They dropped them into the bag without meeting the bomber's eyes. JJ was next. The bomber hunkered down and shook the bag in her face. The contents made a dull jangle, metal clattering against plastic. Up close, she could smell his cheap deodorant, and the cheap detergent he used on his clothes. She could sense his cockiness.

She could feel him watching her.

She was suddenly all too aware of how fragile her life was. If he chose to, this complete stranger could end it in a heartbeat. She glanced up and caught a glimpse of his grey eyes. They were framed by the holes in the balaclava. Cold, uncompromising, judgemental. The whites were shot through with snaking red veins. She quickly removed her Rolex and dropped it in. Her cell followed. JJ wasn't big on jewellery. She'd never had her ears pierced, and she hated the constrictive feel of rings on her fingers. She did wear a plain gold wedding band, though. It was on a chain around her neck.

Her parents had split up when she was thirteen. There had been a big fight and her father had stormed out. Her mother had downed half a bottle of vodka then thrown the ring into the trash. After she'd passed out on the sofa, JJ had retrieved the ring. She'd been going through a *Lord of the Rings* phase at the time and managed to convince herself that the ring had the power to bring her father back.

The magic didn't work. Her father had gone on to marry a woman ten years his junior, her mother married a realtor, and JJ learned to adapt to being the product of a broken home. She'd kept the ring all these years because it reminded her that there were no happy-ever-afters. Fairy tales were for kindergarteners and the seriously deluded.

JJ unclipped the necklace, redid the clasp, then balled the necklace up and dropped it into the bag. The bomber moved on to the next person, and the next. Jewellery and cell phones clattered into the bag. He stopped in front of Elizabeth Hayward and shook the bag at her. The jewellery she dropped into the bag had to be worth at least half a million dollars. Loud, garish pieces with gemstones the size of rocks. Earrings, bracelets, rings.

'I want the watch, too.'

Hayward glanced at the diamond-encrusted Cartier. When she looked back there were tears in her eyes.

'Please let me keep it. This was the last thing my late husband ever bought for me.'

The bomber considered this for a moment. 'How long ago did he die?'

'Six months ago.'

'You must really miss him?'

'I do. More than you can ever imagine.'

'Okay, I'm going to do you a favour. You can keep the watch.'

Hayward's eyes lit up with gratitude. 'Thank you. Thank you so much. You don't know what that means to me.'

'That's not the favour.'

Gratitude turned to puzzlement. 'I don't understand.'

'Say hi to your husband for me.'

The bomber raised his gun and squeezed the trigger.

13:30–14:00

1

Rob Taylor roared into the Palm Tree's parking lot on his vintage Harley and skidded to a halt beside a rusting Pontiac. He bent over to fix his hair in the rear-view mirror. It didn't take long. He'd gone for the just-got-up-look for two reasons. One, it was practical, and two, his fans loved it.

Rob wasn't traditionally handsome, but he had one of those faces that looked great on TV. He'd started in print, working for the *LA Times*. TRN had seen his potential and had brought him on board as their roving reporter. It was the best move he'd ever made. His salary had quadrupled, and every night was party night. The Harley had been thrown in as a sweetener.

Tara Clarke wasn't far behind on her Suzuki. She pulled up alongside him and killed the engine. Tara was twenty-eight, a couple of years younger. She was a blonde-haired, blue-eyed Texan who was as tough as they came. Rob had thought about it. There was no way he'd go there for real, though. She'd eat him alive.

They got off their bikes and made their way across the parking lot. The sun was burning down, the temperature hovering in the nineties. It was too hot for biker leathers. Rob was wearing a shirt and jeans, while Tara had gone for jeans and a white T-shirt.

The Palm Tree was shabbier than Rob had first thought. Maybe it had been grand when it was built back in the sixties, but not anymore. It was an eight-storey high concrete block with crumbling plasterwork. The hotel had once been white, but now it was a filthy grey colour. The windows were covered in layers of grime, and the bulbs in the sign had blown long ago and never been replaced.

A crowd had gathered around the pool, almost a hundred people in total. All of them were staring up at the woman on the wrong side of the rusty top-floor balcony rail. Rob peered into the pool and wondered if it was still a swimming pool when there was no water. Surely a pool without water was just a glorified hole in the ground.

'Fifty bucks we get roadkill,' Tara said in her deep Texan drawl. She took a camera from her backpack and fiddled with it as she walked.

'And why would I bet on something like that? You know roadkill is better for the ratings than a talk-down.'

'Yeah, and I also know that most of these situations end in a talk-down.'

'So, why give your money away?'

'I've just got a feeling this one's going to end messy. Come on, Rob, it's only fifty bucks. It'll make things more interesting.'

Rob considered this for a second. August was always a slow news month, but this was the worst August he'd ever known. When the highlight of your day was a jumper, you knew things were bad.

'Okay, you're on.'

He shielded his eyes and looked up. The fact that the jumper was on the eighth floor indicated they were semi-serious about killing themselves. Anything above the fourth floor and the intention was there. Anything below was just a cry for help. He plotted the downward trajectory and saw half a dozen firefighters working furiously to get the airbag inflated. Someone shouted, 'Jump' and this was quickly picked up by the rest of the crowd and turned into a chant. *Jump, jump, jump*. Tara trained the camera on the top floor and adjusted the zoom.

'What have we got?' Rob asked.

'A white female, black hair, brown eyes. Late twenties. Kind of pretty, if you go for the size zero emaciated look, which I know you do. The police shrink is keeping his distance in case she pulls him over the balcony when she goes. He seems to be doing a lot of talking, but the girl doesn't seem to be doing a whole lot of listening.'

'*If* she goes,' Rob corrected.

'*When* she goes.'

'Okay, stay here in case she decides to jump, and I'll go see if I can find out anything about our mystery girl.'

Rob walked into the crowd and got recognised straightaway. The woman doing the recognising had to weigh in at three hundred pounds. She had four chins and the sickly sweet-and-sour smell of a sugar junky. Her pink smock was large enough to house a family of refugees.

'Hey, you're that guy from the TV. Rob Taylor.'

Rob flashed his trademark smile. 'Got me there.'

It wasn't just the fat lady who was staring. A dozen or so people standing nearby had turned away from the jumper to see what she was shouting about.

'Okay, listen up,' he called out. 'I've got a hundred bucks here for anyone who knows who the jumper is.'

'Make that two hundred and you've got yourself a deal.'

The voice came from somewhere off to the left. Rob turned and saw a Puerto Rican woman pushing through the crowd. He immediately pegged her as a crackhead and a whore. It was the eyes. They were like two dying stars. He gave it a second, hoping someone else would come forward. No one did. Great. He'd been hoping for someone he could put on camera.

‘What’s your name?’

‘You can call me Candy.’

Rob nodded up to the balcony. ‘And who’s she?’

‘Money first.’

Rob fished out a roll of bills, peeled off four fifties and handed them over. The money disappeared into Candy’s bra.

‘Her name’s Sally Jenkins. We shared a place together. At least we used to.’

‘She’s not dead yet.’

‘Well, if she don’t get it right this time, she will next time.’

‘She’s tried to kill herself before?’

‘Man, ain’t you listening? She pulls this shit at least once a month. Usually it’s pills. This is the first time she’s gone this far.’

‘What do you know about Sally?’

‘Nothing you ain’t heard before. She was born and raised in Oklahoma. When she was seventeen she ran away to Hollywood cos she thought she was gonna be a big movie star. That didn’t work out, so she started to drink to help her get by. When the drink didn’t work, she started with the drugs, except that gets expensive real quick. She got into debt with a dealer and next thing she’s selling her sweet ass on the street.’

‘Sad story. You sure you’re not making this up?’

‘Hell, no! And why would I do that?’

‘Well, there’s the two hundred bucks I just paid you for a start.’ Rob eyed her warily. Chances were she was lying, but that didn’t matter. Never let the facts get in the way of a good story. That’s what his first editor had told him. As advice went, it was pure gold. ‘Anything else you can tell me?’

Candy shrugged. ‘Only that if you give me another fifty I’ll blow you. Make it two hundred and I’ll take you to heaven and back.’

A massive cheer suddenly went up and Rob spun around in time to see Sally tumble past the fifth floor. She hit the partially inflated airbag hard, sinking all the way down to concrete. A couple of paramedics rushed in, took a quick look and shook their heads. Rob pushed his way out through the crowd and headed over to Tara.

She grinned and held out her hand. 'Money please.'

Rob found a fifty and handed it to Tara. She stuffed the money into the back pocket of her jeans, then gave him a microphone and hoisted the camera onto her shoulder.

'You ready to roll?'

'Give me a second.' Rob mopped the sweat from his face, shook his shirt a couple of times to make sure it wasn't sticking, then rubbed a hand through his hair to ruffle it up. 'How do I look?'

'Gorgeous, honeybun.'

'Seriously, Tara.'

'Seriously.'

The theme tune from *The Omen* drifted up from Rob's pocket. The sound was muted by denim, shrill in a way that only a ringtone could be. That didn't make the music any less ominous, though. This ringtone was reserved for Jonah, his boss. Jonah headed up the newsroom and had a serious God complex. His real name was Seth Allen, but Jonah was a much better fit. Jonah, after J. Jonah Jameson, Peter Parker's cigar-chomping, permanently stressed editor-in-chief at the *Daily Bugle*. Rob fished out his cell phone and connected the call. He listened, said 'uh-huh' a couple of times, then hung up.

'Change of plan,' he said. 'We're to forget the jumper. It looks like ISIS has finally made it to sunny LA.'

2

'Stand up.'

Everybody looked around uncertainly, waiting for someone else to make the first move. Since the shooting a state of shock had settled over the room. Some people were sobbing quietly, while the rest stared ashen-faced into the middle distance like survivors in a disaster zone. Fear was keeping JJ frozen to the spot. This was alien territory. She was used to calling the shots. She instigated events, she didn't react to them. It was as though all control had been stripped away. She hated herself for being so weak.

Looking around, it was clear that she wasn't the only person trying to make this adjustment. There were some of the most important people in the movie business here today. These were people who lived a life of pampered luxury. Herself included. She was never going to be Learjet rich, but she always flew first class. Her lifestyle now was light years away from her childhood. She'd done well for herself, no doubt about it. Unfortunately, all the money in the world couldn't save her now. It couldn't save any of them. It didn't matter how rich and successful you were, death really was the great leveller.

The room stank of death, a bitter mix of cordite and bodily fluids. Even though JJ had been close enough to Elizabeth Hayward to get a splash of blood on her cheek, she was still struggling to get her head around this. It was just too big and brutal to comprehend. She'd try to convince herself that none of it was happening, but then she'd look over at Hayward lying there with half her head blown away, the diamond-encrusted Cartier glittering on her birdlike wrist, and the denial would stop working.

The bomber clapped his hands. The sound was louder than the gunshot. Everyone shrank into the floor and tried to make themselves smaller.

'I said, stand up. Come on, people, let's hustle.'

Ed Richards got to his feet and everyone followed his lead, thumping and bustling and trying to stay quiet. JJ's legs were made from rubber. It was like gravity had got stronger and was pulling her down towards the floor, down where it was safe. She felt more exposed when she was standing, more vulnerable.

'Take off your shoes.'

Nobody moved. There were puzzled glances all around.

'Come on, folks, this isn't rocket science. Take. Off. Your. Shoes.'

JJ reached down, flicked off her Jimmy Choos, then straightened up again with a shoe in each hand. The bomber moved to the side of the room and leant against the wall under one of the bright paint-splashed canvases.

'One at a time, I want you to bring your shoes over here.' He looked at Ed Richards. 'Since you seem to be the head sheep, you can go first.'

Richards walked over and placed his shoes at the bomber's feet, then walked back and sat down. His footsteps were even and steady, his face completely emotionless. If this had been a World War Two escape movie, he would have been the officer that the other prisoners looked up to for leadership. The problem was that this wasn't a movie. If Richards didn't work that out, and soon, then more people were going to die.

When it got to JJ's turn, she walked as quickly as she dared, laid her shoes on the growing pile, then hurried back. The way the bomber was staring made her skin crawl. The last pair of shoes belonged to Tony. The restaurant owner squared his shoulders and walked over. The dried blood on his face made it look as though he'd been in a car wreck. JJ glanced over at Hayward, then looked back at Tony and thanked God he was still alive. It was only just sinking in how lucky he'd been. She caught his eye on the way back and chanced a quick, reassuring smile. She wanted him to know that he wasn't alone, that they were in this together.

She wanted to know that she wasn't alone.

Tony glanced over his shoulder to make sure the bomber wasn't watching, then chanced a quick smile back. It was a small gesture, but it meant the world. As usual, he'd read her mood perfectly and given her exactly what she'd needed.

The bomber moved a couple of yards left, away from the pile of shoes. 'Take your clothes off. All of them. Pants, shirts, skirts. You can keep your underwear. Then I want you to bring your clothes over here and leave them on the floor.' He clapped his hands and everyone winced. 'Come on, folks, let's move it.'

JJ hesitated, but managed to get moving before she drew any attention. She self-consciously slipped out of her clothes, her pants coming off last. Everyone else was stripping off, too. They no doubt felt as awkward and vulnerable as she did, but no one was arguing, not after what had happened to Hayward.

Being half-naked like this was so humiliating. JJ felt like the whole world was looking at her. That said, the indignity of being half-naked was preferable to being dead. It seemed wrong to be horse-trading with herself like this, but if that's what it took to survive then so be it. It was all about putting the right spin on things. No matter how bad things got, there was always a way to spin things to your advantage. Out of all the things she'd learned from Johnny Wiesner, that was probably the biggest.

Richards went first again. He walked over to the bomber, dropped his clothes on the floor, then walked back. The bomber hunkered down and checked through the clothes, shaking them and patting pockets like he was looking for something. JJ saw his eyes widen with surprise.

'Well, looky what we got here,' he hollered. He straightened up and held the cell phone in the air. 'Didn't I make myself clear to you good folks?'

Everyone flinched and shrank back into the floor. There were some gasps and some sobs. Wherever JJ looked, all she saw was terror.

'Am I speaking a foreign language here? I told you to hand over your cell phones. I made a big speech about it and everything. Would someone mind telling me what part of that was so hard to understand?'

The bomber crossed the room in half a dozen strides. JJ tried to close her eyes, but couldn't. The messages were going out from her brain but they weren't getting through. She glanced over and saw Elizabeth Hayward lying dead on the floor. Then she looked at Richards and wondered how he could have been so stupid.

'Down on your knees.'

Richards didn't move. Head down, he stared at the floor. Despite the air-conditioning there were beads of sweat dotting his forehead. The bomber grabbed him by the shoulder, threw him to the ground, then pressed the end of the silencer against his head. Richards was looking around at the other hostages, his desperate eyes moving from person to person. JJ closed hers and waited for the pneumatic *psst* that would mark the end of his life.

3

'And in breaking news here at TRN, we have reports coming in of a terror attack at one of LA's most exclusive restaurants.'

Up in Mission Control, Seth Allen watched his anchorwoman deliver the news on the main monitor. Caroline Bradley was poetry in motion. Her timing was perfect, the concern on her face absolutely appropriate for the gravity of the situation. It didn't hurt that she had Homecoming Queen genes and was drop-dead gorgeous. Her dark hair was styled into a bob, and the cut and colour of her jacket showed off her curves in a way that was sexy without causing offence to the less liberal-minded viewers.

Caroline touched her ear like she was getting an up-to-date newsflash and Seth had to smile. Boy, she was good. Most of what she said was flashed up on the autocue, even the ad-libs. The last thing you wanted was a news anchor who thought for themselves. Do that and they'd start believing they were real journalists.

Seth was a real journalist and proud of it. He'd started in newspapers and progressed to radio before ending up in TV. Some of his print buddies called him a sell-out, but they weren't earning a six-figure salary, so they could go to hell. He was sixty and wore every single year. There were dark pouches under his eyes, and his lines and wrinkles ran deep. His skin had a yellow tinge caused by too many cigarettes, too much booze, and the fact that he never saw the sun because most of his waking hours were spent in the womb-like gloom of Mission Control.

He was currently on wife number three and had four kids, two of them teenage girls who were hormonal nightmares. He liked to joke that this was the reason he was bald. Whenever he said this he was only half-joking. Seth wasn't physically big, but he had presence. Someone had once described him as a six-foot-four, 280-pound linebacker trapped in a five-foot-three body, and he thought that just about covered it.

'Where the hell is Rob?' he shouted.

'He's only a couple of minutes away.'

This came from one of his assistants. There were three in total, all kids, two boys and a girl. One Asian, one black, one white lesbian. Political correctness was a bitch. Back in the good old days he could have had three leggy, silicon-enhanced blondes and it wouldn't have raised a single eyebrow. All three of the current batch were in their early twenties, fresh from college, and scared half to death of what he might say or do next, which was the way he preferred things. Fear was the best motivator known to man. If you thought you might lose your job at any given moment, it figured that you were going to go that extra mile. In addition to the assistants, he had half-a-dozen technicians to ensure that the constant stream of pictures and sound TRN served up to its viewers kept flowing.

'A couple of minutes!' Seth hollered. 'I need him there yesterday! I want you to get hold of him and tell him that if he doesn't haul ass then I'm going to take away that precious Harley he loves so much and give him a bicycle.'

Seth glanced at his monitors. The one at the top-left of the main screen showed the feed from TRN's Eye in the Sky traffic helicopter. This was currently hovering as close to Alfie's as the LAPD were allowing, which was nowhere near close enough.

The pilot was ex-military and had flown missions in Iraq and Afghanistan, so a little explosion in an LA restaurant wasn't exactly going to faze him. But, no, the cops had ordered him to stay at least three blocks back.

The top-right monitor showed a frozen picture from Natasha Lovett's cell phone. When the footage had arrived at TRN, Seth had thought it was a joke. Then he'd seen who'd sent it and realised it wasn't. Natasha Lovett might have been many things, but practical joker was not on that list.

He'd watched the footage through twice, back to back. It was only fifteen seconds long from start to finish, so it didn't take long. He'd had to watch it a second time because he couldn't believe what he was seeing the first time. By the time it finished all his journalistic senses were twitching. This story wasn't just big, it was possibly the biggest of his career.

Seth had played the footage a third time, and thought about the journalistic Big Five. Who, why, what, where, when. He went for the *where* first. It was Caroline who'd come through on that one. She'd eaten at Alfie's a couple of times and recognised the decor. One call was all it took to confirm that Natasha Lovett was indeed having lunch at Alfie's today, which answered the *when*.

What was the next of the Big Five, and that one was obvious. A masked terrorist wearing an explosive vest had taken a bunch of Hollywood's movers and shakers hostage. ISIS was the logical explanation. *Why* was easy, too. Those lunatics hated America and everything she stood for. What better way to strike a blow against the infidel than to target Hollywood?

In this case, *who* was the least important of the Big Five. There were camps full of kids in Syria and Afghanistan and Pakistan, all of them queuing up for the opportunity to blow themselves to kingdom come and claim their quota of virgins.

'TRN has managed to get exclusive film shot by one of the hostages at Alfie's.' Caroline's delivery was fast and breathless. 'Some viewers may find this disturbing.'

Hopefully, thought Seth.

'And cut to the cell phone footage on my mark,' he said. 'Three, two, one.'

The main screen switched from the studio to the fifteen-second clip that Lovett had shot. The camerawork was shaky, which was understandable, given the circumstances. It actually worked to their advantage since it gave the clip a level of authenticity that would otherwise have been missing. Each time he watched that fifteen-second clip, he was struck by the risk Lovett had taken. The director had bigger balls than he'd given her credit for.

The film opened with a sneaked glimpse of the bomber's back. The silenced Heckler & Koch MP5 slung carelessly across his shoulder was scary enough, but that explosive vest was one of the most terrifying things Seth had ever seen. Considering how long he'd been in this business, that was saying something.

The terrorist was dressed entirely in black. Balaclava, shirt, trousers, boots. He looked like a shadow. The picture jerked away from him, a quick sweep across the hostages, cut to black. Seth already had a team of researchers tasked with putting names to faces.

'And cut to Caroline on my mark,' he said. 'Three, two, one.'

The main screen filled with a close-up of the anchorwoman sitting behind her desk looking suitably grim-faced.

'And now we're going across to Brian Hannigan, TRN's Eye in the Sky,' she said. 'Brian, can you tell us what's happening over there at Alfie's?'

'Cut to the 'copter,' said Seth.

The picture changed to show the view from the camera strapped below the helicopter. The police had cordoned off the street at both ends and crowds were already forming behind the barricades. In addition, there were half a dozen ambulances and a couple of fire trucks.

'The police have managed to evacuate the area around Alfie's.' Brian was shouting to be heard over the roar of the helicopter, but he still sounded like he was gargling warm honey. 'At the moment nobody knows how big the bomb is, so the police are taking no chances and are keeping everyone well back.'

The camera zoomed in and picked out a small, low, L-shaped building with a flat roof. The building was a nondescript concrete structure. It could have dated back to the fifties, or it could have been built yesterday. There were tens of thousands of buildings like this scattered throughout the country, a hundred thousand. The parking lot at the rear of the restaurant was a different story. It was filled with high-end vehicles. Ferraris, a Bentley, even a Rolls. A couple of million dollars' worth, easy.

'The phones are going mad,' the white lesbian called out. 'We've got CNN, Fox and ABC all wanting to buy Lovett's cell phone footage. They're offering silly money.'

'Tell them we're not selling.'

Seth had to smile. These were the moments he lived for, the adrenalin-filled fury of a breaking story. But this was more than that. He'd been in this game long enough to know that he was riding the back of that once-in-a-lifetime story that every journalist lived and prayed for. This story was a monster.

4

The bomber hovered above Ed Richards, legs apart in a combat stance, his gun aimed at the back of the actor's head. Richards was on his knees. He was trembling all over and whispering silently to himself. JJ watched the shapes his lips were making and realised he was reciting the Lord's prayer. It had worked for Natasha Lovett, maybe it would work for him as well. She wasn't holding out much hope, though. Not after the way the bomber had dealt with Elizabeth Hayward.

This was madness. There were twenty-four of them, and only one of him, yet he had all the power. If they worked together, they could take him. But that would take organisation, and organisation required words, and right now everyone was too terrified to say anything. A move like that would also require sacrifice. How many people would get shot before the bomber was taken down? How many would die? These were soft people who were used to a soft way of life. A life they were in no hurry to give up.

Then there was the bomb.

The risks were too great. Twenty-four of them, one of him, and no matter how JJ analysed the situation, the bomber came out the winner every single time. She'd known Richards for years. They weren't particularly close, but she didn't want to see him die like this. A bullet in the back of the head and left to bleed out on a cold restaurant floor. Nobody should have to die like that.

She closed her eyes, but that just made things worse. With her eyes closed the smells got sharper. Food, cordite, that horrific stench of death. JJ opened them again. Richards' head was bowed and he was staring at the floor. His eyes were filled with tears and his cheeks were soaked. There was no acting involved, not this time. She wanted to look away, but couldn't. All she could do was watch helplessly and wait for the gunshot that would end his life.

'Bang!' the bomber shouted.

Everyone jerked involuntarily, and a spreading wet patch appeared on the front of Richards' grey silk boxer shorts. The bomber snapped his gun up and stepped back. He was grinning behind the balaclava again. A cell phone rang and JJ followed the sound to Natasha Lovett's orange canvas bag. Within seconds a confused mix of tunes, buzzes and chirps filled the air.

'Looks like we just made it onto the news, folks.'

The bomber reached into the bag, selected a phone at random, held it up so everyone could get a good look, switched it off, then casually tossed it back in the bag. He plucked out another, held it up, then switched it off. He kept going until all the phones were off. There was something very deliberate about the way he did this. It was like he was driving home the point that they were now completely cut off from the outside world.

'Okay, folks, change of plan. Now, I could have shot Mr Head Sheep, but what does that actually achieve?' He nodded towards Elizabeth Hayward's body. 'A mess on this nice floor is what.'

JJ looked over at Richards again. The actor was still on his knees. His face was buried in his hands and he was biting back his sobs. Even though it was one of the most pathetic sights she'd ever seen, it was still a hundred times better than the alternative.

'Now, I'm thinking that maybe I can use this as an opportunity to educate you people. Do you remember doing Show and Tell when you were kids?'

Nobody answered. Everyone was staring blankly at random spots around the room. Anywhere, so long as they weren't looking at the bomber.

'Of course you do. Well, this is going to be my little Show and Tell.'

The bomber did a slow scan of the hostages, his gaze settling on each person before moving to the next. When it got to JJ's turn, she sat completely still and stared at a scratch on the parquet. He only looked at her for a second, but it felt like a year.

'You and you, come here.'

JJ stole a quick glance and saw Natasha Lovett stand up. She'd never spent any time with the director, but anyone who followed the news knew plenty about her. Natasha was married to David Wills, one of the few black actors to have won an Oscar. The couple were Hollywood's number one black power-couple. They were in the news all the time, particularly at the moment, with diversity being such a hot topic. They might have had matching Oscars on their mantelpiece, but they were all too aware that they were the exception to the rule.

JJ vaguely recognised the man standing beside Natasha. He was in his mid-forties, slightly overweight, with a receding hairline. If she was thinking of the right guy, then he was some sort of accountant. He definitely had the fussy look of someone who wanted to make sure all the columns added up properly. He was standing there in his white boxers and black socks, staring at the floor. His head was bowed and he'd hunched himself up to appear smaller. Natasha looked just as vulnerable. She was wearing a pair of simple cotton burgundy underpants and a matching bra. Her hands were crossed over her little pot belly.

'Don't be shy. Come on, let's have you both over here.'

Natasha and the accountant started walking. Their faces were filled with fear and their legs moved woodenly. The bomber pointed to a spot on the floor in front of Richards.

'On your knees in front of Mr Head Sheep.'

They knelt down.

'Now, we're going have ourselves a little chat about consequences. You see, when you do something there will always be consequences. You put the dinner on the stove and forget about it, then it's going to burn. That's a consequence. You go out and get drunk and drive your car and end up crashing and killing someone, well, that's a consequence, too. Now, if I tell you to do something and you don't do it, then you'd better believe that there will be consequences.'

The bomber turned to Richards. 'I've decided to let you live. However, that decision has consequences. See, if I let you disrespect me and don't do anything about it, what's to stop you doing it again? So here's what's going to happen. You're going to choose which one of these good people is going to die for your sins. Now, in case you're thinking that all you've got to do is keep your mouth shut, think again. Do that and I'll shoot them both.'

He turned back to Natasha and the accountant.

'Now, to keep this fair, I'm going to give each of you thirty seconds to persuade Mr Head Sheep here that you deserve to live.' The bomber looked at the accountant. 'Okay, you're up first.'

'Please don't kill me,' he whispered.

'It's not me you need to convince. It's Mr Head Sheep over there.'

The accountant glanced guiltily at Natasha, then looked at Richards.

'I have a wife and two children.' His voice was shaking, the words as fragile as eggshells. 'My little boy's only three months old. I want to see him grow up. I want to see both my kids grow up. Please, I'm begging you here, don't kill me.'

The bomber did a slow handclap. 'I'm impressed. Playing the kid card was a nice touch. Our director friend here is going to have to come up with something very special to beat that.' He turned to Natasha. 'Okay, your turn.'

Natasha pulled herself up to her full height and stared at the bomber. Her cheeks were wet and shiny and her arms hung loosely by her sides. 'No.'

The bomber stepped closer and cocked his head to one side. Natasha flinched, but stood her ground.

'I'm not doing this,' she said quietly. 'I'm not playing your games.'

'And that's where you're wrong. Whether you like it or not, you're already playing. Darling, right now you're dancing to whatever tune I decide you're going to dance to. Say something or don't say anything, it makes no difference to me.' He paused to let this sink in. 'Now, is there anything you want to say to Mr Head Sheep?'

Natasha stared straight ahead. No words, no gestures, not even a nod or a shake of the head.

'Okay, then.' The bomber turned his attention to Richards. 'It's decision time. Who lives and who dies?'

'Please don't make me do this,' Richards whispered.

'Sorry, I didn't quite catch that.'

'Please. I can't do this.'

'Fine, I'll shoot them both.' The gun rocked back and forth between Natasha and the accountant, like a pendulum. *Tick tock, tick tock*. 'If it helps, look at this as an opportunity to save one of them.'

‘Wait,’ Richards called out.

‘You’ve made a decision?’

The actor nodded and closed his eyes. ‘Natasha,’ he said quietly.

‘And just so we’re absolutely clear. You want her to live?’

Richards nodded again, then glanced at the accountant and mouthed, ‘Sorry.’ He looked like he wanted to say more but just didn’t have the words. He dipped his head and closed his eyes. His face was soaked with tears. The way he did this made JJ think of a scared child. If you can’t see the bad thing, then the bad thing can’t see you.

The accountant sprang suddenly to his feet and made a run for the stairs that led down to the lower level. His legs and arms were pumping, his eyes wild and desperate. The bomber slowly raised his gun, taking his time. JJ couldn’t bear to watch. There was nowhere to run. Nowhere to hide.

The bullet slammed into the accountant’s back, bursting through his chest in a bloody shower of tissue and gore. His arms flew up in the air and he crashed into a table, sending plates and glasses tumbling onto the parquet floor. The candle fell, too, extinguishing itself before it hit the ground. The accountant lay balanced on the table for a moment, then slid slowly downwards before finally coming to rest draped across a chair.

JJ stared in disbelief, an irrational swirl of guilt burning through her gut. Crazy though it was, she felt responsible, like she’d pulled the trigger. This was someone she didn’t know, someone she’d written off as not worth knowing, but that didn’t mean his life hadn’t been worth anything. This guy had been a father and a husband. He’d been loved and he would be mourned. But the biggest tragedy of all was that there was a little boy out there who would never get to know his daddy.

5

Alex King closed the door then sank down to the floor and tried to work out what the hell he was going to do now. The bomber had started killing people. So far there were two dead and counting. King had seen enough hostage films to know that they'd moved up to the next level. When the killing started, that changed everything.

The only thing he knew for certain was that he was not going to die in this restroom. He was the nine-life cat. He redefined the whole concept of lucky. He hadn't survived his shitty childhood to end up dying here. Right now he hated JJ more than he'd ever hated anyone. Even more than he'd hated his mom, and that was saying something. This was all JJ's fault. He hadn't wanted to come to Alfie's, but she'd insisted. She'd told him to jump and he'd jumped right to it. Well, she was going to get those front pages she wanted so badly. Only he doubted this was how she'd imagined things playing out.

King had celebrated New Year's on Saint Kitts, sitting by the pool, welcoming in the New Year with a drink in his hand, while he'd stared into a future that was so bright it was blinding. Man, that had been one hell of a party. The holiday was supposed to mark the start of his new life, the one he'd been dreaming about ever since he'd escaped from Ohio. And up until now, everything had been cool. *Killing Time* had been a blockbuster and the offers had come flooding in. In a word, life was awesome.

And now this. It was just so messed up, and so freaking unfair. How could things be going so amazingly well one second, and so shittily the next? Not. Freaking. Fair. He could feel the dark thoughts pushing in on him again, crushing him. Everything in his world was either black or white. There were no shades of grey. When things were going well, everything was golden. And when things turned to shit, well, all he saw was darkness.

He fished the small Ziploc bag from his jeans and looked at it for a moment. In places, the plastic had gone white and rough from having been inside his pocket for so long. It would be so easy. One snort and he would immediately feel better. But he wasn't going to do that.

Forty-three days and counting.

The first thing he'd done after deciding to go clean was to measure out enough coke for one decent-sized hit. That's what was in the bag. The rest of his stash had gone down the toilet. Since that day, he'd taken the bag out plenty of times and just stared at it, like he was doing now, but he'd never opened it. Not once. And he had no intention of opening it now. That little bag of powder might promise answers, but the reality was that those answers were built from lies.

He put the bag back into his pocket. Rehab might work for some people, but it wouldn't have worked for him. This way did work. Every time the bag went back into his pocket it reconfirmed the promise he'd made to himself forty-three days ago that he was never going to touch this shit ever again.

King shut his eyes and focused on his breathing. Observing the length of the inhale, observing the exhale, just like his yoga instructor had taught him. While he did this he repeated the words 'nine-life cat' in his head, turning it into a mantra. Until this was over he needed to find a place where he could park all his anger and negativity. He needed to keep hold of the positives. That was how he was going to survive this.

He let out a long sigh and opened his eyes. Then he took out his cell phone. There were ten missed calls from his agent, and another three from a number he didn't recognise. He considered calling it, then decided not to. No doubt it was a fan who'd got hold of his number. It was a total bummer when that happened. King had lost count of how many cell numbers he'd gone through.

He brought up his contacts list, then scrolled through the names. One jumped out. He hadn't spoken to this person in years. The truth was that they'd probably never want to speak to him again, which was nothing less than he deserved. Even so, whenever he got a new phone he made sure this number was on it.

King hesitated, then pulled up the text box and typed: *love u. alex x*. Before he could change his mind, he hit send. He knew he was acting impulsively, that he wasn't playing fair, but he needed to reach out to someone, anyone. If the worst happened, then it wouldn't matter. And if he did survive, he'd deal with the fallout then.

He shut his eyes and a picture of his ex jumped into his mind. It was a lazy Sunday morning and they'd just made love. The sun was creeping around the edges of the cheap drapes and the world on the other side of the bedroom door had ceased to exist.

Gold light painting skin.

The smell of coffee and toast.

A perfect moment.

King put his cell away, cracked the door open and tried to tune in to whatever was happening out there. Everything seemed quiet for now. He shut the door, then slid down to the floor and went back to work on the question he'd asked himself earlier.

What the hell was he going to do now?

6

News of the hostage situation had just broken but there was already a crowd of more than fifty people outside Alfie's. Thirty or so pushing up against the barrier at Rob's end of the street, and at least another twenty at the other end. And this was just the start. Within an hour the crowd would have trebled, perhaps even quadrupled. There was nothing like a disaster in the making to get the ghouls and the rubberneckers crawling from the woodwork, and there was nothing like a twenty-four-hour news channel to encourage them. The fact that there were celebrities involved made the story even more alluring.

The demographics of the crowd were interesting. Almost every single category was represented. White, black, yellow, red. Old and young and everything in-between. Kids with skateboards and piercings and attitude, who should have been at school, rubbed shoulders with old folks who should have been at home watching their daytime soaps. The only reason they'd all ended up here was because they could smell the blood.

Rob and Tara were the first news team on the scene. The big advantage with the bikes was that they could get quickly to wherever they needed to go. Unfortunately, now the story had broken, the big boys wouldn't be far behind.

'Shall we?' Tara's camera was slung on her back like a rocket launcher. She looked fearsome, a warrior ready to go into battle.

'After you. But let's hustle, eh?'

Tara headed towards the police barrier. 'Media coming through!' she called out, and the crowd parted like the Red Sea.

The two cops manning the barrier looked pissed at having pulled such a bum detail, which was understandable. All the action was happening further down the street and they were stuck here like glorified babysitters. Rob ducked under the barrier and the cops descended as a pair, stepping up to block his way. The guy calling the shots was five-eight with a worn-out face and a droopy moustache. He had the look of someone who'd been there and done it. His buddy was barely out of college.

'Sir,' the older cop said. 'I'm going to have to ask you to please get back behind the barrier.'

Rob ignored the request and held out his hand. 'Rob Taylor, TRN.'

The cop eyed Rob's hand, then reached out and shook it. Rob felt the hundred-dollar bill slide away. The cop slipped his hand into his pocket, and when it came out it was empty and open. His buddy watched without saying a word.

'You've got two minutes to take your pictures. Then I want you back behind that barrier. And you stay within ten yards of me at all times. Got it?'

'I'm hearing you loud and clear.'

Rob stepped around the barrier, Tara following close behind. She hoisted the camera onto her shoulder and began filming. The view wasn't brilliant, but it was better than it had been on the other side of the barrier. Alfie's was three blocks away. There wasn't much to look at, just a blank white concrete wall facing the sidewalk. No doors, no windows, no signs advertising the place. A narrow access road on the left-hand side of the building led to the parking lot at the rear where the entrance was. The celebs would pull right up to the canopied door and a couple of steps later they were inside, anonymity guaranteed. The paparazzi couldn't get anywhere near them.

The street was deserted now, the stop lights stuck on red. Evacuating the area had been the number one priority. Homes, restaurants, stores, everyone in a three-block radius. The cops had set up their base of operations a block and a half from Alfie's. All the action was centred around a big white truck with 'LAPD MOBILE COMMAND UNIT' on the side in big letters.

A dozen ambulances were parked half a block back from the LAPD truck, engines running, ready to roll. A couple of fire trucks were parked beside them. Rob counted a couple of dozen cops wearing bulletproof vests. They were hovering around, trying to look busy, but not actually doing anything. The scene was static for now, but there was a sense of controlled energy, like everyone was just itching to spring into action.

A large news truck pulled up behind the barrier at the other end of the street. The CNN logo was painted on the side and its satellite dishes were pointed skyward. Looked like the first of the big boys had arrived, which meant the rest wouldn't be far behind.

'What's your name?' Rob asked the older cop.

'Jim Baker.'

'What do people call you? Jim or Baker?'

'My buddies call me Baker.'

'And what does your wife call you?'

Baker laughed. 'You don't want to know.'

Rob didn't smoke, but he carried a pack of Lucky Strikes for situations like this. Empathy was the secret to being a good journalist. Have a tissue ready for the mother whose son has just been killed in a drive-by shooting, and have a cigarette to hand for the bored cop who might just have that vital piece of information that could make or break a story. He offered the pack to Baker. The cop hesitated, but only for a second. A glance down towards the action, a shrug, then he plucked a cigarette from the pack. Rob was quick with his lighter. He flicked up a flame and held it out.

'My wife would kill me if she knew I was smoking again.'

Like your wife doesn't know. 'So what's actually going on here?' asked Rob.

Baker took a long drag. 'This is off the record, right?'

'Sure.'

'It's going to cost you more than a cigarette. Let's say a couple of hundred bucks.'

Rob palmed the money to Baker.

'We've got a suicide bomber who's holding twenty-five people hostage. Customers and staff. What I heard is that al-Qaeda has claimed responsibility.'

'Not ISIS?'

Baker shook his head. 'Not this time. Looks like they've had enough of ISIS getting all the headlines.'

'You're sure about this?'

'You can take that one to the bank. Here's something else you might not know. There's been one person injured so far. The parking valet.'

'Have you got a name?'

'Victor Comaneci. He's an ex-Marine. In addition to parking the cars, he deals with security. What I heard was that he approached the bomber wanting to know what he was doing there. By all accounts there was no warning. The guy just pulled his gun, shot him in the leg, then headed on into the restaurant.'

'How seriously was he injured?'

'His thigh was shattered and he lost a lot of blood, but he's going to live.'

‘What else have you got?’

Baker hesitated. His face betrayed the fact there was something, and that he wasn’t sure how far he should go. Rob kept very still. A wrong move now would shut him up for good. Baker held his hand out and Rob found another couple of hundred bucks.

‘A friend told me there’s someone trapped in the restroom, and the bomber doesn’t know they’re in there.’

This nugget of information was delivered in a confidential whisper. Rob felt his heart accelerate. Now they were getting to the really good stuff. ‘Did your friend mention names?’

‘Alex King.’

‘The actor?’

‘One and the same.’

‘Your friend, how reliable are they?’

‘I’ve known her for twenty years, so you don’t have anything to worry about on that score.’

Her instead of him. Interesting. The LAPD didn’t have that many women in the upper levels, so Baker’s contact was probably closer to ground level. A secretary or a telephone operator, perhaps.

‘I’ve got a favour to ask,’ Rob said. ‘A big one. Before long this place is going to be crawling with reporters. How about we keep this information between the two of us?’

Baker took a final drag on his cigarette and crushed the butt out under his heel. ‘Sure. But it’s gonna cost you.’

7

Alex King pulled out his cell and checked the screen. The little envelope in the top left corner was lit up and that got his heart hammering. His first thought was that it might be a reply from his ex. He navigated to the inbox, and when he saw the text was from the same unknown number as before, his excitement turned to disappointment. He brought the message up on the screen. His eyes widened as he read it.

My name is Brad Carter. I'm the Special Agent in charge of the FBI's LA field office and I need to talk to you urgently. Call me on this number as soon as you can. If you can't talk then text me.

King stared at the screen. This was more like it. The FBI would come up with a plan to get them out. They had to. They were the FBI for Christ's sake. That's what they did. He cracked the door open an inch and listened. Still all quiet out there. He closed it, then tiptoed into the cubicle and pulled the door shut behind him. He hit the button to connect the call and the FBI man answered on the first ring. The voice coming through the earpiece was relaxed and laid-back, more California surf-bum than G-Man.

'Hey there, Alex.'

'Is this Agent Carter?' King whispered.

'It is. And please call me Brad. Now, before we go any further, I want to assure you we're doing everything possible to get you guys out of there. Are you injured?'

'I'm fine.'

'I need to ask some questions. Is that okay with you, Alex?'

'Sure.'

'What's going on in there?'

'The bomber has started shooting people. Two people are dead so far. This guy's a complete psycho.'

'Any idea who the victims are?'

'No, sorry.'

'That's okay, Alex, you're doing great. You're still in the restroom, right?'

'That's right.'

'How much can you hear from where you are?'

'Not much. I can hear when there's shouting, but there's not much of that. The rest of the time all I can make out is the odd word.'

'How many bad guys are out there?'

King had assumed there was only one, but there could be more. He thought about what he'd heard and weighed it against what little he knew. He was pretty sure that the guy with the bomb was working alone.

'There's only one.'

'Tell me something about him. Anything.'

'His English is really good, if you know what I mean.'

'Like he was born in the US?'

'If he wasn't, then he's lived here for a while.'

'Could you make out any sort of accent?'

'No.'

'That's fine, Alex. You're doing great, buddy. Real good. How's the battery on your phone?'

Even before he looked, he knew it would be low. He never remembered to charge the damn thing. He took the phone from his ear and glanced at the screen. The phone was practically running on empty. 'I'm probably okay to talk for another ten minutes.'

'In that case I'm going to hang up now, but keep your phone switched on so I can get hold of you.'

'Okay.'

'And, Alex, I meant what I said. We're going to get you out of there.'

'Sooner would be better than later.'

'I'm hearing you, buddy. Sit tight, okay?'

The line went dead and King stared at the phone. *We're going to get you out of there.* That's what the FBI guy had said. *We're going to get you out.* He just hoped that Carter was a man of his word.

8

A distant telephone started ringing and JJ's head snapped up. She wasn't the only one. Everyone was looking to see where the noise had come from. The sound was as insubstantial as a mirage, but that didn't make it any less real. Judging by the ringtone, this was a landline rather than a cell phone. It was an old-fashioned sound, and heart-achingly lonely, a stark reminder that the world they used to inhabit was both so close, and so far.

'Where's the telephone?' the bomber asked Tony.

'It's in my office.'

'Is it cordless?'

'Yes.'

'Bring it to me.'

Tony hauled himself to his feet and the bomber put a hand up to stop him.

'Don't even think about answering it.'

Tony hurried down the stairs, moving gracefully for someone who was carrying so much extra weight. JJ couldn't get used to his New Jersey accent. Whenever he opened his mouth, she still expected him to sound like a stylist from a high-end hair salon. Compared to some of the adjustments she was being forced to make, this one was relatively minor. The sound of the ringing telephone got louder, and a few seconds later Tony reappeared on the lower level. He hurried up the steps and handed over the phone. The bomber checked the display, then held the phone up so Tony could see the screen.

'Do you recognise this number?'

Tony shook his head.

'My guess would be the cops or the FBI. It's about time they made an appearance, don't you think?'

Tony said nothing. The phone rang twice more, then suddenly stopped. The bomber tossed it casually onto a nearby table, where it landed with a clatter.

'Okay, folks, on your feet.'

This time there was no hesitation. Everybody rose as one. They were moving like robots, limbs stiff and jerky. Ed Richards was one of the last to stand. His eyes were haunted, his spirit shattered. Natasha Lovett didn't look much better. Survivor guilt was written all over the director's face.

'One at a time, I want you to come over here. We'll start with you, Mr Head Sheep.'

Richards sleepwalked over and stopped beside the pile of clothes. The bomber produced a red marker pen from his pocket, flipped the lid off, swept the actor's fringe aside, then wrote ED on his forehead in big capital letters. It looked like the letters had been written in blood. Natasha was next. The bomber wrote NAT on her forehead. Red showed up black against her skin and was barely legible.

JJ tried not to fidget, tried not to stare. Her gaze kept being drawn to the two piles next to the bomber. One for shoes, one for clothes. They reminded her of some old Auschwitz photographs she'd seen where the victims' belongings had been heaped into neat piles on a warehouse floor. Shoes, spectacles, suitcases, toothbrushes. She looked away and saw the bodies of Elizabeth Hayward and the accountant. They were lying awkwardly where they'd died, discarded like trash, limbs at odd angles, eyes wide open. It was the eyes that got to her the most. Empty, unblinking and staring at nothing.

The bomber worked his way along the line until he reached JJ. He waved her across. It was only six strides, but those six strides felt like a mile. JJ kept her head down the whole way. Her breathing was rapid and echoed loudly inside her ears. She stopped walking. The bomber tilted her chin up. He kept tilting until she met his gaze, then brushed the hair from her forehead. His touch was surprisingly tender but it still made her want to squirm. She was close enough to smell his deodorant again, to smell the stale sweat it hid. She wondered if he could smell her fear.

'Name?'

'Jody Johnson.' She stated her name in a blank voice. No emotion, no inflexion.

The bomber inked four letters onto her forehead. J-O-D-Y. She felt the tip of the pen glide across her skin. Greasy, shiny, wet. The smell made her think of her schooldays back in Illinois, those long-ago days of innocence when all that had mattered was who your favourite singer was, and who you wanted to make out with. How on earth had she got from there to here?

Everything went fine until it was Simone's turn. The supermodel walked over slowly and cautiously, just like everyone else had. She stopped in front of him, just like everyone else. The bomber looked her up and down, then asked her name. Simone answered in halting syllables. Her Norwegian accent was more pronounced than JJ remembered. Probably due to the stress.

'Do you work here?' the bomber asked her.

'No. I'm a model.'

'I don't remember seeing your name on the reservations list.'

A sudden flash of how this was going to play out filled JJ's head. Simone was going to tell the bomber all about King, and then he would go looking for him, and when he found him he'd kill him. And then he'd probably come back and kill Simone, too. And JJ would have both their deaths on her conscience because she'd told Alex to bring her here today.

'She's with me.'

JJ blurted out the words without thinking. She hoped to God that Simone wasn't as dumb as she looked. If she said the wrong thing now, it wouldn't be the model who wound up dead, it would be her. The bomber studied JJ closely, his cold, grey eyes crawling over her. *This is it*, she thought. *Any second now he's going to see I'm lying, and then he's going to shoot me.*

'I can explain,' Tony said.

JJ turned and looked at him. What the hell was he doing? It was like they'd both temporarily lost their minds. She opened her mouth to say something and the bomber raised his hand.

'No. This I want to hear.' He turned back to Tony. 'Okay, including the corpses, I count sixteen customers here, yet there were only fifteen names on the reservations list. How does that work?'

'I owed JJ a favour.' Tony's voice was distorted by his broken nose, the syllables all mushy. 'She phoned me last night and asked if she could bring Simone along. I said it would be okay. That's why her name wasn't on the list.'

'It must have been a pretty big favour. From what I've heard, it's easier to get through the gates of heaven than it is to get in here.'

'It was a big favour.'

'Care to elaborate?'

'I will if you want me to, but I'd rather not.'

'That embarrassing, huh? Okay, let's hear it.'

'Allegedly, I was caught with a rent boy. Jody helped smooth things out.'

'That was good of her. So did it actually happen? And I want the truth.'

'Yes.'

JJ went very still. Tony was playing hard and loose with the truth. The stuff about the rent boy was all true, but the story about Simone was only half true at best. JJ had called Tony last night, that much was accurate. But what she'd actually asked for was a table for Simone and Alex. Tony had okayed this, but clearly that information hadn't made it onto the reservations list. She held her breath and prayed that Tony didn't get caught in the lie. He'd stepped up to protect her and Alex. It was one of the bravest things she'd ever seen. It was also one of the dumbest.

The bomber held Tony's gaze for a second, then turned and stared at Simone. JJ didn't dare look at the model, not even a glance. Another thought hit her from left field, one that made her stomach plummet. Simone had been on the lower level when the bomber had come in. If he remembered that, then this whole house of cards was about to come crashing down.

JJ could feel her heart beating. She could feel the blood pounding around her body. She wasn't particularly religious, but she said a quick prayer anyway, figuring that it wouldn't do any harm. Her mom had been an occasional Catholic, which meant that JJ had been dragged along to church from time to time. Christmas and Easter, mainly. Even before Tom's death, she would have described herself as a lapsed Catholic. Afterwards, she'd parted company with God for good. She could still remember how to pray, though. She knew all about guilt, too.

The bomber started moving. *This is it,* JJ thought. *Someone else is going to die.* Instead of reaching for his gun, though, he took a step forward and wrote SIMONE on the model's forehead. He glanced at JJ, then dismissed Simone and called the next person forward. JJ only started breathing again when Simone was safely back with the other hostages.

Last up was Kevin Donahue. The movie producer was pushing sixty and didn't look well. His skin was grey and his eyes were sunk deep into their dark sockets. With his shirt off you could see his ribs. JJ guessed cancer. The bomber asked Donahue for his name, wrote KEV on his forehead, then dismissed him.

'Everyone on the floor.'

JJ sat down. Her hands were in her lap, fingers entwined so they wouldn't take on a life of their own and rub the ink from her forehead. The letters etched onto her skin itched like a healing tattoo. She wanted rid of them. She wanted to scrub at them until every last trace was gone.

It suddenly occurred to her that she might inadvertently have saved King's life. The bomber said that he'd seen the reservations list. Would he have recognised Alex King's name, if it had been on there? Probably. After all, King was a big deal at the moment. And would the bomber have noticed that the actor wasn't here now? Again, it was likely. The fact that this had all been arranged at the last minute was playing in their favour. As far as the bomber was concerned, King didn't exist.

JJ glanced around at the other hostages. Richards looked in a bad way. And no wonder. The accountant had died because of him. He hadn't pulled the trigger, but he might as well have done. It was an impossible choice, yet somehow he'd made it. So, why had he picked Natasha? Was it because she was a woman? Or was it that he knew her? A third possibility was that this was a case of famous people sticking together. Maybe it was as simple as that.

She had assumed that the bomber had chosen Natasha and the accountant at random, but now she was starting to wonder.

This was the second time he'd picked on Natasha. Maybe it was a coincidence, but that explanation still didn't sit well. And if it wasn't a coincidence, why Natasha? And why pick on the accountant? Maybe she was overanalysing, but even if she was, they were questions worth considering.

If this wasn't a coincidence, then it meant that Natasha had been targeted. It was possible. If the bomber had access to the reservations list it would be easy to run checks on the lunch guests. Thirty minutes on Google and he'd know everything worth knowing about everyone in the room. Like Wiesner used to tell her, knowledge was the only power that really mattered. If the bomber had been checking them out, then that implied a certain amount of premeditation. Which, in turn, led back to the question of why the hell he was doing this.

JJ glanced up. The bomber was clearing a space on one of the tables. She watched him take a laptop from his backpack and switch it on. He rubbed his head and face through the balaclava, then reached into the backpack again and came out with a bottle of pills. He shook a couple of tablets into his palm and dry swallowed them.

For the next couple of minutes he was totally absorbed by what was happening on the screen. It was as though everything else had ceased to exist. JJ couldn't see what he was watching, but she could hear enough to know that he was surfing the news channels. CNN, Fox, TRN. She heard the clipped tones of a British reporter, which meant the story had already gone international. No great surprise there. Nothing travelled faster than bad news.

All the channels were running the exact same story. There had been a terror attack on an exclusive LA restaurant. There was a suicide bomber and there were hostages, maybe as many as forty. The LAPD and the FBI were on the scene and they were negotiating with the bomber. Even though al-Qaeda had claimed responsibility for the attack, the situation was being likened to the ISIS attack on the Bataclan in Paris. This in turn led to plenty of lurid speculation about the sort of hell the hostages were going through.

JJ listened with a mounting sense of disbelief. The reporters didn't have a clue what they were talking about. There had been no negotiations, there were nowhere near forty hostages, and al-Qaeda and ISIS didn't have a damn thing to do with any of this. The reporters were filling the gaps with speculation and dressing it up to look like fact. They couldn't have got things more wrong if they'd tried. What worried her most was that the media view was indicative of what the cops were thinking, albeit a distorted, more sensationalised version. She knew only too well how that one worked. This raised two questions.

What were the cops thinking?

And, more worrying, how wrong had they actually got it?

9

'We are now going over to Rob Taylor, our man on the ground at Alfie's.'

Caroline Bradley stared directly into the camera, grim-faced and serious. She'd changed from a red suit to a black one because Seth had felt that red was too frivolous for a story of this magnitude. He counted down from three and the picture on the main monitor switched to the live feed from the scene.

'Thanks, Caroline.' Rob sounded a little out of breath, like he'd been running. It was all an act, but it worked brilliantly, adding a real sense of urgency to the proceedings. 'If you look behind me you can see that there are more than a hundred law enforcement officers on the scene. In addition, I've seen a couple of SWAT teams, agents from the FBI's LA field office, bomb disposal experts, firefighters and paramedics. This is quickly turning into a full-scale emergency situation.'

Rob's head suddenly snapped to the left and the camera followed his gaze. A horde of reporters were pushing towards a small, hastily erected podium. The picture bumped and jolted as he broke into a run. Seth had to smile. It was another nice touch, one that cranked the drama up another couple of notches. You couldn't train someone to do this. You either had it or you didn't, and Rob Taylor had it in spades.

The camera zoomed in on Aaron Walters, the head of the LAPD's public information office. Walters was in his late forties.

He had neat salt-and-pepper hair, a greying moustache, and a politician's face. Today he was wearing his best uniform. His buttons were shining, his shoes gleaming. Everything about his body-language said 'trust me'. Seth had met the PR guy a couple of times and wouldn't trust the brown-nosing, back-stabbing son of a bitch as far as he could spit.

Walters stepped up to the lectern and faced the crowd. His gaze moved from left to right, taking in the cameras, mikes and reporters. A strained silence fell. It was the sound of a crowd of news hounds doing their best to contain themselves.

'Ladies and gentlemen, I'd like to read a short statement. At 13:26 today, we received a 911 call regarding an incident at Alfie's. We mobilised immediately and our first priority was to secure the scene, which we have now done. Everyone in a three-block radius has been evacuated. Because of the nature of the situation, the LAPD is working in close co-operation with the FBI's LA field office to ensure that this matter is brought to a swift conclusion. We would urge you to tell your viewers to please just stay away from Alfie's and the surrounding area. Any questions?'

A flurry of hands shot into the air. Walters pointed to Rob.

'Rob Taylor, TRN. Is this an al-Qaeda attack?'

'At this point we're not ruling out that possibility.'

'Don't evade the question. If this is al-Qaeda our viewers have the right to know. According to my sources, the terrorist is wearing an explosive vest. Alfie's is a high-profile target. The MO is classic al-Qaeda, isn't it?'

'Like I said, at this stage we're not ruling out that possibility.' Walters was suddenly interrupted by a barrage of questions. He put his hand up for silence. 'However,' he added, 'I must emphasise that the terrorist angle is just one angle that we're exploring right now.'

'What other angles are you exploring?'

This question came from a raven-haired, brown-eyed CNN cutie-pie. Seth would have bet a month's salary that she wasn't half as dumb as she appeared. Walters paused and placed his hands on the lectern. His face turned serious, like he was considering this rather than giving answers that followed a carefully agreed-upon script. Tara zoomed in, capturing every gesture and tic.

'At this stage, we cannot rule out the possibility that there may be another explanation. What that explanation might be, I wouldn't like to say. The LAPD is in the business of dealing with facts, not idle speculation.'

'Jim Grieg, Fox News. So, this could be someone with a bomb and a grudge?'

'Your words, not mine, Mr Grieg.'

'How many terrorists are there? The film taken inside Alfie's shows one terrorist. Could he have accomplices with him in the restaurant?'

'We believe there is just the one *perpetrator*.'

'You said the FBI is involved. Does this mean that the LAPD is being edged out?'

The camera angle was all wrong, so Seth couldn't see who had asked the question. It was a woman, though, someone with the throaty rasp of a heavy smoker.

'Not at all. Like I said earlier, we are working in close co-operation with the FBI.'

'Have you managed to talk to the bomber?' Rob asked.

'Not yet. Of course, it goes without saying that making contact is one of our main priorities.'

'Has anyone been killed or injured?' Jim Grieg asked.

'Nobody has been killed. However, one of Alfie's employees has been shot and injured. His injuries aren't believed to be life-threatening.'

'Can you give us a name?'

'Not at this stage.' Walters put both hands up. 'Okay, that's it for now. Thank you for your time, ladies and gentleman.'

Walters made a quick escape flanked by two of the LAPD's largest officers. A barrage of yelled questions followed him towards the Mobile Command Unit.

'And cut back to the studio in three,' Seth said. 'Three, two, one.'

Rob was on the phone seconds later.

'Any luck getting hold of King's cell phone number?' he asked.

'We're working on it.' Seth eyed the main monitor, where Caroline was telling the viewers that the injured employee was fifty-eight-year-old Victor Comaneci, a former marine who doubled as a valet and security guard. Two of the smaller monitors were tuned to Fox and CNN. Neither one had this information yet. Score another home run for the underdog.

'I assume we're still going with the terrorist angle,' said Rob.

'Of course we are. Walters is just playing it down because he doesn't want a full-blown panic on his hands.'

'And here we are fanning the flames.'

Seth laughed. 'Don't you go growing a conscience, now. Do you hear me?'

'Loud and clear, boss.'

Seth killed the call. 'Can someone tell me where the hell my terrorism expert's got to?'

'He's in make-up,' one of the assistants called back. 'He'll be ready in two minutes.'

'Not good enough. I want him ready now. Come on people, let's hustle. We've got news to make here.'

10

'We're going to die, aren't we?'

JJ felt warm breath on her ear and resisted the urge to turn around. The question had been delivered in a barely audible whisper that had come from behind her. She glanced over at the bomber. He was still absorbed by the news reports on the laptop. She had noted a pattern to his behaviour. Every minute or so, he'd look up from the screen, sweep his gaze across the hostages, then turn back to the laptop. He'd done this about twenty seconds ago, so there was a bit of time to play with.

She glanced over her shoulder and saw Dan Stone staring at her. Less than an hour had passed since they'd sat down for lunch, but the pressure had taken its toll. Stone's eyes were wired and his hair was a mess from where he'd been running nervous hands through it. The 'N' on his forehead at the end of 'DAN' was smudged. He looked like he was teetering on the edge of a nervous breakdown, and that was a real concern. If he panicked and did something stupid then he was going to end up as dead as Elizabeth Hayward. That was an absolute certainty. What JJ wasn't so sure about was how many people would die with him. Those sitting closest to him would be in the firing line, and, right now, she was sitting directly in front of him.

'We're not going to die,' she whispered.

A couple of people fired dirty looks at her, but she ignored them. Someone had to talk him back from the ledge. Stone glanced at the bomber, then scooted forward until his arm was touching hers.

'We need to do something. If we all work together, we can overpower him.'

'Like they did on Flight 93? Great idea, Dan. We all know how that one turned out.'

'And we know what happened to the other three planes.'

JJ was watching the bomber's every move. It wouldn't be long until he checked on them again. 'So we're screwed if we do something, and we're screwed if we don't.'

'We can't just sit here and do nothing.'

'Yes, we can. This is not the time to play hero. You can hear the news bulletins as well as I can. The police have the situation under control.'

Even as she said this, she heard how lame it sounded. Stone heard it too and shot her a disbelieving look. A movement from the bomber caught JJ's eye and she froze. Her hand found Stone's leg and she squeezed hard. *Shut up.* The bomber's eyes swept across each hostage in turn, starting with Tony on the opposite side of the room.

He reached Stone, and JJ felt the agent tense. And then those eyes were on her, picking her apart and crawling under her skin. She knew it was just her imagination, but she could have sworn that he looked at her longer than anyone else in the room. The bomber finally moved on and she was able to breathe again. She waited for him to go back to his laptop, then glanced at Stone. The agent was looking as wired as ever.

'Just promise me you won't do anything stupid,' she hissed.

11

'We're now joined by terrorism expert Professor Dorian Michaels, from the University of California.'

Up in Mission Control, Seth gave the order for the camera to pull back. Caroline Bradley turned her chair through a full ninety degrees and faced Michaels. She moved in time with the camera, like this had been carefully choreographed.

'Glad you could join us, Professor Michaels.'

Michaels dipped his head, a gesture that had a patrician quality to it. The professor looked like an academic. He had a white mane of hair, a neat goatee, and his intelligent blue eyes were framed by a pair of spectacles. He was well into his sixties, but the years had been low-mileage ones. He was healthy, tanned and there wasn't an ounce of excess fat on him.

'Al-Qaeda has claimed responsibility for this attack,' Caroline said. 'Do you think they're behind it?'

'Before I answer that, I'd like to make a couple of points that might help your viewers.' Michaels' voice was soft and lilting. There was a trace of Irish in there. Caroline nodded for him to continue, and Seth groaned again. What was it with academics? Was it really so hard to answer a simple question? TRN's usual terrorism expert was attending a conference in Berlin. This was the first time Seth had used Michaels. The first and the last.

'The big mistake people make is to imagine al-Qaeda as a large multinational conglomerate, like McDonald's or Coca-

Cola, say.' Michaels paused for a moment and smiled a smile that lit up his whole face. 'They imagine the person in charge is like the CEO, holding the reins, his orders filtering down to his underlings. This couldn't be further from the truth. Al-Qaeda is an ideology, a belief system. We're talking about the difference between Christianity in its pure form, which is a belief system, and the Roman Catholic church, which is a fully structured organisation with a very clearly defined hierarchy.'

Another short pause, another smile. 'In the same way that anyone can call themselves a Christian, any Islamic fundamentalist terrorist group can claim to be acting on behalf of al-Qaeda. The beauty of this set-up is that no one will contradict these claims, since every atrocity carried out in the name of al-Qaeda ultimately benefits the cause. Simply put, the more atrocities attributed to al-Qaeda, the more widely its doctrine of hatred is spread.'

'Did he just compare al-Qaeda to Christianity?' Seth shouted. 'Please tell me he didn't do that?' He wrenched his microphone closer and told Caroline to get the professor back on track, otherwise they were cutting to Rob. It was the only threat that worked. The thought of someone at TRN getting more face-time killed her.

'In your opinion, professor, are we dealing with an al-Qaeda attack here?'

'The question is irrelevant,' Michaels said. 'It makes no difference if this is an actual al-Qaeda attack or not. What matters is whether people *perceive it* as being al-Qaeda.'

No it is not irrelevant. Seth was seething. It was the only question that mattered. The story they were angling for was so simple a three-year-old could get it. An al-Qaeda suicide bomber had attacked one of LA's most exclusive restaurants and was holding a crowd of the entertainment industry's most powerful people hostage. How difficult was that to grasp?

'But you would agree that this attack was carried out by Islamic fundamentalists?'

'It is possible,' Michaels conceded.

Possible! Seth felt the vein in his temple throbbing. What did the dumb schmuck think this was? An intellectual debate? They were paying him five thousand bucks to come in here and say that this was the work of al-Qaeda. Nothing more, nothing less.

'Enough!' Seth screamed. He gripped the desk, knuckles shining white, and stared at the monitor. 'Next time he pauses for breath, cut to Lovett's video. Then call security and get that asshole escorted out of my studio. As for his fee, tell him we're giving it to the Somalian orphans.' He glared at his assistants. 'I want someone to sit down there in that studio and categorically state that this is an al-Qaeda attack. I don't care what their qualifications are. They could have bought their degree over the Internet for all I care. The point is, they tell the story I want told. Come on, people. Do I have to remind you who makes the news here?'

12

Alex King leant against the door and stared at his cell phone. No calls, no texts. Or rather, no texts from anyone he wanted to hear from. Even though it was never going to happen, he was still hoping for a response to his 'love u' text.

The break-up had not been his finest moment. In the end he'd taken the coward's way out, which was ironic since most people thought he was a hero. They'd gone out for a meal and King had dropped the bombshell. He'd chosen a public place because he didn't want a scene. He just wanted to finish things as quickly and cleanly as possible. The only thing going in his favour was that he hadn't sunk so low as to break up by text.

It felt like hours since he last spoke to Brad Carter, but, in reality, it was only about ten minutes. And, man, how those minutes had crawled by. The lack of activity was really getting to him. He wanted to be doing something, he didn't care what. Sitting around like this was torture. He wanted out of here now. What were the FBI up to? Were they planning a rescue mission? If they were, he wished they'd hurry up.

Dying wasn't something he'd really thought about. Sure, there had been times back in Cincinnati when he'd wished he was dead, but that was different. He hadn't really wanted to die, he'd just wanted the beatings to stop. He was thinking about it now, though. As much as he wanted to believe otherwise, the longer this went on, the more chance there was that his luck might finally run out.

Twenty-six was way too young to be thinking about this sort of shit. His death should be a long, long way into the future. Since his escape from Ohio, he'd been more concerned with the business of living, and that was as it should be. Life was one long party, and he was having the time of his life. And now there was every possibility that the party was about to come to a very abrupt end.

King sat on the tiled floor and wondered who'd be at his funeral. One thing was for sure, none of his family would be there. His grandparents had died before he was born, and his father had split when he was still in diapers. For all he knew, his father might even be dead. Not that he cared one way or the other. He'd never known the guy.

His mom had been dead for almost three years now. The drink and drugs had finally taken their toll. He hadn't gone to the funeral. There had been no point. It would have just dredged up a whole load of memories that he wanted to keep buried. He had tried very hard to forget about that part of his life, to erase it from his memory and pretend it had never happened.

Occasionally, he'd wonder what his mom would have made of his success. Any other mom would have been proud, but not Martha King. No doubt she would have viewed him as her personal ATM. The thing was, he would have ended up feeling sorry for her and given her the money. And she would have just gone out and blown it all on drink and drugs.

King tried to conjure up a good memory from his childhood, but those were few and far between. There was a Christmas when he was about five or six and he'd gone on and on about getting a bike. The one he'd wanted was a bright red Schwinn. The one he'd got was a rusty thrift-store heap that had been painted with black emulsion. None of that had mattered, though, because he'd finally had his own wheels.

That was one of the few times when his mom had actually come through for him, when she'd actually done something right. Those occasions were so rare he could count them on one hand. The thought didn't upset him anymore. He was beyond that. Any tears he'd ever cried for his mom had dried up long ago.

The fact he'd survived his childhood was nothing short of a miracle. Home had been a cockroach-infested hellhole on a trailer park on the outskirts of Cincinnati. There had been a steady stream of uncles, leather-jacketed bikers who were big on substance abuse. King had ended up being beaten almost as often as his mother.

There were two big pluses to having such a shitty childhood. First off, his mom had acted like he didn't exist, so he'd been pretty much left to bring himself up. The only rule was that he didn't get into trouble with the cops. Not for his sake, for hers. The last thing she'd wanted was for the cops to come sniffing around their trailer. That was the deal, and it was an arrangement that had suited him fine. The second plus was that it had made him absolutely determined to get out of Ohio as soon as he could.

He'd left just before his seventeenth birthday. He'd spent the previous two summers pumping gas, working twelve-hour shifts for peanuts. Those peanuts had added up to almost a thousand bucks. His mom would have sniffed the cash out quicker than a bottle of vodka, so he'd bought a cashbox and buried it in the woods bordering the trailer park.

His latest uncle had been six-foot-three with a handlebar moustache, a man who loved his chopper more than life itself. One night he came home drunk. After beating his mom unconscious, he started in on King. The last thing he remembered was curling into a ball with his arms squeezed up together to protect his face, and wishing he was dead.

He regained consciousness to the sound of snoring coming from his mom's bedroom. Deep buzz-saw snores. The rising sun was scraping past the ragged curtains, its gentle orange glow touching his skin. He hurt all over but, miraculously, nothing was broken. He didn't know how much time he had, so he moved fast. He threw some clothes into a bag, then went to the woods to get his money. Before he left, he took a screwdriver to the chopper's tyres, then performed his own customisations to the customised paint job. After that, there was no going back.

He took the Greyhound from Cincinnati to Los Angeles, a journey that lasted more than two days. Within a month his money was gone and he was back pumping gas. He didn't pump gas for long. When a stranger offered him a couple of hundred bucks to do some modelling, he thought it was a joke. The man left his business card and told him to call if he changed his mind. Modelling was a damn sight better than pumping gas. One job led to another, and another. Acting was the natural next step. There had been a few lean years before he landed the audition for *Killing Time*, but even the leanest of those years had been a marked improvement on Ohio.

King gripped his cell phone and willed it to ring. What the hell was Carter doing out there? A gentle scratching sound broke into his thoughts. It was coming from somewhere near the urinal. He tried to ignore it. No doubt it was just a rat, or maybe a mouse. Except the noise was too regular and rhythmical to be an animal. Also, this was a solid wall, which meant there was no hollow crawlspace for a creature to move through.

He made his way over to the urinal, pressed his ear against the tiles, then moved his head around, trying to pinpoint where the sound was coming from. It seemed to be originating from lower down, near where the drainage pipe disappeared into the floor. He knelt so he could hear better. The noise was definitely getting louder. And closer. The sound reminded him of a pepper grinder.

A second later, his cell phone vibrated in his sweaty hand.

14:00–14:30

1

'And the main story here at TRN at the top of the hour: Ed Richards and Oscar-winning film director Natasha Lovett are among those being held hostage by an al-Qaeda suicide bomber at Alfie's, one of LA's most exclusive restaurants.'

Seth had the camera zoom in on Caroline. She was oozing gravitas and he wanted to catch every last drop. The background picture showed a scene from the helicopter. Cops, firefighters, paramedics, and all their vehicles in the foreground, the bland L-shaped building that housed the restaurant behind.

'Twenty-five people are currently trapped in the restaurant,' Caroline continued. 'So far, Victor Comaneci, Alfie's parking valet, is the only casualty. A three-block radius around the restaurant has been evacuated, and the police have made an appeal for members of the public to stay away. We are now joined via satellite by Alistair Noble, a terrorism expert from NYU.'

'Cut to Noble in three,' Seth called out. 'Three, two, one.'

Noble was overweight with a round, flabby face and three chins. He was nowhere near as photogenic as Professor Dorian Michaels, but so long as he told the story Seth wanted told, that wasn't a problem. The backdrop showed the New York skyline, the Empire State Building dominating the scene.

'Mr Noble, what do you make of this situation?'

'It's classic al-Qaeda.' said Noble.

There was no hesitation, no prompting, and Seth could have cheered. The terrorism expert's accent was no-bullshit Brooklyn, albeit with the harder edges smoothed away. It was a great TV voice, confident and believable.

'They've chosen a high-profile target,' he continued, 'which is consistent with their MO. Think back to other attacks attributed to al-Qaeda and you'll see what I mean. The London bombings, the Madrid bombings, 9/11. What these targets have in common is that they're right there in your face. I'm a New Yorker born and bred, and the day the towers came down still haunts me. At the time, it was because footage of the attack was constantly on TV. Nowadays, it's because every time I look at the city I see the space where the towers used to stand.'

'What else makes you think this is al-Qaeda?'

'The fact that there's usually some symbolic significance attached to their choice of targets. On 9/11 they chose to attack the Pentagon and the World Trade Centre, a blow against America's military and financial might, respectively. There's speculation that the fourth plane was intended for the White House. If that's the case, then the symbolic significance of such an attack speaks for itself.'

He gave it a second for this to sink in, then added, 'In this case, al-Qaeda haven't chosen any old restaurant, they've singled out one that's patronised by the entertainment industry. Make no mistake, this isn't an attack on Alfie's, this is an attack on the American Dream.'

Seth smiled at that last bit. *An attack on the American Dream.* He was going to get good mileage from that particular sound bite. He whispered a question down to Caroline. He'd spoken to Noble before he went on air, so he already knew what the terrorism expert was going to say. Live TV was like a courtroom. Never ask a question unless you already know the answer.

'But there are deviations from al-Qaeda's MO,' said Caroline. 'Usually they strike quickly and silently, but that doesn't seem to be the case here. What should have been a straightforward suicide bombing has turned into a siege. Can you shed any light on this?'

'An excellent question.' Noble smiled an encouraging, indulgent smile. 'And you're right, to a point. Yes, they normally attack quickly and quietly, however, another defining feature of their MO is adaptability. They are always changing and refining their techniques. What you've got to remember is that they want to spread their message to as wide an audience as they can. That's what's happening here. By drawing this out, they are able to maximise the media exposure.'

'How do you feel this is going to end?'

Seth saw Noble hesitate. 'Zoom in,' he whispered into the mike.

Noble's face got bigger on the screen. The New York cityscape blurred to grey then disappeared. The terrorism expert's expression was grim. His eyes narrowed and he shook his head.

'I wish I could say otherwise, but I don't see this situation having a happy ending. When that bomber strapped on his explosive vest, his sole intention was to martyr himself. The one thing I am absolutely convinced of is that he *will* detonate his bomb. And when he does, people will die.'

2

According to Rob's watch it was exactly two. He'd known this before he looked. His whole working day was defined by a succession of top-of-the-hour round-ups. He pressed his cell against his ear and counted the rings. Tara was beside him, wearing headphones, a digital recorder set up ready to record everything. They'd found a shaded spot where the temperature was marginally cooler. Somewhere away from the crowds and the noise and the distractions, and, most importantly, away from the twitching ears of the other reporters. King answered on the third ring.

'Who's this?' he whispered.

'My name is Rob Taylor, I'm a TRN reporter.'

'How did you get this number?'

The simple answer was that he hadn't. One of TRN's backroom people had lied and bribed and cajoled, and had eventually got it from a friend of a friend of a friend. Rob had already decided that the best way to play this was to bombard King with quick-fire questions. Nine times out of ten, when you asked a direct question, you got an answer. Conditioning was a hell of a thing.

'You're currently inside Alfie's. Hiding out in the restroom. Is that correct?'

'How do you know that?'

'Are you hurt?'

'No, I'm not hurt.'

'Do you know if anybody else is hurt?'

'He's killed two people.'

Rob smiled. That was scoop number one right there. Aaron Walters had categorically stated that nobody had been killed.

'How many terrorists are there? We're hearing one out here. Can you confirm that?'

'Terrorists? Is that what you think this is? A terrorist attack?'

'Isn't it?'

'There's no way this guy's a terrorist.'

And that was scoop number two. A burst of excitement fluttered through Rob's heart.

'Can you tell me anything about him?'

'Only that he's as American as you and me.'

'Have the police been in touch?'

'No, not the police.'

'The FBI?'

'Yeah, some guy called Brad Carter. He's in charge of the LA office.'

Rob had had a couple of run-ins in with Carter in the past. The agent was your typical G-Man. He had the grey suit and the shades, and he was as inflexible as a steel girder. Your basic everyday asshole, in other words.

'Jesus Christ!' King hissed, and the line suddenly went dead.

Rob looked at Tara. Tara looked at Rob.

'Wonder what got him spooked,' he said.

'Well, there's one sure way to find out, honeybun. Call him back.'

He reconnected the call and put the phone to his ear. There was a moment of ghost static and noise, then an electronic voice told him the line was busy and that he should try again later. He killed the call and looked at Tara. The expression on her face made him nervous. This was her bad-news face.

‘What’s wrong?’

‘We can’t use this interview.’

‘Why not? Is there a problem with the recording?’

Tara rolled her eyes. ‘Like that’s going to happen.’

‘So why can’t we use it?’

She slipped her earphones off and they came to rest around her neck. ‘What if the bomber’s monitoring the news channels and he hears that King’s hiding out in the restroom talking to the FBI? What do you think he’s going to do? He’s going to kill him, right? You heard King. He’s already killed two hostages, so it’s not that big a deal to kill a third.’

‘That’s a big ‘if’, Tara. I mean, what’s the likelihood that he’s sitting there watching TRN? Pretty unlikely, I’d say.’

‘Pretty likely, I’d say. You heard King. This isn’t a terrorist attack. That changes everything. The endgame for a terrorist is a big, headline-grabbing explosion. We don’t know what this guy’s endgame is.’

Rob opened his mouth and Tara showed him the hand.

‘What’s his motive?’ she continued. ‘It could be anything. Money, perhaps. Or maybe he’s out to get his fifteen minutes of fame. If it’s either of those things, then you can guarantee he’ll be following the news. If he is, and we play that interview, then we’re effectively signing King’s death warrant.’

As much as he hated to admit it, Tara had a point. He switched his cell back on. If in doubt, delegate. Just pass that buck on like it’s red-hot and smoking. Jonah could make the call on this one.

3

The drill head broke through the restroom wall with a low-level grinding crunch, and a shard of ceramic tile tinkled to the floor. A shower of powdered cinderblock followed, the particles hanging in the artificial light like dust motes caught in a sun ray. The drill slowly retracted, leaving behind a hole the size of a quarter, and a tantalising glimpse of daylight. King's cell vibrated again. He connected the call in a daze, eyes fixed on the hole.

'Hi.'

'It's good to hear your voice, Alex.' Brad Carter sounded as relaxed and laid-back as ever, but there was a slight edge that hadn't been there earlier. 'I've been trying to get in touch, but I kept getting bounced to your voicemail.'

'I switched my phone off for a few minutes to save the battery,' King lied. The alternative was to tell Carter that he'd been talking to a reporter. He figured that probably wouldn't go down too well.

'Please don't do that again, Alex. I need to be able to contact you.' Carter let out a tiny sigh, and in that sigh King understood what had really been bugging him. The FBI man had thought he was dead.

'What's the hole for?'

'We need you to do something for us, Alex.'

'What?'

Carter started talking and King listened, his disbelief growing with every word. What he was asking was suicidal. It was totally insane. Carter finished by saying, 'If you can't do this, we understand. However, if you can help us out here, we'd really appreciate it.'

'Man, I don't know.'

'It's your call, buddy. No pressure.'

'And if I do this, I'll get out of here quicker, right?'

'Absolutely.'

'You promise?'

'I promise.'

King rubbed his face and shook his head, indecision pulling him every which way. All his instincts were telling him to say no, but that wasn't going to happen. It was all about doing the right thing, and, in this situation, the right thing was to do what Carter asked. Like he'd said, those people out in the restaurant were relying on him.

Then there was his career to consider. If he did this then he wouldn't just be a screen hero, he'd be a hero for real, and that wouldn't do his image any harm whatsoever. Of course, the flipside was that saying no would make him look like a coward. Even JJ would have trouble spinning that into something positive.

'Okay, I'll do it.'

'Thanks, Alex.'

'You can save your thanks. All I want is for you to get me out of here.'

'I'm hearing you, buddy.'

King hung up and pushed the phone into his pocket. His hand was shaking so much it took two attempts. All the blood had drained down into his feet and his heart was beating so hard he was pretty sure he was about to have a heart attack. He'd been scared plenty of times, and what he'd come to realise was that fear came in all different shapes and sizes. The fear he'd experienced back on the trailer park in Ohio was different from the way he felt when he stepped in front of a movie camera. But this was a whole new brand of terror. Basically, the FBI man was asking him to risk his life. The bottom line: if he screwed this up, he was a dead man.

4

'Okay, folks, I'm going to make a quick call here. While I'm on the phone, I want absolute silence. I don't want to hear so much as a mouse fart, got it?'

Nobody nodded or gave any indication they'd heard whatsoever, but JJ knew that every single person in the room had 'got it'. One look at the cooling bodies of Elizabeth Hayward and the accountant was enough to ensure that. The bomber picked up the restaurant phone and punched a couple of buttons. He put the phone to his ear, squashing it hard against the black balaclava. A couple of seconds passed.

'Who am I talking to?'

A pause.

'I'm going to call you Louise. You got a problem with that, darling?'

Another pause.

'And that's the right answer, Louise.'

Another pause.

'And why should I tell you my name? Go on, give me one good reason. Do you think you can use it to build up a bond between us? Is that what it tells you to do in your Hostage Negotiator's Handbook? Next you'll be wanting me to use the hostages' names. If I start using their names then I won't look at them and see targets painted on foreheads, is that it?'

A longer pause.

'Caught you on the wrong foot there, didn't I? You know, they're saying on the news that I'm a terrorist, one of the al-Qaeda bad guys. Now, where on earth do they get a notion like that? I'm offended. Really and truly offended.'

Another pause.

'What do I want? Well, that's an interesting question. I suppose we could start with world peace and work from there.'

Another pause.

'Okay, time's pressing on, so I'm going to stop you right there. Now, much as I'm enjoying gabbing with you, we've got some business that needs to be taken care of. The first thing you're no doubt interested in is this explosive vest that I'm wearing. You're looking at ten pounds of military-grade C4, which, I think you'll agree, is more than enough to reduce me and my good friends here to our constituent parts. The explosives can be detonated in two ways. Manually, using a standard trigger. And automatically.'

The bomber let that last sentence hang there.

'Glad you asked, Louise. You know those watches joggers wear? The ones that monitor heart rate? Well, I'm wearing one of those. Now, where mine differs from a store-bought model is that I've got it wired into the detonator. My resting heart rate is seventy-five beats a minute. If that drops below fifty, the bomb will go off. Similarly, if it hits 180, it'll also go off.'

He paused again and this time JJ could tell he was grinning.

'If you're thinking about pumping the restaurant full of nerve gas or, heaven forbid, mounting a rescue operation where I end up dead, then that would be a really dumb idea. You see, Louise, for every action there's an equal and opposite reaction. Are you starting to get the picture?'

Another pause.

'Right answer, Lou. Clever girl. Okay, earlier you asked what I want. Well, I'm going to throw that question right back at you and the army of shrinks who are no doubt poring over my every word. So here's what's going to happen. I'm going to phone you in five minutes and I want *you* to tell me what I want.'

The bomber killed the call and tapped the phone thoughtfully against his cheek. His eyes were shining bright through the slits in the balaclava. The bastard was still grinning. JJ looked at his watch. Everyone was looking at it. She hadn't paid it any attention before, but she was giving it plenty of attention now. The face was big and round, the digital numbers huge. The time was displayed in twenty-four-hour mode. In the top part of the display was a pulsing heart. The bomber's heart rate was currently eighty-four beats a minute. As she watched, it changed to eighty-three. This was higher than his resting rate of seventy-five, but it was still well within the safe zone.

This latest development was worrying. Up until now, JJ had been holding onto the idea that a SWAT team was going to come storming in at any second. That's the way it worked in the movies. The SWAT team came charging in and the hostage-taker ended up dead. Except if that happened here, then they'd all end up dead. Once again this just highlighted the level of premeditation involved. What it didn't do was take her any closer to working out what his motivation was.

The bomber looked over at the hostages then held his arm up high and pointed to the watch. 'That's right, people. Everyone get a good look.'

5

Alex King rolled up the sleeve of his black silk shirt, scooped up the pieces of broken tile and carried them carefully into the cubicle. He plunged his arm into the cold water, getting right in there, all the way to his elbow. He got as far around the bend as he could before letting go of the pieces. Then he removed his arm and stared into the water until he was satisfied nothing was going to come floating back into the pan.

That done, he stepped from the cubicle and dried his arm on one of the white handtowels piled up on the shelf near the door. He scrubbed until his skin was sore, but it didn't matter how hard he rubbed, his arm still felt dirty. What he really wanted to do was wash it, but there was no way he could do that. The sound of water rushing through the pipes might alert the bomber, and if he came to investigate, a bad situation would end up a million times worse.

King knelt beside the urinal, brushed the cinderblock dust away, then stood back. Unless you were looking for the hole, you wouldn't see it. The metal tube arrived five seconds later, pushed through the hole with a long, thin rod. King caught it before it clattered to the floor. He unscrewed the lid and tipped the contents into his hand.

The camera was tiny, a spy toy. It was so small he had a hard time believing that it was actually a camera. For a second he looked at it lying on the palm of his hand, Carter's words playing inside his head. The thought of what he was about to do made him feel sick.

He took a deep breath, muttered 'nine-life cat' under his breath a couple of times, and did his best not to throw up all over the floor. His feet were glued to the tiles and it took a while to get them moving. He made for the door and inched it open. His heart was racing and the blood was pulsing inside his ears. There was just way too much adrenalin slamming around his body right now.

King could hear the low mumble of the bomber's voice. Good. If he was talking, he was distracted. The more distracted he was, the better. King inched the door open, squeezed through the gap, then pulled it closed behind him. He didn't close it all the way. If things went wrong, he didn't want to be messing around with door handles.

The restaurant's lower level was straight ahead, about ten yards away. Meals had been left half-eaten on the tables, chairs had been hurriedly pushed back and abandoned. A couple of candles were still burning. King saw all this, but it barely registered. All his attention was focused on the dead guy draped across one of the chairs. He'd never seen a dead body before. At least, he'd never seen one for real.

This guy was definitely dead, though. No two ways about it. The only other place he'd seen this amount of blood was on set. This was totally different. It was much darker than the Hollywood stuff. Shinier, too. The man's shirt was drenched, and a puddle of dark crimson had formed around the chair legs, staining the wooden floor. From here it looked like the man was staring straight at him.

For a moment King just stood there feeling sicker than ever. His starter was sitting heavily in his stomach, threatening to make a reappearance. He tried to swallow but his mouth was too dry. How could doing the right thing make him feel so shitty? How the hell did that one work? *Got to get moving. Got to get moving. Got to get moving.* The words went around and around in his head, and still his feet remained glued to the floor. If he didn't move soon then he never would, and that would mean the camera wouldn't get planted, and those people out there would die, and it would be all his fault.

He managed to take a step forward, and immediately froze. The squeak of his leather-soled shoes on the wooden floor was deafening. How could he have been such a dumbass? His heart was racing faster than ever. It felt like it was about to burst through his chest. Any second now the bomber was going to come charging around the corner, all guns blazing.

Nothing happened.

Another dozen heartbeats passed and still nothing happened.

From here, he could hear the bomber talking to the hostages. His tone was casual and relaxed. He didn't sound like he was about to charge anywhere. King unlaced his shoes and slipped them off. Carefully. Quietly. Then he laid them on the floor and made his way along the corridor. The wood felt cold through his socks, but at least he wasn't making so much noise.

At the end of the corridor was a low wall that jutted into the restaurant's lower level, and on top of the wall was a small jungle of green, leafy plants. King crawled behind it, then raised his head until his eyes were level with the top of it. The thick foliage made it difficult to see, but he could just about make out the upper level. All the tables and chairs had been pushed to the sides and the hostages were sitting in their underwear on the floor. Their shoes and clothing had been arranged in two piles near a table that had a laptop set up on it.

The bomber was dressed entirely in black, a balaclava hiding his face. There were three round holes in it. Two for his eyes and a slightly larger one for his mouth. He wasn't small, but he was shorter and less muscled than King had imagined, somewhere around the six-foot mark. In his mind, the guy had been at least seven feet tall and built like a mountain.

King glanced over at the hostages. Their names had been inked in red on their foreheads and they all looked terrified. Simone was near the back in lacy black, hiding behind one of the staff. JJ was on the side nearest him. Her underwear was also black, but it was a lot more substantial than the supermodel's. Ed Richards was sitting near JJ. The actor's chest was rising and falling quickly, and there were beads of sweat on his tanned skin. His grey silk boxers had a dark, wet stain on the front. He looked nothing like the Ed Richards that King had seen in the movies.

The body of an old woman was lying in the space between the hostages and the bomber. King shut his eyes and rubbed his face like this might somehow make her disappear. It didn't work. When he opened his eyes, the body was still there. The way it was lying there brought home how messed up this whole situation was. Before he lost it completely, he took the camera out and pushed it between the plants. Carter had briefed him on how to position it. He double-checked to make sure he'd got it right, then checked again just to be sure.

The bomber suddenly turned around and looked down towards the lower level. For a heart-stopping moment King was convinced he'd been seen. He pressed his back against the wall, then crawled quickly towards the restroom, grabbing his shoes on the way and moving as fast as he dared. All his attention was focused on what was happening behind him. The next thing he'd hear would be quick footsteps heading in his direction. Then he'd hear the *psst* of the silenced gun. And then nothing.

He reached the restroom door and glanced over his shoulder. No one was there. He let himself in and eased the door shut behind him. For a few moments he just sat there, feeling like he was going insane. There was a scream trapped in his chest, more screams trapped inside his head. Gradually, his breathing steadied and his heart slowed. No way was he ever going to do anything like this again. He didn't care what Carter said, it wasn't going to happen.

6

'Yes, I'll hold,' Rob said, 'but I'm not going to hold forever. And another thing. When you speak to Mr Walters, tell him that Seth Allen hasn't forgotten.'

'Hasn't forgotten what?' the LAPD operator asked.

'"Seth Allen hasn't forgotten", that's the whole message. Just pass it on, okay?'

Aaron Walters was on the line less than thirty seconds later. He sounded as bright and breezy as a car salesman. He didn't sound like a man who was stuck in the middle of a major hostage incident.

'What can I do for you, Mr Taylor?'

'I want an exclusive interview.'

Walters laughed. 'I'd love to accommodate you, but the thing is, I'm a little busy here right now.'

'Seth thought you might say that.'

There was a long pause on the other end of the line. A deep breath. 'Okay, you've got your interview, but you tell Seth Allen that we're quits.'

The line went dead and Rob stared at his cell phone.

'Is it a go?' Tara asked.

'Yeah, it's a go.'

'So why the what-the-hell expression?'

'I didn't think it would be that easy. Christ knows what Jonah's got, but it must be good.'

'Child porn?' Tara suggested.

'Child murder at the very least.'

Tara laughed and grabbed her camera. 'Let's get moving.'

'Yeah, "remember who makes the news".'

The impression of Seth was pretty good, but that was because he'd had plenty of practice.

7

Even though Major Tom Gleeson was hitting seventy, he still looked more than capable of kicking some serious ass. Here was someone who did a hundred push-ups, a hundred stomach crunches and a five-mile run every single day without fail. And all before breakfast, thought Seth. The major was ex-Delta Force, and an expert on siege situations. He had medals coming out of his wazoo. A Purple Heart, a Bronze Star, a Congressional Medal of Honour. The guy had served in Vietnam and the first Gulf War and was a bona fide war hero.

All of which paled into insignificance when placed against the fact that he looked great on TV. With his weather-worn face, neat grey flat-top and piercing blue eyes, it was easy to imagine him leading the troops into battle. Today he was dressed in an immaculate dress uniform, every crease perfect. His feet were hidden by the desk, but Seth had no doubt that he'd be able to see his reflection in the major's boots. Caroline Bradley looked tiny beside him, like a little girl.

'Thank you for joining us, Major Gleeson.'

'My pleasure.'

'The police and the FBI have secured the area. What do you think their next move will be?'

'If it hasn't happened already, the next logical step is to establish contact with the bomber.' Gleeson's voice was as wide as it was deep. It was a voice that would easily carry from one end of a parade ground to the other. 'Getting information is crucial. It doesn't matter if you're on the streets of Baghdad or the streets of LA, you want to know what you're dealing with. You need to know your enemy. Once that's done, you need to decide whether you're going to play the long or the short game.'

'How would you decide that?'

'By weighing up the pros and cons, whilst keeping the primary objective in sight. In a situation like this, the primary objective is to get as many people out alive as possible.'

'So you're anticipating casualties?'

'Unfortunately, some collateral damage is inevitable. The aim is to keep that to an absolute minimum.'

'You mentioned the long and the short game, is one better than the other?'

'Generally speaking, the long game is better. With the short game you're talking about going in fast and hard. The problem with this strategy is that it would increase the risk of civilian casualties. If I was in charge, the question I'd be asking is why that bomb hasn't been detonated. Has the bomber lost his nerve, or is he working to an agenda we don't know about? Either way, if he's backed into a corner, how do you think he's going to react?'

The major let the question hang in the air for a second before continuing. 'If the police and the FBI go for the short game, they need to neutralise the bomber before he can trigger the bomb. That's a massive risk when so many lives are at stake.'

'How does the long game work?'

'That's a war of attrition. Psych-Ops, if you will. You're looking to wear the bomber down. The longer this siege goes on, the more likely it is that he'll start to personalise the victims, which will make it harder for him to kill them. He'll also start to tire, both physically and mentally. The negotiator's job is to persuade the bomber that the only solution is a peaceful solution.'

'A tall order.' Caroline's face was serious, eyes searching.

'It is,' Gleeson agreed. 'But that's what these guys are trained to do.'

'When it comes to a rescue operation, the set-up of Alfie's creates a number of problems, doesn't it?'

Up in Mission Control, Seth said, 'Go to the graphic on three.' He counted down with his voice and fingers. The main screen changed to show a 3D computer representation of Alfie's.

The restaurant was housed in an L-shaped single-storey building that bordered onto the street. In the stem of the L there was a split-level seating area with three tables in the upper section and two on the lower. The kitchen occupied the largest space in the base of the L and was reached by a corridor that passed the restrooms and an office. There were no windows and only two external doors. One led directly from the parking lot to the kitchen, the other led to a reception foyer.

'From a tactical point of view the set-up poses a number of challenges,' Gleeson said. 'We know from the video clip that the hostages are being held in the upper level of the restaurant.'

On screen, the upper level flashed.

'With an assault through the main door, the bomber will be alerted straightaway. This can be ruled out since the risk of civilian casualties is too high. An assault via the kitchen can be ruled out for the same reason. Again, there's too high a likelihood that the bomber will be alerted before the SWAT boys can do their thing. The lack of windows means there's no way for a sharpshooter to take out the bomber.'

'What about using gas?' Caroline suggested.

'As was seen during the Moscow theatre siege back in 2002, this is another high-risk strategy. It's believed that weaponised fentanyl was used in that case. Fentanyl is an opioid analgesic that's eighty times more potent than morphine. The rescue attempt was an unmitigated disaster that resulted in the deaths of 133 of the hostages.'

Seth got the camera operator to zoom in on Gleeson's face.

'The situation at Alfie's is just too volatile to use gas. If the bomber feels he's being backed into a corner, he's going to panic. And if that happens, he will detonate his bomb.'

8

Almost an hour had passed since the bomber burst into Alfie's, but to JJ it felt much longer. It was like her whole life had happened in this restaurant. There was no before, no after, only now. Each breath could be her last. There was no way of knowing what was going through the bomber's mind right now, and absolutely nothing she could do to stop him from just hitting the switch.

The initial shock had worn off, replaced by a weird emotional state that fluctuated between terror and numbness. One second she was more scared than she'd ever been, the next she felt completely detached from reality, like her soul had been injected with Novocaine.

She kept drifting into memories from her life with Tom. The first time they met, their wedding day, the time Tom had arranged a surprise trip to New York for their anniversary. Memories both big and small. There were darker, more dangerous memories as well, and whenever one of those threatened to appear, she did her best to push it away.

To survive this thing she was going to have to dig deep. She'd done it before, she could do it again. Focus on the good rather than the bad, the light instead of the dark. When you let the darkness get to you, that was when the real problems began. It had taken a lot of therapy to reach that conclusion, but it was so true.

She glanced sideways at the bomber, being careful not to draw any attention. After talking to the hostage negotiator, he'd sat down in front of the laptop and zoned out. He was still sitting there now, just staring into the middle distance, saying nothing, doing nothing. The laptop wasn't even switched on. It was like he'd powered down. The way he was acting was creepy. JJ didn't know what was worse. Having him marching around giving orders and scaring everyone half to death, or seeing him like this.

She looked across at Elizabeth Hayward and wished she hadn't. The Cartier watch she'd sacrificed herself for was glittering in the light. That as much as anything just seemed to underline how precarious their situation was. It could be any of them lying there. Because the truth of the matter was that the bomber hadn't cared who he'd killed. All he'd wanted was to show them who was in charge. The way he'd executed Hayward had been so cold. He'd brought the gun up, squeezed the trigger, and blown her brains out. There had been no hesitation, no second thoughts, and that scared JJ as much as anything else that had happened. If he could kill a defenceless old woman, then he could kill any of them.

She checked the bomber wasn't looking, then glanced quickly at the other hostages. Everyone was just about holding it together, some better than others. A couple of the women had wet cheeks. Some of the men, too. Almost everyone had that thousand-yard stare that she'd seen so many times on the news. It was an expression that combined shock, terror and disbelief in equal measures. If she could see herself now, she'd no doubt be wearing an identical expression.

Ed Richards was still a concern. The actor looked like he was on the verge of a breakdown. If anyone was a prime candidate for doing something dumb, it was him. She could see him making a run for it like the accountant, and ending up just as dead. The actor had a wife and kids at home, too. JJ had met Catherine a couple of times and she seemed nice enough. The one thing that had come shining through was how much she loved her husband. JJ hoped Richards found the strength to hold it together. For Catherine and the kids, if nothing else.

Kevin Donahue worried her as well. The movie producer looked worse than ever. He was so pale, all skin and bones and as insubstantial as a ghost. Maybe he was on medication and had missed a dose. Keeping him in here seemed unnecessarily cruel. The guy was clearly suffering. JJ had never had any dealings with him, so didn't know much about him. He had a reputation for being hard but fair, which was as close as you got to integrity in this town. She hadn't heard any horror stories. That didn't mean there weren't skeletons in his closet, but if there were, they probably weren't that big.

And what about Alex King? Had he somehow managed to escape? There were no windows in the restrooms, but there was always the kitchen door. Maybe he'd got lucky and had managed to sneak out before the grilles went down. It was a long shot, but it was possible. There had been nothing on the news about him escaping, but that would make sense. If he had got out, the cops would want to keep it quiet. They could be debriefing him right now, picking his brain for anything he might have seen or heard.

JJ hoped that he had escaped. The more information the FBI and police had, the more likely it was that they'd resolve this situation before anyone else died. She glanced over at the bomber. Bad move. He'd come out of his trance and was looking straight at her.

How long had he been staring for? And why was he staring?

The second question was easier to answer than the first. He must have seen her studying the other hostages. She looked away, heart thumping, lungs frozen. She'd screwed up big time. You don't do anything to make the bad guy notice you. That was the golden rule here. The only way to play this situation was to merge into the background. But had she done that? No. And now she was going to pay for that mistake. JJ stared at the parquet, convinced her next breath would be her last. She wondered if she would hear the gunshot.

9

Being escorted by a cop past the slack-jawed reporters from CNN and Fox was pretty cool. They looked totally pissed, and Rob didn't blame them one little bit. If their roles had been reversed, he would have been pissed, too. He felt them shooting daggers into the back of his head and had to smile. *Yeah, you'd better watch out because I'm after your jobs, losers.*

Chasing stories around LA on the Harley was fun, but he definitely had his eye on the bigger prize. And what was wrong with that? He was ambitious. He'd never made any secret of the fact. He wanted the big house, the fast cars, and a wife who turned heads just by walking into a room. Most of all, though, he wanted to tell his father to go screw himself.

Robert Taylor Senior didn't understand what he did for a living. He was a lawyer who worked eighty hours a week. That was real work. What Rob did, in his father's opinion, wasn't. His father had been mostly absent while he was growing up. On the few occasions he had made an appearance, he'd never had a good word to say. Nothing Rob had done had ever been good enough. He'd get As in almost every subject, but it would be that one B that his father would focus on. So, yes, that 'screw you' would be the cherry on the cake.

Tara was right beside him, grinning a big old grin and clearly enjoying the attention as much as he was. The cop took them past the firefighters and the paramedics, and stopped in front of the LAPD's Mobile Command Unit. Rob could sense the tension all around him. It was like a rubber band had been tightened to breaking point and everyone was just waiting for it to snap. The blank wall of Alfie's was a couple of blocks up ahead. Usually this was one of LA's busiest streets. Not today. The stretch of road leading to the restaurant was completely deserted. All the stop signs were on red. It was kind of eerie.

Aaron Walters marched down the steps, shoes clattering on steel. He didn't look happy, but that was the least of Rob's worries. Jonah wanted this interview done yesterday, and Walters had kept him hanging around for almost five minutes, which had meant five minutes of calls from Jonah, each one more abusive than the last. That was not Rob's idea of fun.

Walters stopped in front of him. 'Make this quick.'

Rob looked at him. Despite the fancy title, the uniform and the politician's smile, he was just another PR man, and PR men were one small step up the evolutionary ladder from snake-oil salesmen.

'Alex King,' he said.

'What's he got to do with anything?' Walters' expression was totally blank. No giveaways, no tells, nothing. He had a great poker face.

'Here's the thing,' Rob went on. 'I've just interviewed Alex King and he told me a whole bunch of interesting stuff. For instance, he told me he's currently hiding out in the restroom in Alfie's and that he's helping you guys out. He also told me that two people have died. Now, I'm confused here, Aaron. You see, I remember you standing up before the cameras not so long ago and categorically stating that no one had been killed. So, what's the story?'

Walters took a long breath in and shook his head. 'That stupid asshole. What the hell was he thinking, talking to you?'

Rob shrugged and said nothing.

'You can't use the interview. You realise that, don't you?'

Another shrug.

'Come on, Taylor, we both know that if the bomber finds out about King then he's a dead man.'

'Here's something else I found interesting, Aaron. This isn't a terrorist attack, is it?'

'Jesus Christ, aren't you hearing me? You *cannot* use the interview.'

'Aaron, I'm hearing you just fine. The thing is, if I can't use it, then you've got to give me something I can use.'

'Or what? You're going to condemn a man to death?'

'It's not me you've got to worry about.'

'Seth.' Walters whispered the name like it was a curse. He shook his head. 'No, he wouldn't do that. Even he's not that much of a bastard.'

'Are we talking about the same Seth Allen here? Because the Seth Allen I know would sell his mother in a heartbeat.'

Walters said nothing.

'Look,' Rob added, 'I don't like this any more than you do.'

This was a blatant lie, but sometimes you had to give a little to win the war. Walters shook his head and sighed. He looked into the distance and when he looked back he was still shaking his head.

'What will it take to stop Seth using the interview?'

'An exclusive. You're going to tell me what's really going on in there, and you're not going to speak to anyone else until we've aired.'

'I can't.'

'You can and you will.'

'Okay, but I want to vet the interview before you air it.'

'Not going to happen.'

Rob couldn't help smiling. And no wonder. This was a major coup. Once the interview aired, every news station in town was going to want a piece of him. The future was just looking brighter and brighter. At this rate he'd need a new pair of shades.

10

There had been no gunshot, no retribution. JJ knew she'd had a lucky escape, but it was only just starting to sink in how lucky she'd been. For a moment back there, she'd been convinced she was about to die. The bomber had looked her straight in the eye and she'd thought his next move would be to shoot her. But that hadn't happened.

From here on in she wasn't going to do anything that would mark her out. Nothing at all. Invisible like wallpaper, she told herself, bland and boring and very much in the background. She'd had one strike against her. There was no way she could afford another. She glanced over at the bomber. He was staring intently at his laptop, totally absorbed by what he was seeing. She looked away before he caught her staring.

'And we've got another exclusive here at TRN,' a female voice said. 'Our roving reporter, Rob Taylor, is at Alfie's, where he's talking to Aaron Walters, the LAPD's spokesperson. Rob, can you tell us what's happening over there?'

'We've got breaking news of a major development, Caroline. It would appear this isn't a terrorist attack. Is that correct, Mr Walters?'

'That's correct.' Walters sounded like a politician. Smooth, polished, confident. 'We've now made contact with the bomber and I can confirm that this isn't a terrorist attack.'

'So, what exactly is going on?'

'That's what we're trying to establish. So far no demands have been issued, and until that happens we've got no way of knowing what the bomber's motives are.'

'You can speculate, though?'

'Mr Taylor, speculating is not going to benefit anybody.'

'How are the hostages bearing up?'

'That is something our negotiator will be trying to establish.'

'But, so far as you're aware, nobody's been injured?'

There was a pause, a moment of stillness and silence. 'Unfortunately, there have been two fatalities.'

'Can you tell me what happened?'

Rob's question contained a mix of shock and surprise, but to JJ's practised ear it sounded staged. If the reporter already knew about the deaths, what else did he know? More importantly, *how* did he know? And how had TRN managed to get this interview? Why not CNN or Fox? TRN was tiny in comparison. It made no sense. She re-ran the interview in her head. The only explanation was that TRN had some sort of leverage. But what? It would need to be something big.

An idea occurred to her, one that made her heart sink. Alex King must still be inside the restaurant. That would be big enough. If King was still here, and the police knew he was in here, then they would want to protect him. And if TRN had somehow found out about this, then Seth Allen wouldn't think twice about using it to get an exclusive interview. JJ couldn't be sure if that's what had happened, but it felt right, and it was consistent with the sort of crap that went down in this town all the time.

'At this stage, we're still trying to piece together what happened,' Walters said. 'I'm not prepared to speculate.'

'Can you tell us who the victims are?'

'Once again, that's something we're currently trying to establish. Obviously, the families will need to be notified before we release that information.'

'Thank you very much, Mr Walters. Caroline, back to you.'

'As you can hear, incredible developments over at Alfie's,' Caroline said. 'And another world exclusive for TRN, the station that's always first with the news. For those viewers who have just joined us, two people have died and twenty-three people are being held hostage at one of LA's top restaurants.'

The bomber killed the volume and stood up. JJ watched him pace from the corner of her eye. The silenced submachine gun bumped gently against his back in time with his footsteps. He picked up the restaurant phone, hit a couple of buttons, then pressed it against the side of his balaclava.

'Louise, good to hear your sweet voice again. Any luck with my question?'

A pause.

'It shouldn't be so hard. I mean, "what do I want?". The question sounds simple enough to me.'

Another pause.

'And how did I know you were going to say that? Okay, here's another question. One of your people has been on the news, telling the world that I've killed a couple of hostages. Now, where did they get an idea like that from? And I want the truth, or I might have to kill a couple more.'

The pause was longer this time. The bomber nodded a couple of times as though what he was hearing made sense. 'Infrared and aural scanners. Well, I can't say I'm surprised. If I was in your shoes I'd do the same thing.'

The bomber paused again, but this pause was different from earlier. JJ had the impression he was thinking rather than listening.

'Okay, Louise, the fact I've killed a couple of people no doubt upsets you folks. So here's what I'm going to do, I'm going to let some hostages go. How does that sound? We do it my way, though. Any deviations and everyone stays here with me. Got it?'

A pause.

'And that's the right answer, Louise. Okay, the first thing I need you to do is get in touch with TRN. I've decided they're going to get the scoop on this one. After all, someone's got to root for the underdog.'

11

The reporters on the other side of the barrier were looking more pissed than ever, which figured. Jonah would already have re-run the good bits from the interview, rubbing that salt even deeper into the wound. No doubt they were wondering how some low-life from TRN had managed to get the scoop. It was no secret that TRN was widely regarded as the tabloid news station.

Rob and Tara were twenty yards from the barrier when the cop escorting them came to an abrupt halt and reached for the radio attached to his lapel. He cocked his head towards it, muttered 'uh-huh' a couple of times, then turned to Rob.

'Walters wants to see you again.'

'Why?'

'No idea. I've just been told to bring you back.'

Rob shrugged at Tara, then they turned and headed towards the Mobile Command Unit.

'Hey, where are you taking him now?' The shout came from Jim Grieg. The Fox News man was glaring at them, red-faced and furious. He looked as though he was about to stroke out. 'This is bullshit! Complete and utter bullshit!'

'Come on,' CNN's reporter added. 'Taylor's already had one exclusive. It's someone else's turn.'

Rob grinned and Tara gave them the finger.

Walters was waiting by the command unit steps. 'I need you to do something,' he said without preamble. He was chewing his bottom lip and looked flustered. The admission clearly killed him. This was his version of death by a thousand paper cuts. He took a deep breath and let out a long sigh. 'The bomber has agreed to release some hostages. But he wants the release shown on live TV, and he wants TRN to report on it.'

'And?'

'And he wants you to share your live feed with the other networks.'

'Is that all?'

Walters said nothing.

'So, let me get this straight. You want me and Tara to go down to Alfie's and film the hostages coming out. And then you just want us to hand over the footage. You know, Aaron, I've got to ask, what happens if we're down there and the bomber decides to blow himself up?'

'Don't screw with me Taylor. We both know you're going to do this.'

Rob smiled.

'I need an assurance that there won't be any problems with the other networks getting access to your live feed.'

'Of course there won't be any problems.'

'I'm serious. They're already all over my ass because they think I'm playing favourites.'

'I said it wouldn't be a problem.'

'Thank you.'

'Not so fast. If we don't do this then the hostages won't be released. That's the deal, right?'

The only response from Walters was a careful narrowing of the eyes.

'I've got a couple of conditions.' Rob smiled, then outlined what he wanted. Today was just getting better and better.

12

'Who wants to go home?'

Nobody moved a muscle. All eyes were on the bomber. He was strutting back and forth, stepping over Elizabeth Hayward's body as though it wasn't there. Hopelessness had turned to hope in a heartbeat. JJ felt it. Everyone felt it. There wasn't a single person in the room who didn't want to get out of here.

The suspicious part of her mind was searching for the catch, though. There had to be one. There always was. Read the small print, then read it again. That was something else that Wiesner had drilled into her. Chances were the bomber had no intention of letting anyone go. JJ hoped this wasn't the case, but, based on what she'd seen so far, she couldn't dismiss the possibility.

'Okay,' the bomber said. 'Since eight is my lucky number, I've decided to let eight of you go. But who's going and who's staying? Now, I've thought long and hard about this, but I think I've come up with a solution. What I did was take a good look around at you all and ask myself who *shouldn't* be here. Once I did that, the decision made itself.'

He stopped strutting and faced the hostages.

'Chester, stand up.'

Everyone moved at the same time, bumping and shuffling and turning to see. The head chef stood up on shaky legs, using the back of a chair for support. His large gut was spilling over the waistband of his white boxer shorts.

'Holly, stand up.'

Holly was the head waitress. She was in her early thirties, tanned, athletic, pretty and slim. Beth was called next, another waitress. JJ saw a pattern emerging and did a quick head-count. If you took Tony out of the equation, there were five members of staff left sitting on the floor. Sure enough, one by one, they were told to stand up.

'Tony, please escort these good people to the door.'

Tony's face was looking worse. Both eyes were dark purple and swollen, and his nose was kinked to the right. He stood up and led his staff towards the foyer.

'One more thing,' the bomber called after him. 'Don't even think about sneaking out with them. Do that, and I will shoot someone, and that blood will be on your hands.'

He stared straight at JJ when he said this. She thought she'd been forgiven, but obviously not. She looked desperately at Tony, then back at the bomber. Even if his orders were followed to the letter, he might still shoot her. There were no guarantees here. The bomber sat down at the laptop and pressed the restaurant phone against his ear. Two seconds passed, three seconds, four.

'Okay, Louise, we're good to go here. As soon as I see Alfie's on my screen, I'll give the order for the grilles to go up.'

Another eight seconds passed. Nine. Ten.

'Do you take me for a fool?'

The bomber was holding the phone in front of his mouth and shouting into it. JJ's stomach turned inside out. She glanced at the gun hanging from his back, glanced at the bomb vest. The flashing heart on his watch was registering one hundred and eleven beats a minute.

'Did I not make myself clear? We do this *my* way! What part of that is so hard to understand? Now, you get in touch with whoever's operating that camera and tell them to pull back so I can see both doors. If that doesn't happen within the next two seconds then the deal is off and I start shooting.'

13

'We've got the LAPD on the phone,' one of the assistants yelled out.

Seth glanced down at them. The black kid was looking straight at him, while the other two were doing their best to appear busy. At least that made it easy to work out who'd been doing the shouting. The problem was that the three of them were totally interchangeable. 'And?'

'They need both doors in the shot, and they need it done now or the hostages won't be released.'

Seth pulled his microphone towards his mouth. 'Tara,' he said calmly. 'Be a sweetheart and pull back so we can see the kitchen door.'

The picture on the main screen widened until both of Alfie's doors were in shot. The downside was that too much of the parking lot was now showing. In the middle of the picture was a patch of dried blood that marked the place where Victor Comaneci had been shot. The fact that it had shrunk when Tara zoomed out was a royal pain in the ass, since it diminished the impact. At the moment, that dark patch of blood was the only interesting thing on the screen.

While Tara had been setting up, she'd 'accidentally' swept her camera across the parking lot. Manufacturers, models and number plates had been noted and were now being checked out by the TRN researchers.

One car had stood out amongst all the luxury motors, an old silver Ford Taurus with battered bodywork. The bomber had to get to the restaurant somehow. You never walked anywhere in LA, particularly if you were wearing a balaclava and a bomb vest.

There were no cars in the picture now, but that was intentional. TRN had a chance to beat the big boys to the scoop yet again. Right now, Seth was playing every advantage he could.

'CNN's on the phone.' This came from one of his assistants. The white lesbian this time.

'And?'

'And they want to know why we haven't sent them the live feed yet.'

'Tell them we've got a technical glitch. Ditto for Fox or anyone else looking for their pictures.'

'You want me to lie?'

Seth laughed. 'Yes, sweetheart, that's exactly what I want you to do. Have you got a problem with that?'

'No, sir.'

'And that's the correct answer.'

Seth stared at the main screen, willing something to happen. The lack of activity made him edgy. Dead air was not good for business. To make matters worse, the outside of Alfie's was so boring. The walls were painted white and had no defining characteristics. The gaps in the heavy white door grilles allowed the occasional glimpses of smoked window glass, and the black of the parking lot contrasted with all the white, but neither one made the overall picture any more interesting.

Rob was talking a mile a minute and doing his best to make a whole lot of nothing sound like a whole lot of something. He was like a man drowning in his own bullshit. Seth stared at the big screen and willed something to happen. The banner at the bottom read: 'HOSTAGE RELEASE. ANOTHER TRN EXCLUSIVE'. He hoped he hadn't jumped the gun there.

Another forty seconds passed. Fifty seconds, sixty. A whole minute of dead air. This was a disaster. Rob was rehashing the main points for the third time, and Seth was about to admit defeat and cut to the cell phone footage, when a movement on the monitor caught his eye. Rob broke off mid-sentence.

'The grilles are rising,' he said in a voice that buzzed with excitement. 'Any second now we should see the first hostage coming out.'

14

Even though King was expecting it, the bump and grind of the rising grille still made him jump. He'd managed to tune in to some of what the bomber was saying, enough to work out that he was releasing hostages. As soon as he'd realised what was happening, his brain had gone into overdrive. This was his chance to escape. Perhaps his only chance. He couldn't rely on Brad Carter. That much was obvious. If he was going to get out of here, then it was down to him to make it happen. He edged the restroom door open.

'Nobody move until I tell you!' the bomber hollered.

King froze. It took a second to work out that the bomber wasn't shouting at him. He stepped into the corridor and turned right. He was moving as quickly as he dared, socks gliding across wood. The kitchen door was only six yards away, but it was a long six yards. The door was one of those that swung both ways. There was a rectangular stainless-steel plate at hand level, and a round porthole window at head height. The wood had been varnished to show off the grain.

King peered through the window. The kitchen was empty. He pushed on the door and it opened with a low squeak. King froze with his palm flat against the metal plate, eyes searching frantically over his shoulder. He was listening for any indication that the bomber had heard him. A shout, a footstep, the hiss of a silenced gun. But there was nothing, not so much as a whisper.

He squeezed through the gap and eased the door closed inch by slow inch, absorbing the squeak from the spring with time and patience. He looked around. The kitchen had been abandoned in a hurry. Pots and pans had been discarded, their contents cooling and congealing. All the hobs were switched off, so presumably the bomber must have ordered this to happen when he'd swept through here earlier. Despite the chaos, the kitchen still gleamed, steel shimmering and shining under the bright halogen lights.

The door to the parking lot was directly opposite. Just seeing it was enough to send a jolt of excitement shooting through him. The only thing that stood in the way of freedom was a couple of inches of wood. King crossed the kitchen in half-a-dozen bounding strides and grabbed the handle. The door wouldn't open. He tried again, and it still wouldn't budge. Then he saw the keyhole and it all made sense.

He rattled the handle in frustration, then remembered where he was. He let go, cursing himself for being so dumb. What the hell was he thinking? He stood there paralysed. Seconds drifted past, each one an agony of waiting. Of course the door was locked. What had he expected? The bomber might be crazy, but crazy wasn't the same as stupid. He would have locked the door after rounding up the kitchen staff. The key was probably in his pocket for safekeeping.

But what if that wasn't the only key? King had once worked at a restaurant where the chef kept losing his keys. His solution had been to keep a spare set hanging on a hook next to the door. The kitchen wasn't massive, but there were still too many cupboards and hiding places. King forced himself to take a second to think things through. There was no point wasting time searching places a key would never be kept. He didn't know how long he had. Every second counted.

He started by checking around the door, but that would have been too easy. Next, he tried the drawers to the left of the door. Both were filled with the sort of crap that had nowhere else to go. Birthday candles, a lighter, a torch, shit like that. He didn't find any keys on his first pass, nor his second. He knelt down and checked the cupboards beneath the drawers. Nothing but pots and pans.

He turned a full circle, eyes searching. The cooking range caught his attention, but only because it was so big. It wouldn't be practical to keep the key there. He heard a loud rasping sound and realised it was his breathing. Chill, he told himself. Another glance at the door. This went beyond frustrating. He was inches from freedom, but those couple of inches might as well have been a thousand miles.

King did the only thing he could think to do. He started searching again.

15

'Come over here, Jody.'

Time slipped and JJ felt her heart lurch. Tom had called her Jody right from the start. It was just one of the multitude of small things that form the heart of a marriage. Her mom had been the only other person who called her Jody. After Tom's death, even she had started calling her JJ. The fact that the bomber was calling her Jody was wrong on every level.

'I said, come over here, Jody. I won't ask again.'

JJ glanced left, then right, but nobody would meet her eye. Not that she blamed them. The bomber had put his mark on her. Everyone would be wanting to stay as far away from her as possible. He aimed the gun between her eyes and that got her moving. She stood up slowly and started walking.

The terror was like cement in her stomach, a solid mass of emotion just sitting there. The only reason he'd singled her out was because he planned to kill her. She was tempted to run, but a quick glance at Elizabeth Hayward made her think again. Six steps took her right up to him. She could smell his deodorant, and beneath that, she detected a musky aroma that made her think of wild animals.

For a moment they stood there toe-to-toe, eyes locked. The top of her head came up to his chin and she had to tilt her head to meet his gaze. If she was going to die, she wanted it to happen quickly. The thought came out of nowhere and made her feel ashamed. She'd never been a quitter.

Anger came next, slamming into her and steamrollering the shame out of the way. It tore into her heart and wouldn't let go. She was furious at herself for thinking like a loser, and she was furious with this son of a bitch for putting her in this situation. She hadn't asked for this. None of them had. If she hadn't decided to come here for lunch on this particular day, if she had eaten somewhere else, if she'd been too busy to take a lunch break or she'd been ill, then she wouldn't be here now. She was a random victim, and that somehow made things so much worse.

'Get down on your knees.'

JJ stared at the bomber, defying him. Her hands were shaking and she felt sick. That last burst of adrenalin had made her head go woozy. She knew this was suicide, but didn't care. She'd looked at the situation, and no matter how hard she spun it, she couldn't find one single pro. The bomber was going to kill her as surely as the sun rose in the morning and set at night. As surely as it would continue to rise and set long after she was gone.

The blow caught her by surprise. One second she was standing upright, the next she was on the floor, her head feeling like it was about to explode, her jaw aching. She looked up and saw the bomber turning his gun back around the right way.

'When I tell you to do something, you do it. Now get on your knees.'

'No.'

'What are you doing?' Tony was staring at her in disbelief. 'Come on, JJ, just do what he says.'

JJ surprised herself by laughing. 'Don't you get it? He's going to kill me whatever I do. Isn't that right?'

She looked back at the bomber. He stared at her for a second, then walked over to Tony, covering the distance in a couple of strides. JJ realised what was happening, but it was already too late.

'No!' she shouted. 'You can't do this!'

The bomber pushed the gun into the side of Tony's head. 'Darling, I can do whatever I want.'

JJ knelt. 'Look, I'm on my knees. I'm doing what you told me.'

'You should have done it when I asked.'

The bomber screwed the silencer in a bit deeper and Tony's head tilted to the side. He looked over at her. 'It's gonna be okay,' he whispered. There were tears in his eyes. There were tears in JJ's, too.

'Please don't do this,' she whispered. 'Please, I'm begging you.'

16

The sound of shouting in the main restaurant stopped King in his tracks. He ran across to the kitchen door and pressed his ear against it. He couldn't hear a damn thing. He tried pressing his ear against the window, but that wasn't any better. He inched the door open, just enough to let the sound filter through. He recognised JJ's voice straightaway. She was pleading and sounded desperate, two things King found impossible to comprehend. It just didn't equate to the way he viewed her. If JJ was losing her shit then things were worse than he thought.

He closed the door, then took out the Ziploc bag and ran his thumb over the plastic like it was a lucky rabbit's foot. As he rubbed it, he said a quick prayer for all the craziness to stop. Not that he expected it to do any good. He'd gone through a stage of praying as a kid. His prayers had never been answered back then, so why should things be any different now? The truth was that God didn't have time for losers like him.

If things went bad, he hoped the wood would be thick enough to muffle the shot. He might blame JJ for everything that was happening here, but that didn't mean he wanted to see her dead.

17

The bomber's finger tightened on the trigger.

'Please don't shoot.' The words came out as a sob. JJ hated herself for sounding so weak, but she couldn't help it. She didn't want Tony to die. Not like this. He was looking down at the floor and she was just glad that she didn't have to look him in the eye. If she'd kept her mouth shut, none of this would be happening. That was the bottom line here.

It didn't matter how bad things got, they could always get worse. How many times had she told her clients that? You keep your emotions in check at all times. Let them loose and it will always end badly. At work she was known for her ability to keep a cool head, no matter what. That was her biggest strength. Even during those first few months after Tom died, she'd been able to project like everything was okay. Inside she might have been going to pieces, but outwardly, it was business as usual.

She really should have known better.

Should have, would have, could have. Didn't.

'Give me one good reason,' the bomber said.

JJ's mind was a sudden blank. For the first time in her life, she couldn't think of a single thing to say.

'I'll give you ten seconds.'

He started counting down and that made things worse. As soon as half a thought entered her head, it was gone again, stripped away by those relentless numbers. The bomber reached one.

'I don't know!' she yelled.

The bomber snatched the gun away from Tony's head. He straightened up and turned to face her.

'I don't know,' she whispered.

He looked at her for a moment, then nodded to himself.

'That little admission must have hurt. Looking at you, I'd say you're the sort of person who likes to be in charge. A control freak. Is that a fair assessment?'

JJ nodded.

'This must be tough for you. I mean, you come here thinking you're going to have a nice quiet lunch, and then I appear out of nowhere and turn your world upside down. My guess is that you've got your whole life programmed into your cell phone. Am I right or am I right?'

JJ nodded again.

'I'll bet it not only tells you where you're having lunch a week Tuesday, it probably tells you *what* you're going to have. So, I must be a real shock to the system.'

The bomber paused as though he was thinking things over. JJ could sense her life hanging in the balance. Right now she couldn't see past the next heartbeat.

'Okay,' he said eventually. 'Promise me you'll behave and we'll pretend like this never happened. How does that sound?'

'Fine. That sounds fine,' she said quickly. She looked into his eyes for some sort of assurance that he would keep his word, but all she saw was desolation. There was a part of her that was just waiting for him to raise the gun again. A part that was just waiting for the quiet cough of a silenced shot.

The bomber grinned another of those horrible broken grins. 'Okay, the reason I called you up here was because I've got a job for you. While I'm dealing with the hostage handover I want you to keep an eye on your friends. Anyone even breathes wrong, I want to know. Got it?'

JJ nodded again. She felt both relieved and stupid. Relieved because she was still alive. Stupid because she'd read the situation so wrong. She'd let her emotions cloud her judgement, something she would never have done under normal circumstances. And Tony had almost died as a result. If he had died, she would never have forgiven herself. Never. Whatever happened next, she needed to keep her emotions in check. She couldn't afford to make another mistake like this.

'Right then,' the bomber said. 'Let's go release some hostages.'

18

There was still nothing happening and it was driving Rob nuts. What was going on in there? He heard himself repeating some stats that the viewers had already heard a dozen times, and did his best to sound enthusiastic. The problem was that there were only so many ways you could say the same old thing.

The grilles had gone up almost four minutes ago, and that was the last bit of excitement they'd had. In TV terms, four minutes was a lifetime. Jonah hadn't contacted him for what seemed like a decade, and that was somehow worse than if he'd been hollering and screaming.

Rob's attention kept being drawn to the patch of dried blood on the blacktop. It held the same fascination as a Rorschach inkblot, in that the more you stared, the more patterns you saw. So far he'd seen thunderclouds and desert islands and a horse's head. Mostly, though, he'd seen death. The bloodstain was a vivid reminder of how fragile this situation was. If the bomb went off, would he feel anything? He liked to think he wouldn't. God forbid that that happened, but if it did, he hoped the end would be quick.

Behind him was the small building that doubled as Victor Comaneci's office and a place where the customers' drivers and minders could hang out. It had plenty of windows, and a view of the parking lot. A large air-conditioning unit sat on the flat roof, an absolute necessity in a climate like this. The building was basically a greenhouse.

Rob glanced over at the restaurant's entrance and thought he saw a movement. Even the tiniest movement was enough to get his adrenalin pumping. Could this be it? They'd already had a couple of false alarms. Was this another one? The door opened slowly, and Rob suppressed a smile.

'I can see the first hostage coming out now and I've got to say that I don't think I've ever seen anyone look so relieved.'

His eyes were taking everything in, his brain assimilating what he was seeing, and all that good stuff was just pouring from his mouth. The first hostage was somewhere between fifty and sixty, with a flabby stomach that hung over his white boxers. CHESTER was written on his forehead in neat red capital letters. Rob's first thought was that it was blood, but the colour was too bright. Tears were streaming down Chester's face. What little hair he had was a mess. He waddled over the parking lot on shaky, uncertain legs. Two cops were waiting for him. They wrapped a blanket around him and whisked him away.

Ten seconds later the second hostage appeared. HOLLY was written on her forehead. Her long blonde hair was tied back into a ponytail and she was wearing a white bra and a red thong. Had she known when she got dressed this morning that she was going to be on national television, Rob reckoned that she would no doubt have gone for the matching set. The next person out was a short-haired brunette who was a bit older than the blonde. BETH was etched onto her forehead.

The door opened five more times and five more people came out. Three men and two women. There were tears all around. Jonah was always going on about how the best TV came from getting real-life human dramas up there on the screen. Well, things didn't get any more dramatic or real than this.

19

The kitchen had been a mess before, now it was totally trashed. Every single cupboard lay open, every drawer. King had searched everywhere and it had all been for nothing. The voice of reason was telling him there was no key, but the voice of desperation was screaming out that there had to be one. He glanced over at the door, the one that stood between him and freedom, and wondered how much longer the grille would stay up for.

He went over to the nearest drawer and searched it again, then went to the next drawer and did the same. Nothing and nothing. He knelt down and tried the cupboards underneath. Still nothing. He was moving quicker than he should, making way too much noise, but he didn't care. All he wanted was to get the hell out of here.

He walked into the middle of the kitchen, heart pounding, eyes searching, looking for anywhere he might have missed. He had just reached the work island when he heard the clunk and rattle of the grille coming down. He sank to the floor and put his head in his hands. His one chance had gone. The grille finished closing, the motor cut out, and the silence settled over him like a funeral shroud.

King's hand clenched into a fist and he started pummelling his thigh, punching out his anger and frustration. He punched past the point of pain, kept punching until his leg was numb and he couldn't feel anything at all.

20

'And cut to Caroline,' Seth said. 'Three, two, one.'

Rob's face disappeared from the main monitor and was replaced with Caroline's. She looked directly at the camera and fired off one of her most intense looks. 'Incredible developments over at Alfie's. And we'll be returning to Rob Taylor in a couple of minutes for an exclusive interview with one of the hostages.'

Seth stared down at his assistants and flashed them a rare smile.

'Good work, people. I'm almost impressed.' The smile disappeared and was replaced with a frown. All three assistants were staring expectantly. 'Okay, we've kept ahead of the game so far, and that's where I'd like to stay. Right now, you can guarantee the boys and girls over at Fox and CNN are pretty pissed. And rightly so. They're bruised and bleeding and we've got them on the ropes, but this is only round one. We cannot afford to get complacent, people. We will not get complacent. Nod if you agree.'

Uncertain nods all around.

'And that is the correct answer. In this game you're only as good as your next exclusive. Whatever happened in the past does not matter. Remember that. And remember who makes the news.'

He paused and looked at each of his assistants in turn. 'So, which of you little bunnies is going to hop to it and get Rob on the phone?'

There was a sudden burst of frenzied activity as all three jumped into action. Seth smiled to himself. When you were riding the wave, this really was the best job in the world.

21

The knife was made from the finest steel and had a wicked eight-inch blade. King was clutching it so tightly his knuckles were shining. He turned it slowly from side to side, hypnotised by the way the metal caught the light from the overhead halogens. He was sitting cross-legged on the floor with his back against the door. The wood had been warmed by the harsh LA sun, and was just one more reminder of how close he was to freedom.

JJ was probably dead by now. The thought was enough to make his stomach churn and his head spin. He felt as though he might float away at any second. It was like he was a kid again, like he was back in Cincinnati. This was how it had felt when he'd been cowering in his bed, dreading the door opening, his flimsy blankets wrapped around him like they might somehow shield him from what was about to happen.

It was the sense of utter helplessness that got to him most. Then and now. The feeling that there was absolutely nothing he could do. Once that runaway train got going, nothing could stop it. Then there was the loneliness to contend with. At times like this it didn't matter that there were seven billion people on the planet, nobody could save you from the bad thing. Not the FBI, not the police. No one.

King shut his eyes and a picture of the body he'd seen lying sprawled over the chair flashed into his head. Blood drained from the bullet wound and dripped down the chair leg and pooled on the floor. More blood than a body could hold.

His eyes snapped open. He was breathing too fast, pushing towards a panic attack. He forced himself to calm down and take a couple of deep breaths. He was feeling lighter than ever. If he'd looked down and seen a couple of inches of nothing between his ass and the floor, he wouldn't have been surprised. It was a horrible sensation, like he was turning into a ghost.

Until today the closest he'd come to seeing a dead body was on set. He'd seen plenty of corpses there, but that was make-believe. The real thing had been worse than he could have ever imagined. Whatever it was that had made that dead guy into a person was gone. It was like a switch had been thrown, turning him off forever. King shut his eyes again, and this time a picture of his mom lying passed out on the sofa flashed into his head. She wasn't dead, but she might as well have been. Heroin had stripped away whatever it was that made her who she was. The switch had been flicked to 'off'.

The deep breaths weren't working anymore. Nothing was. His thoughts were getting darker and more threatening by the second. More terrifying, too. There was no way out of here. He was going to die in this place. It might happen in the next couple of seconds, or the next minute, or the next hour, but it was definitely going to happen.

Life was pointless.

Everything was pointless.

King felt angrier than he'd ever felt. It was like there was a red hot ball of fury inside him. He wanted to get it out, but couldn't. It was choking off his breathing and strangling his thoughts. The darkness got denser, and then his anger imploded. Where once there had been rage, there was now a black hole that was sucking everything in and crushing it until it ceased to exist. King opened his eyes and looked down at the knife. He knew exactly how to turn the switch to 'off'.

22

The bomber was watching the news again. Everything else had ceased to exist, even the hostages. In some ways this was a relief for JJ, in others it was a real worry. Considering how volatile this situation was, being able to detach yourself like this couldn't be normal. He looked so relaxed, like he was just hanging out, surfing the net. Give him a latte and he could have been in Starbucks. She watched him rub his head again. She'd seen him do that a couple of times. It was probably a stress headache. It didn't matter how cool he acted, this situation must be taking its toll on him, too.

She took a quick look around at the other hostages. Some were sitting cross-legged, some were holding their knees tight into their chests, and a couple of the older ones were leaning with their backs against chairs and table legs for support. If she counted herself, the total number of hostages now stood at fifteen. Those left included Natasha Lovett, Ed Richards, Kevin Donahue, DeAndre Alexander, Gary Thompson and Simone.

JJ still couldn't get used to seeing them like this. It wasn't just their clothing that had been stripped away, it was everything that made them who they were. Self-respect, status, power. What the bomber had done was totally dehumanising. He'd reduced them to nonentities. Power really was all an illusion. If she wanted proof of that, all she had to do was look around this room.

She wanted to believe that Alex King had escaped, but on the basis of the press conference, she was pretty sure he hadn't. Her guess was that he was hiding out in the restrooms or the kitchen. Tony's office was down there too, so that was another possibility. If he was still here, she hoped to God that he kept his head down and didn't do anything stupid. He might be invincible on the big screen, but in here he was as mortal as everyone else.

The bomber was still staring at his laptop. From here, JJ could see the mustard-coloured parcels of explosives attached to his vest. She could see the flashing heart on his watch. And she could see those cold grey eyes sucking up the light from the screen.

The urge to run overwhelmed her again. The sensation was so strong it was like she was reliving an actual memory. She could feel her legs pumping, feel the smooth coldness of the parquet flooring beneath her feet. She could feel herself flying through the air as she jumped down to the lower level. She was aware of every single ragged breath, every pitter-patter of her heart.

And then what?

There was nowhere to run, nowhere to hide. She might make it as far as the restrooms before the bomber caught up with her. She might even get as far as the kitchen. But in the end he would catch her, and he would execute her.

She closed her eyes and took a couple of deep, steadying breaths. The madness passed almost as quickly as it had come upon her. The only thing she could do now was wait, and hope that the cops knew what they were doing.

23

'I'm joined now by Chester Dugan, the head chef at Alfie's,' Rob said.

Tara panned the camera to the right, bringing Chester into the shot. His face was still ghost-white, but at least he was dressed. The LAPD sweatshirt was too small and strained to keep a hold of his gut. The sweatpants seemed to be coping okay. The interview was taking place near the Mobile Command Unit. Rob had pushed to do it in Alfie's parking lot, but Aaron Walters had nixed that suggestion on the grounds of health and safety, which was part of the story, but not all of it. Walters was looking for excuses to say no to him, anything to reclaim a shred of self-respect. The truth was that Walters couldn't care less if he got blown to pieces.

Rob had positioned himself with his best side to the camera. A couple of cops were looking busy in the background, which added a splash of colour. He conjured up his most serious expression and turned to Chester.

'What was it like in there?'

'Real bad,' the chef replied. 'I thought I knew what it was to be scared, but I didn't have a clue. You've no idea how glad I am to be out here talking to you. I thought I was a dead man. I really did. That guy is a psycho. When he shot that old woman like that in cold blood, it was the sickest thing I've ever seen.'

'Can you tell me exactly what happened?'

'Yeah, sure. He'd gone around us one at a time with this bag, collecting our valuables. You know, jewellery, cell phones, stuff like that. Anyway, he gets to the old lady. I reckon she was about eighty, no threat to anyone.'

'Who was she?'

Chester shook his head. 'Sorry, I don't know, although I did wonder if she was one of those movie stars from way back when. We get a few of those at Alfie's. She looked like one.'

'What happened next?'

The chef let go of a long sigh and shook his head.

'Well, it gets to the old lady's turn and she starts going on about how her watch was a present from her dead husband. I'm sitting there thinking, *just give him the goddamn watch, lady, it's not worth it*. Next thing I know, he shot her in the head. Bam! Just like that. He didn't give her any warning, didn't even stop to think about what he was doing, he just aimed and fired. It was so cold. I've never seen anything like it.'

Rob nodded and kept his face suitably grim. Timing was everything with this sort of interview. You wanted to catch the subject while they were still in a state of shock, because that was when they were least guarded. All the same, you still had to tread carefully. One wrong move and they'd clam up.

'I need you to go back to when you first saw the bomber,' Rob said. 'In your own words, talk me through what happened.'

Chester nodded again. 'I was working in the kitchen when I heard this noise from over by the door. I turned around, and there was this guy standing there dressed entirely in black. He held up his gun and told everyone to keep real still. He said that if we did exactly what he said then no one would get hurt. Well, we all just froze like statues. I mean, who wouldn't? Then I saw the explosive vest and I thought this is it, we're all going to die. Next thing I know, he's telling us to turn off the gas and then he's herding us from the kitchen into the main part of the restaurant.'

'Earlier on you described the bomber as a psycho. Is there anything else you can add that would help us build up a better picture of him? Did he have an accent?'

Chester nodded. 'Yeah, it was a southern one. Louisiana, perhaps. Or maybe Alabama.'

'What else did you notice?'

'Only that he's one twisted bastard.'

The expletive wasn't a problem. The interview was going out live, but there was a seven-second delay for situations like this. The chef glanced guiltily at the camera, then looked back with apologies in his eyes.

'Twisted, how?' Rob asked quickly.

'Well, after he took our valuables, he made us strip down to our underwear. Then he got us to come forward one at a time and used a marker pen to write our names on our foreheads.'

This was the cue for Tara to zoom in on Chester's face. His name had been scrubbed from his forehead, but a faint shadow of the letters remained.

'I mean, that's pretty messed up, right?' Chester added. 'You don't need to be a shrink to see there's something seriously wrong with this guy.'

And now to wind it up. This was the only part of the interview that was staged. Rob wanted a good quote to end on, and that was something you didn't dare leave to chance.

'Is there anything else you want to add?' he asked.

Chester looked into the camera and Tara zoomed in for another close-up.

'Yeah, I just want to say one thing to the cops. Those people in there are scared half to death. You've got to get them out. Please don't let them die in there.'

24

'Louise, it is so good to hear your soft, warm voice again.'

JJ watched the bomber pacing from the corner of her eye. After what had happened during the hostage handover, she didn't dare make eye contact. Stay invisible, she reminded herself. The bomber paused and listened, and JJ glanced around the room. Since the release there had been a distinct change in the atmosphere. Despair had turned to something akin to hope. There had been a definite lifting of spirits, an overall lightening of the load.

'I hear what you're saying, and I want to assure you that we're on the same page here. Nothing would make me happier than to find a peaceful resolution to this sorry state of affairs.'

The bomber stopped pacing and stared at one of the paintings. He studied it while he listened to Louise's response, then started pacing again.

'I'm considering releasing five more hostages, Louise. What do you think about that? And it gets better, because I don't want anything in return. Not a single thing.'

The way he said this sent alarm bells ringing in JJ's head. He sounded like a game show host, or one of those dodgy salesmen who sold useless junk on the higher numbered cable channels. She'd been involved in thousands of negotiations, and if there was one thing she'd learned, it was that there was always a catch.

'Okay, Louise, I'm going to go now, but I want you to stay close to that telephone. I'll call you when I'm ready to do the handover.'

The bomber hung up and gazed across at each hostage in turn. JJ dipped her head when he reached her. She only looked up again when she was absolutely sure he'd moved on.

'That's right, folks, your ears are not playing tricks. Some of you lucky people are going home. But who stays and who goes? Now *that's* the million-dollar question.'

25

King stared at the knife. Dark thoughts were still swirling around his head, but the focus of those thoughts had changed. He was wondering what it would be like to plunge the knife into the bomber's chest. How hard would you have to thrust? How deep would you have to go for the wound to be fatal?

The thoughts of suicide had disappeared as quickly as they'd appeared. Just like they always did. There had been plenty of times where things had got so bad that he'd considered killing himself, times when all he'd wanted was to climb into a warm bath and drag a blade up his arm. But he'd never gone through with it, and the reason was simple. No matter how shitty things were, they would get better. Call it naivety, or blind faith, hell, call it whatever you wanted, the fact was that this simple philosophy had got him through some pretty rough times.

He took out the Ziploc bag and ran his thumb over the roughened plastic. It would be so easy. Just tip out the coke, chop it into a neat line and sniff it up. Unfortunately, it would only be a temporary solution. There was enough coke for one line. Once it was gone, it was gone. And it would just make things worse, because you could never stop at one line. That was the trouble with drugs. They were sneaky and they lied. In the end, all they ever brought was misery.

King put the Ziploc bag away, then stood up and started pacing around the kitchen. Moving around made him feel better. It made it easier to think. Maybe the blood was pumping into his brain more efficiently. Maybe that was it. On a whim, he picked up a pen he found lying on one of the work surfaces and used it to scratch a smiley face into the knife handle. The ink was blue and the handle was made from dark wood, so he needed to keep going over the markings until he'd made an impression in the wood. He had no idea why he was doing this, and didn't really care. For a few moments he was so absorbed in the task he was almost able to forget where he was. Once he'd finished drawing his smiley face, he flipped the knife over and engraved a sad face into the other side of the handle.

King sat down with his back against the sun-warmed door and smiled at the smiley face. Then he flipped the knife over and frowned at the sad face. He turned the knife over again and smiled.

Sad face, smiley face.

Sad face, smiley face.

26

'Everyone on your feet.'

JJ gave it a few moments then stood up. She didn't want to be first because that would mark her out. Kevin Donahue was the last one up, which was just as bad as being first. The film producer was fading fast. The bomber must have noticed how ill he was. How could he not have? JJ couldn't understand why he didn't just let him go. In the end Donahue had to use a table for support. She wanted to help, but couldn't, not with the bomber watching.

'Okay, we're going to play ourselves a little game here. You all like games, don't you? Now, the good news is that five of you lucky people are going home. However, deciding which five is going to be tough. When I said this was the million-dollar question, I wasn't joking. Like my mama used to tell me, you don't get nothing for nothing in this world.'

The bomber grinned behind the balaclava. 'I'm going to let five of you good people go free, but it's going to cost you a million bucks each. I know it's impossible to put a price on a life, but we've got to start somewhere, and a million is a nice, round number. So, here's what's going to happen. Everybody who can afford to play, stay standing. The rest of you, sit down.'

Tony sat first, closely followed by Simone and a man with HARRY written on his forehead. JJ could afford to pay a million, that wasn't the problem. The problem was the gnawing feeling that there was a catch, and that whatever that catch was, it was going to end up with someone dead. Sit or don't sit? She was going to have to decide. Leave it much longer and that would look odd, and looking odd meant standing out. She sat down and stared at the floor, and hoped to God that she'd done the right thing. The bomber was looking at her. She could feel his eyes on her.

'And then there were ten,' he said. 'Okay, if you're not in a position to immediately transfer a million dollars, please sit down.'

A fifty-something woman with JEN on her forehead sat down. Dan Stone wasn't far behind. He had the look of someone who'd been wiped out at poker. JJ guessed he was cursing himself for buying that new Ferrari. If he hadn't done that he might still be standing.

'And then there were eight. Okay, I need to lose a couple more. You and you sit.'

JJ glanced up and saw Kevin Donahue and Ed Richards sit down. Both looked as devastated as Stone had. Natasha Lovett was still on her feet. During the last hour and a half the movie director had aged a hundred years. Her shoulders were hunched, her head bowed, and the spark in her eyes had died. This was not the Natasha Lovett that JJ knew. That person was confident and fiery and opinionated. When it came to her chosen causes, Natasha would have taken anyone on, and won. It was as though everything that had made her who she was had been stripped away and destroyed.

Carrie Preston was standing beside Natasha. She was beautiful and perky, and specialised in girl-next-door roles. Her long red hair was almost as famous as she was. Carrie's revolving-door love life made her a favourite with the tabloids. Every other week she was either stepping out with someone new, or breaking up with them. She gave great pictures, and even better heartbreak. The woman next to Carrie had HAILEY written on her forehead. JJ had never seen her until today. She was in her mid-forties and in pretty good shape, although it looked as though this was due to surgery rather than to a personal trainer. This was a rich body rather than a fit one.

JJ knew two of the men left standing. DeAndre Alexander was a record producer who specialised in R&B acts, and Gary Thompson was the Dreamworks Neanderthal who'd ordered steak. Thompson was thin-faced, mid-fifties, completely bald, and, judging by his sour expression, the last hour and a half had done nothing to make him any less of an asshole.

Alexander was also bald, but bald by choice. He was considerably younger than Thompson, and black. He'd made his first million by the age of twenty, his first hundred-million by thirty. He'd been raised in the Bronx projects and had escaped through a combination of talent and luck. His older brother hadn't been so fortunate. He'd been killed in a gang shooting.

The record producer made regular trips back to New York to talk to the kids in his old neighbourhood. His mission was to show them that drugs and guns were not the answer. If he could escape the vicious circle, then they could, too. That was his message, and it was one that generated great PR. There was a good chance that was his motivation, but JJ wasn't convinced. Very occasionally you found someone who actually believed in what they were doing, as opposed to being forced into it by some PR guru. She had a feeling that Alexander might be the exception rather than the rule.

She did a quick head-count. There were six hostages left standing, which didn't make sense. The bomber had definitely said that he was letting five people go. So what was the catch? What was she missing? She was starting to think that opting out had probably been a good move.

'Nat, step over here.'

The bomber was next to the laptop, holding a chair out like a waiter. JJ could see the terror in Natasha's eyes, and understood it. A short while ago she'd been standing where the film director was standing. It was one of the loneliest places in the world.

'Don't be shy,' the bomber prompted. 'I won't bite.'

Natasha walked over and sat down in front of the laptop. She typed in her log-on details then looked up.

'Where do you want the money sent?' she asked in a shaky whisper.

The bomber removed a slip of paper from his pocket and laid it on the table. Natasha picked it up and inputted the details. Five seconds passed, ten seconds.

'The money's been transferred,' she said.

'And it's a pleasure doing business. Okay, go stand over there.' The bomber waved her towards a piece of empty floor to his left, then turned back to the other five.

'Gary, you're next.'

Gary Thompson kept one wary eye locked on the bomber as he walked over to the laptop. The film executive was wearing a small pair of briefs and had a deep bronze tan. His nails were manicured. He sat at the computer and went through the same process as Natasha. When he'd finished, he walked over and stood beside the director.

The next three hostages transferred their money without a hitch, and then it was DeAndre Alexander's turn. The bomber called him over, but the record producer didn't move. Beads of sweat rolled down his cheeks. He looked ready to bolt. A memory of the accountant's execution flashed through JJ's head. Don't do it, she thought.

The bomber walked slowly towards Alexander, his footsteps cutting through the silence. He raised the gun and pressed the silencer into the record producer's chest, dimpling the skin above his heart.

'I hope you didn't lie about being able to get the money.'

'No, I can get your money.' Alexander hurried the words out. His eyes seemed unable to focus on any single point.

'So what's the problem?'

Alexander nodded to Natasha's big orange bag. 'I need my billfold. It's in there. It's got all my account details in.'

The bomber lowered his gun and Alexander ran over to the bag. He dropped to his knees and rummaged frantically through it, a panicked expression on his face.

'Come on,' the bomber called out. 'Some time this week would be good.'

'Okay, okay, I've got it.'

Alexander held the billfold up, then jumped to his feet and ran back over to the laptop. He crashed into the chair and started clicking the touchpad and pounding the keys. He was concentrating furiously on the screen, lips moving as he repeated the same two words in a seamless rush. *Come on come on come on*. He finished with a sigh.

'The money's in your account,' he said.

The bomber nodded towards the five standing hostages and Alexander hurried over to join them. JJ didn't think she'd ever seen anybody ever look so relieved.

'Right then,' he said to the standing hostages. 'Those of you who can count will notice there are six of you standing there. Five of you will be going home very soon. Unfortunately, one of you won't.'

14:30–15:00

1

Seth ignored the dirty looks being flashed in his direction and lit a Marlboro. This was his newsroom and he could do what the hell he wanted. The health Nazis could go screw themselves. Anyway, what was he supposed to do? They were surfing the crest of a major news story here, one that was big enough for the station bosses to pull the ads. It wasn't like he could leave his post and head out to the smoking area.

He took a long, rebellious drag, savoured it, then reached for his half-empty coffee mug and tapped off the dead ash. It hit the cold coffee with a sizzle. The story was panning out well. Rob was doing a fantastic job over at Alfie's. His interview with the chef had been first-rate, so good that the highlights were being aired again right now. That made the third time and counting.

The curse of the twenty-four-hour news station was repetition. Quite simply, there just wasn't enough bad news to fill a full day's worth of hours, minutes and seconds. The trick was to recycle in a way that made Joe Public think they were getting something new with every airing. Seth was a master at that, which was why TRN paid him that six-figure salary.

The timing of this story couldn't have been more perfect. His contract was up for renewal next month and there were mumblings that, now he'd hit sixty, it might be time for him to head off into the sunset. It was that old battle that had raged in TV since the beginning of time, youth versus experience.

The doubters were arguing that TRN needed someone with energy and vitality and, this was the bit that got him, relevance. Roughly translated, that meant some kid who looked good in a suit but knew nothing about journalism. Well, this story would shut the doubters up once and for all. If they wanted relevance all they had to do was look at the way this story was being presented. Seth had no intention of retiring any time soon and if anyone thought they could edge him out, then they were going to find out just how much fight he still had left in him.

Relevance. What a crock.

He still couldn't believe he was sixty. Aside from those days when he woke up hung-over, he didn't feel sixty. Nor did he act sixty. It only seemed liked yesterday that he was back in Arkansas, stepping into the newsroom of the *Jonesboro Gazette* for the first time. From the get-go he'd loved being a journalist. The excitement of wrestling down a good story. The buzz of seeing his byline on the front-page lead. He'd always known he was bigger than Arkansas, and aged twenty he'd headed off to the *New York Post*. He only stayed there a couple of years. He'd hated being a small fish in such a big pond, hated the harshness of the New York winters. The west coast had been the obvious place to go.

He'd got a job as a reporter on the *Los Angeles Times* and, although he'd still been a small fish, the climate had made it bearable. He'd progressed steadily through the ranks and had ended up as a news editor. The move from print to radio had broken his heart, but it was inevitable. The money was better and, by then, he was already on wife number two. The move to TV had happened ten years later and had coincided with his divorce from wife number two. And somehow he'd ended up being sixty.

His kids had organised a surprise party to soften the blow. It had been a touching gesture, one that he really hadn't expected, but that particular hangover had been a killer. Out of everything that had happened when he'd hit sixty, that was the thing that had brought home the fact he wasn't getting any younger. Back in his *Jonesboro Gazette* days he could shake off a hangover without even trying.

Seth took a final drag on his Marlboro and dropped the butt into his coffee mug, where it extinguished with a hiss. Over the years he'd been involved in some pretty major stories, but this was without a doubt the biggest. It had everything. Drama, the human interest angle and, most of all for LA, celebrities. Having a megastar like Ed Richards involved would keep the viewers glued to their screens. A real-life celebrity in a real life-or-death situation. It didn't get much better than that. And having Alex King in there wouldn't hurt ratings, either, that was for sure. Seth wondered how he could exploit that angle. The Hollywood old guard and the new kid on the block, there had to be some way to use it.

He was still wondering about this when the interview clip finished and Caroline Bradley came back on screen. She stared deep into the camera and gave a quick round-up of the latest developments over at Alfie's. Seth smiled to himself. He couldn't help it. He was hearing the facts laid bare for the umpteenth time and they still hadn't lost any of their impact. This was the story that just kept giving. It really was a thing of beauty.

2

The bomber rummaged around inside his backpack and brought out an old wooden box that was about fifteen inches long and ten inches wide. It was varnished, the grain running deep and dark. He placed the box beside the laptop.

'Dan, come over here. I've got a job for you.'

Dan Stone looked around desperately, like he was hoping there might be another Dan in the room. The stress was getting to him. His hair was a mess and the red ink on his forehead was smudged. For once, he looked every one of his forty-two years.

'Well, don't just sit there, Dan. On your feet.'

Stone got up reluctantly. He took a step forward, then glanced over his shoulder and fired a dirty look at JJ. It was like he was trying to make out that this was all her fault. But how could this be anybody's fault? Did he honestly think that she wanted to be here any more than he did? How dare he try to lay this on her?

It was a case of wrong place, wrong time. That's all. It was always happening. Some guy gets held up because he burns his toast and ends up leaving for work five minutes later than usual, and winds up dead in a car wreck. Stories like that were a daily occurrence. They happened seven days a week, three-hundred-and-sixty-five days a year. JJ had originally planned to meet Dan tomorrow, and, had that happened, then she'd be in her office right now, glued to the TV, watching events unfold from the safety of her desk.

The bomber nodded towards the table with the wooden box on it. 'Go stand over there, Dan.'

Stone glanced at the submachine gun, then followed this up with another quick, hate-filled glance for JJ. She met his gaze without flinching or turning away. She wasn't going to give him the satisfaction.

'What's this?' the bomber asked. 'Have we got some issues we need to work through here?'

JJ looked away quickly. She could have strangled Stone. What was the idiot playing at? They were in enough trouble as it was. Getting pissed and acting like a sulky teenager was not going to help.

'Much as I'd like to help you kids out, it's going to have to wait. But rest assured, we will come back to this. That's a promise.' The bomber turned to the six standing hostages. 'Okay. Spread out and get yourselves into a circle. Once you've done that, sit down on the floor, legs crossed, hands resting on thighs.'

Natasha looked uncertainly at the other five hostages, then shuffled into position and sat down. The others weren't far behind. The bomber rearranged them until he was satisfied, then went back to the table and opened the box. JJ's heart sank when she saw what was inside.

3

Alex King took out his cell phone and checked for texts. There were a load of new ones, most of them from his agent. The one he wanted wasn't there, but what had he expected? He'd been a complete asshole to his ex. The cold shoulder was nothing less than he deserved. He pulled up the list of recent callers, selected the one at the top and connected the call. Brad Carter answered on the first ring.

'Alex, how are you doing?'

'I want out, and I want out now.'

'I'm sorry, Alex, I can't do that.'

'What do you mean *you can't*? Come on, you're the FBI. You guys can do anything.' King took a deep breath. 'Look, I've done what you asked. I risked my life to plant your goddamn camera. It's time for you to keep your side of the deal. Please, just get me the hell out of here.'

'If we could, we would. You've got to believe that, Alex.'

King almost laughed. 'And why should I believe you, Brad? Tell me that. Why should I believe a single word that comes out of your mouth?'

'Because it's the truth.'

'Look, I'm standing beside the kitchen door right now. I'm just one door away from getting out of here. We're talking a couple of inches of wood. Now, are you honestly telling me that the FBI can't get me out?'

'It's not that simple, Alex.'

'Yes, it is that simple. All you've got to do is cut through the grille, break down the door, and let me out.'

'If we do that we'll be putting the other hostages' lives at risk. I'm sorry, Alex. I really am.' Carter paused. 'I know this isn't what you want to hear, and I know you're scared, but I need you to sit tight and hang on in there, okay? I promise we're doing everything we can to get you out. You and all the other hostages.'

'Forget the other hostages.'

The silence coming from the other end of the phone went on long enough for King to realise what he'd said. He sank to the floor and rubbed his face. 'Shit, I'm sorry, man. I didn't mean that. I don't want anyone else to die.'

'There's nothing to apologise for, Alex. I think you're handling this amazingly well. There aren't many people who could handle this as well as you.'

King took another deep breath and wondered for the millionth time how the hell he'd ended up in this situation. 'Okay, what happens now?'

'Now you sit tight and let us do our thing. We are going to get you out of there. That's a promise. In the meantime, why don't you go back and hide in the restroom? You'll be safer there. Can you do that?'

'Yeah, I can do that.'

'And Alex? Be careful.'

King hung up and shook his head. *Be careful.* What the hell else was he going to do?

4

The bomber took out the revolver and held it up for everyone to see.

'This is a Smith & Wesson Model 29. The very same gun that Dirty Harry will tell you is the most powerful handgun in the world. Please don't confuse this model with the 629. The 29 was made from carbon steel, whereas the 629 was fashioned from stainless steel.' He turned the gun lovingly in his hand. 'It really is a beautiful piece of precision engineering. Crafted in America and made with pride.'

He placed the gun next to the laptop and took a single bullet from the box. Once again he held it up for everyone to see.

'The core of the bullet is brass. However, the problem with using brass is that it'll wear a gun barrel out in no time. To get around this, some bright spark came up with the idea of coating bullets in Teflon. This little baby is capable of piercing metal and bulletproof vests, so you've got to wonder what it's going to do to someone's head. Anyone ever seen a watermelon being used for target practice?'

The bomber scanned faces and JJ looked at the floor, avoiding eye contact. One gun, one bullet, five out of six people going home. It was clear where this was headed. She wanted to be wrong, but she wasn't. Choosing to opt out might just be the best decision she'd ever made.

'I'll take that as a "no". Well, let's just say that it gets pretty messy.'

The last two words were drawn out. The bomber grinned, then held the gun and the bullet out to Dan Stone. The agent just stood there with his arms at his side, uncertainty written all over his face.

'Go on,' the bomber prompted.

Stone took the gun and the bullet.

'Can you confirm that these are real?'

Stone glanced down. The revolver was in his left hand, the bullet in his right. 'Yes,' he whispered.

The bomber cupped a hand to his ear. 'Sorry, Dan. I didn't quite catch that.'

'Yes, they're real.'

'Thank you very much, you've been a big help. Okay let's have a round of applause for Dan.'

Nobody moved.

'I said, let's have a round of applause. Don't make me ask again.'

The sound of weak, embarrassed clapping drifted around the room. It died almost as soon as it started. The bomber held out his hand, and Dan gave him the revolver and the bullet.

'Go and sit down.'

Stone didn't need asking twice. He hurried across the room and crashed to the floor. The bomber flipped the gun open and slotted the bullet into a chamber. Carefully, reverentially. Then he flicked the gun closed and spun the cylinder. Once, twice, three times. The mechanical clicking sent a shiver crawling across JJ's skin. The bomber walked over to the circle of hostages and tapped the gun barrel against his watch.

'In case anyone is tempted to shoot me, just remember that if my heart stops, then the vest goes bang.'

He turned the revolver around and offered it handle-first to Hailey.

'I think you know how the game works.'

Hailey took the gun and pressed it to her temple. The barrel was juddering like it had a life of its own, marking her skin with little red lines. She lowered the revolver.

'I can't do this.'

'Sure you can, honey. Just press the gun against your head and squeeze the trigger. It couldn't be simpler.'

'But I don't want to die.'

'Sorry to be the bearer of bad news, but we're all going to die. It might happen today, it might happen twenty years from now. The thing is, it is going to happen. That you can guarantee.'

'I've got kids, a husband.'

'And you've also got a five in six chance of seeing them again real soon, a chance you paid a million bucks for. In this game, those odds are as good as it gets.'

Hailey raised the revolver, hesitated, then pushed it against her head and pulled the trigger. The dull click sounded much louder than it should have done. The gun tumbled into her lap and she started to sob.

'Hush now,' the bomber soothed. 'It's over. You're going to get to go home.'

5

Alex King wiped the knife blade on his shirt, removing the fingerprint smudges and making the metal shine, then he wedged it into the waistband of his jeans and arranged the shirt to hide the handle. He walked across to the door and peered through the small porthole window. The corridor appeared empty. He cracked open the door and listened through the gap. The bomber was talking in a calm voice. King could pick out the odd word, but what he was hearing didn't make sense.

He pushed the door open inch by slow inch. The occasional microscopic squeaks and creaks sounded over-loud in the stark silence, but he kept going. He opened it as far as he dared, then squeezed through the gap and closed it behind him, only letting go when it had settled snugly back in the frame. Up ahead, beyond the end of the corridor, he could see the dead man draped across the chair. The lake of blood congealing around the chair legs turned his stomach.

'Go on,' he heard the bomber say.

'No.'

A sigh, then, 'When are you people going to realise that passive resistance just won't cut it?'

King frowned. The person the bomber was talking to had only said one word, but that one word was enough to give him a vivid picture of what they were like. Self-assured, confident, someone used to calling the shots. The voice was deep and male.

Curiosity got the better of him and he tiptoed along the corridor to get a better look. It was risky, but he wanted to see what a real hero looked like. He ducked down behind the wall that jutted into the lower level of the restaurant, then raised his head until his eyes were level with the top and peered through the thick foliage.

He could see the camera he'd hidden for Brad Carter, and, beyond that, he could see the bomber pressing the barrel of a big handgun into the back of a black dude's bald head. King remembered the black guy coming in. He hadn't recognised him, but Simone had. He racked his brains for a name. DeAndre Alexander, that was it. The guy was some hotshot record producer. Simone had dated him, and from the way she spoke, it was clear she still liked him. What's more, judging by the way Alexander had kept looking over at her before the bomber had come in, the feeling was mutual.

Why did relationships in this town have to be so complicated? King would have given anything to be back with his ex, and Simone would rather be with Alexander, yet she was with him. And the reason for that was that this town was all about how things appeared. Looks were everything. When you thought about it like that, it was insane.

The bomber increased the pressure on the trigger and King's breath caught halfway into an exhale. This was wrong on so many levels. It was wrong on *every* level. The hammer flew forward, but there was no bang, just a dull click. What the hell was going on? He didn't get it. *Really* didn't get it. The record producer should be dead by now, his brains and blood splattered all over the floor. But that hadn't happened. There he was, sitting cross-legged on the floor, hands on thighs and staring straight ahead.

'Your little act of resistance has just cost you your chance of getting out of here.' The bomber clicked his fingers. 'A million bucks gone, just like that. You know, that's got to ruin your day.'

JJ suddenly turned and looked towards the lower level, and King ducked behind the wall, convinced she'd spotted him. He could hear the bomber talking, but what he was saying wasn't registering. He did a slow count to ten then put his head up again. The scene had changed, and the new picture made even less sense.

Carrie Preston now had the gun. The actress's long red hair was her trademark. Whole magazine articles had been written about that hair. Usually there wasn't so much as a single strand out of place, but today it was a total mess. CARRIE was scrawled on her forehead in bright red ink.

She suddenly raised the gun and pressed the barrel against the side of her head. Her face was expressionless, her eyes blank. She reminded King of a mannequin. She squeezed the trigger, but the gun didn't go off. It was only when she passed it to the man on her left that he finally worked it out.

6

Three chambers left. Two empty, one containing a bullet. The three people still to go were Natasha Lovett, Gary Thompson and Harry, a middle-aged guy JJ had never seen until today, but whose haggard face was now permanently etched into her memory. Carrie Preston was shaking all over and weeping silent tears. The overriding emotion that JJ was seeing was relief, but this was tempered with guilt, which was completely understandable. The woman had tallied up the cost of her survival and it had come to a lot more than a million dollars. She'd survived, which meant someone else was going to die.

JJ glanced around at the people sitting beside her. Everyone was looking as horrified as she felt. The horror was mixed with relief, though. They were staring at the gun and no doubt thinking the same thing. *Thank God it's not me.* Next up was Gary Thompson. He was staring at the gun too, the difference being that it was cradled in his hands.

'In your own time,' the bomber said. 'And remember what I said about passive resistance.'

The movie exec glared at the bomber. 'Why are you doing this?'

'Do you really need to ask?'

'Yeah, I think I do. If I'm going to die, I'd like to know why.'

'Fair point. Although the reason should be obvious, since I'm now six million dollars richer.'

Thompson held up the gun. 'If this is just about money, why all this bullshit? There are a lot easier ways to make money.'

'Maybe for you, Gary. But what you've got to bear in mind here is that you've got your own unique skill set and I've got mine. It's all about playing to your strengths, right? You can make six million bucks by screwing over the little guy, whereas someone like me, well, the only way I'm going to make six million bucks is by doing something like this.'

'You realise that most hostage situations end up with the hostage-taker dead or in prison? If you do manage get out of here alive, then the only thing you've got to look forward to is the lethal injection.'

'And I'm starting to think you talk too much, Gary.'

Thompson looked at the gun, then aimed it at the bomber. His finger was on the trigger, his hand rock steady. JJ couldn't believe what she was seeing. What the hell was he thinking? It was suicidal, not to mention crazy. Was he trying to get them all killed? All around her people were holding their breath. Everything had gone still.

'And I'm starting to think that you've got no intentions of letting any of us go. You know what I think? I think you're full of bullshit.'

'Shoot me if you want, but know this. If you do that then you'll be condemning every single person in this room to death. It's like I said earlier, there are consequences to every action.' The bomber paused a moment to let that one sink in. 'Anyway, we both know you're not going to shoot me. You're someone who lives for the bottom line, and the bottom line is that you've got a two in three chance of getting out of here alive, and you'll take those odds because right now you'll do anything to save your sorry excuse of an ass. Now, are we going to play ball or not?'

Thompson pushed the gun into his temple and pulled the trigger.

Another dull click.

'Like pulling teeth from a hen. Okay, pass the gun to Nat.'

Thompson handed the gun over. Like Hailey and Carrie, the main emotion that JJ was seeing was relief. Unlike them, his relief was tempered with anger, and there were no signs of survivor's guilt. Thompson was a real hothead on the outside world, someone used to getting his own way. She hoped he'd keep his rage in check. For all their sakes.

'And then there were two,' the bomber said. 'Okay, you're up next, Nat.'

Natasha was staring into the middle distance, not really focusing on anything. It was heart-wrenching. She looked like she'd had some sort of breakdown. She lifted the gun to her head and pulled the trigger. There was no hesitation, no emotion. The sound of the gunshot was enormous.

JJ saw the side of the director's head explode in a shower of blood, brains and bone, and even though she was witnessing this with her own two eyes, she still couldn't reconcile what she was seeing with what was happening. Natasha tipped to the side and the gun tumbled from her fingers. All signs of life were gone and there was so much blood. It poured from her shattered skull, collecting into a crimson halo that crept slowly across the floor.

'Congratulations, Harry,' the bomber said. 'Looks like you get to go home.'

Harry was gazing at Natasha's motionless body without really seeing it. One of his hands came up and he absent-mindedly wiped some of the splatter from his face. Then the other hand came up to join it. He started to scrub manically with both hands, trying to get rid of the blood and gore. It wasn't working.

He was just smearing the blood deeper into his skin, turning it a sickly brown-yellow colour.

'Tony,' the bomber called out. 'Please escort these four lucky people to the door. DeAndre, you get to go sit back with the others.'

Tony walked over to the circle of hostages and helped them to their feet. He was whispering soft words of encouragement under his breath, assurances that everything was going to be okay. He led them in single file towards the foyer. JJ caught one last glimpse of their broken, haunted faces, and then they were gone.

The bomber picked up the telephone. While he waited for his call to connect, he scanned the faces of the remaining hostages. When he reached DeAndre Alexander, he lingered for a while. JJ was glad she wasn't in the record producer's shoes. Stay invisible, she reminded herself.

'Hey there, Louise. How's it going? You know, we've been having ourselves some real fun and games back here.'

7

Rob watched the grilles go up for the second time. By his reckoning twenty-five minutes had passed since the first batch of hostages had come out. His interview with Chester had happened twenty minutes ago and since then they'd been hanging around just waiting for something to happen. Those twenty-five minutes had been long minutes. That was the downside to what he did. For every minute of adrenalin-soaked activity, there would be an hour of boredom so mind-numbing that watching paint dry would be a mercy.

Aaron Walters had contacted him just in time. He'd been driving Tara mad and it was only a matter of time before she took a swing at him, probably with the camera, and those things were heavy. The message from the PR guy was short and sweet. Four more hostages were coming out and the bomber wanted TRN to cover the handover.

Rob was standing side-on to the main entrance of Alfie's, while Tara stood front-on. She had positioned herself far enough back so she could get both Rob and the doors in the shot. Helicopters buzzed behind them. The loudest was about a block and a half away, while the rest were swarming about three blocks away. The closest one belonged to the LAPD. The rest belonged to the news channels. TRN's pilot would be jockeying for the best position, pushing right up to the edge of the exclusion zone. If he hadn't had at least three warnings to get back then you could bet that Seth would have ripped him a new asshole.

Rob was talking with no real awareness of what he was saying. His full attention was focused on the main entrance, and he was just waiting for something to happen. He thought he saw a shadow pass behind the door, but it was difficult to say for sure because of the smoked glass. Maybe this was it. Maybe it wasn't. They'd already had two false alarms.

In case this was the real thing, Rob started to wind things up. He was choosing his words more carefully now, so he could make the link as seamless as possible. Sunlight flashed on the glass panel of the door as it swung open.

'We're just waiting for our next hostage to come out,' Rob said. 'We should be seeing them any second now.'

Right on cue, a woman stepped out of the door. Her hand was up to shield her tear-stained eyes from the sun. Rob didn't recognise her, and the position of her hand meant he couldn't see what the bomber had written on her forehead. He thought there might be an 'H' in there, a 'Y', too. The woman broke into a stumbling run. Her stride was uneven, her balance all over the place. Two cops in full body armour and helmets ran out and met her halfway across the lot. The one on the left grabbed her before she fell, while his partner wrapped a blanket around her. They wasted no time in whisking her away to safety.

Next out was Gary Thompson. Rob recognised him immediately. He was one of the high-ups at Dreamworks, a top-level player who was a top-level asshole. Rob didn't have any first-hand experience, but he'd heard the stories. Thompson didn't run, he strode. He was walking across the lot like walking through LA in a pair of black silk briefs was something he did every day. There were no tears from Thompson. His face was grim, his mouth tight. He looked like he was getting ready to punch someone out. A couple of cops rushed out to meet him and he shrugged them away. He grabbed the blanket, threw it around his shoulders and strode off in the direction the first woman had disappeared.

'And that was Gary Thompson from Dreamworks,' Rob said, just in case anyone had missed it the first time. He was giving a constant commentary on events, a seamless narrative to match what was happening. Keeping the delivery slow was a real challenge. His blood was up and those words were crashing out of his mouth like an avalanche.

Thirty seconds later, a woman wearing a red bra and panties came out. CARRIE was written on her forehead. The trademark red hair was a mess and the make-up was smudged, so it took Rob a second to place the face.

'And that's Carrie Preston, the Emmy Award-winning actress who first found fame in the TV sitcom *All About Me.* Her last film was the box-office hit, *Heartriders.*'

Carrie crossed the parking lot quickly, glancing back a couple of times at the front door like she was waiting for someone to come after her. The haunted look on her face was light years away from the infectious smile that had made her famous. She fell dramatically into the arms of the first cop who reached her. A second cop wasn't far behind. He swirled a blanket around the actress, covering her up. Carrie was petite, five-two at a rough guess, and the blanket touched her feet. Her eyes were filled with tears and her chest was hitching like she was having an asthma attack.

The last person out was some guy called Harry. Rob didn't have a clue who he was, which meant the viewers wouldn't have a clue, either. It would have made much better viewing if Carrie had come out last. That way they could have ended on a high instead of an anticlimax. Ten seconds later the metal grilles came back down. Tara repositioned herself and zoomed in on Rob.

'More incredible developments here at Alfie's. Back to you in the studio, Caroline.'

8

Seth lit another Marlboro and got a dirty look from the Asian kid.

'Is there a problem?'

'No, sir.'

'And that's the correct answer.'

The kid looked away and got real busy, real fast. Seth took a moment to smoke and to bask. For now, the story was taking care of itself, the parts turning like well-oiled cogs in a giant machine. They were right up there on the crest of the wave, the good times were rolling, and the view was just fantastic.

'Sir, I've got Carrie Preston's agent on the line.'

This came from the Asian kid. The eager-beaver was clearly anxious to make amends for his earlier sin. Two minutes had passed since a dishevelled Carrie Preston had stumbled from Alfie's. Two minutes and her agent was already calling.

Because they had deeper pockets, CNN and Fox would have been first in line for a call. Being third in line didn't bother Seth. He knew how the game was played. He also knew this was a courtesy call, and the only reason he was getting it was because TRN was leading the story. And he knew one more thing. Judging by how tight the timescale was, the one person the agent hadn't contacted was Carrie. Not even a quick call to check she was okay. It didn't matter how long he worked in LA, this town never ceased to amaze him.

Seth took a last lingering drag on his cigarette, blew a cloud of smoke up towards the ceiling, then positioned the headset mike and barked a terse, 'Seth Allen,' into it. The agent didn't bother with introductions, or small talk. She got right down to business. Seth understood exactly where she was coming from. Time was money. Carrie Preston might be hovering at the lower end of the A-list, but right now she was the hottest actress in town. The reason was simple. She was the highest-profile celebrity to come out of Alfie's so far.

The crucial words there were *so* and *far*, because there was no telling how long that would last. At any second the bomber could release someone higher up the food chain. Ed Richards, for example. If he released Richards, then Carrie Preston became yesterday's news. That's why the agent was talking at a hundred miles an hour, and that's why her client hadn't received so much as a courtesy call to see how she was doing.

The agent reeled off a figure for an exclusive interview. The sum was obscene. It was an amount that the higher-ups at TRN would never authorise. Seth agreed to it without haggling, and the agent hung up without a thank you or a goodbye.

Worst-case scenario, he won the auction and ended up being fired. But that wasn't going to happen because Fox and CNN wouldn't let it happen. TRN had bloodied their noses enough for one day. They'd be looking for a way to claw back some of that lost ground at any cost. An exclusive interview with Carrie Preston would go some way to putting one of them back in the game.

9

Alex King sat paralysed behind the low wall on the lower level, and stared blankly at the painting on the wall opposite. There was a rainbow of colours splashed onto the white canvas, but all he saw was red. He'd always thought of red as being the colour of blood. He knew differently now. Blood wasn't red. It was shiny and black and it glowed with a dark crimson tint when the light caught it a certain way.

He had been hiding behind this wall when the gun had gone off. He'd seen Lovett bring the gun up to the side of her head. He'd seen her finger tightening on the trigger. He'd prayed for another click, but that hadn't happened. There had been a moment of stillness, a moment where he'd truly believed that Lovett would be okay, and then the big handgun had boomed. An echo of the gunshot still rumbled around inside his head. His ears still sang. The smell just made it worse. The sharp tang of gun smoke was mixed with the dead stench of slaughtered animals. It was a smell that made him want to puke. This was something else that was missing from the movies. The smell.

Above King's head, the leaves stirred gently on the currents made by the air conditioning. Hidden in all that green was the camera he'd planted, and beyond the green was a huddle of terrified people. He hoped the FBI was getting all this. Anything that might shake them into action. If Carter and his buddies hadn't come up with a plan to get them out, then they'd better come up with one soon. How many more people had to die before they did something?

He knew he should get back to the restroom, but he couldn't move. It had been like this ever since Lovett had died. His limbs were frozen solid, his ass was glued to the cold, hard floor, and his head was filled with a swarm of butterfly thoughts, ideas that flitted here, there and everywhere and wouldn't settle. He forced himself to get moving. He had to use the wall for support because he didn't trust his legs. He reached the restroom, checked behind one last time, then inched the door open and slipped through the crack. The smell of oranges hit him straight away, but it still couldn't erase the stench of gun smoke and death. That smell seemed to be permanently stuck in his nose.

He closed the door, easing it back into place with his left hand while his other hand worked the handle, slowly and carefully, in case it squeaked or creaked or made any sort of noise that might give him away. For a second, he just stood there with his heart thundering and his forehead touching the cool wood. The door dulled the sound from the restaurant, turning it into a background hum. And that was good.

As he stood there, he pictured himself lying by the pool on Saint Kitts, and the kaleidoscopic splash of fireworks lighting up the midnight sky. He could smell the sea on the wind. He could feel its pleasant chill on his naked arms. Slowly, he detached himself from the reality of his situation. This was something he'd taught himself to do as a kid. He'd needed to. When things were at their worst, the only way to survive was to imagine himself into a better world, one where his mom was a normal, loving mom. One where he didn't have to worry about how he was going to hide the bruises.

When he opened his eyes again he was feeling a little better. The memory of Lovett's death was already fading, squashed down into that place where all the bad stuff was kept safely locked away. He inhaled deeply, then exhaled. Inhaled then exhaled. Long, calming yoga breaths. Then he moved over to the urinal and crouched down until he was level with the hole. Sunlight and the hot breeze of LA in August brushed his face. He was so close to freedom, close enough to feel it, yet he might as well have been stranded on the dark side of the moon.

10

The hostages were sitting in a tight group, two deep and shoulder to shoulder. Ten in total, if JJ counted herself. They were huddled together, as though sitting in close proximity could somehow protect them. The problem was that it was all an illusion.

She recognised six of the remaining hostages. Tony, Ed Richards, Simone, Kevin Donahue, Dan Stone and DeAndre Alexander. There were three others she'd never seen before, two women and a man. Bev, Jen and Frank. Chances were they worked behind the scenes. Executives or producers, probably. If they'd been actors, she would have recognised them. And if they'd been screenwriters or composers or any of the other hundreds of people that were needed to make a film, they wouldn't be here, because they weren't rich enough or important enough.

Then there was Alex King.

JJ was convinced that he was still in the restaurant. While the bomber had been engrossed in his game of Russian roulette, a movement from the lower level had caught her eye. She'd glanced over and seen some of the plants moving. It might have been a rogue air current pushing through the leaves, but she was certain it was King. There was no hard evidence to back this up, just a feeling that they were being watched.

As recently as this morning she would have laughed at anyone who made decisions based on anything as flaky as a feeling.

She would have grouped them with those people who freaked out if they broke a mirror. As far as JJ was concerned, superstition was for people who had too much time on their hands. Those things had no place in her world. Bad stuff happened, good stuff happened. It didn't matter how many rabbit feet you possessed, or how many ladders you avoided walking under, or even how many red cars passed you on the street, that was just the way it was.

Her world was a world of cold, hard facts. You got those facts together, you made a plan, and then you executed that plan. As far as she was concerned, gut instinct was right up there with palm reading, tarot cards and horoscopes. But the person sitting here this afternoon was very different from the person who'd walked into Alfie's less than two hours ago. Current events had given her a new perspective, one where she was happy to concede that there was a time and place for trusting your instincts.

'Anyone hungry?'

The question came out of left field, pulling JJ from her thoughts. She might even have let out a small gasp, although she didn't think so. At least, she hoped she hadn't. A scratch on the parquet floor a yard in front of her was suddenly the most interesting thing she'd ever seen.

If the bomber was talking about food, that meant a trip down to the lower level of the restaurant where the kitchen was situated. Assuming Alex King was still here, then any trip to the kitchen would increase his chance of being found. JJ was suddenly hit by a wave of guilt that threatened to engulf her. If King died, it would be her fault. She'd told him to come here today. She was the one who'd set the whole thing up. The buck had to stop somewhere, and that somewhere was with her.

'Am I talking to myself here? It's a simple question. Is anyone hungry?'

JJ was still staring at the scratch on the floor. She was aware of heads shaking all around her. Someone whispered 'no'.

'So nobody's hungry? Well I've got to tell you, I am starving.'

This is it, thought JJ. *He's going to march us down to the kitchen, and King is going to be discovered and then he'll be executed and it will be all my fault.*

But that didn't happen. Instead, he picked up the restaurant phone and thumbed it to life. He pressed the handset to the side of his head, wrinkling the balaclava. A couple of seconds passed, then, 'Louise, darling, have you missed me? How are you getting on with working out what I want?'

A pause.

'Relax. We can save that for later. I've got to tell you, though, I could kill for a pizza.' A short pause, a laugh. 'Sorry about that, Lou. I probably just gave you guys a heart attack. When I said I could kill for a pizza, I wasn't talking literally. It was just a turn of phrase. I guess I should choose my words more carefully, right?'

Another pause.

'I'd like an extra-large deep pan with ham, mushroom, pepperoni and extra cheese. Actually, make it two. My friends here tell me they're not hungry but you know how it is when someone walks in with a pizza. The smell gets those stomach juices going and suddenly everyone wants a slice.'

Another pause, another laugh.

'Now, there's a question. What am I going to give you in return? Now, why don't you say what you really mean? You want me to release another hostage, right? They say you can't put a price on a life, but it looks like you just did. Two pizzas in exchange for a life sounds about right to me, but, I've got to tell you, this better be mighty fine pizza. And one more thing, Lou. In case you're tempted to add a little something to the sauce to put me to sleep, remember the watch. If my heart-rate drops below fifty, then it's a case of tick, tick boom. Understand? Call me when the pizza gets here.'

The bomber disconnected the call and put the handset down beside the laptop. He turned to face the hostages, staring each one down in turn. 'I'm guessing the question you're all asking right now is who gets to go home.'

JJ looked at the scratch on the floor, hardly daring to breathe. That wasn't the question she was asking. Not even close. The question she was asking was what's the catch this time?

11

'I don't get why the cops don't just go in there. I mean, there's got to be like a couple of hundred of them and only one of him. Sure, there'd be some collateral damage, but it's better to get some hostages out rather than them all dying. Ten per cent of something is always going to be better than ten per cent of nothing, am I right or am I right? The cops are the ones with the guns, and they've got their SWAT team, and I say they use it. I mean, what the hell's the point in having all that firepower if you don't use it? It makes sense to me. Send in the big guns, that's what I say.'

Rob Taylor was at the periphery of the crowd, holding out a microphone and nodding like the guy doing the talking was a candidate for Mensa rather than some dumb redneck with a two-figure IQ. MOTS was one acronym guaranteed to strike the fear of God into him. The Man-on-the-Street interview. Basically, he got to stick a microphone in front of a bunch of opinionated assholes and record their views for posterity. Soul-destroying didn't even begin to cover it.

These jerks could always do it better than the pros, and they always had the answers. Ironically, the one question Rob desperately wanted to ask was the one he couldn't ask. If they had the answers, then why were they standing talking to him when they could be out there righting all those perceived wrongs?

The redneck guy was still droning on. He'd moved on from the mess the cops were making to the mess that the governor was making over in Sacramento. The next stop would be the mess the president was making at the White House. The guy paused for breath and Rob jumped in to wind the interview up. He could have happily strangled Jonah for making him do this.

The interviews weren't going out live, which was just as well. If these people could hear themselves they'd probably die on the spot. They thought they sounded so clever, but they didn't. The way they saw themselves was light years from the reality. The interviews would have to be edited so the dumbass doing the talking didn't sound quite so dumb, then they'd be used between the main stories to add colour. They also helped filled up airtime, which went back to the twenty-four-hour news station curse of too much time and not enough content. The theory was that they helped make the crisis more accessible to the Average Joe. Rob knew all this, but he still hated doing them.

A small crowd had gathered around him, which was no real surprise. Drop a camera crew anywhere in the US and you could pretty much guarantee a crowd would form. LA was more jaded than the rest of the country because it was the centre of the entertainment industry, but it was still as true here as it was anywhere else. Next up was a middle-aged woman who'd been attractive once upon a time, although that time was long gone. Her roots were showing, and the make-up was there out of necessity rather than for enhancement.

'So, what do you think of today's events?' Rob asked after he'd gone through the preliminaries. Name, age, that sort of thing. It was difficult to dredge up any enthusiasm, artificial or genuine, but he dug deep and managed to find something passable.

'I love Ed Richards,' she shrieked in a voice guaranteed to give a headache. 'I've seen all his films. Every single last one. I Just pray to God and Jesus and all the saints that he's going to be all right. I don't know what I'd do if anything happened to him.'

Her sad little life would carry on exactly as it had always done, thought Rob. The only change would be the object of her obsession. Ed Richards would be replaced by someone else, it didn't matter who, so long as there was a white knight there to fuel her fantasy of being whisked away into a life of money and privilege. The fact that it was never going to happen was irrelevant. All that mattered was the fantasy. Rob bit his tongue and wished a biblical plague down upon Jonah.

'Is there anything else you want to add?'

'Only that I'm thinking about his family. Thinking and praying for them. God only knows what that poor woman and those kids are going through. This must be hell for them.'

The woman went on in this vein for a while, and Rob tuned her out. That voice was like a dentist drill. On the basis of that alone, he doubted Seth would use the interview. Then again, you never knew with Seth. The man was a law unto himself. Rob wound up the interview and looked around for his next victim. A guy in a suit caught his eye, mostly because of the suit. Everyone else was dressed casually. Jeans, T-shirts, shorts, sneakers. Rob walked over to him.

'What's your name, sir?'

'I'd rather not say.'

Rob didn't push it. Seth wouldn't use the interview without a name, but there was something about this guy that had got him curious. Part of it was the way he was dressed, although that wasn't all of it. He was giving off a different vibe to the rest of the crowd. Everyone else was here because they could smell blood, but that wasn't the case here. This guy exuded an air of detachment, like he was observing from a distance rather than getting carried away by the mood of the mob.

'So, why have you come here today?' The enthusiasm in Rob's voice was real this time. He was genuinely interested in what the guy had to say.

'Because, I've got a vested interest.'

'You know someone in Alfie's?'

The guy shook his head and laughed cynically. 'You're way off the mark there, my friend.'

'So why are you here?'

'Because I've got a hundred bucks at five-to-one on Ed Richards being the next person to get a bullet.'

12

'This better be good,' Seth barked into the phone. 'It's coming up to the top of the hour. I don't need to tell you that you could have picked a better time.'

'You're going to want to hear this,' Rob said.

'And you've got ten seconds.'

'People are betting on who's going to die next.'

'You're kidding, right?'

'I've never been more serious. I've just spoken to a guy. One buck gets him five that Richards is next.'

'No legitimate bookie's going to touch that sort of action, but I'm guessing there are plenty of backstreet guys who would.'

'*Backstreet guys*. Seth, this is the twenty-first century. You've got to stop thinking like Kennedy's still president.'

'And you'd better watch your mouth or you'll be looking for a new job.'

'The Internet is where it's happening these days,' Rob said. 'Online gambling is a multi-billion dollar a year enterprise. You can bet on anything you want. *Anything*. And the reason for that is because most of the action is controlled by organised crime. They couldn't care less what you gamble on. All they care about is that the punters are losing more money than they're winning. And they are. It doesn't matter if the casino is on an Indian reservation or it's based at a web address in cyberspace, the house always wins.'

'Nice work.'

Seth hung up as Rob started to say thanks. He reached for his Marlboros, lit one, then looked down at his assistants. He was about to start barking out orders, but something about the way they were staring at him made the words choke in his throat. They were huddled together, arms almost touching. The way they were standing grouped like that made him think of a bunch of kids standing in front of an angry principal. The quick, shared glances made it obvious they'd been whispering together while he'd been on the phone, and that the news wasn't good.

'Spit it out,' he hollered, and all three just about jumped from their skins.

More whispering, more jostling, then the white lesbian stepped forward.

'Fox has a story,' she said.

'Fox has lots of stories, sweetheart. They're a news channel. It's what they do. I'm going to need you to be more specific.' His voice sounded calmer than he felt, but it was a stretched calm. This was the sort of calm you got when you passed through the eye of a hurricane.

'LA Abuse has just received a six million dollar donation from the bomber.'

'And you know this how?'

She nodded towards one of the smaller monitors. Fox News had been playing on it non-stop since the crisis began. The banner at the bottom of the screen read: 'ALFIE'S BOMBER DONATES SIX MILLION DOLLARS TO LA ABUSE ... STAY TUNED FOR MORE'.

'Who the hell is LA Abuse?

'It's a charity that helps people who can't afford to go to Betty Ford. People on food stamps, the homeless, prostitutes, people right down on the bottom rung of the ladder.'

Seth glanced at the cigarette burning away between his fingers. The vein in his temple was throbbing, and he could feel that unpleasant tingle you got when nicotine and caffeine mixed with adrenalin.

'Okay, here's my question.' He widened his gaze to take in his three assistants, and then he let rip. 'Why is the world hearing this from Fox and not from us? For Christ's sake, do I have to remind you who makes the news here? You're all fired. Get the hell out of my sight.'

All three assistants had expressions on their faces like they were trying to work out if he was serious. No one was looking at Seth. They shared some glances and a couple of shrugs, then sat down and got on with their work. Seth glanced at the clock above the hi-tech screens. Twenty seconds until the top of the hour. TRN's title sequence was playing on the main screen. The graphics were funky and cutting edge, the music suitably dramatic. On one of the smaller screens, a make-up girl was working on Caroline Bradley.

Ten seconds to go.

The make-up girl hustled out of shot and Caroline turned to face the camera. She rubbed her lips together, flicked away an imaginary stray hair, then straightened the papers on her desk.

'Everyone get ready,' Seth said.

There was no enthusiasm in his voice, just weariness. He would get back up on the board. He always did. All he needed was a second or two to get his breath back, that's all. Or maybe he was getting too old for this game. He shook this last thought away. It was so ridiculous it wasn't even worth entertaining.

'Cut to Caroline on my mark,' he said. 'Three, two, one.'

15:00–15:30

1

'And the main story here at Fox News at the top of the hour is a major worldwide exclusive. The bomber holding ten people captive in the Alfie's siege has just made a six million dollar charity donation to LA Abuse. The move has got people calling him a modern-day Robin Hood.'

The bomber pulled the lid of the laptop closed, cutting the anchorman off in mid-flow. Those last few words were still playing in JJ's head. *A modern-day Robin Hood.* What was that all about? She looked over at the bomber and saw him rub his head again. He pulled a small white tub from his pocket, shook a couple of pills into his hand, then dry swallowed them, throwing his head back to help them down. For a moment he just sat there looking down towards the restaurant's lower level, his hand resting on the lid of the laptop. He was staring at the dead accountant, but JJ had a feeling that he wasn't really seeing him. There was a faraway look in his eyes, like he was puzzling something out. But puzzling out what?

Since he'd last spoken to the hostage negotiator, the energy in the room had become more positive again. Everyone was no doubt thinking the same thing. Someone was getting out, and there was a one in ten chance it could be them. Everyone except her. She was still wondering what the catch was. And now she was wondering something else, too. What was the bomber's real agenda?

Earlier, when he'd collected six million dollars, she'd assumed his motivation was money. It made sense. With a couple of keystrokes and a couple of clicks he had become a multimillionaire. All he had to do was escape from Alfie's and he'd have enough money to comfortably live out the rest of his days. A tall order, but doable. He'd got this far through careful planning, so it followed that he must have an escape plan. Mexico wasn't far. If he managed to get there, he could disappear for ever. With six million dollars in the bank it would be easy to ensure that nobody ever saw him again. Except that wasn't how it was going to go down.

That donation to LA Abuse was a game changer. The media was renowned for getting things wrong. It was inevitable. News stories were fluid and organic. They grew and changed and took on a life of their own. Trying to pin down a big story was like wrestling an alligator. But JJ was confident that Fox had called this one right. Since the siege had started, they'd been playing catch-up with TRN. This was their chance to regain some of that lost ground, so they would have made damn sure that they'd got their facts straight. If they hadn't been one hundred per cent certain they wouldn't have led with the story.

Which brought her back full-circle to the question of motivation. Why was the bomber doing this? What was his agenda? Because he must have one. Every single person on the planet had an agenda.

JJ shut her eyes and tried to clear her mind. Since the siege had started she'd been reacting to events rather than instigating them. Usually she was on the outside, looking in. That's what gave her the clarity of perspective she needed to get the job done. Being on the inside, looking out, was a whole new ballgame.

The doubts and what-ifs made it almost impossible to think straight. She'd seen this time and time again with her clients.

Their precious little worlds had been blown apart, so they started questioning everything in the hope that a solution would magically present itself. The irony was that nine times out of ten, *they* were the problem, and that was the one place they never looked. They were happy to blame everyone else. They never blamed themselves.

But this situation was the one in ten. Whichever way JJ looked at it, she couldn't see how any of this could be her fault. She'd been in the wrong place at the wrong time, and that was that. End of story.

Giving the money to charity was a shrewd move. She had to concede that much. It was the sort of move she'd suggested to her clients on numerous occasions. JJ loved charities. It was amazing how much goodwill you could buy with a large donation. It was amazing how much damage could be undone. Of course, you always got a few cynics who were quick to pour scorn on the gesture, but they were in the minority. The majority loved the big gesture.

The only thing better than giving away money was giving time, actually getting out there and getting your hands dirty. Anything that provided a good photo op was fine in JJ's book. Dishing up food to the homeless at Thanksgiving, or a trip to an African orphanage to play soccer with the kids. It didn't matter what it was, so long as the client was smiling when they did it.

What JJ found most interesting was the bomber's choice of charity. There were more than a million registered public charities in America. Some massive, most tiny. He could have given the money to the American Cancer Society or the Red Cross, but he hadn't. Instead, he'd chosen LA Abuse, a charity so obscure she doubted anyone had ever heard of it. She certainly hadn't. There was a good chance that donations to LA Abuse hadn't hit seven figures in the entire time it had been in existence. A cash injection of six million would be like a gift from God.

The six-million-dollar question was why had the bomber chosen LA Abuse. The answer was to be found in the last part of the news report. *A move that has got people calling him a modern-day Robin Hood.* From a PR point of view it was pure genius. With one gesture, he'd transformed himself from bad guy to anti-hero. When this had all started everyone had thought he was an al-Qaeda suicide bomber. Now he was the new Robin Hood. Despite everything, JJ was impressed. She couldn't have done a better job of spinning this herself.

Question: if money wasn't his motivator, then what the hell was?

From where JJ was sitting, fame was looking more and more likely. Maybe he was after his fifteen minutes of fame, after all. The reason he'd made the donation was because he was clearly looking for history to remember him in a favourable light. Whatever the reason, the bottom line was that you didn't just burst into a restaurant with a bomb and a gun and start killing people for no reason. And the stats really weren't on his side. Like Gary Thompson had pointed out, most hostage situations ended up with the hostage-taker either dead or in custody. Not that there was much difference between the two. There wasn't a single jury in California that wouldn't return a guilty verdict on this guy. And there wasn't a single judge who would hesitate to pass the death sentence.

2

Seth stared at each of his assistants in turn, fixing them with a stern look. They were shuffling their feet and avoiding eye contact at all costs. No one seemed to know what to do with their hands.

'I've come up with a way for you three to redeem your sorry selves,' he said.

'How?' asked the Asian kid, and this won him a couple of Brownie points. At least he'd had the balls to open his mouth, which was more than could be said for the other two.

'I want you to find out who the bomber is.'

'How?' the Asian kid asked again, wiping off the Brownie points he'd just earned.

'Jesus Christ, don't they teach you anything at those fancy colleges you allegedly graduated from?'

'Obviously not,' murmured the black kid, earning himself a dirty look.

'Look, I don't care how you get it. I don't care who you have to bribe or how many laws you have to break. All I care is that you get me that name.'

'You want us to break the law,' the white lesbian said.

'No sweetheart, what I want is for you to grow a pair and go out there and pretend for two seconds like you're a real journalist.'

'LA Abuse is one possibility,' the black kid suggested. 'The money must have been wired to them. They should have a record of who sent it.'

'Hallelujah and praise be to Jesus. Maybe there's hope for you yet. But remember, Fox didn't get the name, which means that LA Abuse is being cagey. You're going to have to be more persuasive than they were. Can you do that?'

The black kid nodded. 'Yeah, I can do that.'

'Good. Have the researchers had any luck tracking down the owners of the cars in the lot?'

'They're still working on it,' the Asian kid said.

'Well, tell them to work faster.'

3

The bomber stopped in front of Ed Richards and let his gaze wander from person to person. Once again, JJ was convinced that he looked longer at her than at the others, but she put this down to paranoia. No doubt every single person was thinking the exact same thing.

'I wish you folks could see yourselves right now. You know, I'm sure I've seen more smiles at a funeral. Okay, I want everyone on their feet. It's time for a party game. That should help blow those dark clouds away.' He clapped his hands. 'I said everyone up! Come on people, let's hustle.'

JJ timed it so she was fifth. The first person up would stand out. So would the last. The ones in the middle, the fours, fives and sixes, wouldn't be so noticeable. Kevin Donahue was the last person up again. Her heart went out to him. Getting to his feet had been a major test of endurance. He was looking worse than ever, like he was about to collapse. His breathing was shallow and quick. She wanted to say something, but kept her mouth shut tight. The bomber had singled her out once and she'd somehow survived. She doubted her luck would stretch far enough to save her a second time. She chanced a quick glance. Nobody was about to step up and fight Donahue's corner. Not even Tony. The restaurant owner looked utterly defeated.

One of the things she loved most about Tony was his laugh, particularly when he was trading gossip. Right now he looked like he might never laugh again. His eyes were swollen to narrow slits, the skin around them turning from red to dark purple. In a sunset those colours would look glorious. On Tony it was just another reminder of how much danger they were in. And if she needed another reminder, there was the ache in her jaw from where she'd been hit.

The bomber was marching up and down in front of them, the silenced submachine gun cradled in his hand. He stopped and faced them.

'I take it everyone's heard of musical statues, the kids' party game? The rules are simple. You dance around and when the music stops you stand absolutely still. Just like statues. First to move is out, and the last one standing is the winner.'

There was something about the way he said this that troubled JJ. *The last one standing.* It sounded too final, like a death sentence. The bomber hit a couple of keys on the laptop and the tinkly, rainbow-soaked sound of 'The Wheels on the Bus' came out of the computer's speakers. The female singer had a bright, bouncy voice, like she'd OD'd on sugar. The sound was thin and reedy and lacking in bass, and that was creepy enough, but the choice of song made it even creepier. JJ felt like she'd been transported into a horror movie.

'What are you waiting for?' the bomber yelled. 'Get dancing.'

He pointed the gun at Ed Richards and sighted along the barrel. Richards started shuffling his feet. He looked ridiculous, like an embarrassing old uncle at a wedding. He was a mess, a car wreck just waiting to happen. If his fans could see him now they wouldn't believe this was the same man who'd stolen their hearts.

'All of you, get dancing!'

JJ started shuffling her feet. She no doubt looked as ridiculous as Richards, but didn't care. Looking stupid beat the hell out of being dead. Staying alive trumped everything else. The longer she stayed alive, the more chance there was of being rescued. The music stopped, and JJ stopped, too. The way she was positioned she could see Richards and Simone but she couldn't see anyone else. She wouldn't make that mistake again. Next time she would position herself so she could see everyone. The room had fallen completely silent. This was the sound of ten people desperately trying to stay still. JJ already had her strategy worked out. She was going to bail out at number five.

'Kev, looks like you lose round one.'

JJ glanced over her shoulder. Kevin Donahue looked paler than ever. He was as white as a ghost. The bomber raised his gun and aimed at the producer's head.

4

'I can get you odds of fifty to one on Kevin Donahue winning,' Tara said.

Rob looked over her shoulder, angling himself so he could see her cell phone. They were standing apart from the crowd, waiting for something to happen. Anything. They'd done as many MOTS as Rob could stand doing, which was six. And Tara had plenty of background shots of cops, firefighters and paramedics doing what they did in these situations, which basically amounted to hanging around waiting for something to happen as well. It was like being trapped in an airport departure lounge.

'Who's the favourite?' he asked.

Tara jabbed at her cell. 'Ed Richards. You're only going to get evens on him.'

'Who's favourite to take the next bullet?'

More jabbing, then a laugh. 'You're not going to believe this. Ed Richards is favourite for that, too. The odds are slightly better, though. You'll get two to one on that.'

Rob thought about this for a second. 'Actually, I do believe it.'

Tara looked up from her phone. Her eyes narrowed. 'You've got your thinking face on.'

'It's nothing.'

'No, it's something. Look, Rob, just tell me what's on your mind. Maybe I can help. Hell, maybe just putting your thoughts out there will help to clarify them.'

Rob bit his lip then pulled out his cell phone. He went to CNN's live feed first, then Fox's, then TRN's. Everything he was seeing and hearing was a variation on the same theme. The bomber was the new Robin Hood. Tara was hovering at his shoulder, watching him.

'What are you seeing, Rob?'

He turned to look at her. 'We can agree this guy's a complete puzzle, right?

She nodded. 'Yeah, he's the original riddle wrapped up in a mystery trapped in the middle of whatever the hell it was he got himself trapped inside.'

'An enigma. He's a riddle wrapped in a mystery inside an enigma. Anyway, to start with, we think he's a terrorist, right? Then he's a psychopath, murdering people for kicks. Then he's Robin Hood. And now people are making bets on who's going to live or die. I've got to tell you, this situation is starting to look less and less like a hostage situation and more and more like a popularity contest.'

Tara was nodding. 'Do you know what this reminds me of? A reality show. Granted, it's the world's most screwed up reality show, but that's what it is nonetheless.'

'Exactly. But what's motivating this guy? So far we've ruled out the political angle. And we can rule out the idea that he's doing this for money. So where does that leave us? There needs to be a reason. You don't just wake up one morning and decide that today's a good day to strap a bomb to your chest and hold a restaurant full of people hostage.'

'Back up a second. What if the motivation *is* financial?'

'In that case, you're not going to give away six million bucks.'

'You would if you stood to make more than six million.'

'And how does that work?'

'You told Jonah earlier that Internet gambling was a billion-dollar business, right? Maybe he's after a slice of that.'

Rob shook his head. 'It doesn't work. The bomber's in there dealing with his hostages, dealing with the cops, and he still finds time to go online and post bets. Sorry, I'm not buying that. It takes multitasking to a whole new level.'

'I'm telling you, it could work, Rob.'

'It can't. What's he going to do? Put a million on Kevin Donahue and walk away fifty million bucks richer?'

'That's exactly what he's going to do.'

Tara had grown an inch taller and had a look on her face like she was daring him to argue. As a general rule, he didn't argue with her. The fact was, she'd won every argument they'd ever had.

'Okay, let's say you're right. So the bomber puts a million bucks down at fifty-to-one. He can control the outcome, so why not? It's a sure thing, right?'

Tara said nothing.

'Okay, problem number one: he has to get out of Alfie's without being killed or captured. Problem two: he needs to collect his winnings. Do you think the Russian mob, or the Serbians, or whoever the hell he made his bet with is just going to hand over fifty million bucks? Don't you think they might be just a little bit suspicious? Suspicious enough to put out a contract on him?'

'You're assuming he's going to place one massive bet. Of course he's not going to do that. That would be stupid. He's going to spread those bets around. He's going to use false names and multiple accounts. He's going to fly under the radar. He's going to gamble with the Russians and the Serbians and anyone else who'll take his money. If he plays this right then he can make six million bucks look like pocket change.'

Rob shook his head again. 'Still not buying, and I'll tell you why. It comes back to multitasking. There's no way one person can keep that number of balls in the air.'

Tara smiled the sort of smile you sometimes saw when you'd laid down a straight flush and were reaching for the chips. It was the sort of smile that said, *not so fast buddy*. 'What's the biggest assumption we've made here? And by *we* I mean you, me, the cops, everyone?'

'No idea, but I'm guessing you're about to tell me.'

'What if he isn't working alone?'

5

JJ watched in horror as the bomber firmed his grip on the gun. His finger curled around the trigger, applying a fraction more pressure. Everyone had shuffled away from Kevin Donahue. The producer was standing completely alone, stranded on his own patch of floor, three feet of empty parquet stretching out in all directions.

'Please God, don't shoot me,' he pleaded. His accent was from somewhere up north. Chicago was JJ's best guess. There was no such thing as an LA accent. Everyone in LA was an immigrant to one degree or another.

'What's wrong with you?' the bomber asked.

'What's wrong?' Donahue replied incredulously. 'What's wrong is that you're pointing a goddamn gun at me and you're about to blow my head off.'

'No, what's *wrong* with you? You're sick, right? Either that or Halloween's come early.'

'It's cancer. I'm riddled with it.'

'How long have you got?'

'According to the doctors I should have been dead six months ago.'

'But what do they know, eh?'

Donahue gave a death's-head grin. 'Yeah, what the hell do they know?'

'So, if I was to shoot you, I'd be doing you a favour, right?'

'That's one way of looking at it.'

'Convince me there's another way.'

Donahue glanced down at his feet and let out a long sigh. When he straightened up he looked like he was one breath away from being laid out on a mortuary slab. 'Shoot me or don't shoot me. I don't really care anymore. If murdering me means you won't kill someone else, then maybe that's for the best. You know, when I wake up in the morning the first thing I do is thank God that I've lived to see another day. The second thing I do is curse him for exactly the same reason.'

'Then you have a cigarette and a coffee and head to the office.'

Donahue grinned another of those death's-head grins. 'I had to quit the smokes. Doctor's orders. But, yeah, that pretty much covers it. I might have a month left. Then again, I might have a day. These people, on the other hand, they've got years ahead of them.'

'Nice speech. What are you? A screenwriter?'

Donahue laughed. 'You think they'd let a screenwriter in a place like this? Not a chance. I was one once upon a time, though, when I first arrived in town, but that was a century ago.'

'Do you know what I think? I think you're full of shit.' The bomber reaffirmed his grip on the gun, his finger tightening on the trigger. 'Come on, Kev. Do you really expect me to believe that someone in this town is capable of a truly selfless act? *Selfish* acts, I can believe, but not *selfless* ones. You're a survivor, which means you're not about to willingly roll over and die anytime soon, not if you can help it. As for all that crap about praising God. Give me a break. Your first thought when you wake up is that all those doctors with their fancy educations and big houses don't know diddlysquat. So how does this work, Kev? You tug at my heartstrings and I don't shoot you? Is that it?'

Donahue lowered his head and said nothing, The way he was standing there made JJ think he was just waiting for the bullet. And the way the bomber's whole body had tensed made her think that he was about to deliver it.

'Here's what I don't understand,' the bomber went on. 'Your life's hell, right? You're in constant pain and the pills are getting to be less and less effective with every passing day. The fact you've lasted this long means you've had chemo, probably more than once, which I'm betting was no picnic. So, I'm asking myself why you wouldn't want to die, and the only reason I can come up with is that whatever's waiting for you on the other side must be pretty bad.'

'I don't expect you to understand.'

'Try me. You might be surprised.'

'I've got a boy and a girl. Well, I say a boy and a girl, but they're both in their thirties now. Anyway, I wasn't around while they were growing up, and now I'm dying *they're* not around. Last time I saw them was five years, two months and thirteen days ago. It was at their mother's funeral. I tried to talk to them but they didn't want anything to do with me.'

'And they haven't talked to you since. That's why you're so determined to hang on in there. You're waiting for that Hallmark moment. The big reunion, tears all around.'

'Something like that. I don't blame them, though. It's my own fault. I should have been there. But I wasn't, and now it's too late.'

'You know, Frank got a lot of things right, but he was off the mark with all that stuff about regrets in 'My Way'. When you get to the end, it's not the things you achieved in life that you focus on, it's all those things you didn't do. All those missed opportunities. All those regrets. And the truth is that everyone's got more than a few. Every last one of us. Let's face it, nobody lies on their death bed and wishes they'd spent more time at the office. Nobody.'

The bomber shifted his feet to get more comfortable and re-affirmed his stance. His fingers relaxed then tensed, relaxed then tensed. He inhaled, exhaled. Another inhalation and JJ knew this was it.

'Bang!'

Donahue crumpled to the floor and it took JJ a second to realise he hadn't been shot. The lack of blood was the first giveaway. The fact Donahue was on his knees weeping was the clincher.

'Okay, folks, on to round two.'

The bomber hit a key on the laptop.

'The wipers on the bus go swish, swish, swish.'

6

A replay of the last hostage handover was playing on the main screen, but Seth wasn't watching it. His attention was fixed on one of the smaller screens. CNN had wasted no time whisking Carrie Preston through make-up and getting her in front of a camera. She was wearing a grey sweatshirt with LAPD in big black letters on the front, which was a nice touch. A big public thumbs-up for the cops always went down well when there was a disaster unfurling. Her long red hair had been brushed through and tidied up and was pulled into a neat ponytail.

The interviewer was reeling off her credentials, stretching her thin résumé to make it sound like she was a double Oscar-winning heavyweight rather than a two-bit actress who'd managed to grab her fifteen minutes of fame by appearing in a sitcom and a couple of mediocre movies. He asked his first question and Preston took a moment to compose herself, a moment she'd no doubt been rehearsing in her mind since she'd got out of Alfie's. She looked down at her hands lying in her lap. When she looked back up there were tears in her eyes.

Seth figured she was probably thinking about that pet kitten who'd died when she was a little girl, anything to get the waterworks going. It was so contrived, but nobody at home would care about that. They'd just love her all the more because she was showing her "human" side. If she'd been in front of TRN's cameras, Seth wouldn't have given a damn, but she wasn't, so he did.

Just hearing the actress's affected, whispery voice was enough to get his blood boiling.

He cast a dirty look in the direction of his assistants. The white lesbian and the black kid had their heads down and were studiously avoiding his gaze. The Asian kid was staring at him, but not saying anything. The impression Seth had was that he'd drawn the short straw and wasn't sure where to begin.

'Spit it out. I don't have all day.'

'Rob's on the line.'

'Well, what are you waiting for? Patch him through.'

Something clicked in his headset, then Rob was there.

'What if the bomber's not working alone?' he asked without preamble.

'A conspiracy theory. Fantastic. I love it. Okay, I'm listening.'

'It's actually Tara's idea. She thinks this could be some sort of gambling sting. She reckons there could be a whole gang working this thing.'

'And this is happening on the Internet?'

'Got it in one. She thinks this gang's putting bets on everything from who's going to be the next person out to who's going to be the last person standing.'

'How many people do you reckon are involved?'

'Including the bomber, Tara reckons a minimum of three. They need to keep the bets small and they need to spread them around so it doesn't appear suspicious. However, the more people involved, the more chance there is that someone's going to say the wrong thing and screw the whole thing up, so they're going to want to keep the numbers as small as possible.'

'Okay, you've told me what Tara thinks. What do you think?'

Rob hesitated. 'The truth is, I don't know. It makes as much sense as anything else that's happened today. To start with, everyone's saying it's a terrorist attack. I mean, the guy's got a bomb strapped to him, what else are we going to think?'

On the small screen, Carrie Preston was describing how the bomber had forced them to play Russian roulette.

'I think we can definitely rule out the terrorist angle,' Seth said.

'And then he threw us a curveball when he donated six million dollars to charity.'

'Which is why I'm not convinced by this gang theory. Why give away six million bucks if you're doing this for the money?'

'It's all about maximising your earning potential.'

'And that's the sort of bullshit I'd expect to hear from an economist. You're a journalist, Rob. At least, that's what you keep telling me. Start talking like one.'

'That donation has given his public image a huge boost. Yes, he's the bad guy, and yes, he's killed hostages, but you'd better believe that there are people sitting out there glued to their TV sets right now who are actually rooting for him. You've heard what everyone's calling him. He's the new Robin Hood.'

'All well and good, but how does that help him "maximise his earning potential"?'

'Simple. It makes it easier to drag the situation out. The longer this goes on, the more bets his buddies can place, and the more money they can make. If they play it right then six million will look like nothing.'

'Again, all well and good, but why does it make it easier to drag the situation out?'

'And, again, the answer's simple. The police and the FBI are going to be treading on eggshells. Can you imagine the PR fallout from killing Robin Hood?'

7

Five down, five to go.

Each round had ended the same way. The music had stopped and the bomber had called out a name. He'd aimed his gun and shouted 'bang!'. Everyone had flinched even though they were expecting it, then the loser had dropped to the floor and joined all the other losers.

Ed Richards had gone out after Kevin Donahue, then Tony, then Jen. Simone had been number five. The supermodel had been devastated when she'd lost. She'd cursed herself under breath. At least, that's what JJ had thought she was doing. She'd been speaking in Norwegian, so it was difficult to be sure. Simone knew that Alex King was probably hiding out in the restroom, and that still worried JJ. What was to stop the model trading that information for her freedom? JJ had talked to her a couple of times and wouldn't put it past her. Simone was so self-obsessed she made Dan Stone look as selfless as Mother Teresa. The only real surprise was that she hadn't tried to trade the information already.

JJ shuffled from foot to foot, her arms and legs working as stiffly as everyone else's. 'The Wheels on the Bus' had been replaced by 'Camptown Races', but the same woman was singing, and that sugary voice was like fingernails on a blackboard. JJ had positioned herself so she could see the other dancing hostages. She needed to make this look good. If the bomber thought for a second that she was deliberately trying to lose, then she'd end up like Elizabeth Hayward. The music stopped and JJ froze to the spot. She was watching the other four carefully. They were all doing their utmost to stay completely still. She did a slow count to three then made her left hand tremble.

'Frank, you're out.'

JJ had been watching Frank. He hadn't moved a muscle. None of the others had. Frank hadn't moved and she had. It should be her going out, not him. The bomber aimed his gun and everyone shuffled out of the way. This time JJ was ready and waiting for the shouted 'bang!', so she didn't jump. The suppressed *phht* didn't really register, but the sound of Frank's body hitting the ground did. So did Simone's scream.

'Damn, these triggers are sensitive. Guess I'm going to have to be more careful in future.'

JJ barely heard him. She was staring down at Frank. There was a small dark hole in the middle of his forehead, and the back of his head was a mess of blood and gore and brain tissue. She kept staring, one thought going around her head. *It should have been me.*

She'd planned on being the sixth person out, and if that had happened it would have been her lying there with half her head blown away. Her hands started shaking for real, her breathing sped up to the point where she was almost hyperventilating. So what now? Did she play it so she was the next person out and end up dead like Frank? Or did she play to win even though she was sure the winner would never be set free?

'Tony and Ed, clear away this mess,' the bomber said.

Richards and Tony got up slowly. Both of them were moving like they were sleepwalking. Tony grabbed Frank under the shoulders, Richards got the feet, and they dragged the body to the side of the room. The restaurant owner was walking awkwardly and doing his best to avoid the mess spilling from the hole in Frank's head.

'And then there were four.'

The bomber hit play, and JJ started to dance.

8

Up in Mission Control, Seth watched the big screen and quietly seethed. Alison Trevane, TRN's showbiz editor, was sitting at the side of a funky-looking pink desk. She had short black hair, bright blue eyes, and was possibly the most annoying person he'd ever met. She was originally from North Carolina but she had that whole Valley Girl act down to a fine art. Nothing was ever just good in Alison's world, it was super-fantastic. The woman had mastered the knack of being able to open her mouth and fill a silence with absolutely nothing. Vacuous didn't even begin to cover it.

A thirty-second conversation was exhausting, which was why Seth avoided her. Unfortunately, the viewers loved her, and that was why she was on screen now. The suits upstairs had decided that things were getting "a little on the heavy side" and they'd wanted Alison brought in to lighten the mood.

When Seth had heard this he'd almost choked on his coffee. Heavy! Of course it was heavy. It was a goddamn siege, for Christ's sake. A major news story. A major *international* news story. This thing wasn't just heavy, it had the weight and gravity of a black hole. He'd said no. He'd said no in a number of interesting and colourful ways. But the suits had been adamant, and Seth was savvy enough to realise that this was one battle he wasn't going to win.

Alison finished telling the viewers a whole bunch of facts they already knew about Ed Richards, and the actor's picture disappeared from the screen behind her. A second later it was replaced by a picture of a bald-headed black guy. There were diamond studs in both his ears and a diamond pinkie ring on his finger. The jewel-encrusted watch he was wearing had to be worth a cool quarter of a million bucks, easy.

'Music mogul DeAndre Alexander is also being held hostage,' Alison said.

Just the sound of her voice was enough to get Seth fuming all over again. It was all wrong for a story of this magnitude. If the brightness was dialled all the way down it would still be completely wrong. It might be fine for trading gossip, but this was a hard news story, goddamn it!

'What can you say about DeAndre Alexander that hasn't already been said?' she continued. 'Alexander has been called the Angel of the Bronx for his charity work. Every year he donates millions to help the kids from his old neighbourhood. There are hundreds of kids out there today who owe their futures to him.'

Jesus, thought Seth, pass me a sick bag. The guy wasn't a saint, he was just someone who'd got lucky.

'Kill the sound before I kill her,' he hollered.

One of the technicians hit a button and Mission Control fell silent. He didn't know who'd jumped to it. He didn't care. All that mattered was that he didn't have to listen to that woman massacring his story. He stared at the screen, the vein in his temple throbbing unpleasantly, coffee sloshing uncomfortably in his stomach. A strained silence had fallen across the room. There was a sense of people biting their tongues in case they said the wrong thing, a sense of people not daring to breathe in case they breathed the wrong way. Underpinning this was the electric hum of the machines and the gentle *brrr* of the air-conditioning.

'So, how close are we to naming the bomber?'

The question was fielded by the black kid. 'We're working on it, sir.'

'Which is another way of saying that the three of you are a bunch of incompetent screw-ups.'

'We've got a couple of leads we're chasing.'

'Well, chase harder. I want that name. And someone get Rob on the phone.'

Seth adjusted his headset and positioned the mike in front of his mouth. Rob answered on the first ring.

'Hey, Seth.'

'If we're going to prove Tara's theory, we need to ID the bomber.'

'No problem. Let me go grab my crystal ball.'

'Shut up and listen, Rob. The bomber's car is in Alfie's parking lot, which means the cops will have run the plate, which means they know who he is. I want you to lean on Aaron Walters and get that name.'

'What if the car's stolen?'

'If it's stolen then we try something else. Go do some leaning, Rob. I want that name.'

9

Eight down, two to go.

'Camptown Races' had been replaced by 'Twinkle Twinkle Little Star'. Same annoying singer. Same annoying sound that made JJ think of horror movies. The nursery rhyme was eating into her brain and driving her insane. The singer's voice was too bright. It hit all the wrong frequencies.

JJ was one of the last two standing. She'd wanted to bail out at number four, and number three, but hadn't been able to. The music had stopped and she'd just stood there, rooted to the spot, images of Frank's death swirling through her mind. Dan Stone had been the fourth person out, and then DeAndre Alexander. Now it was just her and Bev left dancing.

Bev was the same age as her, and a couple of inches shorter. She had brunette hair, hazel eyes and expensive white underwear. They were facing one another and trying to psych each other out. JJ had glimpsed a faint reflection of the two of them in one of the picture frames, and the way they were moving reminded her of two boxers rather than two dancers. Bev would make a move and she would match it, then she would do something and it would be Bev's turn to match her.

JJ still hadn't decided if she wanted to win, because she still couldn't shake the feeling that there had to be a catch. Then again, she didn't want to lose either, because she didn't want to know what the runner-up prize was. This was the ultimate rock and a hard place. To make matters worse, it was her fault that she'd ended up in this situation. She could have bailed out earlier. She *should* have bailed out.

Bev didn't have the same dilemma. She was going all-out to win. It was only after Frank had been shot that JJ had started taking notice of her. Since then she'd been paying very close attention indeed. Bev was a born winner, that much was obvious. Here was someone who always had to be first, whatever the cost. She had the same look of grim determination that you saw on sprinters when they took their positions at the start line. In Bev's world, all that mattered was winning. There were no prizes for second place.

The music stopped.

JJ stood dead still. No movement whatsoever. She held her breath and waited. The lack of oxygen was making her head spin. Bev was standing directly in front of her, no more than half a foot away. A stray hair had fallen over her eye and JJ could sense her irritation. She was trying to keep still, but that hair must have been driving her mad. Time stretched out and JJ battled to keep still. She had no idea how much longer she could keep this up for. She'd finally made a decision. She wanted out. Yes, this might be a trick, but if there was even an outside chance of escaping this nightmare, she was willing to take the risk.

Beads of sweat burst out on Bev's forehead. That stray hair was still there, tickling and niggling and making her crazy. JJ could see the bomber out of the corner of her eye. His head was moving between her and Bev, like he was watching a tennis match. All she had to do was hold on for a few more seconds.

'And we have a winner,' he suddenly announced.

JJ let go of the breath she'd been holding onto. Her shoulders slumped as a wave of relief washed over her. Just before the bomber spoke, she'd seen Bev's fingers move. She hadn't imagined it. Her fingertips had twitched and then he'd announced that they had a winner.

'It's been a closely fought contest, folks. A contest that's seen its share of drama.' The bomber glanced over at Frank's body as he said this, and everyone followed his lead. 'But there can only be one winner. Jody, please step forward.'

JJ stepped forward. She was standing close enough to smell the bomber's aftershave again, to smell the base animal stink that it hid.

'Sorry, but you're not going home.'

Bev let out a small whispered, 'Yes,' and JJ felt the hope inside her die. The bomber aimed the gun at her. Maybe he was going to pull the trigger. Maybe he wasn't. She didn't care anymore. A bullet would be a mercy right now. Anything to escape from this hell.

'Bang,' he whispered.

The bastard was grinning again.

10

Rob sprinted towards Alfie's parking lot. He was doing his best to keep up with Tara, but the camerawoman was already five yards in front, the gap widening. Her legs were longer, and she was a damn sight fitter than he was. They reached the parking lot as the grilles were coming up. Tara pointed her camera at the blank white face of the building, positioning herself so she could get both doors in. The bloodstain left by the valet looked blacker than ever.

Aaron Walters was waiting for them. He started to say something and Rob put a hand up. *Give me a second.* He placed his other hand on the hood of a brand new Ferrari and quickly pulled it back. The metal had been cooked under the fierce sun and was hotter than a barbecue. He took a couple of deep breaths, a stitch niggling at his side. Tara wasn't even breathing hard.

'I want the name of the bomber,' Rob said.

'Not going to happen.'

'I want that name.'

'And you can have it when this is over and the hostages are all safely out. Just like everyone else.'

'Give me the name.'

'Or what? You're going to walk away from this? I don't think so.'

'The bomber specifically asked for me.'

'Mr Taylor, a word of advice. A threat is only effective if the person issuing the threat is willing to follow through, or the person being threatened thinks that's going to happen. Neither of those scenarios is appropriate to what's happening here.' Walters smiled. 'And one more thing, Mr Taylor. Tell Seth to quit with the stalling tactics. The feed goes through to the other networks immediately. Understand? Immediately. I've got enough on my plate right now without having to deal with his bullshit games.'

Rob watched the PR guy walk away, happy to let him go. He was smiling, too, although his smile was more subtle, just a slight turning up at the corners of his mouth. It was an expression that could have meant anything. He'd known before he'd asked that Walters would never give up the name. It just wasn't going to happen. But that wasn't what he'd been angling for.

'You ready, Rob?' Tara called over.

'One second.'

Rob wiped the sweat from his forehead, then ran a hand through his hair to try and tame it a little. The sun was burning down hotter than ever and there wasn't a scrap of shade. He glanced over at Walters. The PR guy was standing next to a Bentley, watching him. The junker that the bomber had turned up in was beside the Bentley. It was an old Ford Taurus with rust-streaked silver bodywork and dents in both front fenders. It looked a hundred years old and probably had 200,000 miles on the clock.

Walters smiled and tipped him a wink, and Rob resisted the urge to fire a sunny one right back at him. Instead, he frowned and did his best to look annoyed. The PR guy seemed blissfully unaware of the fact that he'd royally screwed up. Rob was now in possession of one crucial piece of information that he hadn't had thirty seconds ago. He now knew for certain that the cops had identified the bomber.

11

Alex King sat on the tiled restroom floor playing sad face, smiley face with the knife. He hadn't started talking to it yet, but if this went on much longer then he probably would. He wasn't sure if that made him crazy or just plain lonely. He wasn't sure if there was much difference. The bomber had stormed into Alfie's two hours ago, two hours that already felt like a lifetime. He could barely remember his life from before. It was like it had ceased to exist.

Luck. That word had been thrown at him so much lately, and the people doing the throwing were right. He was lucky. Basically, he was one of the Chosen Few. Give it another couple of years and he would be richer and more famous than he'd ever imagined. Yes, sir, he was one of the luckiest people on the planet.

Unfortunately, all the money and fame in the world didn't mean a damn thing if you were dead. Because the truth was that his luck was about to run out. He could feel that the same way you could feel a coming storm. At some point one of the hostages would need to take a piss, and when that happened he would be discovered. It was only a matter of time. The only real surprise was that it hadn't happened already.

Just thinking about this made him want to go. There was no way he was going to do that, though, because it would make too much noise. That would be a hell of a way to go. Shot in the head while your dick was in your hands. In a weird-ass sort of way it would be kind of fitting. Most of his life had been lacking in any real sort of dignity, why should his death be any different? And maybe that was the reason everyone was sat out there with their legs crossed. An aching bladder had to be better than a bullet in the head any day

King heard the distant rumble of thunder. Except that couldn't be right. The sky had been a cloudless blue when he arrived, and he hadn't heard any news reports of bad weather on the way. No, not thunder, the grilles were going up again. He pushed the knife into his waistband, then moved quickly to the door and cracked it open. Everything was quiet out there. Nothing from the bomber. Nothing from the hostages. He slipped into the corridor and hurried to the kitchen, socks gliding over the wooden floor. He'd given up with his shoes. They were hidden beneath a pile of handtowels on one of the restroom shelves.

He eased the kitchen door open and slid inside, then used both hands to ease it closed again. The kitchen looked like a tornado had ripped through it after his search for the door key. One glance and the bomber would know someone had been back here. There weren't that many places to hide, so it would take all of ten seconds to find him. A millisecond to pull the trigger and his life would be over.

Who would mourn him? His agent would, but only because of all the money he'd lose. And his fans would miss him for the whole five seconds it would take until they moved on to someone new. And that was about it. As for accomplishments, *Killing Time* was the only thing of note that he'd done. Yes, it had been a blockbuster, and yes, it had earned big bucks, but, at the end of the day, it was just another action movie. There had been a thousand movies like it in the past, and there would be another thousand movies like it in the future. A couple of years from now no one would remember it.

King ran to the back door and pulled out his cell phone. Brad Carter answered on the first ring, like he was sitting there with his phone in his hand.

'Hi, Alex.'

'You've got to get me out of here, man.' His voice was just a hiss, like air escaping from a tyre.

'I wish I could, I really do. But that would mean compromising the safety of the other hostages. We've talked about this, buddy.'

'What about my safety? Doesn't it bother you that that's being compromised? And how about this? The longer I'm stuck in here, the more it's being compromised. Have you thought about that? You could save me. You know that. Blow this door and I'll be out in seconds.'

'Alex, we're doing everything possible to get you out. To get *all* of you out. And our strategy's working. That's another hostage just about to be released. You've just got to hang on in there.'

King laid his hand against the warm wood. A couple of inches lay between him and freedom. Two goddamn inches. The panic grew until there was only one thought in his head. *Got to get out.* He looked around for something he could use as a battering ram. Everything was either too big and heavy, or too small to even dent the wood. He spotted the fire-extinguisher. Big, red, heavy. It could work.

'Break the door down or I'll break it down,' he said.

'Alex, listen to me. Whatever you're planning, I'm begging you, please don't do it.

'Either break it down, or I swear to God, I will.'

'Listen to me. That door is solid wood. There's no way you're going to break through it. All you're going to do is make a noise, which will alert the bomber. If you do that, we cannot protect you. Are you listening? We *cannot* protect you. Four people have died already, do you want to be the fifth?'

'Four dead. By my count there's only three.'

'Another hostage was shot a couple of minutes ago. And that's my point, Alex. This situation is too volatile. I'm pleading with you here. Do not do anything rash. Your best chance of getting out is to sit tight and let us do our job.'

'Are you going to break down this door or not?'

'Please, Alex, just let us do our jobs.'

'I'll take that as a "no".'

King killed the call and shoved the cell phone back into his pocket. He glanced around the trashed kitchen. He had to get out. Had to get out now. He pulled the fire extinguisher off the wall and walked over to the door. It was heavier than he'd imagined, but was it heavy enough? He took a couple of deep breaths, filling his lungs. He could do this. He could make this work.

But what if it didn't work? What if the door refused to open? What if he just made a whole lot of noise? If that was the case then he might as well just walk into the next room and ask the bomber to shoot him. King stood there, indecision pulling him every which way. Being this close to freedom made him want to scream. In the end the decision was taken out of his hands. A motor hummed, metal rattled, and the steel grille started to descend.

12

The latest hostage to be released was someone named Bev. Rob had never seen her before, and doubted he'd ever see again. A producer or executive, he guessed. She looked the type, a real ball-breaker. He'd been hoping for a face the viewers would recognise. Still, any hostage was better than none. Anything that kept the story with him rather than Caroline Bradley was okay with him. CNN was watching.

The actual handover had gone smoothly enough. The front door had opened and a cop dressed in a Kevlar vest and helmet had walked over and placed the pizza boxes in the doorway. Thirty seconds later a shadowy arm had pulled them into the building, and thirty seconds after that Bev had come out. Rob's first thought was that the arm must have belonged to the bomber, but that would have been dumb. Why put himself at risk like that? No, it must have been one of the hostages. And if that was the case, then they had more self-discipline than he did. If it had been him looking out of that open door, there was no way he would have been able to stop himself from making a run for it.

Rob sidled up alongside Tara. 'We need to get out of here, and fast,' he whispered.

'What's the hurry?'

He didn't have time to reply because Aaron Walters was stalking towards them. The PR guy came to a halt in front of him. He was smiling, but there was no joy in it.

'This guy has a real hard-on for you. Maybe you should stay close by for when he lets out the next hostage.'

'No can do.'

Rob had positioned himself so Walters wouldn't be able to see Tara's face. He had his back to her but he could imagine her expression. Her jaw would be hitting the floor right about now. She'd be staring like he'd lost his mind. He understood exactly where she was coming from. All the other reporters were stuck on the wrong side of the barrier, while they had the equivalent of front row seats, and here he was saying thanks but no thanks.

'You sure about that?' Walters asked.

'Not my call. Seth wants us to record some MOTS. He likes to get his money's worth.'

Before the PR guy could respond, Rob grabbed Tara's arm and led her away from the lot.

'Jonah has more than enough MOTS,' she whispered. 'What's going on, Rob? And this better be good. It's not just you that he's going to crucify. You know how he likes to spread that love around.'

Rob didn't reply until they were well out of Walters' earshot. 'We need to find that cop I was talking to earlier. Jim Baker.'

Tara dragged him to a halt. 'You've got two seconds to start making sense or I'm hauling your ass back to the parking lot. Maybe it's not too late to save our jobs.'

'The cops know who the bomber is, and we're going to persuade Baker to get that name for us.'

'Just like that?'

'Have you got any better ideas?'

Tara shook her head.

'Let's go then.'

They found Baker where they'd left him, manning the barrier and looking bored to death. The younger cop was there as well, looking just as bored.

'You distract the kid while I talk to Baker. Can you do that?'

Tara tugged her T-shirt tight, then pulled herself to her full height. 'Easy,' she said.

'Baker,' Rob called out. 'You got a minute?'

Baker laughed. 'How many minutes do you want? It's not like I'm rushed off my feet here.'

From the corner of his eye, Rob saw Tara make a beeline for the younger cop. The kid's gaze drifted to her breasts, then shot back to her eyes. Tara was going to eat him alive. Rob herded Baker to a quiet spot where they wouldn't be overheard. He held up the pack of Lucky Strikes. This time he didn't need to ask twice.

'Your contact, how good is she?'

'I get you Alex King's name, and you've really got to ask?'

'I need her to get another name. This one's going to be tougher.'

'If it's in the system, she can get it.'

'I want the name of the bomber.'

Baker paused with the cigarette dangling from his mouth. He took a drag, blew out a cloud of smoke, then shook his head and sighed like a mechanic. 'That's a tough one.'

'Tough but doable, right?'

'Tough but doable,' Baker agreed. 'But I've got to ask. How much is that information worth to you?'

'Name your price,' Rob said.

13

'Anyone want some pizza?'

The bomber held the box up like it was a trophy. The smell alone was enough to turn JJ's stomach. Pizza was a once-a-week Tuesday-night indulgence. A Meat Feast, full-fat Pepsi, Ben and Jerry's Chocolate Fudge Brownie, and a double workout at the gym the next day. If she got out of this alive, she doubted she would ever eat pizza again.

'No takers? I've got to tell you that you're missing out on a real treat here. It's mighty fine pizza.'

He lifted the balaclava and took a bite. It was up long enough for JJ to catch a quick glimpse of his chin and mouth, long enough to notice the cheap dental work. With teeth like that she doubted he was a native of California. If he was then he was on the lowest rung of the income ladder. Which didn't make sense. If he was that broke, why on earth give away six million dollars?

The bomber finished eating and wiped his hands on his trousers. For a while he paced up and down in front of the hostages. JJ was watching him from the corner of her eye. He was walking casually, shoulders rolling. She'd seen that walk before, but couldn't place where. And then she got it, and the answer wasn't good. She'd seen soldiers walking like that on news reports from Afghanistan and Baghdad, faraway places seared to sand by the sun.

JJ knew she'd called this one right. The reason she'd been so successful was that she had a knack for reading people, and the story this guy was telling her was that he'd been a soldier, and that he had seen action. She reckoned he was too old for the second Gulf War and too young for Vietnam, so chances were he'd served in Desert Storm.

That would explain why he was so comfortable with guns and explosives. And it would also explain how he could be all action one second and completely disassociated the next. A soldier was deployed for months at a time. They couldn't stay in a constant state of battle readiness because it would drive them insane. In order to survive mentally they needed to be able to switch off during the down times. To disassociate, just like this guy had.

Two things clinched it. First was the way he was carrying his gun. His left hand was supporting the barrel and his right index finger was curled around the outside of the trigger guard. It was held high, ready to use at a second's notice. This was the way a soldier carried a gun. It was completely different from the way a hunter carried one. Hunters carried their guns low, like they had all the time in the world. When they used them, they took careful aim, waited for the perfect moment, then squeezed the trigger. If you were in a war zone you didn't have that luxury, because more often than not the people you were shooting at were shooting back.

The second reason was the way he'd killed without hesitation. The army claimed to train recruits. It didn't. Conditioning was a much better word for what they did. The bottom line was that a soldier who froze on the battlefield was useless. They needed to pull that trigger without hesitation, just like this guy had. The ability to do that came from firing thousands upon thousands of rounds at cardboard man-shaped targets, firing so many rounds that pulling the trigger came as naturally as breathing.

Even though JJ knew she was right, she wished she wasn't. The idea that she was trapped in here with a trained killer was somehow worse than the idea that she was trapped in here with a lunatic. It all came back to the question of motivation. Why would an ex-soldier risk life and liberty to do something like this? And why would he want to sell himself to the media as a modern-day Robin Hood?

Whichever way she looked at the situation there were just too many questions and nowhere near enough answers. She could analyse a situation better than anyone, but not this time, and the reason was because she was too close to what was happening here.

The bomber stopped pacing and grabbed another slice of pizza. He glanced around the room, the pizza slice held up for everyone to see.

'Still no takers?'

14

King looked around the trashed kitchen and wondered where you even began to tidy up a mess like this. He started by putting everything back in the drawers, working quietly and carefully and trying to make as little noise as possible. Getting things back into their proper place wasn't important. All that mattered was getting everything out of sight and creating the illusion that the place hadn't been searched by someone who was so desperate that all common sense had flown out the window.

His phone vibrated and he pulled it out. No doubt it was Brad Carter again. The FBI guy was probably pissed at being hung up on. Well, screw him. He wasn't stuck in here. It wasn't his ass on the line.

But it wasn't Carter. "Unknown number" flashed on the screen. For a moment King was convinced it was his ex. Clearly, they'd changed their number. That's why his phone hadn't recognised it. It was possible. He'd had plenty of numbers since they broke up, so why not? A spark of hope flared in his chest, only to be extinguished a second later when he worked out the flaw in his thinking. If his ex had changed numbers, they wouldn't have received his text.

The phone was still vibrating, the screen still flashing. Answer or don't answer? King connected the call.

'Who's this?' he whispered.

'Rob Taylor. How you holding up in there?'

King recognised the journalist's voice from earlier. He wanted to hang up, he knew he should hang up, but the loneliness wouldn't let him.

'Not so good, and I need to keep the line free, so whatever this is about, you best make it quick.'

'I'm just calling to see if you're okay. I thought you might appreciate hearing a friendly voice. You know, Alex, I've no idea how you're holding it together. If I was in your shoes, I think I'd be shitting myself right about now.'

'And who says I'm not? So, how are things looking out there?'

The silence on the other end of the line said more than a thousand words.

'That bad, huh?' he added.

'The bomber is releasing hostages.'

'Yeah, he's releasing the hostages that he's holding in the main part of the restaurant. What do you think he'll do if he finds me?'

The question was followed by another silence that spoke volumes.

'Probably best you don't answer that one,' King said.

'People are getting out.'

'And people are getting killed. The body count's up to four. If he hits the switch, he can add a whole load more to that figure.'

'Four,' said Taylor, puzzled. 'Last I heard it was three.'

'He killed someone else just before the last hostage handover.'

'Any idea who?'

'Sorry, man, I was in the restroom when it happened.'

'And who says the life of a big-time Hollywood actor isn't glamorous?'

King stifled a chuckle. He was actually starting to like this guy. Probably because he was the first person he'd spoken to in forever who wasn't Brad Carter. But he was a journalist. The thought was a sobering one. Taylor was doing a good impression of being his best buddy, but it was all an act. There was no reason to believe that Taylor was any different from every other journalist he'd met. All they ever cared about was the story.

'You're going to get out,' Taylor said. 'The cops and the FBI, they're on the case. You want to see it out here. It's like a circus.'

'Bullshit. The FBI could have got me out by now but they haven't. All they had to do was open the kitchen door while the hostage handover was going on.'

'They couldn't do it, Alex. The handover was televised, and the bomber was very specific about having both of Alfie's doors in the shot.'

'Because he thinks someone might try and escape,' King whispered. 'Jesus, he knows I'm here, doesn't he?'

'No, no, it's nothing like that,' Taylor said quickly. 'He just wants to make sure the FBI don't try anything while the grilles are up. It's okay, Alex. Just chill.'

'Easy for you to say, man.'

There was no response. King looked at his phone screen. It had gone black. He tapped it and pressed the on button, but nothing happened. He tried again and got the same result. Realisation dawned and he swore to himself. The battery had finally died.

15

Dr Sally Jenkins was on the main screen of Mission Control. She was an attractive forty-something brunette who came loaded with a list of credentials and diplomas longer than her cellulite-free legs. Finding a shrink in LA hadn't posed much of a problem. Throw a stone in any direction and you'd hit either a lawyer, a psychiatrist, or someone claiming to be an actor. Finding a shrink who wanted to appear on TV posed even less of a challenge. The fee was obviously an incentive, but that paled into insignificance when measured against the amount of free publicity a TV appearance would generate.

Caroline Bradley was sitting side-on to her desk, facing the psychiatrist. 'Dr Jenkins, we're now well into the third hour of the siege, how are the hostages going to be holding up?'

'That depends very much on the individual,' Jenkins replied smoothly. 'We all deal with stress in different ways. Some people internalise, some externalise. At the moment, the ones who hold it in will be faring better than the ones who need to vent because they can rely on well-established coping strategies. The ones who vent will be having a much tougher time.'

'Can you expand on that?'

'Certainly. Because of the circumstances, nobody will be doing anything that makes them stand out. This means that everyone is being forced to internalise their feelings, which, psychologically speaking, is never a good thing. Of course, the big problem is that a large percentage of the people who patronise Alfie's are leaders rather than followers.'

'People who are used to calling the shots?' Caroline suggested.

'Exactly. These people don't hold back, and they don't do deferred gratification. If they have an opinion, you can be sure that you're going to hear it. If they want to get something out there, they get it out. If they need something, they can get it with a click of their fingers. And now they're in a situation where they need to suppress their desires, because if they don't, they could die. That's tough for anyone, but it's going to be even tougher when you're used to everyone jumping when you say jump.'

Seth liked what he was seeing and hearing. Not only did Jenkins look great on TV, she had a straightforward delivery that avoided psychobabble. She was doing an excellent job of keeping it simple without being patronising. A large section of the TRN demographic would have trouble spelling "IQ", so having tough ideas and concepts broken down into easily digestible chunks was crucial.

'What about their emotional state?' Caroline asked.

'The hostages will be feeling a whole host of different emotions,' Jenkins replied. 'Obviously, they're going to be scared. That goes without saying. This will be the most terrifying situation that any of them have ever experienced. But they will be experiencing other emotions, too. Anger and guilt being the main two.'

'Guilt?'

'Absolutely. People have died. Now, we don't know exactly what happened there, but it's highly likely that the surviving hostages witnessed those deaths. This will lead to survivor guilt. That's a condition where a person thinks that they're to blame because they survived where others have died. The situation at Alfie's is a hothouse for survivor guilt.'

Caroline nodded like this was the most profound thing she'd ever heard. 'Some of the hostages have already been released, and we're obviously praying that the police manage to negotiate the safe release of the rest of them, but what happens afterwards?'

'They're going to need counselling for PTSD, that goes without saying.'

'Post-traumatic stress disorder?' Caroline said.

Dr Jenkins nodded. 'That's right.'

Of course they will, thought Seth, *and who's going to be first in line to offer that counselling at a gazillion bucks an hour?*

'Can you tell our viewers a little more about post-traumatic stress?'

'PTSD is an anxiety disorder that's caused by exposure to a major trauma. Sufferers often relive the event through flashbacks and nightmares, and they frequently make a conscious effort to avoid situations that remind them of the incident. In extreme cases this can be severely limiting, leading to agoraphobia and panic attacks. Sleep disorders and anger management issues are also common.'

'Rob's on the line,' the white lesbian called out.

'Well, patch him through.' Seth positioned his microphone closer to his mouth, and tried to ignore what was happening on the big screen. 'Rob, what have you got for me?'

'Good news and bad.'

'Let's start with the bad news.'

'The LAPD know who the bomber is, but my contact hasn't been able to get the name. He's going to keep trying, but they're keeping a tight lid on this one, Seth.'

'Have you tried leaning on Aaron Walters?'

'It won't do any good, not this time. I don't care what you've got on him, Seth, it's not going to be enough. If this information gets leaked, and that leak gets traced back to Walters, then he'll lose his job. Whatever you've got on him, if that gets out, I'm guessing that could also get him fired. We're talking rocks and hard places. Incidentally, what have you got on him? Tara's money's on kiddie porn.'

Seth chuckled. 'Ask no questions. So what's the good news?'

'I think I know how we can get the bomber's name, but it's going to cost us.'

'Whatever it takes.'

'Yeah, I thought you'd say that. And that's not the only good news.'

'I'm listening.'

'We might also have come up with a way to get Alex King out.'

16

The cell phone was dead. It didn't matter how much King poked and prodded, it wasn't about to come back to life any time soon. What had he been thinking, talking to that journalist? He thought he'd been alone before, but that was nothing compared to what he was experiencing now. At least when the phone had been working, he'd had a link to the outside world. It didn't matter that most of his conversations had been with Brad Carter, it was better to have someone to talk to than no one.

There would be no more calls from Carter. And no more texts. That second one cut deeper than the first. Every time King had picked up his phone, he'd hoped to see that little text envelope. He knew there was little to no chance of getting a reply to his "love u" text, but just thinking that he might had reminded him what it meant to hope.

For a split second he considered asking the FBI to push a new battery through the hole in the restroom wall, but that was a dumbass idea. To start with, a battery was far too big. And secondly, how the hell would he get in touch to ask them? Thinking about the hole got him thinking about the spy camera. If the FBI could come up with a miniature camera, they must have a two-way radio that was just as small. Again, the problem he kept coming back to was that he had no way to contact the FBI.

Except there was a way, he suddenly realised. It would be risky, but it wasn't like he had any other option. King scrambled to his feet and pushed the kitchen door open. Everything seemed quiet enough out there. He could hear mumbled voices but there was something artificial about them, like the sound was coming through low quality speakers. He listened more closely and realised he was hearing a news report playing on the laptop. The volume was too low to make out what was being said, but the tone of the voices contained that sense of urgency you heard on news channels.

King slipped into the corridor, gently pulling the door closed behind him. His socks shushed against wood, making a whispering noise that seemed as loud as thunder. In the silence, he imagined he could hear his heart beating. When he reached the threshold to the restaurant's lower level, he got down on his knees and crawled the last few yards. Every squeak and scrape sounded enormous. He'd never felt more exposed. For a second he sat with his back to the wall, eyes shut, willing his heart to calm. The greenery above his head swished gently in the currents created by the air-conditioning. He opened his eyes and glanced at the swaying leaves.

All he had to do was reach up and grab the camera. What could be simpler? He raised his arm and pushed his hand carefully into the thick forest of plants, slowly parting the foliage, fingers searching. He could feel the cold smoothness of the leaves brushing against his skin, but where the hell was the camera? His stomach was in his mouth and he felt sick. He was sure he was searching in the right place.

He moved a little higher and peered over the lip of the wall. Beyond the swaying leaves, he caught glimpses of bodies. The scared huddle of hostages on the upper level, and the blood-soaked corpses lying discarded around the room. The camera was off to his left, a couple of inches from where he'd been searching.

He reached for it, and the bomber suddenly stood up. King stopped dead with his hand frozen among the leaves. For a moment he just knelt there with the wooden floor digging into his knees and tried to keep as still as possible. It was like everything had gone into slow motion. An impression of the knife was burning into his thigh. King was expecting the bomber to turn towards him and start down the stairs. He didn't. Instead, he walked over to the hostages.

'On your feet, Tony.'

King didn't recognise the restaurant owner at first because his face was so messed up. Both eyes were puffy and bruised, and it looked like his nose was broken. He let go of the breath he'd been holding onto and shrank behind the wall. His eyes were now level with the top. A fraction of an inch lower and he'd be staring at the brickwork. The upper level was a green blur, but he could just about make out what was happening up there, and he could hear every word.

'You know what goes well with pizza?' the bomber said. 'A nice cold glass of cola. You'd think the all-seeing, all-knowing FBI might have thought of that, wouldn't you? I can't say I'm surprised, though. That's the problem with the world today. Everybody's too wrapped up in themselves. Where's the giving? Where's the love?'

'I can get you a cola,' Tony said. 'It's no problem.'

'A regular cola? Sugar, caffeine, ice?'

Tony nodded.

'Well, what are you waiting for?'

The restaurant owner hurried towards the stairs, and King shrank back down behind the wall. He was about to race back to the restroom when he remembered why he was out here in the first place. He reached up, grabbed the camera and stuffed it into his pocket. There was no time for subtlety, no time to be careful. He just reached up and grabbed and hoped for the best.

Tony was on the stairs now, his naked feet padding heavily on wood. King glanced anxiously along the corridor. There was no way he'd make the restroom in time. The men's or the women's. The office was closer, but he probably wouldn't reach that either. The kitchen was all the way at the end of the corridor, so that was a complete non-starter.

He hurried along the corridor anyway, moving as fast as he dared. Tony had already reached the lower level. He could hear his footsteps getting closer. The door to the women's restroom was only a few feet away. King reached it and grabbed for the handle, knowing that it was already too late. He glanced over his shoulder just in time to see the restaurant owner turn into the corridor.

17

'This better be good.'

Aaron Walters might have been smiling, but Rob wasn't fooled. Walters was a PR man. He smiled when he was happy, he smiled when he was pissed, and his smile was just as broad and beaming when he was jamming a knife into your back. Tara made up the threesome. They were standing at the bottom of the Mobile Command Unit's stairs, continually stepping aside to let people past like it was a new kind of dance.

'Let's move over there,' Rob suggested, indicating an empty stretch of sidewalk.

'I don't have time for this.'

'Make time.'

Walters sighed heavily, then followed Rob over to the sidewalk.

'You've got my complete and undivided attention for the next thirty seconds. Whatever you've got to say, make it quick.'

'I know how we can get Alex King out.'

'Okay, before we go any further, this conversation is most definitely off the record.' Walters glanced at Tara. 'If you have any recording devices currently activated, please turn them off.'

'No recording devices.' She smiled sweetly and put her hands up in mock surrender. 'Promise and cross my heart.'

Rob opened his mouth to speak and Walters shushed him with the hand.

'Furthermore, if you make any mention of Alex King before this situation is resolved then you will effectively be signing his death warrant. If King dies, I will have you arrested on every charge I can think of. Your thirty seconds starts now.'

'This guy is smart,' Rob said quickly. 'You've only got to look at where he's chosen to make his play to realise that. Alfie's is basically a concrete bunker. There's no way to storm it without a ton of collateral damage, and there's no way that's going to happen because of who's inside. Can you imagine the fallout if the LAPD or FBI attempt a rescue and Ed Richards winds up dead? That would make Waco look like the PR coup of the century.'

'If you've got a point, get there fast. You've got ten seconds.'

'The fact he's so smart is his Achilles' heel. Each time he's released a hostage, he's wanted both doors in the camera shot. And each time there's been at least a minute or two where nothing's happened. We've basically had our camera trained on a blank wall.'

'So what?'

Rob sighed. He couldn't believe he was having to spell out something that was so obvious. Either Walters was a complete idiot, or he was being purposefully obtuse.

'So, we have film footage of a wall and two doors and nothing much happening. The next time any hostages are released we broadcast that footage instead of broadcasting live. That'll give your people time to get the kitchen door open and get King out. As soon as the front doors are about to open we switch to the live feed and the bomber's none the wiser. It could work.'

'It could,' Walters agreed. 'Except for one thing. We've lost contact with King.'

'What do you mean you've lost contact? How?'

'We think his cell phone battery has died. We know it was running low, so hopefully that's the case.'

'And if it's not the battery, then the bomber has found him.'

Walters didn't respond. He didn't have to. If the bomber had found him then he was probably already dead.

'Shit,' Rob said.

'Look, it's a good idea. And if we manage to get in touch with King again, it's definitely something that's worth pursuing.'

Walters reached out but stopped short of patting Rob on the shoulder. He turned and headed back to the Mobile Command Unit. Rob watched him go.

'He might still be alive,' Tara said.

Rob answered with a cynical look.

'Yeah, you're right,' she added. 'Chances are he's dead. Has Baker got back to you with the bomber's name yet?'

Rob took out his cell and switched it on. No missed calls, no voicemails, no texts. He shook his head. 'No, nothing yet.'

He pulled up Baker's number and connected the call. It rang five times then went to voicemail. He didn't leave a message. The cop would see his number and know why he was calling. That would be enough to hurry him along. Baker would be in as much of a hurry to get the name as he was. The dollar signs flashing in front of his eyes would ensure that.

'So what now?' Tara asked.

'Now I guess we just wait for something to happen.'

18

The restaurant owner kept on coming towards King. 'TONY' was scribbled on his forehead in big red capitals, and his enormous gut was hanging over his silk boxer shorts. He was heading straight towards him like he wasn't there, calm and self-assured, one foot following the other. He must have seen him. How could he miss him when he was stood here like a deer pinned in the headlights of an eighteen-wheeler Mack?

Then he got it. The bomber would be listening. Any hesitation, any change in the sound of Tony's footsteps, and he would come to investigate. The restaurant owner's quick thinking had probably saved his life. Tony met his eye and placed a finger on his lips. He pointed to the kitchen door as he breezed past, and King fell in step behind him.

The sound of the kitchen door clattering open was shocking because he'd got so used to opening it quietly. He glanced over his shoulder, then realised it was okay. The bomber would be expecting to hear certain noises, and Tony was delivering in line with those expectations. That's why he wasn't tiptoeing around like the world was made from eggshells. The door swung shut on its spring hinge, locking them into a bubble of silence.

'I wondered where you'd disappeared to,' Tony whispered. His voice was muffled as a result of his busted nose, and his accent had changed dramatically, a seismic shift from affected camp to the rough growl of a blue-collar worker from the tri-state area. New York or New Jersey, somewhere up there on the Eastern seaboard. This came as no great surprise. King knew better than anyone that everyone had a past they wanted to bury.

'The FBI have been in contact,' he whispered back.

'Are they going to get us out?'

'I don't know. They say they're working on it, but they're all talk. I'm not seeing much in the way of action.'

Tony rummaged around in a drawer for a bottle opener, then went over to the refrigerator, pulled out a Coke and flipped the top off. 'You've got to tell them to hurry up. There's a whole bunch of scared people in there.'

'I'm with you on that one, man. The problem is that my cell's died.'

The restaurant owner stopped what he was doing and faced him. 'Shit.'

'I know, I know. It's a disaster. I'm going crazy back here. I keep expecting to be discovered at any second.'

Tony grabbed a glass, threw in a few ice cubes, and poured the Coke. He glanced around the kitchen like he was just seeing the mess for the first time. 'What the hell happened here?'

'I'm sorry. I was looking for the back door key.'

Without a word, Tony walked over to the drawers nearest the door.

'It's not in there. I checked it like a dozen times.'

Tony ignored him, pulled the top drawer open, then reached underneath. There was a tearing sound of tape coming away from wood. He walked back over and handed King the key.

'Here you go. Not that it's going to do any good.'

'How do you figure that?'

'Next time the grilles go up, you're going to make a run for it? That's the plan, right?'

King remembered what the journalist had said about the TV crew keeping both doors in the shot, and realised where Tony was going with this. 'The bomber's watching the news?'

Tony nodded. 'If you try to escape, he'll see you.'

'So why give me the key?'

'Because it's always best to have options. Who knows what's going to happen next?'

'I guess.'

'Look, I need to go before I'm missed.'

Tony patted him on the shoulder then turned to leave. He reached the door and turned back.

'Good luck, Alex.'

The door crashed open, then swung closed, and Tony was gone.

15:30–16:00

1

JJ forced herself to sit still. It wasn't easy. The tsunami of nervous energy crashing through her body had no outlet. It just kept building and building and building. She resisted the urge to chew her fingernails and twist her hair around her finger, two nervous habits she hadn't indulged in since she was a kid.

It seemed like Tony had been gone ages, but it was only a couple of minutes. What was he doing back there? Nothing stupid, she hoped. If he was cooking up some crazy scheme with King, chances were it would probably end in failure and result in even more deaths. JJ looked over at the bomber. If he was concerned about how long Tony was taking, it didn't show. He'd powered down again. Even though he was looking at the laptop screen, he wasn't really seeing it. She was more convinced than ever that he'd been a soldier. It was like he was conserving his energy, ready to spring into action at any moment.

A distant door banged shut. The kitchen door, judging from the way it was flapping back and forth. Out of the banging came the sound of bare feet padding along the corridor that lay beyond the lower level. A couple of seconds later Tony walked around the corner. His face looked worse than ever, the bruises turning all the shades of purple. He was carrying a tall glass of cola and there was a slight tremble in his hand. He walked up the stairs and stopped in front of the bomber. Everything went still, like the pause button had been hit, then the bomber suddenly stood up.

'Tony, you're back. It's real good to see you.'

Tony just stood there with the glass trembling at the end of his outstretched arm, ice cubes tinkling. The bomber took the glass and put it down on the nearest table.

'Turn around.'

Tony turned around and the bomber patted his boxer shorts. JJ felt her stomach drop. He was going to find a knife hidden in there. She was sure of it. The bomber stepped back and she breathed again.

'Open your mouth.'

Tony hesitated and JJ's stomach plummeted yet again. The idiot was hiding something in his mouth. But what sort of weapon could you hide in your mouth? The restaurant owner opened wide and the bomber peered inside, gazing intently through the slits of the balaclava.

'Always best to be careful, that's what my momma used to tell me. Measure twice, cut once. Okay, sit down.'

Instead of going back to where he'd been sitting, Tony came and sat beside her. Eyes down, she stared at the grain in the wood. She was aware of him settling alongside her, shifting his massive bulk to get comfortable. He was breathing through his mouth rather than through his broken nose. Low, wheezing gasps. The bomber smacked his lips together and JJ glanced over. His balaclava was rolled up to reveal his mouth and he was staring at his glass like it contained an expensive Bordeaux. He sipped the drink, smacked his lips together again, then let out a satisfied, 'Ah.' He looked up. 'Now, that really hit the spot. Anyone thirsty? It's got to be a couple of hours since you last had a drink.'

JJ was parched, but there was no way she was going to admit that. Stay invisible. Chances were, she wasn't the only one feeling thirsty, and chances were she wasn't the only one sat here biting her tongue.

'I'll take that as a no. I've got to tell you, though, you don't know what you're missing.'

JJ heard the grin in his voice. The sick bastard was getting a kick out of taunting them. She just didn't get it. The entertainment industry was cut-throat, but nothing she'd seen in Hollywood came close to this. This guy made the sharks that swam around this town look as threatening as minnows. She figured that was the difference between real violence and the posturing, pretend variety.

'So, do any of you good folks need to take a piss?'

JJ's bladder suddenly felt fuller than it had ever felt. Judging by the way everyone was shuffling around, she wasn't the only one suffering. The bomber wiped his hands on his pants, then pulled a pack of adult diapers from his backpack. He held them up for everyone to see.

'You need to piss, you use one of these. Understand? Anyone makes a puddle on this nice floor and I will not be happy.'

He moved around the hostages, dropping diapers. One landed next to JJ. She pulled it closer and wedged it under her leg. She was working hard to keep her disgust from showing. This was just another way to screw with them. The bomber stopped when he reached Tony. He hesitated, then dropped a diaper in his lap.

'It's one size fits all, I'm afraid. You'll just have to do the best you can.'

He finished distributing the diapers then grabbed another slice of pizza. Everyone was glancing uncertainly at each other, but no one was putting on their diaper. JJ reckoned she could hold on for a while longer. She had to. The alternative didn't bear thinking about. The bomber folded the pizza slice in two, took a large bite, chewed for a while, then chased it down with a swallow of Coke. His chin was square and stubble free. It was a strong chin. The pulsing heart on his big jogger's watch was flashing well within the safe limit.

'King's back there. He seems to be holding up okay.' Tony was leaning against JJ's shoulder. His lips were so close she felt the whisper rather than heard it. She wanted to reply, but couldn't without turning around. She couldn't take that risk. Any movement would alert the bomber. She'd already had one strike. Two and she'd be out.

'He's been talking to the FBI, but his cell phone's died.'

JJ glanced over at Natasha Lovett's orange canvas bag, then went back to staring at the floor. There had to be thirty cell phones in that bag. It was crazy. This was the age of communication. You took it for granted that you could connect to anyone in the world in seconds, by computer or phone. And the thing was, most of those communications were meaningless, a waste of breath and words. Then, that one time when you really needed to contact someone, the technology let you down. The signal died or the computer crashed. Or the battery ran out. If that didn't define irony, JJ didn't know what did.

The weight on her arm eased as Tony settled back into his own space. She quickly tallied up the pros and cons in her head, but all she could see were a whole load of negatives and very few positives. The fact that the authorities hadn't been able to get King out was the biggest negative on her list. It was right there at the top, filling the number one slot. Up until now she hadn't realised how much she'd been clinging onto the slim hope that he'd somehow escaped. If even one person could escape, then there was a chance for the rest of them.

The other big negative was that King was an unknown quantity. JJ hated unknown quantities. She liked certainties. She liked to know the answers to questions before she asked them. Knowing how a film or a book ended did nothing to reduce the enjoyment for her. Tony said the actor was holding up, but that was based on spending a couple of minutes with him, and a couple of minutes was nowhere near long enough to make that sort of assessment. JJ had lost count of the number of times she'd sat down with a client who'd tried to convince her everything was A-okay, when it obviously wasn't.

There was no telling how King was holding up. He was isolated and alone and probably bouncing from one emotional extreme to another. The only positive she could come up with was that if he'd lasted this long without getting caught, then maybe he'd manage to keep his head down until the cops made their big play.

But what were the cops up to out there? JJ tried to put herself in their shoes. Maybe there wasn't going to be any big play. Maybe that was just wishful thinking. What if they were playing the long game? That would be consistent with what had happened so far. Thirteen hostages had been released, thirteen people who'd live to see another day. It was easy to see how that could be spun into a PR win.

Perhaps the strategy was to get them out one at a time. But what happened when they got down to the last person? Would the bomber just open the doors and let that person go, then come out with his hands up? Or would he go out with a bang, taking that hostage with him?

The restaurant phone rang, fracturing the silence. The bomber glanced over but didn't answer it. He finished his pizza, then tugged his balaclava back into place. The phone was still ringing.

'Jody, stand up and come on over here.'

JJ felt as though her heart was being crushed in a vice. The bomber had heard Tony whispering and assumed it was her. This was her second strike. Her final strike. She stood up slowly on legs made from rubber. The ringing telephone was burrowing into her brain like a migraine. The bomber was grinning again, his expression partially hidden behind the balaclava. The bastard was toying with her. Any second now the rug was about to be pulled from under her feet. The telephone stopped ringing and an awful silence claimed the room. JJ started walking. It was the longest walk of her life.

2

'I've got the bomber's name.'

Mission Control went very still. Every single pair of eyes turned towards the Asian kid. He was on his feet, hardly able to contain himself. Seth was staring along with everyone else. One of the MOTS was playing on the main screen. Rob Taylor was talking to a low-IQ specimen who had a buzz cut and no doubt knew a great recipe for roadkill stew.

'Ted Marley,' the Asian kid said.

'And you're sure about that?'

'Absolutely certain. I got the name from LA Abuse. They didn't want to give it up, but I can be very persuasive.'

'How much did you offer?'

'Ten thousand,' the Asian kid said quietly.

'Which is coming out of your salary, I suppose.'

The kid's face turned white.

'Relax,' Seth said. 'What else have you got?'

'The payment came from the Allied Bank of Idaho.'

'Never heard of it.'

'I'm not surprised. It's tiny. It's based in Twin Falls. The city only has a population of 44,000.'

Seth considered this for a second.

'Okay people, listen up and listen good. This guy's way too smart to make a dumb mistake like using some piddly little bank nobody's heard of when he could have used the Bank of

America. The only reason he'd make a move like this is because he wants us to find out who he is, and to do that we start by looking in Twin Falls. Okay, everyone who isn't crucial to keeping the pictures flowing to the homes of our esteemed viewers hit the phones and the Internet. I want to know everything there is to know about Ted Marley. Has everyone got that?'

A wave of nods and murmured yeses went around the room.

'Then why in the name of all that's holy are you just sat there gawping?'

Seth rocked back in his big leather chair as Mission Control exploded into a frantic whirlwind of motion and sound. He grinned to himself. It was almost like being in a real newsroom again.

3

After Tony had disappeared through the flapping kitchen door, King had snuck back along the corridor to the restroom. He was sitting on the tiled floor now, the tiny spy camera in his hand. Freedom was blowing through the hole in the wall, and the choking heat-seared stink of an LA summer had never smelled so good. The tiles were cold and hard against his back and butt.

He stared into the camera's tiny lens and made two distinct gestures. First, he held his hand up to the side of his head in the universally acknowledged mime for a telephone. Thumb and little finger sticking out, the other fingers curled into his palm. Then he held his hand up and moved his fingers slowly toward his thumb to indicate small. All those hours of acting lessons, all that time, money and effort, and it boiled down to this, a mime that any kid could do. He needed to get in touch with Brad Carter. Right now, he would do anything to hear the FBI guy's voice again.

He pointed the camera at his face and whispered, 'Miniature radio.' He wasn't sure if the camera had a microphone. It probably did, but even if it didn't, there had to be someone out there who could read lips. He peered through the hole in the wall, hoping to see one of those metallic tubes being pushed through, but all he saw was daylight.

He held the camera at arm's length and repeated his mime. Then he moved the camera towards his face and whispered,

'Miniature radio.' He peeked through the hole and saw nothing but daylight.

He did it all again.

Mime, whisper, look.

Still nothing.

Mime, whisper, look.

4

The bomber swung a chair around and JJ lowered herself carefully into it. She felt sick. Mostly because of what was happening, but the smell wasn't helping. When she'd arrived here two and a half hours ago the restaurant had smelled like heaven. Now it smelled like hell. Old pizza, older food, the burnt acrid tang of spent ammunition, the smell of death. *This is the moment my life ends*, she thought. *This is the time and this is the place.*

The restaurant telephone rang again, and again the bomber ignored it. Half the hostages were staring at her, the rest were staring at the telephone. The sound drilled into JJ's head, shrill and annoying. The bomber positioned a second chair opposite hers, a distance of four feet separating them.

'Dan, get over here.'

Dan Stone glanced around warily. He looked like hell. He'd been running his nervous fingers through his usually immaculate hair, leaving it a spiky porcupine mess. Stray strands stuck out in all directions. The red letters on his forehead were smudged. The bomber levelled his gun and took aim. The silence in the room was punctuated by the ringing telephone.

'Come on, Dan. Surely you must have worked out how the game's played by now. Do you really want to become another example of the futility of passive resistance?'

The telephone rang one final time, then went quiet. The sudden silence was somehow worse. JJ willed Stone to stand up. She didn't care much for the agent, but she didn't want to see him die. Not here. Not like this. There had been too much death today. She kept her mouth shut, though, her eyes fixed on one of the paint-splashed canvases. The bomber raised his gun and aimed it at Stone. He didn't say anything because he didn't need to. Stone stood slowly and padded across the room. He sat down in the empty chair and stared at the floor.

'I picked up on some tension earlier. Now, you two need to get things talked out.' The bomber was looking at JJ as he said this. She held his gaze even though it was uncomfortable. The way he was staring made her want to squirm. 'Jody, is there anything you want to say to Dan?'

She broke eye contact and stared at the floor.

'What about you, Dan? Anything you want to share?'

Stone glanced up at the bomber, then went back to staring at the floor.

'Let me put it another way. You've got ten seconds. If you're still not talking after those ten seconds are up then I'm going to shoot both of you in the head. It's all about choices, remember? Choose to live, choose to die.' The bomber looked at his watch. The heartbeat was pulsing quicker than it had been earlier. 'Your ten seconds start now,' he said, and started counting down.

JJ wanted to say something, but the connection between her brain and mouth was broken. The countdown wasn't helping. Every time she got even half a thought in her head, she'd get distracted by the numbers and her mind would go blank. The bomber reached three and she braced herself for the gunshot. She was about to shout, 'No!', figuring that it had to be better than saying nothing, but Stone beat her to it.

'I wouldn't be here if it wasn't for her,' he said quietly. 'She made the reservation. She told me she could get us in here no problem because she was best friends with the owner. She wanted to show off, wanted me to know what a big shot she was.'

'And you agreed to come, Dan. So enough with all that "poor me" crap. You might remember differently, but the way I remember it, you bit my hand off when I offered to bring you here.'

JJ glared at Stone, and Stone glared back.

'Okay, Dan,' the bomber said. 'Jody's just called you a freeloading son of a bitch. How are you going to respond?'

Before Stone could reply, the telephone rang again. The sound made JJ jump. Each ring was jangling her nerves closer to breaking point. The bomber marched over and snatched it up.

'Louise, honey, you obviously don't know how to take a hint, so let me spell it out. If I'm not calling you, it means I don't want to talk. Phone me again and I'll shoot a hostage. You can even choose which one.'

The bomber killed the call and slammed the phone down on the table. The jolt banged the laptop back to life and he looked over. For a moment he stared at the screen, then he turned the computer around to face the hostages. It took JJ a second to realise she was looking at a photograph of herself. This picture had been taken at a charity event she'd attended back in March. The reason she was able to place it was because it had been one of those rare occasions when she'd worn a dress.

'Shall we see what they're saying about you, Jody?'

The bomber hit a key on the laptop. A beat of silence, then the news reporter on the screen said, 'Jody Johnson has single-handedly built up a highly successful PR company, but her life has not been without its share of tragedy.'

The ball of ice that had settled in JJ's gut was slowly pushing outwards to fill her chest, her stomach, her limbs. *Please, God, don't go there*, she thought. Except the woman on the screen was going there. It didn't matter how much she wished or prayed, she couldn't stop that happening. She knew how this game was played. If you wanted public sympathy, if you wanted empathy, you had to show them some humanity, a glimpse of the real. The background picture changed to a picture of a man, and JJ's heart broke all over again. She felt the love, felt the loss. Most of all, though, she felt the guilt.

'Two years ago, her husband, movie executive Tom Sanderson, committed suicide. He was only thirty-six when he died.'

The bomber closed the laptop lid with a snap that sounded like the end of everything. JJ shut her eyes but she couldn't stop time sliding backwards. She was back in the house she'd shared with Tom for all those years. She'd been working late and it was dark. Tom's Mercedes was parked in the drive and every light in the house was blazing.

The second she'd walked through the door she'd known something was wrong. A cold wind had blown through her, freezing her momentarily to the spot. She'd told herself to get it together, then forced herself to walk through the house. To start with she'd called out his name in a voice that sounded just like her own. By the end, she was screaming it.

She'd found him face down in the pool, swirls of beige vomit contrasting against the bright blue.

'Looks like you've got lots to share,' the bomber said.

The bastard was grinning again.

5

Tara leant against a wall, eyes glued to her cell phone. The screen was too small for Rob to work out what she was up to, but he could see that she was logged on to a gambling site.

'Who's favourite to get the next bullet?' he asked.

'It's still Ed Richards. But you can only get odds of two to five, so it's really not worth the effort. The odds of him being last man standing is evens, which is almost as bad.'

'So who's your money on?'

'I've got fifty bucks at five to one on DeAndre Alexander being the last man standing. I've got a good feeling about him. And I could do with the money. I'm behind with my rent.'

Rob laughed. 'Like that's something new. So, what are the odds on Kevin Donahue?'

Tara tapped the screen of her phone. 'Best I can get you there is four dollars on a buck.'

'Put me down for a hundred.'

The theme from *The Exorcist* drifted up from Rob's pocket. He connected the call and put it on speaker so Tara could hear.

'Hey Seth, what's new?'

'We've got the bomber's name.'

'How?'

'One of my minions got it from LA Abuse.'

Rob felt his heart kick up a gear. It didn't matter that the name hadn't come from Baker. Whatever got the job done. The important thing was that TRN were first with the story. Anything that kept the spotlight angled in his direction was fine by him. 'I hope you said thank you.'

Seth barked out a laugh then turned serious again. 'Look, don't get too excited. When I say we've got his name, what I mean is that I'm ninety-nine point nine per cent certain that we've got his name. Which is why I'm calling. We need to get Aaron Walters to confirm it.'

'Not going to happen, Seth. There's no way Walters is going to play ball with us on this one.'

'Jesus H Christ, am I surrounded by idiots?' Seth was roaring so loud the sound was distorting. Tara grimaced then made a sympathetic face at Rob. 'You don't need verbal confirmation, you just need to arrange a meeting with the guy, drop the name and watch his reaction. It's not exactly rocket science.'

The phone went dead. For a second Rob just stood there staring at it and shaking his head.

'So what are you waiting for?' Tara said. 'Best jump to it before Jonah tears you a new asshole.'

'There's one slight problem. Before I can get confirmation of the name, I need to know what the name is.'

Tara made another face. This one translated as "ouch". 'And to do that you need to phone Jonah back,' she finished for him.

'And that's one conversation I'm really looking forward to.' Rob sighed. 'To think I used to believe being a reporter was all glitz and glamour and good times.'

'And now you're procrastinating. There's no point postponing the inevitable, Rob. You'll have to talk to him eventually.'

Rob sighed again, then made the call.

6

Mime, whisper, look.

Alex King peered into the hole, but all he saw was daylight. He went through the routine again. Mime, whisper, look. He'd lost count of how many times he'd done this. It could have been a hundred, or a thousand, or even a million. His plan was to keep going until those FBI dumbasses worked it out. He could feel his frustration growing. Any idiot could work out what he was getting at, so what was the hold-up?

Mime, whisper, look.

He peered into the hole again and was about to repeat the routine when a noise stopped him dead. It was a kind of scratching sound, like someone out there was doing their best to move around stealthily. The daylight was suddenly eclipsed as a new tube was pushed through the hole. Metal scratched against cinderblock, the noise getting closer and louder.

King caught the tube and unscrewed the lid. It took longer than it should have because he was in too much of a rush. He wanted what was inside, wanted it now. He tipped the tube upside down but nothing came out. He peered into it and saw something jammed in there. A tangle of wires and bits of plastic. He gave the tube a hard shake and a loop of wire dropped out, just enough so he could pull the rest of the device free. At one end of the curly wire was an earpiece, at the other was a throat mike.

For a second all he could do was stare. Somehow his plan had worked. Hand shaking, he fitted the earpiece, stuck the mike to his throat, then arranged the wires. This was so cool. Give him a pair of shades and a dark suit and he could have passed for a secret service agent. He touched the throat mike.

'Are you there, Brad?' he whispered. He paused a second, then added, 'Over.'

7

In the end Rob didn't need to call Aaron Walters because the LAPD spokesman came looking for him. The first he knew about it was when Tara elbowed him in the side and nodded towards the Mobile Command Unit. Rob looked up from his cell phone and saw Walters striding towards them. The PR guy was a man on a mission, and clearly not happy.

'Wonder what's got him all hot and bothered,' Tara said.

'Aside from the fact we're still alive and breathing, I can't think of anything we've done in the last couple of minutes to piss him off.'

Walters pulled up in front of them. His face was hard and unreadable, which was telling in itself. This was a negotiator's face. The PR man clearly wanted something, and that made Rob very happy.

'So, what can I do for you, Mr Walters?'

'This idea of yours for getting King out, will it work?'

'It'll work.'

'And you're absolutely certain about that? Certain enough to risk King's life? To risk the lives of the other hostages? Because I want us to be very clear about something, Mr Taylor. If this goes wrong and he dies then I will make it my personal mission, my *only* mission in life, to make sure that you are held accountable.'

'It's a simple piece of TV trickery,' Tara said. 'And do you know what the great thing with TV is? People know they shouldn't believe what they hear and see, but they still go right on believing anyhow.'

Walters fixed her with a hard stare. 'I hope to God you're right.'

'I take it this means that you're back in touch with King?' Rob said.

'This is strictly off the record?'

Rob nodded.

'Yes, we're back in touch with him.'

'Can I ask how?'

'You can ask, but I'll politely decline to answer.'

'Remember, it was you who came to us asking for favours.'

'And remember, you could be stuck on the other side of the barrier with everyone else, so don't even think about playing that card.' A tight smile. 'Okay, I want you two to wait here. I'll let you know when we're ready to do this.'

'Works for me,' Rob said. 'How about you, Tara?'

'Yeah, works for me, too.'

Walters shook his head, then marched back towards the Mobile Command Unit. Rob waited until he'd got a couple of yards, then called out, 'One more thing.'

Walters stopped and turned.

'Does the name Ted Marley mean anything to you?'

'Never heard of him.'

Walters spun on his heels and carried on walking, and Rob took out his cell phone. He'd been watching the PR guy carefully, looking for any tic or tell, no matter how subtle. Seth answered on the third ring.

'I've got that confirmation you wanted,' he said. 'Ted Marley is definitely the bomber.'

8

'Tell me what happened, Jody.'

'I can't.'

The words were barely a whisper. There was no way she was going back there again. It wasn't going to happen. It had taken a long time and a load of therapy, but she'd eventually managed to move to a place where she could live with the darkness that had followed in the wake of Tom's death. Life was about light. It was about living. That was her mantra. The room had fallen totally silent. Breathing and movement were being kept to an absolute minimum. It was like being underwater.

'It's good to share, Jody.'

'I'm not doing this,' she said quietly.

The bomber walked over to Dan Stone and pushed the gun into the back of the agent's head. 'Maybe you need a moment to reflect on that. Please don't take too long, though.'

Stone's eyes went wide. 'Jesus, JJ, tell him what he wants to know. For Christ's sake, just do it.'

'Careful,' the bomber warned. 'Blasphemy's a sin. It's right up there at number three on the list. Believe it or not, it comes before "thou shalt not kill", which has got to tell you something about the Big Guy's priorities. In my humble opinion, any God who values words more than a life has really lost their way.'

JJ looked down at her hands. Her fingers were knotted tightly together to stop the shakes, but it wasn't working. So much for being invisible. That spotlight was shining down so brightly it was blinding. Why had he singled her out like this? It wasn't fair. Then again, life wasn't fair. She'd learned that one a long time ago. If it had been fair then Tom would still be alive. As to the question of why the bomber was doing this, when it came to his reasons for doing anything, he was a law unto himself. At the end of the day, he was a sadist, and that was all JJ needed to know.

'You have five seconds starting now,' the bomber said.

'JJ, just tell him what he wants to know,' Stone pleaded. 'I'm begging you here.'

'Shut up!' she screamed back at him. 'Shut up, shut up! Shut! Up!'

'This is good, Jody,' the bomber said. 'Let it all out, honey. But bear in mind that you've only got three seconds left before I pull the trigger and decorate the floor with the contents of Dan's head.'

'You bastard.'

The bomber laughed. 'Sweetheart, believe me when I tell you that I've been called a lot worse.'

JJ glared, then looked away. A single candle was still burning on one of the lower-level tables. The flame was flickering orange and yellow and casting graphite shadows that danced on the wall.

'Three, two.'

The bomber reaffirmed his grip on the gun. His finger tightened on the trigger. Stone had his head in his hands, weeping and blubbering and pleading.

'It was all my fault,' JJ said quietly. 'I'm the reason Tom's dead.'

9

'Good to hear your voice again, Alex.'

King pressed the throat mike. 'And yours,' he whispered. 'Over.'

'It distorts the sound when you press the mike against your throat. And you don't need to keep saying "over". They only do that in the movies.'

'Sorry.'

'Hey, don't be. I've got some good news. We've come up with a plan to get you out of there.'

A surge of hope flooded through King. 'How?'

'I don't want to say too much at this stage.'

King picked up on the reason immediately. If he was discovered back here, then the less he knew, the better. That was the only reason for keeping him out of the loop. What he didn't know, he couldn't tell. It was that simple.

'There's something we need you to do for us first,' Carter said.

'You want me to put the camera back, right?'

'I'm sorry buddy, but we need to see what's happening in there.'

King opened his mouth to speak, then shut it again. The suspicious side of his mind was suddenly working overtime.

'You okay, Alex? You've gone quiet.'

'This plan of yours, it doesn't actually exist. You're lying to me, aren't you?'

'And why would we do that?'

'Oh, I don't know, Brad. Maybe if I think I'm getting out then I'll be more likely to say yes when you want me to do something. Like put your camera back. A little hope goes a long way, right?'

'You've got it all wrong, Alex.'

'Do I? In that case tell me what the plan is.'

Brad sighed. 'I can't, Alex. I've already told you that. You've just got to trust me on this one.'

King snorted. 'Trust you? Yeah, that's a good one. The truth is that I'm more use to you in here than I am out there. If I get out, then who's going to plant your damn devices? That's what's really going on here, right?'

'There is a plan, Alex.'

'Okay, let's assume for a second that you are telling the truth. What happens if I don't put the camera back?'

'That's your prerogative.'

'No, it's not. If I say no then you'll drag your heels and I'll never get out.'

'That's not how we work. Our goal is to get everyone out alive. You and all the other hostages.'

'But to do that you need to know what's happening in the restaurant, so if I don't plant the camera, then I don't get out. That's the way this works. Then again, if I don't plant the camera and by some miracle I manage to get out of here but the rest of the hostages die, then I'm going to spend the rest of my life wondering if planting the camera would have made a difference.'

'I didn't say that, Alex.'

'You didn't have to, *Brad*.'

'So you'll put the camera back?'

'Yeah, I'll put your damn camera back. If there is a plan, then I've got to keep you sweet. And if there isn't one, then I'm probably going to end up dead, so what the hell.'

'Thanks, Alex. I really appreciate this. Okay, once the camera's back in place, I want you to go to the kitchen and wait there. We're going to get you out.'

'Whatever, man.' The "over and out" he tagged on the end was thick with sarcasm.

10

JJ slid back in time as events that she'd tried hard to bury tumbled through her mind. The arguments, the silences. The funeral. The good times, too. There had been plenty of those. Not so many at the end, but lots at the start. Whenever she thought about Tom, the memories she went to were always from the early days. She was staring down at her trembling hands. In her peripheral vision she saw the bomber step away from Stone.

'I knew he was depressed.'

'But?' the bomber prompted. 'I'm sensing a "but" in there, Jody.'

Tony caught her eye and gave a little nod. The gesture was practically non-existent, but it meant the world. She might be feeling more alone than she'd ever felt, but she wasn't. Tony was there for her. Just like always.

'But I was too busy to help him. I was working twelve-hour days, building up my business. He was working fourteen-hour days. We occasionally passed each other over breakfast, and we'd see each other for an hour or two in the evening, if we were lucky.'

'That doesn't sound like much of a relationship.'

'Perhaps, but it was a fairly typical Hollywood marriage.'

'Did he have any affairs?'

'A couple that I knew about. There might have been more. There probably were.'

'And you?'

JJ hesitated. 'Yes, but only one.'

'Was it serious?'

'Not really. It was with someone a lot younger. It was never going to end up being anything.'

'Why did you do it?'

'I'm not sure. The opportunity was there, so I took it.'

'That kind of sums you up, doesn't it? You're an opportunist? So what was the trigger? What was it that finally pushed him over the edge?'

'I don't know if there was a trigger.'

'Believe me, there was a trigger. There always is.'

The bomber stared at JJ, and JJ stared right back. He shook his head and aimed the gun at Stone's head.

'Okay, okay. Just please lower the gun.'

He pushed the gun into the side of Stone's head, and kept pushing. The agent's head slowly tilted to the right. Stone was sobbing, his face filled with fear. She'd thought she couldn't hate the bomber any more than she already did. She was wrong.

'About six months before Tom killed himself he got passed over for a promotion,' JJ said in a dull monotone. 'It wasn't the first time. After that he became more and more distant. We'd go for days without talking, and then when we did finally talk, he just kept going on about getting out of LA. He wanted to move to Seattle or Miami, anywhere, really. Except that wasn't going to happen. We were trapped by debt and our lifestyle. There was no way he was going to get a job outside LA that paid well enough. And my business was just starting to take off, so there was no way I was going to leave.'

The bomber lowered the gun and Stone's head slowly came upright again.

'Okay, here's a question. If you had been willing to give up your life here, do you think your husband would still be alive today?'

JJ glanced at Tony. The nod he offered up was almost non-existent, but it was enough.

'Every problem has a solution,' the bomber continued. 'You could have liquidated your assets, packed your bags, bought an umbrella and headed off to rainy Seattle. You could be living there right now in a little cookie-cutter house. Two point four kids, a dog, school runs, trips to the gym to shift the baby fat. Just think, your husband could still be alive.'

'Please don't do this,' she said quietly. That awful smell had got into her nose again, unsettling her stomach. All of a sudden there wasn't enough air in the room.

'Am I getting a little too close to the bone here? Too close to the truth? Am I making you uncomfortable, Jody?'

'Yes,' she screamed at him. She glanced down at her knotted fingers, then looked back at the bomber. 'Okay, I admit it. I killed my husband. Is that what you want to hear?'

'What I want is the truth.'

'The truth? You want the truth? The truth is that those last six months were hell. Tom had always been a drinker, but his drinking spiralled out of control. Towards the end I hardly ever saw him sober. I told myself I'd get him help, but I kept putting it off until tomorrow. And then there were no more tomorrows.'

'You found him, didn't you?'

JJ nodded. 'I came back from work one night and found him in the pool. He'd used a bottle of vodka to wash down a load of sleeping pills.'

The bomber went silent, then nodded to himself. 'He blamed you. That's why he engineered it so you'd find him.'

JJ felt like an icicle had just been rammed into her heart. Her face was soaked with tears. 'You bastard,' she whispered under her breath.

11

Alex King let himself out of the restroom, eased the door shut behind him, then tiptoed along the corridor. His breathing was as loud as a siren and the friction rub of his socks on the wooden floor sounded like a chainsaw. He was still wearing the earpiece and mike because there was nothing to be gained from taking it off. If he got caught, the bomber would search him. He'd find the camera and would want to know all about it, and King would tell him everything.

He reached the wall and crawled behind it. Above his head, the leaves rustled gently. He could make out two voices on the other side of the wall. The bomber's and JJ's. It was weird, but the way they were talking, it sounded like they were having a therapy session. Even weirder, it sounded like JJ was crying. The idea of her shedding real tears like a real person just didn't compute.

King sat with his back hard against the cold wall, the knife pressing into his leg. Just having it there made him feel more in control. He took the knife out and smiled at the smiley face, then turned it over and his smile turned into a frown.

Smiley face, sad face.

Smiley face, sad face.

One thing he'd learned growing up in Cincinnati was that people cheated and lied to get what they wanted. His mom had been an expert at that. It looked like Brad Carter was an expert, too. The FBI guy had to be lying. There was no escape plan.

There never had been. Carter had just said that to keep him from going postal and trying to break the door down again. It all came down to the bottom line. It *always* came down to that. Basically, he was more use to the FBI in here than he was on the outside. No matter how King looked at the situation, there was no getting away from that fact.

But what if he was wrong? What if there was a plan? Another idea occurred to him. A new and different way of looking at things. If the FBI were able to get him out, then that meant they could get their people in. It was possible. Hell, it was more than possible, it was more or less a certainty. And it would go a long way to explaining why Carter was being so cagey.

Up until now, King had been too wrapped up in himself to realise what was actually going on here. The problem with being Hollywood's man of the moment was that he was surrounded by people trying to convince him that the universe did in fact revolve around him. Hear that enough times from enough people and anyone would become a believer. He'd been thinking about everything from his own point of view, but the FBI would have been looking at things very differently. Carter had told him as much when they last spoke. He'd said they wanted to get everyone out. *Everyone*. That was their goal, and any plan they hatched would be based around that.

King had made it this far without being caught. He could go that extra yard. All he had to do was get back to the kitchen in one piece and the FBI would get him out. He pulled the camera from his pocket, pushed it between the leaves, then peered over the lip of the wall to make sure it was positioned properly. He shifted it slightly to the left and checked again. It looked okay. He'd got halfway to the kitchen when JJ's voice stopped him in his tracks. It rang out as clear as if she'd been standing right beside him.

'If you're going to shoot me, then shoot me.'

What she was saying was bad enough, but the way she said it made it so much worse. The resignation in her voice was all wrong. It was almost as alien as her tears. The JJ he knew was a fighter. She was scary as hell. King didn't recognise this person at all.

12

The bomber drilled the silencer deeper into the nape of JJ's neck and time slowed to a crawl. She was aware of every heartbeat. Each breath seemed loaded with added significance. The bomber leant in closer, invading her personal space. She could smell his aftershave, and the musky animal aroma that lingered below it. His lips brushed her ear.

'Bang,' he whispered.

'Go to hell,' she whispered back.

The bomber laughed and the solid, insistent pressure of the gun disappeared. He stepped back and a faint trace of aftershave lingered in his wake.

'Well, you've got some balls. I'll give you that much.' He turned to Dan Stone. 'I know Jody's been hogging the limelight, but rest assured that I haven't forgotten about you. So where were we before we got side-tracked by Jody's heart-wrenching story? Ah, that's right. She'd accused you of being a freeloader. So, what's your opinion of Jody then? I'm figuring that you've got one, so let's hear it.'

'I think she's a cold-hearted, money-grabbing bitch who'd sell her own mother if she could make a buck.'

The bomber shook his head and took a dramatic intake of breath. 'And that's harsh. Very harsh indeed. So what have you got to say about that, Jody?'

'He's right,' she replied quietly.

'What? You're just going to sit there and let him trash your good name?'

'Don't you get it? I don't care anymore. I don't care what Dan thinks or says about me. And I care even less what you think. I'm done playing your games.'

The bomber swooped in close and the smell of his after-shave filled her nose again. There was pizza and Coke on his breath. 'Sorry, sweetheart, but that's not your decision to make.'

He fired the gun and the back of Stone's head exploded in an angry shower of red and grey. Bone fragments and gore pattered onto the floor, glittering and shining in the light. The force of the gunshot sent the agent tumbling backwards. He hit the floor with a solid thump. The small black hole in the middle of his forehead looked like a third eye. The blood splatter on the tablecloth reminded JJ of the Pollock-inspired paintings that hung around the room.

Simone screamed. The sound stopped so suddenly JJ was convinced that she'd been shot as well. She looked over and saw the model sitting with her hands clasped tightly over her mouth to hold back the scream. JJ turned back to the bomber. The flashing heart on his watch was fast approaching a hundred beats a minute. He saw where she was staring and held up his hand.

'It's really not a good idea to get me too excited, Jody.'

'Or what? You're going to kill me anyway, so it's not like it makes any difference. Not really.'

The bomber swooped in close, and she cringed against the chair-back.

'Just so we're absolutely clear here,' he said. 'You killed Dan as surely as you killed your husband. Remember, passive resistance just doesn't cut it with me.

JJ said nothing.

'Okay, go sit with the others. I'm done with you for now.' He looked over at the hostages. 'Tony and Ed, get over here and clean up this mess.'

13

'And in another world exclusive, TRN has discovered the identity of the bomber who is holding a group of the entertainment industry's most powerful people hostage at Alfie's.'

Caroline Bradley delivered this in a tone of voice that combined excitement with just the right amount of sincerity. She was on her third outfit change. The latest offering was a simple black pant suit over a white blouse.

'Sergeant Ted Marley is a forty-nine-year-old former bomb disposal expert,' she went on. 'A veteran of both Gulf Wars. He received a Bronze Star during Desert Storm, and a Purple Heart during the 2003 conflict. He retired from the armed forces in 2005. Three months ago, Denise Marley, his wife of twenty-six years, was killed in a hit-and-run accident.'

On Seth's cue, the camera pulled back to reveal Dr Sally Jenkins. Caroline turned her chair so she was facing the psychiatrist, then glanced at her clipboard as though she was seriously considering which question to start with. The random words written on there were pure gibberish. The only questions Caroline asked were the ones Seth whispered down from Mission Control, or those on the autocue.

'Dr Jenkins, thank you for joining us again.'

'My pleasure.'

'The question our viewers are asking themselves right now is how can a decorated war hero turn into a murderer? Can you shed any light on that?'

The psychiatrist nodded like this was the most penetrating question she'd ever heard.

'I believe the trigger was the death of Marley's wife. The death of a spouse is one of the most traumatic life events that any of us will ever experience. When it comes out of the blue, as seems to have been the case here, then the effects are amplified. It's bad enough to lose your husband or wife after a long illness, I'm not disputing that, but in those situations there is a sense of inevitability, which can provide some comfort. Can you imagine how devastating it must be to get a telephone call or a visit from the police to inform you that your wife is dead?'

'But it doesn't necessarily follow that the husband is going to go on a murder spree. So why did Marley suddenly snap like this?'

'Every situation is unique,' Jenkins replied. 'The death of Marley's wife was the trigger, but to understand how he ended up on this highly destructive path of behaviour, we need to know more about his life. Now, there are a number of assumptions we can make. The fact he's a decorated war hero means he has seen military action. Also, the fact that he's a bomb disposal expert means he was subjected to the possibility of death on a regular basis. Every time he defused a bomb he would have been hyper-aware of his own mortality. He would also have had first-hand experience of the devastation caused by explosives. Combine these two factors, and it becomes inevitable that he will be suffering from post-traumatic stress disorder.'

'Again, the situation you've described is not unique,' Caroline said.

'Marley's time in the army is only part of the story. What happened after he left the army? How well did he make the transition from military life to civilian life? Was he unemployed? Does he have a drink problem? A drug problem? Any of those issues would have impacted on his life. It's possible that some or all of them may have led him to the place he finds himself in today. There are probably other factors, too, but those are the main ones. Now, rewind to last June, and the question I'm asking myself is what happened to the hit and run driver?'

'And that's a damn good question,' Seth shouted out. 'Anyone got an answer?'

The three assistants shook their heads in unison.

'Well, go find one. And quick.'

On the big screen, Dr Jenkins said, 'My guess is that one of three things happened. Either the driver was never caught, or they were caught but the authorities failed to secure a conviction. The third possibility is that they did get a conviction, but it was so lenient that Marley couldn't accept that justice had been done. The fact he gave six million dollars to charity is significant. More than once today I've heard him being referred to as a modern-day Robin Hood, and I truly believe this is how he views himself. Any of the scenarios I've just outlined would be consistent with him wanting to be viewed as an avenging angel.'

And that was a perfect line to end on. Seth gave Caroline the cue to wind things up.

'Dr Jenkins, thank you very much for joining us again.' Caroline turned her chair to face the camera and laid her clipboard on her lap. 'We're now going back to Rob Taylor, our man on the ground at Alfie's.'

'On my mark,' Seth said. 'Three, two, one.'

Caroline disappeared from the big screen and was replaced by a close-up of Rob. He flashed his trademark smile, but only for a second. The expression disappeared as quickly as it had appeared, replaced with something more serious. He stared intently at the camera.

'Thanks, Caroline. The siege is now well into its third hour. So far, four lives have been claimed, including that of Oscar-winning director Natasha Lovett. The atmosphere around Alfie's right now is beyond tense. Everyone here is just hoping that the situation can be resolved without any further bloodshed.'

Yeah right, thought Seth. He was picturing the crowds gathered behind the police barriers. No way were they looking for a peaceful resolution. They'd turned out because they smelled blood. Basically, they wanted to be able to tell everyone that they'd been there when the bomb went off. The same could be said of the viewers watching at home. They hadn't tuned in because they were expecting a warm, fuzzy Oprah moment, they'd tuned in because they wanted to watch the body count rise. It was the same basic drive that had brought the crowds flocking to the Colosseum in Rome to watch the lions tearing the Christians apart.

Seth glanced at the small monitor that was tuned to CNN. Another glance for the monitor tuned to Fox. Neither of the big boys had the bomber's name yet, which must hurt. Right now they would have every spare man and woman frantically searching for information on Ted Marley. If he'd been in their shoes, that's what he would have done.

He'd purposefully held back the name of Marley's hometown because he didn't want to make life too easy for them. He'd also held back on one vital piece of information that would have given Sally Jenkins a light-bulb moment. That particular bombshell was going to have the big boys eating his dust. He was waiting until the top of the hour when viewing figures were at their peak before dropping that one.

There was a risk that one of the big boys might get hold of the information before then, but it was a gamble worth taking. And anyway, there was no way they were going to scoop him. It just wasn't going to happen, not now that he was back on top of the wave again.

14

Alex King had just reached the kitchen door when the gun went off. The single silenced shot was followed by the dead, dull thud of a body hitting the wooden floor. He put his hands over his face and bit into his palms to stop any sound escaping. He'd never liked JJ, but that didn't mean he wanted her dead.

'Hey, Alex, you okay, buddy?'

King didn't dare answer. He was too exposed out here. The idea that his luck was about to run out hit suddenly, and it hit hard. If the invincible Jody Johnson could die, then any of them could. Even a nine-life cat would eventually run out of lives. He eased the kitchen door open and squeezed through the gap. Then he eased it closed again and sank to his knees.

'Come on, Alex, talk to me, buddy. I just want to know you're okay.'

Okay? Was that some sort of joke? This situation was so far from okay you'd need a freaking map to find your way back again.

'If you can't talk, just tap the throat mike twice.'

King took a deep breath and somehow managed to find his voice. 'I'm fine.'

'That's good to hear. And Alex? Thanks for putting the camera back. You have no idea how grateful we are.'

'Brad, I don't want your gratitude. What I want, the *only* thing I want, is for you to get me the hell out of here.'

15

'Two million dollars,' Kevin Donahue said. 'I'll give you two million dollars if you let me go.'

JJ barely heard him because she was trapped back in the moment when Dan Stone had died. It kept playing over and over in her head and wouldn't stop. She could still hear the echo of the gunshot, and she could see him falling, and she wanted to save him but there wasn't a damn thing she could do. It was just like the night Tom had died. Back then, she'd been hypnotised by the beige swirls on the translucent rippling blue water of the pool. Now it was the bright red spatters on the dazzling white tablecloths that held her captivated.

'Two million dollars,' Donahue repeated. 'I can wire it wherever you want. Anywhere in the world. The Caymans, Switzerland, wherever. Just tell me where you want it to go.'

JJ shook herself free from the past and forced herself to focus on the present. There would be time for recriminations later. Assuming there was a later. From where she was sitting she could just about see Donahue. The old guy looked like a corpse. The last few hours had taken its toll on all of them, but the producer had been hit hardest. If he suddenly dropped dead, it wouldn't be a great shock.

'Two million bucks,' the bomber mused. 'You say that like it's nothing, like it's pocket change. It's not. My daddy worked in a Tennessee steel mill his whole life and I doubt he earned half a million dollars in all that time, never mind two million. The harsh truth is that most people will never see money like that in their whole lifetime, yet, with a click of your fingers you can make me a millionaire. Doesn't that seem wrong to you?'

'What do you want me to say? That life's unfair? That I'm sorry I'm rich? Well here's a newsflash, buddy. Life isn't fair. I've got plenty of money in the bank, and do you know something? I'd give away every last cent if I could buy another year. But the harsh truth is that all the money in the world won't buy me another year. However, a couple of million so I can live long enough to see the sun come up tomorrow? Well, from where I'm sitting, I've got to tell you, that sounds like money well-spent.'

The bomber cocked his head to one side like he was giving this some serious consideration, then he stepped back. JJ saw the gun come up. She saw his finger curl around the trigger. She wanted to shout a warning, but the words were trapped in her throat. There was no gunshot, though. Not this time.

'Okay, Kev, on your feet.'

The producer stood slowly. It was pitiful to watch. He winced with every movement and barely had the strength to hold himself up. JJ closed her eyes. She didn't want to witness any more deaths. Unfortunately, what she wanted didn't come into the equation. Donahue was about to die and there was nothing she could do change that. She wouldn't see it happening, but she'd still be able to hear. And at some point she would have to open her eyes again, and Donahue would be lying there with all the other corpses.

'Two million bucks could really change a person's life.' There was a tremor in Donahue's voice. 'Just think. No mortgage, no debts. Budget carefully and you'd never have to work again.'

'You're assuming I'm doing this for money. Remember, I just gave six million dollars to charity.'

Donahue shook his head. 'It's always about the money.'

'So why did I give away six million bucks?'

'To get the public on your side. This town's one big popularity contest, and, like everything else in this world, you get popularity by buying it.'

JJ had been involved in enough negotiations to recognise one when she saw one. Somehow during the last ten seconds this had turned into a negotiation. That's the way it worked. One second you were shooting the breeze, the next you were bargaining. Donahue was back on familiar ground. That's why he was suddenly sounding more sure of himself. A negotiation was a negotiation. It could be a film deal, or it could be that you were bargaining for your life, but in the end it was all the same thing. One person had something the other person wanted, and the trick was finding a price that made both parties come away from the table feeling like winners.

Donahue glanced over at the other hostages, eyes moving from Ed Richards to DeAndre Alexander then back to the bomber. 'There's still plenty of money in this room. We both know that. I'm willing to pay two million. Do you think I'm alone here? Play your cards right and you could walk away with ten million, easy. You know, I've got to hand it to you, what you're doing here is total genius. I've been involved in some pretty major deals, but even on my best day I never came close to earning ten million bucks.'

'Four million.'

'I could get that for you, but it would take a couple of hours on the Internet. I'd need to liquidate some assets. Three million would be easier. I could have that in your account straight away.'

For a time the only noise in the room was the gentle shushing of the air-conditioning, and the tiny sounds made by a group of people desperately trying to keep quiet.

'Three million,' the bomber mused. 'That would be a real life-changer. Okay, Kev, you've got yourself a deal.'

He stepped aside and waved Donahue over to the laptop. The old guy walked over quickly. The adrenalin was masking any discomfort and making him move like a younger, much healthier man. He sat down at the laptop and started pecking at the keyboard.

JJ's mind had already gone into overdrive. Even Stone's death had momentarily slid into the background. After the bomber had given six million to charity she'd assumed this wasn't about money, but after what had just happened, she was reassessing that one. At a push, she could get her hands on a million and a half. In Hollywood terms, that was nothing. She was virtually a pauper. When you got down to it, so was Donahue, and he was able to get hold of three million.

So how much could DeAndre Alexander get hold of? Or Ed Richards? Donahue reckoned the bomber could net himself a cool ten million, but that figure was a massive underestimate. Richards alone could probably pay ten million without it creating so much as a ripple in his bank balance. She didn't even want to think what his net worth was. He was definitely Learjet rich.

Donahue was right. This scam was genius. The only part JJ couldn't figure out was the escape plan. Everything else had been carefully thought through, so he must have one. Otherwise, what was this all for?

'I'm going to need your account details,' Donahue said.

The bomber pulled the laptop closer and began typing. JJ's eyes were drawn back to the blood-stained tablecloth and the wide smear of Dan Stone's blood on the floor. Maybe the killing was over. Maybe this was how things were going to play out from here on in. The bomber would call them up one at a time, negotiate a price, then let them go. For the first time since this all began, she was starting to believe that she might get out of here alive.

'Okay, I'm done.' Donahue struggled to his feet and gave the bomber another one of those death's-head grins. 'Congratulations, you're now three million dollars richer.'

'You know, Kev, there was one thing in that bullshit speech you gave earlier that really resonated with me. You're right. Life isn't fair.'

The bomber raised the gun and pumped two bullets into Donahue's chest.

16:00–16:30

1

The TRN graphic faded out, the studio faded in, and Seth took a long drag on his Marlboro and prayed his gamble would pay off. Up until now he'd been convinced it would. But this was the moment of truth and that changed everything. The farm had been bet, the dice rolled, and he would either walk away from the table with everything or nothing. There were butterflies in his chest and stomach, and no amount of nicotine seemed to be soothing them. Caroline Bradley was on the big screen. Her black jacket had been straightened, her make-up retouched. She smiled a serious smile and said, 'Good afternoon.'

'Swap to the photograph on my mark,' Seth said. 'Three, two, one.'

The TRN logo disappeared from behind Caroline and was replaced with a picture of Ted Marley. Seth glanced over at the two small screens on the left. One was tuned to Fox, the other to CNN. A millisecond after the picture had appeared on TRN, similar pictures had appeared on the other two channels. Good. TRN's was out there first, which meant they were still ahead of the game. It didn't matter that it was only by a fraction of a second. A fraction of a second was the difference between gold and silver, and nobody ever remembered who won silver.

Both Fox and CNN had gone with photos that made Marley look like a criminal. They weren't prison mugshots, but they might as well have been. In both pictures, Marley's head was turned to the left so that your eye was drawn immediately to the ragged scar on his right cheek. The impression these photographs gave was that this was someone who'd lived life on the wrong side of the law. If you saw this version of Ted Marley walking down the sidewalk, you'd definitely cross the street and hide the kids.

Portraying the bomber like this was understandable, but it was a mistake. Like Rob had pointed out, a large section of the public actually liked this guy. They were more than happy to buy into the whole Robin Hood act, while conveniently forgetting that he was a murderer. This didn't surprise Seth. He'd stopped being surprised by the sheer stupidity of Joe Public decades ago. The sad truth was that violence and death had become such an integral part of everyday life that the shock value had eroded away to nothing. The irony was that he was partly responsible. It was an irony that had not escaped him.

By contrast, TRN's photograph showed Ted Marley in full dress uniform. He was standing to attention, medals pinned to his chest, and he looked every bit the hero. His head was turned to the right so the scar was hidden. If the viewers wanted Robin Hood, then who was he to deny them?

Marley was handsome in a rugged, outdoorsy sort of way. He had strong features and piercing grey eyes. His skin was tanned to the colour of mahogany. Seth could imagine him walking to the South Pole, or heading out into the wilderness to hunt deer and sleep under the stars. He could also imagine him living in one of those communes in the Midwest, holed up with enough guns and ammunition to start a small war, waiting for the End of Days. It was the eyes. Those were the eyes of someone who had everything to prove and nothing to lose.

On the big screen, Caroline looked straight and serious at the camera. 'The latest from the siege at Alfie's is that the bomber has been named as Sergeant Ted Marley, a forty-nine-year-old former army bomb disposal expert. Marley is originally from Tennessee, but since retiring in 2005 he has been living in Twin Falls, Idaho.'

Usually, this would be the point where Caroline would give a rundown of the headlines in a series of easily digestible bullet points. The number of dead, their names, that sort of thing. Seth glanced over at the screens on his left. The sound was muted, but he didn't need sound to confirm that Fox and CNN were heading down that old familiar route.

'Okay, Caroline,' he whispered into his microphone. 'We've got the exclusive. It's show time.'

On the big screen, Caroline touched her earpiece. 'I'm just getting a report coming in of a new development. This is another world exclusive for TRN, the station that's always first with the news.'

2

Simone put her hand up and everyone turned to look. The bomber responded immediately. It was almost as though he'd been waiting for this.

'Can I help you?'

'I need to go to the bathroom.' Her Norwegian accent was more pronounced than JJ remembered. Probably the stress.

'Well, go on then. No one's stopping you.'

Simone broke eye contact and stared at the floor. The bomber walked over slowly. The sound of his boots hitting the parquet sounded like a series of small explosions. He levelled his gun and aimed at her head.

'Is there a problem?'

Simone glanced down at the diaper and said nothing.

'I said, is there a problem?'

Just do it, JJ thought. *Put on the goddamn diaper.* She could see where this was headed. Simone was going to keep sitting there, and the bomber was going to give her maybe one more chance, and then he was going to blow her head off. She didn't particularly like the model, but she did feel responsible for her. The bottom line: she was the reason that Simone was here.

'Let me make this real simple, sweetheart. You want to go pee-pee, you put on the diaper. You mess up the floor, you die. "Diaper" and "pee-pee" aside, that's words of one syllable. Are we understanding one another here?'

Simone nodded, then picked up the diaper. Everyone except the bomber turned away. JJ could see him from the corner of her eye. He'd lowered his weapon and had his head cocked slightly to the side, watching. Everything went quiet for a long time.

'All done?' the bomber asked.

Simone didn't say anything, but she must have made the right response because she was still alive.

'Anyone else need to go? And before you decide to keep your legs crossed, remember what I said about making puddles.'

Jen and DeAndre Alexander put their hands up, and JJ turned away again. She could hear them shuffling around. She could sense their embarrassment. She needed to go as well, but not that badly.

'Okay, Jen, you're on clean-up duty. Collect the dirty diapers then dump them over there in the corner.'

There was more shuffling as the diapers were removed, then footsteps. JJ chanced a glance and saw Jen walking across the room. She was in her fifties, but wearing the years well. Dye to keep her hair golden and regular workouts at the gym to keep in shape. The pressure was getting to her, though. It was there in the stiff way she moved and the worry lines cutting deep into her face. Jen put the used diapers on a table, then walked back over and sat down.

'Anyone else need to go?'

This time there were no takers. The bomber gave it another second then walked over to the laptop. JJ glanced around the room. There was death everywhere she looked. Look left and there was Elizabeth Hayward. Look down at the lower level and there was the accountant. She didn't dare look to her right because that was where Dan Stone and Kevin Donahue's bodies had been dumped. Even thinking about Stone was enough to bring a wave of guilt crashing in on her.

Donahue's death took the total number of hostages to six. Tony, Simone, Ed Richards, DeAndre Alexander, Jen, and herself, of course. They were the only ones left now. A quick look confirmed that they were all in pretty bad shape. Ed Richards was handling it the worst. He looked like a man who'd fallen over the edge and was tumbling into the abyss. If they got out of this it was going to take a lot of therapy to put him back together again. Simone worried her, too. Not because she was about to do something stupid, but because she was such a cold-hearted bitch. If she had to sacrifice every single person in this room to get out of here alive, she wouldn't think twice about it.

Keeping positive was hard. Less than five minutes had passed since Ed Richards and Tony had dragged Donahue's corpse away and dumped it unceremoniously on top of Stone's. Five minutes filled with guilt, recriminations and doomsday scenarios. JJ was more convinced than ever that she was going to die. Here, now, today. The only person who had any control over this situation was the bomber, and it seemed that he was on course to self-destruct. What she didn't know was how many people he'd end up taking with him.

But what was motivating him? People didn't do things without a reason. Whether that reason was good or bad was irrelevant. Junkies knew they were pumping poison into their veins, but they kept using because the alternative was the hell of withdrawal. That was all the motivation they needed. Likewise, a Hollywood A-lister would do or say anything to save their precious career because the alternative was a hard, cruel slide into infamy, followed by an equally cruel slide into obscurity.

JJ had made it her business to work out what made people tick. She'd got real good at it, too. Usually she could suss someone out within seconds of meeting them, but the bomber had her baffled. By now they must be fast approaching the three-hour mark and she still had no idea what was motivating him. Money was the obvious reason, but even though he'd just taken three million from Donahue, she still wasn't convinced.

And if money wasn't the motivator, what was?

She'd ruled out a political agenda back at the start, but had she been too hasty there? She knew how the media worked. They were almost three hours into the siege, which meant the story would have gone global. Nothing could have stopped that happening. A story like this would have gone global by the end of the first hour. Was that what the bomber wanted? Was he waiting for the stage to get big enough before he outlined his agenda? The idea had merit, but, again, JJ wasn't convinced. Something about this theory just didn't sit right. From what she'd seen, the bomber wasn't an activist or a militant. He didn't seem to have any sort of political axe to grind.

He was a sadist, though. That much was evident from the way he'd been toying with them. He was also a psychopath, which was evident from the way he could kill an innocent person without batting an eyelid. Maybe he just got off on killing people. Maybe that was all the motivation he needed. It was possible she was just trying to over-complicate a situation that was, in fact, very simple. Maybe he killed for the sake of killing.

But something must have happened to cause him to snap and go on a killing spree. You didn't wake up one morning and decide to do something like this. There was usually a trigger, and, if that was the case, then things were even worse than she'd thought. He'd crossed the line and there was no turning back. The only way this could end was with his death.

JJ looked up from the patch of floor that had been holding her hypnotised. Everyone was looking more terrified than ever. Faces were pinched, eyes were darker and deader, and those thousand-yard stares just kept getting longer with each passing minute. Then there was that smell to contend with. Given enough time you were supposed to be able to get used to any smell. Bullshit. JJ knew she'd never get used to this one. Not in a day, or a week, or even a century. This was a smell that got right inside you and wouldn't let go.

The bomber was at his laptop, watching the news headlines on TRN. JJ couldn't see the screen, but she could hear everything the anchorwoman was saying. The first thing that jumped out was a name. Ted Marley. The name meant nothing to her. The only Marleys she could think of were Bob and Jacob. If the news networks had got hold of his name, you could guarantee they'd got hold of a photograph. She was wondering what he looked like. She liked to have faces to go with names. That was why she was such a big fan of video conferencing.

The anchorwoman fell silent, and when she spoke again her voice was edged with excitement.

'I'm just getting a report coming in of a new development. This is another world exclusive for TRN, the station that's always first with the news. According to our sources, Ted Marley is suffering from an inoperable brain tumour. When the tumour was diagnosed six months ago, doctors gave him less than a year to live.'

It took less than a second to process this, and then the implications hit. JJ had thought things were bad before, but they'd just got a whole lot worse.

3

King had been careful to make sure he didn't overdo it when he cleared up. If the kitchen looked too tidy that would be as bad as it being too messy. Anything out of the ordinary would stand out. And standing out was bad, because it led to questions. Questions like who was hiding back here? Those were the sorts of questions that got a person killed. King had seen enough hostage movies to know that much.

He glanced around, trying to decide if he'd gone too far. Everything looked all right, but the problem with *all right* was that it might be a whole world away from *right*. No matter how hard he tried, he couldn't remember what state the kitchen had been in before he'd trashed it. He took out his phone and stared at the dead screen. He'd give anything to talk to Stuart right now, even if it was for the final time. Stuart had been his first serious relationship, and the way things were going it could well be his last.

The relationship had happened before *Killing Time*, and it had happened before his agent signed him up with the promise that he would make him the biggest action movie star in the world. His agent had made it clear that long-term romantic relationships were bad for business. *Any* sort of relationship. King had said he understood, and since then he'd been discreet. And he had understood. He was an action hero, and action heroes did not go out with other men. That was not how things worked in Hollywood.

Then there were his female fans to consider. They had to believe he was romantically available. That was one of the things that made him so marketable. It didn't matter that it was never going to happen, the illusion just needed to be out there. One-night stands and short-term relationships were okay, so long as the person he was dating was female. His fans would expect to see him going out with someone like Simone hanging from his arm. It would be weird if he wasn't. It was all part of the image. All a part of the act.

JJ had spent a long time explaining this to him. Even when he'd told her for the millionth time that he'd got it, she'd still kept on, browbeating him until he'd wanted to strangle her. Thinking about JJ made him feel bad, so he stopped thinking about her. He still couldn't believe she was dead.

He looked around the kitchen again. Had he gone too far? Stuart used to call him a neat freak, which was crap. The truth of the matter was that he was tidier than Stuart, that was all. Being tidy did not make you a neat freak, it just meant that you didn't want to live in a mess. A picture of Stuart filled his mind. His ex was so good-looking, and the really cool thing was that he had no idea how handsome he actually was. But what King loved most about him was his sense of humour. Stuart was always laughing and joking. It didn't take much to set him off, and sometimes when he got started laughing, it was like he'd never stop.

Remembering the good times made King's heart shrink. He'd traded love for fame, and, at the time, he'd thought he was getting a good deal. That had been back when the whole of his golden future had been stretching out in front of him. There would be more Stuarts, he'd told himself, and he'd really believed that, too.

When he'd signed his pact with the devil, he'd thought he fully understood the terms and conditions. Now he knew differently. Money and fame could never equate to happiness and love. In hindsight, he could see that where he thought he'd traded up, he had in fact traded down. He'd swapped stability for a series of one-night stands, each one sapping a little more of his heart and soul.

Had Stuart received his text and, if so, what had he done? There was a good chance he'd taken one look, then deleted it. King wouldn't have blamed him. Then again, there was a slim chance that Stuart had sent a reply, and the reason he hadn't received it was because his cell phone was dead. Even though it was unlikely, King still clung to the idea. Thinking that there was someone he loved reaching out to him, even if it was just by text, made things slightly more bearable.

He sank down onto the floor with his back to the door. The key was pulsing inside his pocket and the knife was pushing against his hip. It was so frustrating. That door was only a couple of inches thick. He was two inches from freedom, and two inches was the length of his little finger. It was nothing. Yet, at the same time, it was everything.

If he got out, he was going to make some big changes. Firstly, he was going to get himself into therapy so he could deal with his demons once and for all. Secondly, he was going to come out. His agent could go to hell. If he didn't like it, tough. King would just find a new one. He couldn't live a lie anymore. That was why his life had got so screwed up in the first place. Well, it was one of the reasons. His childhood had obviously played a part, but he'd let the shrinks help him to unravel that mess.

Last, but not least, he was going to apologise to Stuart. He wasn't expecting them to get back together. After the way he'd treated him, there was no way that was going to happen. He just wanted to be able to look him in the eye and say sorry.

Big changes.

King pressed his fingers against the throat mike, then remembered he didn't have to do that. He took his hand away and whispered through his tears, 'Brad, if you're listening, please, please, please just get me out of here.'

4

'Relax,' Tara said.

Rob looked up from his cell phone. Caroline Bradley was on the small screen and getting all the glory, and that just made the frustration worse. He was standing a hundred yards from the Mobile Command Unit, closer to Alfie's than any other member of the media, yet he might as well not exist. This was the part of the job he hated. The waiting. It drove him nuts. Basically, he was stuck here until the next hostage came out. That could happen in the next couple of minutes, or the next couple of hours.

'I am relaxed.'

'Honeybun, if you were any more wound up you'd snap.'

Rob nodded towards the Mobile Command Unit. 'What do you think's going on in there?'

Tara shrugged. 'No idea. Why not knock on the door and ask?'

'Yeah, right.'

'I'm serious.'

Rob studied her face carefully, and realised she was.

'And what good's that doing to do? Walters will just say he's too busy, or that he doesn't have anything for us.'

'Or maybe he'll give us the story of the century. Look, right now I'm in favour of anything that's going to turn your frown upside down, even if it is temporary. The truth is, I don't care what you do, so long as I get my happy, smiley Rob back.'

He tried for a smile but it came out as a grimace.

Tara laughed. 'Is that the best you can do?'

'Sorry, that's all I've got.'

Her face turned serious. 'Remember, until this thing's over, we own Aaron Walters. So, what have you got to lose?'

'I guess you're right.'

'No guessing about it. That one's gospel.' She paused. 'Look, I know what's really eating you up here. You're pissed because Caroline Bradley is currently getting all the glory.'

'Am I really that petty and shallow?'

'Sure you are. It's one of the things I love about you. I don't have to go digging too hard to discover your hidden depths, because you don't have any.'

Rob laughed. 'That's harsh.'

'Harsh but true. Basically, the way I see it, you've got two options. Either stand around moping, or go bang on that door and get Walters to give you an exclusive that's going to knock Caroline Bradley off of her perch.'

'Put like that, I guess I don't have an option.'

'Damn right you don't.'

5

The light bulbs went on in JJ's head one after the other. It was all starting to make sense. She'd wanted a trigger and now she had two. After dropping the bombshell about the tumour, the anchorwoman had gone on to talk about the hit-and-run driver who'd killed Marley's wife.

That was the thing when you had all the pieces. Everything suddenly became crystal clear. Discovering he was dying had pushed Marley right to the brink. JJ guessed the only thing that had stopped him plunging over the edge was the fact that his wife had been there. When she'd died something inside him had finally snapped.

Marley closed the laptop lid and sat very still. JJ was watching him from the corner of her eye. Everyone was watching. She really didn't like the way he was just sitting there. The lack of movement was almost as disturbing as the gun and the bomb. He was too calm. Too composed. If this had been a film, this would be the moment when the director called for a close-up. The screen would fill with a picture of the bad guy with his finger on the trigger. A calmness would wash over him as any doubts dissolved. And then he would detonate the bomb.

JJ searched deep inside for a single happy thought to carry her from this world to the next. The memory she came up with was a childhood one. She was seven, still young enough to believe in Santa Claus. That year she'd written to him to say she'd been a good girl and could she please have a new bike because her old one was too small.

On Christmas morning there had been a pink Schwinn wrapped up under the tree. It was the exact one she'd wanted, the very same model that was circled in the catalogue hidden under her bed. She couldn't believe that Santa had got it so right. That morning she'd gone for a bike ride with her dad. They'd gone for miles, just the two of them. It was the best Christmas ever. Back then her parents had still loved each other, and they'd loved her, and life had been easy and uncomplicated. Good times.

Marley stood up and raised his hand. JJ expected it to stop at the explosive vest since that was the obvious place to have a trigger. It didn't. Instead, it kept going, past the vest. He grabbed the bottom of the balaclava and pulled it over his head.

JJ wasn't sure what she'd expected, but it wasn't this. Aside from the scar, he looked so normal. If she had passed him on the street she wouldn't have given him a second glance. At a rough guess she'd put him in his mid-fifties, but he could just as easily have been a hard-worn late forties. He had the deep tan of someone who worked outdoors, as opposed to someone who'd bought a tan because it fitted an image.

His salt-and-pepper hair was razor short, not quite cut back to the scalp, but not far off. It was a practical haircut. A military haircut. If she hadn't heard the anchorwoman saying he was ex-army, the scar on his right cheek would have been the clincher. It had been sewn up quickly with big baseball stitches. This was battlefield surgery. No hospital in the US would produce work like that, not even the poorest ones.

JJ realised she was staring and looked away. Her palms were slick with sweat and her fingers kept twisting together like puzzle pieces, interlocking and unlocking. Judging by the muted sounds of movement coming from all around her, she wasn't alone in her discomfort.

She stole another quick glance. Marley was studying the hostages, eyes moving from person to person and momentarily pausing on each one. JJ was able to properly see his grin for the first time. There was nothing out of the ordinary about it, nothing evil, which surprised her. Her imagination had turned it into something from a horror movie, a grotesque parody of a grin. It wasn't. It was warm and friendly and filled with good humour.

'I think this is a good time to put my cards on the table,' he said. 'I'm afraid I haven't been entirely honest with you.'

6

'The hit-and-run driver is dead.'

The black kid was on his feet, hiding his nerves by pretending to play it cool. Seth wasn't fooled for a second. He wanted to shout "boo" just to see if he'd piss his pants.

'Who, why, what, where, when?' he snapped.

'The hit-and-run driver went by the name of Alan Atkinson,' the Asian kid put in. 'He was murdered in his home some time yesterday morning. Atkinson lived in Dartford, a small town a couple of miles from Twin Falls. The killer strung him up by his feet in the garage then eviscerated him. His wife found him hanging there with his guts hanging out.'

'Based on that I reckon I can work out the "why" for myself. The police have issued an arrest warrant for Marley, right?'

The Asian kid nodded.

'And I'm also guessing that Alan Atkinson escaped a prison sentence on some sort of technicality, hence the reason he was at home rather than in prison.'

Another nod.

'Okay, I want to know everything there is to know about Atkinson. And I want an interview with the wife. There's nothing like a grieving widow to give those heartstrings a tug.' Seth clapped his hands, making everyone jump. 'Come on people. What are you waiting for? The news does not make itself.'

'Yeah, remember who makes the news,' the white lesbian muttered under her breath.

Seth fixed her with his hardest stare. 'Got something to add, sweetheart?'

'I said, "will do".'

'Sure you did. And I'm a complete idiot, so I believe you.' Seth shook out a Marlboro and lit it. His eyes were fixed on his assistants. He paused for effect and took a drag. 'Okay, folks. Back to work. And don't you dare forget who makes the goddamn news here.'

7

JJ had waited for Marley to expand on his comment about not being honest. She was still waiting. He'd done his grand unveiling, made his grand proclamation, then he'd walked over to the laptop. He was standing there now, watching them. The restaurant phone was pressed hard against his ear.

'Louise, it is so wonderful to hear your sweet voice again. Any luck with my question? You know the one I'm talking about. The *big* question. The one that's got you all running around out there like headless chickens. What do I want?'

Marley looked directly at JJ when he said this. There was no room for misinterpretation. No maybes, no doubts. The way he was staring it was like he was expecting an answer. But how would she know why he was doing this? She'd never met him before today. If she had, she would have remembered that scar. He was a war hero from some small town in Idaho that nobody had heard of. She was a Hollywood PR consultant. This wasn't a case of different worlds, it was a case of different universes. JJ was suddenly fascinated by the patterns on the floor again. She stared at them like she was studying a Picasso. The sound of her thoughts was deafening her to the point of distraction. None of them were happy thoughts.

'Are you telling me that you still don't have an answer, Lou? You know, I've got to tell you I'm disappointed. I mean, there you all are with your fancy degrees from Harvard or Yale or whichever Ivy League college you attended, and you can't even answer a simple question.'

Marley paused. 'Tell you what. You make sure those listening devices are pointed in my direction because I'm just about to make things real simple for you.'

He killed the call and placed the phone carefully on the table. For a moment he just stood there, lost in thought. Then he turned and looked straight at JJ.

'On your feet, Jody.' He nodded to the chair she'd been sitting in earlier. 'Come and take a seat.'

JJ was trembling so much she didn't think she'd make it. Getting to her feet was hard enough, but walking those few short steps to the chair was even harder. She sank into it. All she could see was the upturned chair that Dan Stone had been sitting on, and the smear of his blood on the parquet. She tried not to look at his corpse, but couldn't help herself. The agent's eyes were wide open and staring blank accusations at her. Like she needed to be guilted out by a corpse. She knew she was the reason he was dead. She didn't need any reminders.

'Look at me'.

Marley's voice was calm and rational. For a split second, JJ almost believed that here was someone she could do business with. The illusion was shattered when she glanced up and saw the explosive vest and the pulsing red heart on his watch.

'You have no idea what this is all about, do you, Jody?'

JJ shook her head. Marley was shaking his, too.

'And you have no idea how sad that makes me.'

8

In the end, Rob took the easy way out. Instead of knocking on the door of the Mobile Command Unit, he called Aaron Walters on his cell. He could sense Tara hovering at his shoulder, listening in. The phone was on speaker so they could both hear.

'Mr Taylor, to what do I owe the pleasure?'

'I want everything you've got on Ted Marley.'

'And little boys who want, rarely get.'

'I'm serious.'

'So am I.' Walters sighed. 'Just for a second look at this from my point of view. Your rivals are saying I'm playing favourites, and they're right. I'm really getting it in the neck here. The next hostage comes out, you'll cover the story. When this is all over and everyone discovers that it was you who came up with the plan to get Alex King out, you're going to be a hero. I can't give you any more. This well has run dry. I've already gone above and beyond. Whatever debt I've got with Seth Allen, it's paid in full.'

'The fact that you're under pressure is your problem, not mine.'

'No, Mr Taylor, it is very much your problem.'

Rob considered asking for an off-the-record interview, and dismissed the idea almost as quickly as it occurred. First, it would take the boys and girls over at Fox and CNN all of two seconds to work out where TRN had got the information from. Secondly, and more importantly, this wasn't about getting information, it was about getting face-time. Unless he was standing in front of Walters holding a microphone, Jonah would take any information he got and have Caroline Bradley deliver it.

'Okay,' Rob said. 'I'm hearing plenty about what you can't do. How about you tell me what you can do?'

Walters sighed then went quiet, like he was thinking this over. 'I can arrange another press conference. And you can have the first question.'

The way he said this made it sound like he was doing him a huge favour, but there was something in his tone that rang a false note. Rob replayed the last thirty seconds and the reason became obvious.

'Come on, Aaron, do you take me for a complete idiot? You've already agreed to do the press conference to get the other networks off your back.'

Silence on the other end of the phone.

'I'll definitely get the first question?'

'So long as your hand's up first, I don't have a problem with that.'

Rob hung up.

'A press conference works,' Tara said. 'Jonah will have to air it, so that brings the story back to us. And it sure as hell beats standing around watching Caroline Bradley on our cell phones.'

'I would have preferred a one-on-one with Walters.'

Tara laughed. 'But little boys who want, rarely get.'

9

'Relax,' Marley said. 'This will all be over soon. That's a promise.'

A shiver shot through JJ. What was that supposed to mean? *Over soon.* She wanted to believe that he'd let her go, but she'd made a career from facing the facts, and the facts right now were not encouraging. There was an air of resignation in the way he spoke that scared her. This was a man on a ledge who'd finally made the decision to jump.

Or maybe he was planning to let them go.

No, that last thought wasn't even worth entertaining. Marley was done letting people go. They were heading into the final act. This was the endgame. The hostages that were left were either destined to die here, or they would be rescued. Right now, the prospect of rescue seemed increasingly unlikely. If there was a plan to get them out, why hadn't it been implemented?

The answer was as obvious as it was disturbing. There was no viable plan. If there had been, she wouldn't be here now. The cops were listening in with their scanners, so they would know that people were dying. That was a game changer. They would be looking at every angle, trading off the numbers of potential survivors against collateral damage. The fact they'd done nothing meant the numbers weren't adding up. Too much collateral damage, not enough survivors. Until the cops and the FBI came up with a plan that tipped the scales the other way, they were stuck here. Unfortunately, as Marley had demonstrated, even doing nothing had consequences.

'Ed, get on your feet,' Marley called out.

Ed Richards stood slowly. His skin was bleached white and his hair was a mess. The bright red letters on his forehead were smeared from where he'd been rubbing at them. He was staring at the floor, hollowed out and broken. It was hard to equate this version of Ed Richards with the version who appeared on cinema screens across the globe. Even when he was made up to look like he'd been to hell and back, he still looked good. The difference here was that this was real. No pretence, no artifice, no make-up and no acting.

Marley picked up the chair Dan Stone had died on and positioned it so it was facing the other hostages. He motioned Richards over. The actor shuffled across the room like every step might be his last. He sat down heavily, the chair creaking under his weight.

'Jody, why don't you turn around and face the rest of these good folks, too?'

JJ got up and repositioned the chair, then sat back down.

'Okay, here's a question for the both of you. What's the value of a life?'

10

Caroline Bradley looked deep into the camera and said, 'I am now joined by Professor Eric Bartholomew, a leading neurosurgeon based at Cedars-Sinai Medical Center here in LA.'

Bartholomew was sat facing the camera. His legs were crossed and he looked relaxed. Everything about him was precise and tidy. His suit, his dark hair, the way he moved. Seth had the distinct impression that this was someone who was always thinking a dozen moves ahead. Caroline turned to the professor.

'Thank you for joining us, Professor Bartholomew.'

'My pleasure.'

Caroline glanced down at her clipboard of non-existent questions. Her expression contained just the right amount of serious. 'Professor, can a brain tumour affect personality?'

Bartholomew considered this. 'In a word, yes. However, this is dependent on where the growth is situated in the brain. What you have to understand is that the brain is a highly complex organ. Different parts control different things. For example, the cerebellum controls complex motor functions such as walking, balance and posture.'

Up in Mission Control, Seth groaned. What was it with experts and plain speaking? Why were the two things mutually exclusive? 'In English,' he whispered into his mike. 'And quickly or I'm cutting to one of Rob's MOTS.'

'And what about personality? Which part of the brain controls that?' The question was delivered as smoothly as ever, but Seth could tell that his anchorwoman was rattled.

'The frontal lobe.'

'English,' Seth hissed.

'How extreme can the personality change be?'

'It can be massive. For example, a normally placid person can suddenly turn violent. This can be terrifying for loved ones and carers.'

'Is it possible for a war hero to turn into a psychopath?'

'Good girl,' Seth whispered, and he could have sworn that the tiniest shimmer of a smile appeared on Caroline's face. It was there and gone in a flash.

'Hypothetically speaking, yes. Obviously, there are a number of factors that need to be taken into consideration. For example, the size of the tumour and the position it occupies in the brain. A predilection toward violent behaviour would also have an influence. It's worth pointing out that not everyone who gets a brain tumour automatically becomes a psychopath. This is an incredibly rare occurrence. It's the result of a unique series of factors.'

'Wind this up before I die of boredom,' Seth whispered. He moved the mike from his mouth, rocked back in his chair and lit another cigarette. On the big screen, Caroline was thanking Bartholomew for joining them in the studio.

'Rob's on the line,' the Asian kid called up.

Seth blew out a plume of smoke, then repositioned his mike. 'Please tell me you've got some more hostages coming out.'

'Sorry, no hostages. Aaron Walters is organising another press conference, though.'

Seth sighed.

'I get the first question,' Rob added quickly.

'Well, I guess that's better than nothing. When is it happening?'

'Walters said ten minutes.'

'Which means it'll be closer to fifteen minutes. Okay, go get yourself set up, and I'll sort everything out at this end.'

'Will do.'

The line went dead. Seth sighed and took another drag on his cigarette. The revelation about the tumour was already old news. They needed another big exclusive if they were going to keep the story. One thing was for sure, they weren't going to get it from a goddamn news conference.

11

Alex King sat with his back to the door and turned the key over in his hand. He'd spoken to Brad Carter a couple of minutes ago, and the FBI man had promised they were doing everything humanly possible to get him out. He'd finished up by telling him to sit tight.

The problem was that he'd given him that exact same bullshit line the last time they spoke. And the time before that. As for sitting tight, King had been sitting tight for so long his ass was numb.

The key turned in his hand. Over and over and over. The metal caught the bright halogen lights and sent tiny sparks shooting in all directions. Before he knew what he was doing, he was up on his feet. He pushed the key into the lock and turned it until he felt resistance. It made sense to unlock the door. He couldn't believe Carter hadn't suggested this. When things finally got moving, they'd move fast. Every second saved could be crucial. He turned the key a fraction of an inch more. Then stopped.

What if the door was connected to an alarm? Maybe that's why Carter hadn't told him to open it. King was ninety-nine per cent sure that opening the door would not set off any alarms. This was based on the fact that no alarms had gone off during any of the hostage handovers. The problem was that one per cent of doubt. No matter what he told himself to the contrary, he couldn't shake the feeling that bad things would happen if he unlocked the door.

'Brad, are you there?'

'Yeah, I'm here buddy.'

'I want to unlock the door. I think it'll help speed things up when you finally get around to doing your thing. I'm just worried that I might trip an alarm.'

'Okay, let me check and get back to you. Just sit tight for a second. Don't do anything until I tell you, okay?'

The earpiece fell silent. *Sit tight.* The silence seemed to go on for ever. King could imagine a bunch of FBI experts with their heads together, throwing ideas around. The thing was that they didn't have a clue. Not really. They had no idea how high the stakes were. How could they? They were out there, while he was trapped in here. There was no way they could understand what he was dealing with, not in a million years.

If the alarm went off they still got to go home and kiss their wives and kids. Their consciences might hassle them, but they'd learn to live with that. Given enough time, they'd learn to live with the fact that they had killed him. Given enough time, you could learn to live with anything. King knew that one from experience.

'Hey Alex, you're good to go for unlocking the door. The alarm's not activated.'

'You're sure about that?'

Carter laughed. 'We're the FBI. We've got gadgets that you film people can only dream about. And, Alex? Good call, by the way.'

'Thanks.'

The earpiece fell silent again and King stared at the key. Do something or do nothing? The atmosphere in the kitchen had suddenly got heavier. He didn't have to do this. He could just sit back down and pretend like this was the dumbest idea ever. Before he could talk himself out of it, he turned the key, hoping to God that Carter had called this one right. The lock released like a sigh. There was no click, just a moment of gentle pressure, then a sense of emptiness that felt like a long, slow dive into nothing. King held his breath and waited for the alarm to go off. He was expecting bells and sirens, but all he got was a whole lot of nothing.

The world had moved on by a fraction of a degree, yet everything was exactly as it had been a second ago. The kitchen was still in a state of controlled mess. Maybe too much, maybe not enough. And there was still a lunatic with a bomb strapped to his chest strutting about in the main part of the restaurant. And if he called Brad Carter right now, the FBI guy would no doubt tell him that they were doing everything humanly possible to get him out, and that he should just sit tight.

Nothing had changed, yet everything had changed. The door was unlocked, which meant that he was one step closer to being free. Right now the only thing separating him from freedom was the steel grille. He reached for the door handle and started to push down, then realised what he was doing and stepped back as though he'd been electrocuted.

He sank back to the floor and for a moment just sat there staring at his hand like it might not be attached to his body. Unlocking the door was one thing. Opening it was a whole different ball game. He knew the bomber was monitoring the news. What he didn't know was whether there were any TV cameras currently trained on the doors. If the bomber saw the kitchen door opening, that would be it.

He couldn't believe how close he'd come to screwing everything up. At the same time, he fully believed it. Up on the big screen, he might be indestructible, but deep in his heart he'd always be just another trailer-trash loser. He fished the small Ziploc bag of coke out and stroked the rough plastic a couple of times. It would be so easy. *Too* easy. He pushed the bag back into his pocket and found the knife. The sad face was looking at him. He flipped the knife over and forced a smile. A single tear slid down his cheek and dripped onto his jeans, leaving a small, dark wet patch.

12

'What's the value of a life?' Marley asked again. He nodded towards Kevin Donahue's cooling corpse. 'According to Kev over there, it's three million dollars. You know, he lied about how much he could afford to pay. His life was hanging in the balance, and he chose to lie, gave me all that hogwash about having to liquidate assets. He could have afforded four million, easy. Hell, he could probably have managed five. I have a highly tuned bullshit detector. You people might want to bear that in mind.'

He looked at JJ and she met his gaze. There was no point pretending to be invisible anymore. She could see exactly where he was going with this. He was going to call them up two at a time, and he was going to ask them to put a value on their lives, and they were all going to come up with their very best offer. After what had happened to Donahue there was no way anyone would short change him. It looked like it was about the money, after all.

JJ glanced around at the other hostages and estimated that Marley could clear thirty million dollars easy. Ed Richards and DeAndre Alexander alone could probably raise ten million apiece without breaking a sweat. Big money by any standard. What she didn't get was why. If Marley was dying, what use was thirty million? Or a hundred million? Or a billion?

Unless he was planning on giving it all away to charity. But even that didn't make sense. Yes, it made for good headlines, but when the dust settled, the lawyers would be queuing up to recover the money for the families. If there was big pot of cash going wanting, the one thing you could guarantee was that the lawyers and relations would be hovering nearby.

'Okay,' Marley said. 'Let's go back in time to the Forties. Do you know why the Nazis stopped shooting the Jews and started gassing them? It was because they couldn't justify the cost of the bullets. Basically, it was cheaper and more efficient to gas them. So, for Hitler and his buddies, the cost of a life was less than the cost of a bullet.' He shook his head and smiled a tight smile. 'Okay, for argument's sake, let's assume the cost of manufacturing a bullet is fifty cents. If you do the math, then Kev's three million dollars equates to six million lives. Or, to put it another way, we're talking every man, woman and child who died in the Holocaust. Kind of puts things in perspective, doesn't it?'

He looked over at the hostages.

'Fifteen million dollars,' Richards said in a voice that was as quiet as air. 'I can have the money wired anywhere you want. I just want to see my wife and children again.'

Marley turned slowly and faced the actor. 'Interesting. So your life is worth five Holocausts. That's thirty million people, and thirty million people is a country.' He turned to JJ. 'What about you, Jody? How many Holocausts are you worth?'

'I could only manage a million and a half.'

'Only a million and a half,' said Marley. '*Only.* You realise that's still half a holocaust. You reckon your life is as valuable as three million people?'

'No. You asked how much I could afford to pay, and that's what I can afford. My life isn't worth any more or any less than anyone else's.'

'Careful. My bullshit detector is starting to light up.'

'It's the truth.'

'No, it's not, Jody. We all place ourselves slap-bang in the centre of the universe. You, me, everyone.'

Every time he called her Jody, it was like a smack in the face. What's more, she was sure that he'd worked this out and was doing it on purpose. 'Don't ever compare us. We are nothing alike.'

'Aren't we? You see something you want, you take it. Just like I'm doing here today. We've both lost people we love. Face it, Jody, we're more alike than you could ever begin to imagine.'

'I've never killed anybody.'

'Haven't you? What about poor old Dan over there? What about your husband?'

There was no response to that. What Marley was saying was true. Tom was dead because she'd run out of tomorrows, and Stone was dead because she'd invited him here today.

'Okay, here's another question for you. How much was Tricia Marley's life worth?'

Marley smiled, and JJ felt as though she'd stepped into a trap. It was like her foot had been snagged by a loop of rope and she was now dangling upside down with her stomach left twenty feet below. Despite the fact she no longer knew which way was up, a small part of her brain was still functioning enough to ask one very important question.

Who was Tricia Marley?

13

'I've got something,' the Asian kid yelled.

Seth stubbed out his cigarette and lit a new one. The thin fog of smoke that hung around his head was stinging his eyes and scratching at his throat. A dozen Marlboros and Mission Control was turning into a proper newsroom. The Asian kid had a telephone cradled in the crook of his neck, and had turned around in his chair so he was facing Seth.

'I'm listening.'

'Marley's just made another donation to LA Abuse. Three million this time.'

'And you know this how?'

'Because I asked my contact to call if any more donations were made.'

'And you promised another donation if they did.'

The kid blushed and looked down at the back of his chair.

'Relax. You've done good. Better than good. And better than your two compadres. Hell, who knows, Pinocchio, maybe one day you'll turn into a real journalist.'

Seth glanced over at the small monitors on the left. So far, neither Fox nor CNN had made any mention of the donation. On the big screen, Caroline Bradley was reeling off the main headlines. He positioned his mike and whispered, 'Caroline, be a doll and inform our esteemed viewers that Ted Marley has made another donation to LA Abuse. Three million this time.

And make sure you get the word "exclusive" in there somewhere.'

Seth watched Caroline raise a hand to her ear. He watched her eyes light up like she was getting a message from God Almighty Himself. He watched her shoot her most intense expression into the camera. He could have watched her all day.

'And in another exclusive, we've just heard that Ted Marley has made a three-million dollar donation to LA Abuse. That's the second seven-figure donation that this modern-day Robin Hood has made to the charity, and brings the total up to nine million dollars.'

Seth tuned Caroline out. The feeling that he'd missed something was nagging like an itch he couldn't reach. Why had Marley singled out LA Abuse? What was that all about? Nine million bucks was a serious amount of money. At face value it was a noble gesture. With a cash injection like that the charity would be able help thousands of people. Chances were, they wouldn't need to do any fundraising for the next century.

Ultimately, though, the gesture was a futile one. LA Abuse dealt with the homeless, the destitute, junkies and prostitutes. Most of the people it helped were back on the streets and using as soon as their programs were finished. But nobody did anything without a good reason, particularly something as massive as this. Seth reckoned that nine million bucks might even have pacified his ex-wives.

'Okay, people, listen up,' he shouted. 'I want to know what the connection is between Ted Marley and LA Abuse. You don't give nine million bucks to a no-account charity working out of a single office in an LA back street unless there's a very, very good reason. I want to know what that reason is, and I want to know now.'

14

Was, thought JJ. Marley had asked how much she thought Tricia Marley's life *was* worth? Was, as in the past tense. This thought was quickly followed by another that was equally as disturbing. *Not good.*

'Let me tell you about Tricia,' Marley said. 'Tricia was an angel sent down from Heaven above. She was the happiest kid you'd ever wish to meet. Always smiling, always laughing. She was one of those kids who could light up a room just by walking into it.'

Marley pulled up a chair and positioned it opposite JJ and Ed Richards. For once, he wasn't grinning. Instead, he had a broad smile on his face. Whatever memories he was lost in, they were good ones.

'And she was so bright, too. A real crackerjack. She could have been anything she wanted. A doctor, a scientist, anything. Hell, if she'd set her mind to it she could have been the president or cured cancer.' Marley's smile was replaced by a frown. His eyebrows crept closer together. The heart on his watch flashed faster. 'All that potential, and do you know what she wanted to be?'

He stared at JJ, stared at Ed Richards. The other hostages had ceased to exist. It was just three of them. JJ stared back and kept her mouth shut. The question was rhetorical.

'She wanted to be an *actress.*' The last word was spat out like acting was on a par with being a serial killer. 'Tricia won a scholarship to UCLA to study Law. The first year she finished in the top one per cent of her class. That's how bright she was. I can't even begin to tell you how proud I was. It was during her second year that things started to unravel. She quit college and moved into a small apartment with her boyfriend. She'd decided that being a lawyer was too much like hard work. Instead, she was going to be a movie star. "I'm going to be as big as Angelina Jolie," she told me. I told her she was crazy, that she was throwing her life away. She told me she was old enough to make her own decisions and that I could go to hell. We went back and forth like that for a while and then she hung up.'

Marley shook his head, then smiled one of the saddest smiles JJ had ever seen.

'That was the last time I spoke to her. I don't have many regrets, but I do regret that. Every single day I regret it. My wife always said I was too proud, and she was right. I am too proud, and that pride contributed to the death of my daughter. I am absolutely convinced of that. If I'd been able to pick up the phone and call her, if I'd been able to say sorry, then she'd probably still be alive today.'

Marley wasn't looking at JJ anymore. Or Ed Richards. He wasn't talking to them, either. He was staring at a point in the distance with a faraway look on his face. JJ wondered if he was seeing his daughter standing there. If so, which version? The idealised child? The college kid? The wannabe actress?

'I used to tell myself that we'd make up one day. She'd eventually come to her senses and realise what a huge mistake she'd made, and I'd be there to help her pick up the pieces, because that's what fathers do. Unfortunately, it didn't work out that way.'

Marley looked at JJ. 'I have no problem with the fact that I'm going to die here today. Everyone's got to die, this just happens to be my time. It's strange, though, every tour I did, I didn't think I'd come home. I was convinced my destiny was to die on some dusty street, blown up by a bomb that some asshole had built in their kitchen. I came close. That's how I got this scar. But the good Lord must have been looking down on me that day. If I'd been standing a couple of feet to the left, I wouldn't be here now. As it was, I caught some shrapnel in my face and got a Purple Heart to pin on my chest for my troubles. A couple of my buddies weren't so lucky. They didn't come home. The thing I could never work out was what made me so special. Why should they die while I carried on living? It all seemed so arbitrary.'

Marley nodded towards the corner of the room where Kevin Donahue's body was piled up on top of Dan Stone's and Frank's. 'But death is arbitrary. It can strike at any time and any place, and that's the truth. A car wreck, a plane crash, a brain tumour. A drug overdose.'

JJ waited for more, but there wasn't any more. Marley had his head down and was staring at his boots. He sat like that for an eternity. Completely still, not moving a muscle. As suddenly as he'd tuned out, he tuned back in again. He looked up at JJ and Richards.

'So, the name Patricia Marley means nothing to you?'

It was another rhetorical question, but this time JJ answered with a slow shake of her head. Marley fixed her with his intense grey eyes.

'What about Sabrina? I'll bet that name rings a bell or two.'

15

'Marley's got a daughter,' the black kid shouted out.

Seth glared down at him. The kid's smile was broad and filled with bright white teeth. If he'd had a tail he would have been wagging it.

'At least, he had a daughter,' the kid added.

'Okay, I get it. She's dead. Please don't do subtext with me. It really pisses me off.'

'Sorry, sir.'

'I don't want an apology, damn it! I want the who, why, what, where and when.' Seth lit his last cigarette and crumpled the pack. 'You!' he shouted down at the white lesbian. 'I've got a really important job for you, honey.'

'Fire away,' she replied, as eager to please as the black kid was.

'I need you to run out and get a pack of cigarettes. Marlboro full strength. None of those crappy Lights.' The girl's face fell. 'What? You think you're too good for that? From where I'm sitting, it's the boys who are doing all the hard work, while you're just sat there dreaming the day away. You might as well make yourself useful.'

Seth took a drag on his cigarette. Caroline Bradley was on the big screen, as large as life and twice as beautiful. She was telling everyone to stay tuned because they were going back over to Alfie's any minute now for a press conference. Seth turned back to the black kid.

'You were saying?'

'The daughter's name was Patricia Marley. She was born and raised in Twin Falls, and moved to LA because she got a scholarship at UCLA.'

Seth put his hand up and the kid ground to a halt. 'Please get to the good bit before I die of boredom.'

'Patricia Marley dropped out of college in her second year to become an actress. Things didn't work out as she'd planned and she ended up on the streets working as a prostitute.'

'And that's when she got hooked on drugs?'

The kid nodded.

'And that's where LA Abuse comes into the story. She went to them because she wanted to get clean. So what happened?'

The kid smiled. 'That's where things get really interesting.'

16

Sabrina. JJ remembered a long-ago early morning phone call, and a chill rode through her. She glanced over at Ed Richards. The actor looked completely panicked. She stared down at the parquet flooring. The lines and the patterns mesmerised her. The scratches were fascinating. She was trying hard not to look at the smears of blood. Trying and failing. Marley was at the edge of her peripheral vision, studying her, his head cocked a little to the right. The scar tissue on his cheek was shining softly in the restaurant's subdued mood lighting.

'Judging by the startled rabbit expressions, I'm guessing you remember Sabrina,' he said.

JJ didn't respond. She glanced at Richards again. Panic had given way to fear. His hands were shaking and he was trembling from head to toe. If she could see herself in a mirror, she'd no doubt see the same expression of disbelief and horror. She'd wanted to know what motivated Marley, and now that she knew, she was desperate to unlearn that knowledge.

'So, what was the value of Sabrina's life? What price do you put on a drug addict who sells her body to pay for her addiction?'

Marley looked over at Kevin Donahue's body. The producer looked as grey and pallid in death as he'd looked in life.

'That one doesn't run to three million bucks, that's for damn sure. You know, I'd almost given up on getting the two of you here together. What with your busy schedules and all. But I waited, and I told myself to be patient. Now, that's something I excel at. I have more patience than anyone you'll ever meet. Steady hands and plenty of patience.'

Marley's laughter sounded all wrong in the forced stillness of Alfie's. It bounced off the walls, displacing the silence. Richards' head jerked up, He was looking more terrified than ever. And no wonder. He'd seen what Marley had done to Hayward and Donahue and all the others. That had been bad, but how much worse could it get? This was now personal, and that changed everything.

'Every Sunday I'd hack into Alfie's booking system, and every Sunday I'd end up disappointed. Jody, you weren't too much of a problem, what with you being a regular. But Ed here was another matter altogether. I suppose that's the thing with being the big shot movie star. You're always jetting off somewhere or other on your private plane, never staying in one place too long.'

Marley smiled, then sighed.

'A month ago you missed each other by seven hours. Jody, you were booked in for a one o'clock lunch, and, Ed, you were booked in for an eight o'clock dinner. Seven lousy hours. You have no idea how pissed I was about that one. And the thing is it had to be Alfie's. Strategically speaking this place is about as perfect as you're going to get. The lack of windows makes it ideal for holding hostages. It's like a prison. Then there's the fact that there's no way for a sharpshooter to draw a bead on me. The cops and feds must be driving themselves crazy out there. Like I say, it's just about perfect.'

He paused again. 'Anyway, I got over myself and went back to waiting. But now the doubts were creeping in. The longer this went on, the more convinced I was that I'd never get you both together at the same time. It was getting to the point where I thought I was going to have to choose between you. But I told myself to be patient, and do you know something? It's true what they say. Everything does come to those who wait.' Marley gestured like a principal actor acknowledging his supporting cast. His arms flowed outwards and his head dipped in mock respect. 'So I waited and waited and here we all are. You know, the three of us have lots to talk about.'

JJ just sat very still and stared at the floor. Voices whispered through her head. Echoes of memories past.

'You're really that good?'

'For your sake, you better hope I am.'

17

'You're going to love this,' the black kid said.

'And you're really starting to piss me off,' Seth replied. Mission Control had gone very still. All eyes were on the black kid and he was just lapping up the attention.

'Marley's daughter went to LA Abuse a couple of times to get clean. The problem is that their success rate isn't brilliant. For every person who stays clean, another dozen relapse. It's not the charity's fault, it's a sociological issue.'

Seth put his hand up and the kid stopped in mid-flow. 'Get to the point, and fast.'

'The daughter's last client was Ed Richards.'

'You mean she was *that* hooker? And you're only thinking to mention this now?'

The kid nodded.

Seth didn't need him to expand. Everyone knew about *that* hooker. You could be living in an igloo in the Arctic and you'd still know. The story was massive. Hollywood's number one actor had been found in a sleazy motel with a dead hooker and a load of cocaine. To top things off there was even a blurry photograph of Richards using a straw to blow coke up the hooker's ass. As stories went, it didn't get much better, or bigger. The scandal had almost destroyed Richards. The only reason it hadn't was because Hollywood could be incredibly forgiving when it came to its royalty, particularly when they made as much money as Ed Richards.

After the story broke Richards' people had gone on a massive PR offensive. Whoever was in charge of the damage limitation had done an incredible job. Richards had begged forgiveness through the media, his wife and kids standing loyally at his side. It had all been a massive lapse of judgement. A one-off. He had never done anything like this before, and he'd never, ever make the same mistakes again. He'd gone to rehab, and promised to be a good boy in future. It had been the performance of his career. It had needed to be.

The dead hooker hadn't fared so well. After all, she was just another dead prostitute. She'd basically ended up as a postscript to the story, a minor detail. Hollywood might treat its megastars with the utmost reverence, but everyone else was there to be chewed up and spat out.

Except that was all about to change. Marley's daughter was going to become a very big deal indeed.

Seth's mind was racing. He was projecting twenty moves into the future, searching for the endgame. This could destroy Richards. The death of a hooker was one thing. That was forgivable. Being responsible for the deaths of some of Hollywood's top people was a whole different matter. From this moment on, whenever anyone thought about Ed Richards they'd think about what had happened at Alfie's. Something clicked inside Seth's head. He scrambled through the loose sheets of paper littering his desk until he found the hostage list. The name he was looking for was right down at the bottom.

'Okay,' he called out. 'I want one of you jokers to confirm that Jody Johnson handled the publicity when Ed Richards got caught with his dick hanging out his pants.'

Thirty seconds later he had his answer. This time it was the Asian kid who came up with the goods. Yes, Brightlight had handled that story. And, yes, the person who'd made sure those plates kept spinning was none other than Jody "JJ" Johnson. Seth grinned to himself. He finally had an answer to the question that had been bugging him pretty much from the start. *Why?* It was all about revenge. Nothing more, nothing less. And *that* story was as old as time itself.

The black kid was talking again, but Seth wasn't listening. He reached for his cigarettes, remembered the pack was empty, and cursed loud enough to make everyone in the room jump.

'Anyone got a smoke?' he shouted.

'I've got some,' one of the techs called back.

The tech fished out a pack of Lucky Strikes and tossed them over. Seth caught the pack one-handed, lit a cigarette, then rocked back in his chair. He closed his eyes to block out any distractions and thought about what he'd just learnt. Then he took a long drag and thought about how he could use it to his advantage.

18

'Please tell me that you guys are going to get me out soon?' King said quietly.

'We're working on it, buddy,' Carter replied.

'You said that last time we spoke.'

'Just hang on in there. We are going to get you out. That's a promise. Just sit tight, okay?'

'You said that, too. Come on, Brad, I need to see some action from you guys. And soon. I'm going insane here.'

'No you're not, Alex. On the contrary, we were just talking about how well you're holding it together.'

'And you sound like a director who's trying to get his lead actress back on set after she's had a meltdown.'

The FBI guy's laughter filled his ear. 'Seriously, buddy, you're doing great. Better than great.'

King didn't respond. There was nothing to say that hadn't already been said. He leant back against the door. The *unlocked* door. Being this close to freedom was too much. He shut his eyes and rubbed at his temples. The combination of stress and the bright kitchen lights was conspiring to give him a headache. He rubbed harder, willing his headache away, and wished he had some Tylenol.

A sudden, excruciating pain shot through his left thigh. It felt like someone had grabbed hold of the muscle and twisted it through a full 360 degrees. He'd had cramp before, but nothing like this. The pain was unbelievable. King shot to his feet and the muscle pulled even tighter. He rubbed frantically at his leg. All he wanted was to get away from the pain, but no matter what he did, it was still there.

'Hey, buddy, you okay?'

King couldn't answer because all the air had been stolen from his lungs. He rubbed harder, but still couldn't find any relief. In desperation he started hopping across the kitchen, figuring that moving around might help. It didn't. If anything, it made things worse. He swung to the left and his elbow clipped a pan on the centre island. For a long, stretched-out moment it teetered on the edge, rocking and rattling, then gravity took over and it tumbled to the floor. King lunged and almost caught it. His fingers brushed against copper, and then the pan hit the tiles with a clatter that was louder than a nuclear blast.

19

'What the hell was that?'

Marley's head snapped towards the bottom level of the restaurant. He was staring at the wall that separated the main room from the corridor like he could see through it. JJ had heard the noise, too. Everyone had heard it.

'Something you want to share?' Marley aimed the question squarely at Tony.

'I don't know what you mean.'

Marley held his arm up and pointed to the pulsing red heart. 'See the way it's flashing faster? This thing's a pretty good lie detector, so let's try again. Something you want to share?'

'I have no idea what you're talking about.'

Tony was staring at the floor and trembling all over. It was one of the bravest things JJ had seen. Brave but stupid. Marley would keep pushing until Tony gave up Alex King. That was an absolute certainty. The only real question was whether there would be one or two corpses joining those already littering the room.

Marley aimed the submachine gun at Tony's head. 'Third and final time. You were back there only a short while ago. I want to know who made that noise, and I want to know now.'

Tony said nothing.

'When are you people going to realise that passive resistance just does not work?'

Marley let out a long, weary sigh, then shifted his aim a fraction to the right and squeezed the trigger. A bloom of red appeared on the left side of DeAndre Alexander's chest, a momentary look of surprise filled his face, and then he toppled backwards and landed in Simone's lap. The supermodel screamed, and tried to wriggle free. More screaming. More wriggling. The other hostages had moved out of the way, leaving a wide exclusion zone around her.

Marley aimed at her head. 'Shush now, honey.'

'Alex King,' she whispered.

'What did you just say, sweetheart? I didn't quite catch that.'

'Alex King is in the restrooms.'

'And you know this how?'

'Because he was my date. He went to use them just before you came in.'

Silence. The watch was flashing at a hundred and eight beats a minute. A second later it jumped to a hundred and thirteen. 'I don't remember seeing Alex King's name on the reservations list.'

'That's because it wasn't on there,' JJ said. 'He was here with Simone. For some reason their names didn't make it to the list. I asked Tony to squeeze in an extra table for them. It was a publicity stunt. I'd arranged for them to be photographed together when they drove away from the restaurant.'

Marley looked at Simone. 'Is this right?'

The model nodded.

'Okay, let me get this straight. For the last three hours you've known that Alex King was hiding back there and you're only telling me now. Did God really make you as dumb as you are pretty?'

'I'm sorry. I should have said something.'

'Yes, you should have.'

Marley squeezed the trigger.

20

The pan rattled to a standstill and King just stared at it. The cramp was starting to ease, adrenalin masking the worst of the pain.

'Alex, buddy, you okay?' All the cool was gone from Brad Carter's voice.

'Not really.'

'What was that noise?'

'I knocked a pan over.'

'Okay, don't panic. We'll think of something. Just hang on in there, okay?'

King actually felt calmer than he'd felt since this all kicked off. The back door was right in front of him. He had no recollection of walking over to it. Nor did he have any recollection of reaching for the handle.

21

'Something's going down,' Tara said.

Rob looked up from his cell phone and saw she was right. Everyone was suddenly moving with more purpose. The cops, the FBI, the SWAT guys. There was a buzz in the air that hadn't been there a couple of seconds ago. Tara was already on the move, adjusting her camera as she ran. She covered the hundred yards to Alfie's parking lot in less than twenty seconds. By the time Rob came skidding to a halt beside her, the camera was already aimed at the restaurant. She thrust a microphone into his hand.

'The kitchen door,' she said.

Rob looked over. At first he couldn't see anything because the sun was in his eyes. He put his hand up to his forehead and could just about make out a figure pressed against the grille. It could have been a ghost or a mirage, but he knew it wasn't.

'Jesus. Is that Alex King?'

'One and the same.'

'This is not good.'

'Okay, Rob, find those happy thoughts. I need you to start talking right now. It's time to do your thing.'

22

Alex King stood with his nose almost touching the grille. He wanted to push against it, anything to get closer to freedom, but the metal was too hot. The sunlight shining against the grille painted bright bars on his skin and clothes. It was like being in prison. He inhaled deeply and his nose filled with the hot black-top smell of summer, a smell that reminded him of his Ohio childhood. Back then, he'd spent his days dreaming of escape. All these years later and he was dreaming much the same thing.

'Alex, buddy, you need to get back inside and close the door.'

King took another deep breath. Beneath the smell of hot tar was the traffic stink of gasoline, and beyond that smell was the soft aroma of a city baked under a hot sun.

'Alex! Please get back inside now! You've got to hide.'

But that was the problem. There was nowhere to hide. The FBI guy just didn't get it, and King couldn't be bothered to explain. Life was too short. *His* life was too short. He could taste freedom in the hot air. It was so close. He glanced up and imagined that the slice of blue he could see went on for ever. An endless sky. The idea appealed to him because the only thing his future held right now were endings.

Footsteps in the corridor. This was it. He didn't want to die, but if that's what was going to happen, he wanted his last breath to taste of freedom and his last view to be a blue-sky view.

The kitchen door opened.

'I'm sorry,' said a voice.

The world shifted beneath King's feet. He felt light-headed and unreal. He would have recognised the bomber's voice anywhere, and this wasn't his voice. He turned and saw Tony standing in the doorway. His massive bulk was blocking the light from the corridor.

'I need you to come with me.'

23

'Seth,' the Asian kid called out. 'We've got the LAPD, Fox, CNN and a dozen other news channels burning up the phones. They all want to talk to you, and they want to talk now.'

'Stall them,' Seth called back.

'Stall them how?'

'Tell them I've left the country. Hell, tell them I've been indicted for my part in Princess Di's assassination. Whatever it takes.'

Seth stared at the main screen. 'LIVE FROM ALFIE'S' was printed in big letters on the banner, just in case anyone hadn't worked it out. Rob was talking up a storm, making this sound like the most exciting thing that had ever happened. This was pure TV gold. Alex King was pressed up against the grille. You could see the desperation on his face. You could feel his terror.

As TV moments went it was as compelling as that kid and the tank in Tiananmen Square. This was one of those rare moments where real history and media history collided. It had started in 1937 with the Hindenburg disaster. That had been the first major historical event to be captured by the TV cameras. It hadn't been the last. The Kennedy assassination, the first man on the moon, the Berlin Wall coming down, 9/11. That list would go on for as long as there were people out there willing to document the news, and people willing to bear witness.

The phones were ringing off the hook. The news stations were calling to see where their pictures had got to, and the LAPD were no doubt calling to tell him to kill the feed before Marley killed King. Seth was letting the pictures run, not because he was heartless, but because it was already too late. Unless the SWAT guys got out there with their metal cutters in the next two seconds, King was a dead man.

Seth stared at the screen and counted the seconds off in his head. He reached five. There was a blur of movement at the door, and then the actor disappeared. Seth stared at the empty space behind the grille, hoping King would make a miracle reappearance, and knowing it wasn't going to happen.

'Seth,' the black kid shouted. 'I've got the head guy over at Fox on the line and he's threatening legal action if we don't send those pictures now.'

'Tell him we're sending the footage over, and apologise profusely for the delay.'

This part of the story was all played out, and it was another home run for TRN. Fox could have as many damn pictures as they wanted. It really didn't matter anymore. In life, first place was all that mattered. Nobody remembered the losers.

24

'The prodigal son returns,' the bomber said. 'Come on up here so I can get a good look at you.'

King climbed the stairs to the upper level on legs made from lead. It was a real effort to keep moving. He could barely breathe. The air seemed thinner in here, like he was at the summit of Everest.

'Sit down, Tony, I'll deal with you later.'

King watched as the restaurant owner lowered himself to the floor beside a woman who had JEN written on her forehead. For some reason, JJ and Ed Richards were sitting on chairs away from the other two. Their faces were white, the stress showing. They both looked like the world was about to end. The fact that JJ was alive came as a shock. It looked like he wasn't the only nine-life cat in this town. Twice now he'd been convinced that she was dead, yet here she was, alive and breathing.

The bodies of DeAndre Alexander and Simone were lying in a lover's tangle at the side of the main group. Like Romeo and Juliet, if Tarantino had been directing. The supermodel's head was surrounded by a pool of coagulating blood. From the front she looked as beautiful in death as she had in life. If it wasn't for the small, neat bullet hole in her forehead, she could have been sleeping.

The back of her head was another matter. When the bullet had exited it had taken a large section of skull with it. Her blood had spilled out onto the floor and was still seeping into the cracks. King just stared. It was such a waste of a life. He glanced around and saw the other corpses. This wasn't like the movies. Not even close. The smell of death seemed to have got right inside him. This whole thing was just too much. He sank to his knees and threw up all over the floor. The smell was so bad it made him double over and puke again. He kept retching until the vomit turned to bile and his stomach was empty.

'Feeling better?'

King looked up and saw the bomber staring at him. The question was heavy on sarcasm and light on concern.

'Grab a napkin and get yourself cleaned up. Then come on over here, son.'

King struggled to his feet and grabbed a napkin from the nearest table. He wiped his face then walked over on legs that were shaking so much he could barely feel them. He stopped in front of the bomber. His eyes went straight to the explosive vest, then the gun, then the watch with the flashing red heart. Vest, gun, watch. In that order. The watch puzzled him. It looked like the sort of thing a jogger would wear. Judging by the precision of his marksmanship, there was nothing wrong with his eyesight, so what did he need such a large watch for?

The bomber looked him up and down. 'Take off the microphone.'

King did as he was told. He bundled the earpiece, mike and wires together and handed them over. The bomber dropped the device onto the floor and crushed it under his boot heel. He looked King up and down again.

'So this is what the next big thing looks like. I've got to say, I'm not impressed. I thought you'd be taller. And that whole frightened-little-boy act you've got going on kind of jars with the whole action-hero thing. You know, I saw that film of yours.

What a joke. You wouldn't have lasted a day in the real army. You would have been eaten alive. Special Forces? I don't think so.' He paused. 'Okay, how about you tell me what you've been up to back there for the last three hours?'

The bomber raised the gun and sighted along the barrel, and King started talking.

25

JJ was only half-listening so all she picked up was the odd word. FBI, hidden camera, throat mike. She was trying to find the positives in the situation, while desperately trying to work out a move that would keep her alive. Mostly, though, she was trying hard to pretend that it wasn't King standing there because the guilt was too much to bear.

The actor was little more than a kid, and he was going to die because of her. She tried to tell herself that she wasn't holding the gun, that it wasn't her who was about to pull the trigger. She tried to tell herself that she couldn't take responsibility for other people's actions, that she *shouldn't* take responsibility, but it didn't work. This was her fault. She'd arranged the date with Simone. She'd made the lunch reservation. And it was her who'd dragged him here kicking and screaming.

King finished talking and Marley told him to empty his pockets. He dropped everything onto a nearby table. Cell phone, billfold, a small scuffed Ziploc bag. Marley picked up the bag and held it to the light.

'Heroin or cocaine?' he asked.

'It's coke.'

Marley tipped the bag upside down and watched the contents drift like snow to the floor. He shook his head.

'You dumb son of a bitch. You've got the whole world at your feet and you've got to go and stick this crap up your nose.'

'It's just coke.'

'Just coke! Next you'll be telling me you're not an addict.'

'I'm not an addict.'

'So what? You use it every now and again? Just the occasional line to make the party swing a little harder, is that it?'

'No man, you've got it all wrong. I've stopped.'

Marley barked out a laugh. 'Of course you have. That's why you've got that bag in your pocket. What is it with the people in this town? Are you all stupid? You know, I could have stayed in bed today, just let that whole survival of the fittest thing take its course. Leave it long enough and you're all going to end up extinct anyway.' He shook his head. 'I don't get it. I really don't. You've got everything going in your favour yet you want to go and screw it all up by taking drugs. Come on, help me out here. Why would you do that?'

King shrugged. 'I don't know.'

'And that's the best you can come up with?'

'I'm sorry.'

JJ felt her heart breaking. King didn't just look like a scared, lost kid, he sounded like one, too. The actor shrugged again, then shook his head and stared straight at Marley.

'What? Have I got pizza around my mouth? Is my fly undone?'

King let out a small, self-deprecating laugh and shook his head. 'This is stupid, but when I was hiding back there I promised myself that if I ever got out of here I was going to start over. I was going to go the whole nine yards. Get myself into therapy and get my head sorted out once and for all. I really meant it, too.' He shook his head. 'I don't even know why I'm bothering telling you any of this since you're just going to shoot me anyway, but it's been forty-three days since I last had any coke. I keep that bag on me because I find it helps. It's like a smoker keeping a pack with one cigarette in. I know how lame that sounds but it's the truth. I swear on my life. If you don't believe me, look how beat up the bag is. If I was still using, that bag would be new.'

Marley glanced at the bag, then stared hard and long at King. The actor broke eye contact and looked at his socks.

'And that's the God's honest truth? And don't even think about lying to me, son. As I'm sure these good folks will testify, I've got a bullshit detector the likes of which you would not believe.'

King nodded, and Marley stared some more.

'I guess everyone deserves a second chance,' Marley said eventually. 'After all, that's why we're here today. If I'd given Tricia a second chance, then things would have worked out very differently.'

King said nothing.

'Alex, I'm going to be honest with you because you've been honest with me. I was going to kill you, but I've changed my mind. I'm going to let you go.'

King sagged with relief. He opened his mouth to say something and the bomber shut him up with a wave of his hand.

'Before you get too excited, there is a condition. When you get out of here, you're never going to use that crap again. Do you understand? Never. Again. You're not even fit to breathe the same air as my Tricia, but if I can save even one person from the same fate, then that's got to be worth something. But bear this in mind. If you ever use drugs again, even once, even a little bit, I will come back and haunt you until the end of time. Do I make myself clear?'

King nodded. JJ doubted he knew who Tricia was. She doubted he cared. All that mattered was that he was getting out of here. She heard Marley tell him to get undressed and that's when everything turned to shit. King reached under his shirt, and JJ saw the glint of steel and knew exactly how this was going to play out. There was no time to think. She launched herself from the chair and hurtled towards the actor, desperate to stop him, but knowing it was already too late. This was her worst nightmare come to life. The idiot was trying to play the hero.

Time went long, but it wasn't long enough. It didn't matter how fast she moved, there was no way to reach King in time. It was like that long-ago night when Tom had died. Whether you were a second too late, or ten minutes, or an hour, it was all the same. Marley's arm came up to defend himself and it was like everything was moving in slow motion. King countered the move and lunged with the kitchen knife, burying it deep into Marley's neck. A second later, JJ crashed into them. Her last thought was that, yet again, she was too late.

26

JJ opened her eyes and saw Marley lying on the floor beside her. His eyelids fluttered as he fought to stay conscious, but he was fighting a losing battle. You didn't need a medical degree to see that he was in a bad way. There was just too much blood pulsing from the knife wound. His eyes closed again and this time they stayed shut. The heartbeat on the watch was flashing at ninety beats a minute. As she watched, it dropped to eighty-nine.

JJ jumped to her feet and pushed past King. She grabbed some napkins from one of the tables then dropped to her knees beside Marley. She knew from TV that removing the knife would make the injury worse, and she knew you had to apply pressure to the wound, but that's all she knew. She arranged the napkins around the knife and pressed down hard. The sad face that had been carved into the knife's handle seemed oddly fitting. King was getting to his feet beside her, a look of dumb incomprehension on his face. He kept glancing at his empty hands like he couldn't work out what they were.

'You idiot!' she shouted at him.

'I had to do it. He was going to find the knife.'

JJ glared at him.

'What? I've just saved our lives.'

'No, you've probably just got us killed.'

'I don't get it.'

'And there's no time to explain.' JJ turned to Tony. 'Get everyone out. Now!'

The restaurant owner struggled to his feet and started ushering Ed Richards and Bev towards the foyer. Their faces were worried, eyes scared. JJ looked at Marley's watch. His heart rate was down to eighty-seven. Only thirty-seven beats to go. King was hovering at her shoulder, glued to the spot.

'Get out of here!' she screamed at him.

The actor jumped like he'd been electrocuted, then sprinted after the others.

'JJ, come on,' Tony shouted over his shoulder. 'You need to get out.'

'I can't,' she called back. 'If I go now, Marley will die quicker. You'll never get clear in time.'

'You can't stay here'.

'Please, Tony, just go.'

Tony looked at her one last time, then disappeared into the foyer. JJ pressed harder on the wound, blood seeping between her fingers. If she left now, Marley would bleed out more quickly. His heart rate would plummet and she'd probably be dead before she made it to the lower level. If she stayed then his heart rate would slowly fall until it reached fifty. Either way, she was dead.

She suddenly felt more alone than she'd ever felt, even more alone than she'd felt during those dark days after she'd buried Tom. This was crazy. She never acted on impulse, yet here she was, kneeling on the floor with the hot blood of a murderer covering her hands.

Her eyes locked onto the sad face carved into the knife handle. It was almost as though it was mocking her. What's more, she deserved to be mocked. You gathered the facts, formulated a strategy, then executed that strategy. That's how things worked in her world. But not this time. She'd acted without thinking, and now she was facing the consequences of those actions. JJ almost laughed at that. Like Marley had said, it was all about consequences.

A second later an explosion ripped through the restaurant. JJ instinctively shut her eyes. When she opened them again, she was still alive. Her ears were ringing, her head was full of noise, but her heart and lungs were still pumping. There was a second explosion. This one sounded smaller because she'd been deafened by the first. The doors and grilles, she realised. It had to be.

Eighty beats and counting.

JJ grabbed some clean napkins and laid them on top of the blood-soaked ones. She pressed down hard, careful not to move the knife. There was blood on her fingers and hands. Alarm bells were chiming inside her head. She glanced at the watch and saw Marley's heart-rate drop by another beat. The stink of him had got into her nose again. Cheap aftershave and soap, but eclipsing all that, the hot smell of his blood.

'Don't die.' She whispered the words under her breath, repeating them over and over. 'Don't die, don't die. Don't you dare die, you son of a bitch.'

Seventy-eight beats.

Marley's eyes suddenly flickered open and he reached up and grabbed her wrist. There was no strength in his grip. It was like being grabbed by a ghost. He opened his mouth to speak, but all that came out was a wet, gurgling sound. It took JJ a second to realise he was laughing at her.

Seventy-six beats.

Had Tony reached safety yet? She hoped he had, otherwise this had all been for nothing. The irony of the situation hadn't escaped her. For someone who spent her whole life divining the future, she'd really screwed this one up.

A heavy hand landed on her shoulder. She looked up and saw a SWAT guy in full battle gear. He motioned for her to move aside.

JJ shook her head. ‘I can’t. I need to keep him alive.’

A second SWAT guy grabbed her, threw her over his shoulder, and sprinted towards the stairs. She glanced back at Marley. There were two SWAT men working on him. One was keeping pressure on the wound, while the other attempted to defuse the bomb vest. The guy carrying her jumped from the last step, then sprinted across the lower level and into the foyer. They crashed through the wreckage of the front doors and burst out into the parking lot. The sunlight touching her naked skin felt like the kiss of an angel.

EPILOGUE

So, how are you going to play this one?

First, you're going to remove the battery from your cell phone. The concept is completely alien, and it takes a couple of attempts before you manage it. You feel like you're unplugging yourself from civilisation, which is exactly what you are doing. When the cops finally returned the phone to you, there were 236 missed calls and texts. Some were from friends, but most were from the news channels.

TRN's footage of you being carried half-naked from Alfie's has been playing non-stop since the siege ended. Stills from the footage made the front pages of the morning papers. All of them. The *New York Times*, the *South China Morning Post*, the *Sydney Morning Herald*. Inadvertently, you've become the face of the siege. The only saving grace is that your underwear matched and was relatively modest. The fact that the whole world has now seen your cellulite is something you'll learn to live with. When placed against the fate of the eight hostages who died, it means nothing. You've orchestrated plenty of media circuses, but this is the first time you've been the main feature. It is not a comfortable place to be.

The SWAT guys managed to keep Ted Marley alive just long enough to defuse the bomb. It was a close thing. Marley hadn't been bluffing. The bomb was big enough to take out a whole city block. If his intention was to ensure that Tricia wasn't forgotten, then he has succeeded. Her name and face are all over the news, too.

Tricia's death was a tragedy, but the biggest tragedy of all is that it changes nothing. There will be more Tricia Marleys in the future. Nothing can stop that. For as long as movies are made, there will be no shortage of young girls trampling over each other to star in them. And the hard truth is that for every girl who makes it big, there will be hundreds who don't. Hundreds of lives destroyed, and for what? Who are the winners here? Are there any?

Ed Richards' people have severed all ties with Brightlight. You haven't lost any sleep over this. After what happened there is no way you'll ever be able to look at him the same way again. The feeling is no doubt mutual. His new PR firm has already gone on a major offensive, which is understandable. After all, Richards is a billion-dollar brand. Whether or not this will do any good, time will tell. You've got your doubts, though. Something like this is going to leave scars. The Ed Richards who's smiling for the cameras today is not the same Ed Richards who walked into Alfie's three days ago.

His marriage will be the first casualty. It survived the Sabrina scandal, but only just. The fact that all that bad history is being dredged up again will be the final nail in the coffin. His next film will probably do well on the back of what happened, but then the decline will start. Three years from now he'll be struggling to get parts in B-movies. Five years from now he'll either have made it through rehab or he'll be dead. That's the way you see it going. Maybe you're wrong, but you don't think so. You know how this town works better than anyone.

As for Alex King, he's disappeared off the face of the planet. The first rumour you heard was that he's gone to India to find himself. Your guess is that his management company will find him first. Right now he's more golden than ever. Give it a few years and he'll be a billion-dollar brand in his own right.

The second rumour you heard was that he isn't alone. If that one turns out to be true, then you wish him all the luck in the world. You think he'll probably be okay. At least you hope he will. You kind of like the kid.

Tony is doing okay. One of the hundred and one things you love about him is the fact that nothing much fazes him for long. His broken nose will heal and the bruises will fade, and he'll eventually find a way to move on. The offers are already flooding in. Film, TV, books. Out of respect for the victims he has kept his silence. He says he has no intention of talking, but that won't last forever. The money being offered will climb higher and eventually he'll cave. When it reaches that point you'll suggest he hands a percentage over to LA Abuse. That would go a long way to stemming any accusations of cashing in.

Alfie's is currently closed and will remain so for the foreseeable future. When its doors do eventually reopen it will be harder than ever to get a booking. People will naturally be curious, and they'll happily pay good money to have that curiosity satiated. The fact they'll get a great meal pales into insignificance next to the kudos they'll gain by saying they've eaten at Alfie's.

Now that you've unplugged yourself from the twenty-first century, you can move on to phase two of your plan. Skipping the country. LAX is a total paparazzi magnet, so this is a no-go. Instead, you're going to hire a car. Something cheap and anonymous. In other words, something that's the complete opposite of your Maserati. Then you're going to drive south to the border and slip quietly into Mexico.

Maybe you'll stay in Mexico, or maybe you'll catch the first plane to the most remote island you can find. Wherever you end up, your cell phone will remain switched off, and you will avoid the Internet, newspapers and TV. For the next two weeks the Amish will be more plugged in than you are. During that time the only thing you need to work on is your tan, and the only thing you need to worry about is where you're going to eat dinner.

You reckon two weeks is long enough for a media storm of this magnitude to blow over. Five days to a week is the usual length for a full-on Hollywood mourning period, but this situation is unique, so it's bound to stretch on a bit longer. Nothing like this has happened before, and you pray nothing like it will ever happen again. You can imagine how things will play out. There will be plenty of fake tears, empty platitudes and heartfelt soliloquies. Then, after a couple of weeks, the tears will dry up and it will be business as usual.

At the end of the day the only real winner here is the media. Their job is to stoke the fire then stand back and let everyone else deal with the aftermath. That's the way things have always been. The way things will always be. This story still has some life left in it, but the news channels will already be searching for the next big thing, whatever that might be. An airplane crash, a terrorist attack, a celebrity scandal, whatever. Give it another couple of weeks and nobody will care about you anymore, which suits you fine.

Once things finally die down you'll move on to phase three of your plan.

You've been given a second chance and that means you're going to take a long, hard look at your life. As usual, you're going to make two lists. One for the pros and one for the cons. Then you're going to pick your life apart piece by piece. Some things will end up in the pros column, but, inevitably, most will end up under cons. There will be no bending or shaping, not this time. There will be no spin. You're going to visit places you don't want to visit. You're going to face up to some uncomfortable truths. You won't want to do this, but you'll do it anyway, because to do otherwise would be an insult to the memory of all those who died.

Your name is Jody Johnson and, for once, you have no idea what the future holds. All you know for certain is that you have a future, and for that you are eternally grateful.

A LETTER FROM JAMES

Dear reader,

Thanks for spending some time with me. It's been a blast. Hopefully I traumatised you; at the very least maybe I scared you a little. If nothing else, I'd like to think that I've entertained you, since that's what this game is all about. You know, the best compliment I ever received was from a woman who'd taken her kids on holiday to Florida. The kids were waiting at the door of their apartment, desperate to go and meet Mickey and the gang, while she was telling them that they had to wait because she needed to finish the book. I didn't know whether to feel sorry for the kids, or pleased that my book had had the desired effect.

If you've come this far, then maybe you'd like to go a little bit further and post a review. As a reader, one of the things I like most is discovering new books and new writers, and the way I do that is through word of mouth. Someone tells me they love a book, I just have to go and check it out. That's the way it works.

And feel free to drop me a line. It would be great to hear from you. The easiest way is through my website. That's where you'll also find information about my new books. There's always something in the pipeline. It might be another Jefferson Winter tale or one of these standalones. Whatever it is, hopefully it'll be tempting enough for you to pick up a copy, pull up a chair, and lose yourself for a few hours.

Use the link below to sign up to my mailing list; that way, I can let you know when my next book will be released. And don't worry, your email address will never be shared, and you can unsubscribe at any time.

www.bookouture.com/js-carol

Anyway, happy reading, and if you do come across any good books, please let me know!

Until next time,

James

@JamesCarolBooks

www.james-carol.com